Jack Reacher – a hero for our time

'**Clint Eastwood**, **Mel Gibson** and **Bruce Willis** all rolled into one, a **superman** for our time' *Irish Times*

'Thinking girl's beefcake'
The Times

'TOUGH-BUT-FAIR'
Mirror

'ONE OF THE GREAT ANTIHEROES'
Independent

'**Admired** by his male readers and **lusted** after by his female ones' *Daily Express*

'Arms the size of **Popeye's**'
Independent

'The lonest of **lone wolves**... **too cool** for school' *San Francisco Chronicle*

'Part-**Robin Hood**, part-**gorilla**' *Sunday Times*

'One of the truly memorable tough-guy heroes' Jeffery Deaver

'This is Jack **Reacher** for pity's sake, he'll **eat you** for breakfast!' *Los Angeles Times*

Have you read them all?

KILLING FLOOR
Jack Reacher gets off a bus in a small town in Georgia.
And is thrown into the county jail, for a murder he didn't commit.

DIE TRYING
Reacher is locked in a van with a woman claiming to be FBI.
And ferried right across America into a brand new country.

TRIPWIRE
Reacher is digging swimming pools in Key West when a detective
comes round asking questions. Then the detective turns up dead.

THE VISITOR
Two naked women found dead in a bath filled with paint.
Both victims of a man just like Reacher.

ECHO BURNING
In the heat of Texas, Reacher meets a young woman whose
husband is in jail. When he is released, he will kill her.

WITHOUT FAIL
A Washington woman asks Reacher for help. Her job?
Protecting the Vice-President.

PERSUADER
A kidnapping in Boston. A cop dies.
Has Reacher lost his sense of right and wrong?

J ck Reacher: CV

Name: Jack Reacher (no middle name)

Born: 29 October

Height:
6 foot 5 inches/
1.95 metres

Weight:
220-250 lbs/
100-113 kg

Size:
50-inch/127cm chest,
3XLT coat, 37-inch/
95cm inside leg

Eyes: Blue

Distinguishing marks:
scar on corner of left
eye, scar on upper lip

Education:
US Army base schools in
Europe and the Far East;
West Point Military Academy
.

Service:
US Military Police,
thirteen years; first CO
of the 110th Division;
demoted from Major to
Captain after six years,
mustered out with rank
of Major after seven

Service awards:
Top row: Silver Star, Defense
Superior Service Medal,
Legion of Merit
Middle row: Soldier's Medal,
Bronze Star, Purple Heart
Bottom row: 'Junk awards'

Last known address:
Unknown

Family:
Mother, Josephine Moutier
Reacher, deceased, French
national; Father, Career US
Marine, deceased, served in
Korea and Vietnam; Brother,
Joe, deceased, five years in
US Military Intelligence,
Treasury Dept.

Special skills:
Small arms expert, outstanding
on all
man-portable weaponry
and hand-to-hand combat

Languages:
Fluent English and French,
passable Spanish

What he doesn't have:
Driver's licence; credit cards;
Federal benefits; tax returns;
dependents

WORTH DYING FOR

Lee Child

BANTAM BOOKS

LONDON · TORONTO · SYDNEY · AUCKLAND · JOHANNESBURG

TRANSWORLD PUBLISHERS
61–63 Uxbridge Road, London W5 5SA
A Random House Group Company
www.transworldbooks.co.uk

WORTH DYING FOR
A BANTAM BOOK: 9780553825480

First published in Great Britain
in 2010 by Bantam Press
an imprint of Transworld Publishers
Bantam edition published 2011

A CIP catalogue record for this book
is available from the British Library.

Addresses for Random House Group Ltd companies outside the UK
can be found at: www.randomhouse.co.uk
The Random House Group Ltd Reg. No. 954009

The Random House Group Limited supports The Forest Stewardship
Council® (FSC®), the leading international forest certification
organisation. All our titles that are printed on Greenpeace approved
FSC® certified paper carry the FSC® logo. Our paper procurement
policy can be found at www.randomhouse.co.uk/environment

Typeset in 11/14pt Century Old Style by
Kestrel Data, Exeter, Devon.
Printed in the UK by
CPI Cox & Wyman, Reading, RG1 8EX.

2 4 6 8 10 9 7 5 3 1

MIX
Paper from
responsible sources
FSC® C016897

For Ruth
my daughter

WORTH DYING FOR

ONE

Eldridge Tyler was driving a long straight two-lane road in Nebraska when his cell phone rang. It was very late in the afternoon. He was taking his granddaughter home after buying her shoes. His truck was a crew-cab Silverado the colour of a day-old newspaper, and the kid was flat on her back on the small rear seat. She was not asleep. She was lying there wide awake with her legs held up. She was staring fascinated at the huge white sneakers wobbling around in the air two feet above her face. She was making strange sounds with her mouth. She was eight years old. Tyler figured she was a late developer.

Tyler's phone was basic enough to be nothing fancy, but complex enough to have different ringtones against different numbers. Most played the manufacturer's default tune, but four were set to sound a low urgent note halfway between a fire truck siren and a submarine's dive klaxon. And that sound was what Tyler heard, in the late afternoon, on the long straight two-lane road in Nebraska, ten miles south of the outlet store and twenty miles north of home. So he fumbled the phone up from the console and hit the button and raised it to his ear and said, 'Yes?'

A voice said, 'We might need you.'

Tyler said, 'Me?'

'Well, you and your rifle. Like before.'

Tyler said, 'Might?'

'At this stage it's only a precaution.'

'What's going on?'

'There's a guy sniffing around.'

'Close?'

'Hard to say.'

'How much does he know?'

'Some of it. Not all of it yet.'

'Who is he?'

'Nobody. A stranger. Just a guy. But he got involved. We think he was in the service. We think he was a military cop. Maybe he didn't lose the cop habit.'

'How long ago was he in the service?'

'Ancient history.'

'Connections?'

'None at all, that we can see. He won't be missed. He's a drifter. Like a hobo. He blew in like a tumbleweed. Now he needs to blow out again.'

'Description?'

'He's a big guy,' the voice said. 'Six-five at least, probably two-fifty. Last seen wearing a big old brown parka and a wool cap. He moves funny, like he's stiff. Like he's hurting.'

'OK,' Tyler said. 'So where and when?'

'We want you to watch the barn,' the voice said. 'All day tomorrow. We can't let him see the barn. Not now. If we don't get him tonight, he's going to figure it out eventually. He's going to head over there and take a look.'

'He's going to walk right into it, just like that?'

'He thinks there are four of us. He doesn't know there are five.'

'That's good.'

'Shoot him if you see him.'

'I will.'

'Don't miss.'

'Do I ever?' Tyler said. He clicked off the call and dumped the phone back on the console and drove on, the little girl's new shoes waving in his mirror, dead winter fields ahead, dead winter fields behind, darkness to his left, the setting sun to his right.

The barn had been built long ago, when moderate size and wooden construction had been appropriate for Nebraska agriculture. Its function had since been supplanted by huge metal sheds built in distant locations chosen solely on the basis of logistical studies. But the old place had endured, warping slowly, rotting slowly, leaning and weathering. All around it was an apron of ancient blacktop that had been heaved by winter frosts and cracked by summer sun and laced with wiry weeds. The main door was a slider built of great baulks of timber banded together with iron, hung off an iron rail by iron wheels, but the gradual tilt of the building had jammed it solid in its tracks. The only way in was the judas hole, which was a small conventional door inset in the slider, a little left of its centre, a little smaller than man-sized.

Eldridge Tyler was staring at that small door through the scope on his rifle. He had been in position an hour early, well before dawn, a precaution he considered prudent. He was a patient man. And thorough. And meticulous. He had driven his truck off the road and followed winding tractor ruts through the dark, and he had parked in an ancient three-sided shelter designed long ago to keep spring rain off burlap fertilizer sacks. The ground was frozen hard and he had raised no dust and left no sign. He had shut down the big V-8 and stepped back to the shelter's entrance and tied a tripwire across it, made of thin electric cable insulated with black plastic, set shin-high to a tall man.

Then he had walked back to his truck, and he had climbed into the load bed, and he had stepped on the roof of the cab, and he had passed his rifle and a canvas tote bag up on to a half-loft built like a shelf under the shelter's peaked roof. He had levered himself up after them, and crawled forward, and eased a loose louvre out of the ventilation hole in the loft's gable wall, which would give him a clear view of the barn exactly a hundred and twenty yards north, just as soon as there was light in the sky. No luck involved. He had scouted the location many years before, the first time his four friends had called on him for help, and he had prepared well, driving in the nails for the tripwire, pacing out the distance to the barn, and loosening the louvre. Now he had once again gotten comfortable up on the half-loft, and he had kept as warm as he could, and he had waited for the sun to come up, which it had eventually, pale and wan.

His rifle was the Grand Alaskan model built in America by the Arnold Arms Company. It was chambered for the .338 Magnum and fitted with a 26-inch barrel and had a stock carved from exhibition-grade English walnut. It was a seven-thousand-dollar item, good against most anything on four legs, better than good against anything on two. The scope was by Leica, a nine-hundred-dollar Ultravid with a standard crosshairs engraving on the reticle. Tyler had it zoomed through about two-thirds of its magnification so that at a hundred and twenty yards it showed a circular slice of life about ten feet high and ten feet across. The pale morning sun was low in the east, and its soft grey light was coming in almost horizontal across the dormant land. Later it would rise a little and swing south, and then it would fall away into the west, all of which was good, because it meant even a target wearing a brown coat would stand out well against the brown of the faded timber baulks, all day long.

Tyler worked on the assumption that most people were right handed, and therefore his target would stand a little left of centre so that his right hand when extended would meet the handle in the middle of the judas hole's narrow panel. He further figured that a man who was stiff and hurting would stand in close, to limit his required range of movement to what was most comfortable. The door itself was less than six feet high, but because it was inset in the larger slider its lower edge was about nine inches above the grade. A man six feet five inches tall had the centre of his skull about seventy-three inches off the ground, which in terms of the vertical axis put the optimum aiming point about six inches below the top of the judas hole. And a man who weighed 250 pounds would be broad in the shoulders, which at the moment of trying to open the door would put the centre of his skull maybe a foot and a half left of his right hand, which in terms of the horizontal axis would put the aiming point about six inches beyond the left edge of the door.

Six inches down, six inches left. Tyler reached back and pulled two plastic packages of long-grain rice from his canvas tote bag. Brand new from the grocery store, five pounds each. He stacked them under the rifle's forestock and tamped the fine walnut down into them. He snuggled behind the butt and put his eye back to the scope and laid the crosshairs on the top left corner of the door. He eased them down, and eased them left. He laid his finger gently against the trigger. He breathed in, and breathed out. Below him his truck ticked and cooled and the living smells of gasoline and cold exhaust drifted up and mixed with the dead smells of dust and old wood. Outside, the sun continued to climb and the light grew a little stronger. The air was damp and heavy, cold and dense, the kind of air that keeps a baseball inside the park, the kind of air that cradles a bullet and holds it straight and true.

Tyler waited. He knew he might have to wait all day, and he was prepared to. He was a patient man. He used the dead time visualizing the sequence of possible events. He imagined the big man in the brown coat stepping into the scope's field of view, stopping,

16

standing still, turning his back, putting his hand on the handle.

A hundred and twenty yards.

A single high velocity round.

The end of the road.

TWO

Jack Reacher was the big man in the brown coat, and for him that particular road had started four miles away, in the middle of an evening, with a ringing telephone in a motel lounge at a crossroads, where a driver who had given him a ride had let him out before turning in a direction Reacher didn't want to go. The land all around was dark and flat and dead and empty. The motel was the only living thing in sight. It looked like it had been built forty or fifty years earlier in a burst of commercial enthusiasm. Perhaps great possibilities had been anticipated for that location. But clearly the great possibilities had never materialized, or perhaps they had been illusions to begin with. One of the four crossroads lots held the abandoned shell of a gas station. Another had a poured foundation, perhaps for a large store or even a small mall, with nothing ever built on it. One was completely empty.

But the motel had endured. It was an adventurous design. It looked like the drawings Reacher had seen as a kid in boys' comic books, of space colonies set up on the moon or on Mars. The main building was perfectly round, with a domed roof. Beyond it each cabin was a circular domed structure of its own, trailing away from the mothership in a lazy curl, getting smaller as they went to exaggerate the perspective. Family rooms near the office, individual accommodations down the line. All the siding was painted silver, and there were vertical aluminium accents spaced to frame the windows and the doors. Concealed neon lighting in the eaves of the circular roofs cast a ghostly blue glow. The paths all around were made of grey gravel boxed in with timbers that were also painted silver. The pole the motel sign was set on was disguised with painted plywood to look like a space rocket resting on a tripod of slim fins. The motel's name was the Apollo Inn, and it was written in letters that looked like the numbers on the bottom of a bank cheque.

Inside, the main building was mostly an open space, except for a slice boxed off for a back office and what Reacher guessed were two restrooms. There was a curved reception counter and a hundred feet opposite there was a curved bar. The place was basically a lounge, with a pie-shaped parquet dance floor and huddles of red velvet chairs set around cocktail tables equipped with lamps with tasselled shades. The interior of the domed roof was a concave cyclorama washed by red neon. There was plenty more indirect lighting everywhere else, all of it red or pink. There was tinkly piano music playing softly over hidden loudspeakers. The whole place was bizarre, like a 1960s vision of Las Vegas transplanted to outer space.

And the whole place was deserted, apart from one guy

at the bar and one guy behind it. Reacher waited at the reception counter and the guy behind the bar hustled over and seemed genuinely surprised when Reacher asked him for a room, as if such requests were rare. But he stepped to it smartly enough and coughed up a key in exchange for thirty dollars in cash. He was more than middle-aged, maybe fifty-five or sixty, not tall, not lean, with a full head of hair dyed a lively russet colour that Reacher was more used to seeing on Frenchwomen of a certain age. He put Reacher's thirty bucks in a drawer and made a fussy notation in a book. Probably the heir of the lunatics who had built the place. Probably worked nowhere else his whole life, probably making ends meet by pulling quintuple duty as manager, desk clerk, barman, handyman and maid. He closed the book and put it in a different drawer and set off back towards the bar.

'Got coffee over there?' Reacher asked him.

The guy turned and said, 'Sure,' with a smile and a measure of satisfaction in his voice, as if an ancient decision to set a Bunn flask going every night had been finally vindicated. Reacher followed him through the neon wash and propped himself on a stool three spaces away from the other customer. The other customer was a man of about forty. He was wearing a thick tweed sports coat with leather patches at the elbows. He had those elbows on the bar, and his hands were curled protectively around a rocks glass full of ice and amber liquid. He was staring down at it with an unfocused gaze. Probably not his first glass of the evening. Maybe not even his third or his fourth. His skin was damp. He looked pretty far gone.

The guy with the dyed hair poured coffee into a china mug decorated with the NASA logo and slid it across the bar with great pride and ceremony. Maybe a priceless antique.

'Cream?' he asked. 'Sugar?'

'Neither,' Reacher said.

'Passing through?'

'Aiming to turn east as soon as I can.'

'How far east?'

'All the way east,' Reacher said. 'Virginia.'

The guy with the hair nodded sagely. 'Then you'll need to go south first. Until you hit the Interstate.'

'That's the plan,' Reacher said.

'Where did you start out today?'

'North of here,' Reacher said.

'Driving?'

'Hitching rides.'

The guy with the hair said nothing more, because there was nothing more to say. Bartenders like to stay cheerful, and there was no cheerful direction for the conversation to go. Hitching a ride on a back road in the dead of winter in the forty-first least densely populated state of America's fifty was not going to be easy, and the guy was too polite to say so. Reacher picked up the mug and tried to hold it steady. A test. The result was not good. Every tendon and ligament and muscle from his fingertips to his ribcage burned and quivered and the microscopic motion in his hand set up small concentric ripples in the coffee. He concentrated hard and brought the mug to his lips, aiming for smoothness, achieving lurching, erratic movement. The drunk guy watched him for a moment and then looked away. The coffee was hot and a little stewed, but it had caffeine in it, which was really all it needed. The drunk guy took a sip from his glass and put it back on its coaster and stared at it miserably. His lips were parted slightly and bubbles of moisture were forming in their corners. He sipped again. Reacher sipped again, slower. Nobody spoke. The drunk guy finished up and got a refill. Jim Beam. Bourbon, at least a triple. Reacher's arm started to feel a little better. Coffee, good for what ails you.

Then the phone rang.

Actually, two phones rang. One number, two instruments, one over on the reception desk, the other on a shelf behind the bar. Quintuple duty. The guy with the hair couldn't be everywhere at once. He picked up and said, 'This is the Apollo Inn,' just as proudly and brightly and enthusiastically as if it was the establishment's first-ever call on opening night. Then he listened for a spell and pressed the mouthpiece to his chest and said, 'Doctor, it's for you.'

Automatically Reacher glanced backward, looking for a doctor. No one there. Beside him the drunk guy said, 'Who is it?'

The bartender said, 'It's Mrs Duncan.'

The drunk guy said, 'What's her problem?'

'Her nose is bleeding. Won't stop.'

The drunk guy said, 'Tell her you haven't seen me.'

The guy with the hair relayed the lie and put the phone down. The drunk guy slumped and his face dropped almost level with the rim of his glass.

'You're a doctor?' Reacher asked him.

'What do you care?'

'Is Mrs Duncan your patient?'

'Technically.'

'And you're blowing her off?'

'What are you, the ethics board? It's a nosebleed.'

'That won't stop. Could be serious.'

'She's thirty-three years old and healthy. No history of hypertension or blood disorders. She's not a drug user. No reason to get alarmed.' The guy picked up his glass. A gulp, a swallow, a gulp, a swallow.

Reacher asked, 'Is she married?'

'What, marriage causes nosebleeds now?'

'Sometimes,' Reacher said. 'I was a military cop. Sometimes we would get called off-post, or to the married quarters. Women who get hit a lot take a lot of aspirin, because of the pain. But aspirin thins the blood, so the next time they get hit, they don't stop bleeding.'

The drunk guy said nothing.

The barman looked away.

Reacher said, 'What? This happens a lot?'

The drunk guy said, 'It's a nosebleed.'

Reacher said, 'You're afraid of getting in the middle of a domestic dispute?'

No one spoke.

'There could be other injuries,' Reacher said. 'Maybe less visible. She's your patient.'

No one spoke.

Reacher said, 'Bleeding from the nose is the same as bleeding from anyplace else. If it doesn't stop, she's going to pass out. Like a knife wound. You wouldn't leave her sitting there with a knife wound, would you?'

No one spoke.

'Whatever,' Reacher said. 'Not my business. And you'd be no good anyway. You're not even fit to drive out there, wherever she is. But you should call someone.'

The drunk guy said, 'There isn't anyone. There's an emergency room sixty miles away. But they're not going to send an ambulance sixty miles for a nosebleed.'

Reacher took another sip of coffee. The drunk guy left his glass alone. He said, 'Sure, I would have a problem driving. But I'd be OK when I got there. I'm a good doctor.'

'Then I'd hate to see a bad one,' Reacher said.

'I know what's wrong with you, for instance. Physically, I mean. Mentally, I can't comment.'

'Don't push it, pal.'

'Or what?'

Reacher said nothing.

'It's a nosebleed,' the doctor said again.

'How would you treat it?' Reacher asked.

'A little local anaesthetic. Pack the nasal cavities with gauze. The pressure would stop the bleeding, aspirin or no aspirin.'

Reacher nodded. He'd seen it done that way before, in the army. He said, 'So let's go, doctor. I'll drive.'

THREE

The doctor was unsteady on his feet. He did the usual drunk-guy thing of walking across a flat floor and making it look like he was walking up a hill. But he got out to the lot OK and then the cold air hit him and he got some temporary focus. Enough to find his car keys, anyway. He patted one pocket after another and eventually came out with a big bunch on a worn leather fob that had *Duncan Transportation* printed on it in flaking gold.

'Same Duncan?' Reacher asked.

The guy said, 'There's only one Duncan family in this county.'

'You treat all of them?'

'Only the daughter-in-law. The son goes to Denver. The father and the uncles treat themselves with roots and berries, for all I know.'

The car was a Subaru wagon. It was the only vehicle in the lot. It was reasonably new and reasonably clean. Reacher found the remote on the fob and clicked it open. The doctor made a big show of heading for the driver's door and then ruefully changing direction. Reacher got in and racked the seat back and started the engine and found the lights.

'Head south,' the doctor said.

Reacher coughed.

'Try not to breathe on me,' he said. 'Or the patient.'

He put his hands on the wheel the same way a person might manoeuvre two baseball gloves on the end of two long sticks. When they got there he clamped his fingers and held on tight, to relieve the pressure on his shoulders. He eased out of the lot and turned south. It was full dark. Nothing to see, but he knew the land was flat and infinite all around.

'What grows here?' he asked, just to keep the doctor awake.

'Corn, of course,' the guy said. 'Corn and more corn. Lots and lots of corn. More corn than a sane man ever wants to see.'

'You local?'

'From Idaho originally.'

'Potatoes.'

'Better than corn.'

'So what brought you to Nebraska?'

'My wife,' the guy said. 'Born and raised right here.'

They were quiet for a moment, and then Reacher asked, 'What's wrong with me?'

The doctor said, 'What?'

'You claimed you knew what's wrong with me. Physically, at least. So let's hear it.'

'What is this, an audition?'

'Don't pretend you don't need one.'

'Go to hell. I'm functioning.'

'Prove it.'

'I know what you did,' the guy said. 'I don't know how.'

'What did I do?'

'You strained everything from your flexor digiti minimi brevis to your quadratus lumborum, both sides of your body, just about symmetrically.'

'Try English, not Latin.'

'You damaged every muscle, tendon and ligament associated with moving your arms, all the way from your little fingers to the anchor on your twelfth rib. You've got pain and discomfort and your fine motor control is screwed up because every system is barking.'

'Prognosis?'

'You'll heal.'

'When?'

'A few days. Maybe a week. You could try aspirin.'

Reacher drove on. He cracked his window an inch, to suck out the bourbon fumes. They passed a small cluster of three large homes, set close together a hundred yards off the two-lane road at the end of a long shared driveway. They were all hemmed in together by a post-and-rail fence. They were old places, once fine, still sturdy, now maybe a little neglected. The doctor turned his head and took a long hard look at them, and then he faced front again.

'How did you do it?' he asked.

'Do what?' Reacher said.

'How did you hurt your arms?'

'You're the doctor,' Reacher said. 'You tell me.'

'I've seen the same kind of symptoms twice before. I volunteered in Florida after one of the hurricanes. A few years ago. I'm not such a bad guy.'

'And?'

'People who get caught outside in a hundred-mile-an-hour wind either get bowled along the street, or they catch on to a cyclone fence and try to haul themselves to safety. Like dragging their own bodyweight against the resistance of a gale. Unbelievable stress. That's how the injuries happen. But yours aren't more than a couple of days old, judging by the way you look. And you said you came in from the north. No hurricanes north of here. And it's the wrong season for hurricanes, anyway. I bet there wasn't a hurricane anywhere in the world this week. Not a single one. So I don't know how you hurt yourself. But I wish you well for a speedy recovery. I really do.'

Reacher said nothing.

The doctor said, 'Left at the next crossroads.'

They got to the Duncan house five minutes later. It had exterior lighting, including a pair of spots angled up at a white mailbox, one from each side. The mailbox had *Duncan* written on it. The house itself looked like a restored farmhouse. It was modest in terms of size but immaculate in terms of condition. There was a front lawn of hibernating grass with an antique horse buggy parked on it. Tall spoked wheels, long empty shafts. There was a long straight driveway leading to an outbuilding big enough to have been a working barn back when work was done around the place. Now it was a garage. It had three sets of doors. One set was standing open, as if someone had left in a hurry.

Reacher stopped the car level with a path that led to the front door.

'Show time, doctor,' he said. 'If she's still here.'

'She will be,' the guy said.

'So let's go.'

They got out of the car.

FOUR

The doctor took a leather bag from the back of the car. Then he repeated his uphill drunk-guy stumble all the way along the path, this time with more reason, because the gravel surface was difficult. But he made it unassisted to the door, which was a fine piece of old wood with glassy white paint carefully applied to it. Reacher found a brass button and laid a knuckle on it. Inside he heard the sound of an electric bell, and then nothing for a minute, and then the sound of slow feet on floorboards. Then the door opened a crack and a face looked out.

Quite a face. It was framed by black hair and had pale skin and frightened eyes at the top, and then a red-soaked handkerchief pressed tight at the apex of a triangular red gush that had flooded downward past the mouth and neck to the blouse below. There was a string of blood-soaked pearls. The blouse was silk and it was wet to the waist. The woman took the handkerchief away from her nose. She had split lips and blood-rimed teeth. Her nose was still leaking, a steady stream.

'You came,' she said.

The doctor blinked twice and focused hard and turned down his mouth in a frown and nodded. He said, 'We should take a look at that.'

'You've been drinking,' the woman said. Then she looked at Reacher and asked, 'Who are you?'

'I drove,' Reacher said.

'Because he's drunk?'

'He'll be OK. I wouldn't let him do brain surgery, but he can stop the bleeding.'

The woman thought about it for a moment and then she nodded and put the handkerchief back to her face and opened the door wide.

They used the kitchen. The doctor was drunk as a skunk but the procedure was simple and the guy retained enough muscle memory to get himself through it. Reacher soaked cloths in warm water and passed them across and the doctor cleaned the woman's face and jammed her nostrils solid with gauze and used butterfly closures on her cut lips. The anaesthetic took the pain away and she settled into a calm and dreamy state. It was hard to say exactly what she looked like. Her nose had been busted before. That was clear. Apart from that she had good skin and fine bone structure and pretty eyes. She was slim and fairly tall, well dressed and solidly prosperous. As was the house itself. It was warm. The floors were wide planks, lustrous with a hundred years of wax. There was a lot of millwork and fine detail and subtle pastel shades. Books on the shelves, paintings on the walls, rugs on the floors. In the living room there was a wedding photograph in a silver frame. It showed a younger and intact version of the woman with a tall reedy man in a grey morning suit. He had dark hair and a long nose and bright eyes and he looked very smug. Not an athlete or a manual worker, not a professor or a poet. Not a farmer, either. A businessman, probably. An executive of some kind. An indoors type of guy, soft, with energy but no vigour.

Reacher headed back to the kitchen and found the doctor washing his hands in the sink and the woman brushing her hair without the help of a mirror. He asked her, 'You OK now?'

She said, 'Not too bad,' slow and nasal and indistinct.

'Your husband's not here?'

'He decided to go out for dinner. With his friends.'

'What's his name?'

'His name is Seth.'

'And what's your name?'

'My name is Eleanor.'

'You been taking aspirin, Eleanor?'

'Yes.'

'Because Seth does this a lot?'

She paused a long, long time, and then she shook her head.

'I tripped,' she said. 'On the edge of the rug.'

'More than once, all in a few days? The same rug?'

'Yes.'

'I'd change that rug, if I were you.'

'I'm sure it won't happen again.'

They waited ten minutes in the kitchen while she went upstairs to take a shower and change. They heard the

32

water run and stop and heard her call down that she was OK and on her way to bed. So they left. The front door clicked behind them. The doctor staggered to the car and dumped himself in the passenger seat with his bag between his feet. Reacher started up and reversed down the driveway to the road. He spun the wheel and hit the gas and took off, back the way they had come.

'Thank God,' the doctor said.

'That she was OK?'

'No, that Seth Duncan wasn't there.'

'I saw his picture. He doesn't look like much to me. I bet his dog's a poodle.'

'They don't have a dog.'

'Figure of speech. I can see a country doctor being worried about getting in the middle of a domestic dispute where the guy drinks beer and wears a sleeveless T-shirt and has a couple of pit bull terriers in the yard, with broken-down appliances and cars. But apparently Seth Duncan doesn't.'

The doctor said nothing.

Reacher said, 'But you're scared of him anyway. So his power comes from somewhere else. Financial or political, maybe. He has a nice house.'

The doctor said nothing.

Reacher asked, 'Was it him?'

'Yes.'

'You know that for sure?'

'Yes.'

'And he's done it before?'

'Yes.'

'How many times?'

'A lot. Sometimes it's her ribs.'

'Has she told the cops?'

'We don't have cops. We depend on the county. They're usually sixty miles away.'

'She could call.'

'She's not going to press charges. They never do. If they let it go the first time, that's it.'

'Where does a guy like Duncan go to eat dinner with his friends?'

The doctor didn't answer, and Reacher didn't ask again.

The doctor said, 'Are we heading back to the lounge?'

'No, I'm taking you home.'

'Thanks. That's good of you. But it's a long walk back to the motel.'

'Your problem, not mine,' Reacher said. 'I'm keeping the car. You can hike over and pick it up in the morning.'

Five miles south of the motel the doctor stared all over again at the three old houses standing alone at the end of their driveway, and then he faced front and directed Reacher left and right and left along the boundaries of dark empty fields to a new ranch house set on a couple of flat acres bounded by a post-and-rail fence.

'Got your key?' Reacher asked him.

'On the ring.'

'Got another key?'

'My wife will let me in.'

'You hope,' Reacher said. 'Goodnight.'

He watched the doctor stumble through the first

twenty feet of his driveway and then he K-turned and threaded back to the main north-south two-lane. If in doubt turn left, was his motto, so he headed north a mile and then he pulled over and thought. Where would a guy like Seth Duncan go for dinner with his friends?

FIVE

A steakhouse, was Reacher's conclusion. A rural area, farm country, a bunch of prosperous types playing good-old-boy, rolling their sleeves, loosening their ties, ordering a pitcher of domestic beer, getting sirloins cooked rare, smirking about the coastal pussies who worried about cholesterol. Nebraska counties were presumably huge and thinly populated, which could put thirty or more miles between restaurants. But the night was dark and steakhouses always had lit signs. Part of the culture. Either the word *Steakhouse* in antique script along the spine of the roof, all outlined in neon, or an upmarket nameboard all blasted with spotlights.

Reacher killed his headlights and climbed out of the Subaru and grabbed one of the roof rails and stepped up on the hood and then crouched and eased himself up on the roof. He stood tall, his eye line eleven feet above the grade in a flat part of the world. He turned a full 360 and peered into the darkness. Saw the ghostly blue glow of the motel far off to the north, and then a distant pink halo maybe ten miles south and west. Maybe just a gas station, but it was the only other light to be seen. So Reacher drove south and then west. He stopped twice more to fix his bearings. The glow in the air grew brighter as he homed in on it. Red neon, made slightly pink by the night mist. Could be anything. A liquor store, another motel, Exxon.

It was a steakhouse. He came up on it end-on. It was a long low place with candles in the windows and siding like a barn and a swaybacked roof like an old mare in a field. It was standing alone in an acre of beaten dirt. It had a bright sign along its ridgeline, a bird's nest of glass tubing and metal supports spelling out the word *Steakhouse* in antique script and red light. It was ringed with parked cars, all of them nose-in like sucking pigs or jets at a terminal. There were sedans and pick-up trucks and SUVs, some of them new, some of them old, most of them domestic.

Reacher parked the doctor's Subaru on its own near the road. He climbed out and stood for a moment in the cold, rolling his shoulders, trying to get his upper body comfortable. He had never taken aspirin and wasn't about to start. He had been banged up in the hospital a couple of times, with IV morphine drips in his arms, and he remembered that experience quite fondly. But outside of the ICU he was going to rely on time and willpower. No other option.

He walked to the steakhouse door. Inside it was a small square lobby with another door. Inside that was an unattended maître d' lectern with a reading light and a reservations book. To the right was a small dining room with two couples finishing up their meals. To the left, the exact same thing. Ahead, a short corridor with a larger room at the end of it. Low ceilings, unfinished wood on the walls, brass accents. A warm, intimate place.

Reacher stepped past the lectern and checked the larger room. Directly inside the arch was a table for two. It had one guy at it, eating, wearing a red Cornhuskers football jacket. The University of Nebraska. In the main body of the room was a table for eight. It was occupied by seven men, coats and ties, three facing three plus the guy from the wedding photograph at the head. He was a little older than the picture, a little bonier, even more smug, but it was the same guy. No question. He was unmistakable. The table held the wreckage of a big meal. Plates, glasses, serrated knives with worn wooden handles.

Reacher stepped into the room. As he moved the guy alone at the table for two stood up smoothly and sidestepped into Reacher's path. He raised his hand like a traffic cop. Then he placed that hand on Reacher's chest. He was a big man. Nearly as tall as Reacher himself, a whole lot younger, maybe a little heavier, in good shape, with some level of mute intelligence in his eyes. Strength and brains. A dangerous mixture. Reacher preferred the old days, when muscle was dumb. He blamed education. The end of social promotion. There was a genetic price to be paid for making athletes attend class.

Nobody looked over from the big table.

Reacher said, 'What's your name, fat boy?'

The guy said, 'My name?'

'It's not a difficult question.'

'Brett.'

38

Reacher said, 'So here's the thing, Brett. Either you take your hand off my chest, or I'll take it off your wrist.'

The guy dropped his hand. But he didn't move out of the way.

'What?' Reacher asked.

The guy asked, 'Are you here to see Mr Duncan?'

'What do you care?'

'I work for Mr Duncan.'

'Really?' Reacher said. 'What do you do for him?'

'I schedule his appointments.'

'And?'

'You don't have one.'

'When can I get one?'

'How does never work for you?'

'Not real well, Brett.'

'Sir, you need to leave.'

'What are you, security? A bodyguard? What the hell is he?'

'He's a private citizen. I'm one of his assistants, that's all. And now we need to get you back to your car.'

'You want to walk me out to the lot?'

'Sir, I'm just doing my job.'

The seven men at the big table were all hunched forward on their elbows, conspiratorial, six of them listening to a story Duncan was telling, laughing on cue, having a hell of a time. Elsewhere in the building there were kitchen noises and the sharp sounds of silverware on plates and the thump of glasses going down on wooden tabletops.

Reacher said, 'Are you sure about this?'

The young man said, 'I'd appreciate it.'

Reacher shrugged.

'OK,' he said. 'Let's go.' He turned and threaded his way back around the lectern and through the first door and through the second and out to the cold night air. The big guy followed him all the way. Reacher squeezed between two trucks and headed across open ground towards the Subaru. The big guy followed him all the way. Reacher stopped ten feet short of the car and turned around. The big guy stopped too, face to face. He waited, standing easy, relaxed, patient, competent.

Reacher said, 'Can I give you some advice?'

'About what?'

'You're smart, but you're not a genius. You just swapped a good tactical situation for a much worse one. Inside, there were crowded quarters and witnesses and telephones and possible interventions, but out here there's nothing at all. You just gave away a big advantage. Out here I could take my sweet time kicking your ass and there's no one to help you.'

'Nobody's ass needs to get kicked tonight.'

'I agree. But whatever, I still need to give Mr Duncan a message.'

'What message?'

'He hits his wife. I need to explain to him why that's a bad idea.'

'I'm sure you're mistaken.'

'I've seen the evidence. Now I need to see Duncan.'

'Sir, get real. You won't be seeing anything. Only one of us is going back in there tonight, and it won't be you.'

'You enjoy working for a guy like that?'

'I have no complaints.'

'You might, later. Someone told me the nearest ambulance is sixty miles away. You could be lying out here for an hour.'

'Sir, you need to get in your car and move right along.'

Reacher put his hands in his coat pockets, to immobilize his arms, to protect them from further damage. He said, 'Last chance, Brett. You can still walk away. You don't need to get hurt for scum like that.'

'I have a job to do.'

Reacher nodded, and said 'Listen, kid' very quietly, and the big guy leaned in fractionally to hear the next part of the sentence, and Reacher kicked him hard in the groin, right-footed, a heavy boot on the end of a driving leg, and then he stepped back while the guy jackknifed ninety degrees and puked and retched and gasped and spluttered. Then Reacher kicked him again, a solid blow to the side of the head, like a soccer player pivoting to drive a volleyed crossfield pass into the goal. The guy pinwheeled on the balls of his feet and went down like he was trying to screw himself into the ground.

Reacher kept his hands in his pockets and headed for the steakhouse door again.

SIX

The party was still in full swing in the back room. No more elbows on tables. Now all seven men were leaning back expansively, enjoying themselves, spreading out, owning the space. They were all a little red in the face from the warmth and the beer, six of them half listening to the seventh boasting about something and getting ready to one-up him with the next anecdote. Reacher strolled in and stepped behind Duncan's chair and took his hands out of his pockets. He put them on Duncan's shoulders. The room went absolutely silent. Reacher leaned on his hands and pulled them back a little until Duncan's chair was balanced uneasily, up on two legs. Then he let go and the chair thumped forward again and Duncan scrambled up out of it and stood straight and turned around, equal parts fear and anger in his face, plus an attempt to play it cool for his pals. Then he looked around and couldn't find his guy, which took out some of the cool and some of the anger and left all of the fear.

Reacher asked, 'Seth Duncan?'

The bony man didn't answer.

Reacher said, 'I have a message for you, pal.'

Duncan said, 'Who from?'

'The National Association of Marriage Counselors.'

'Is there such a thing?'

'Probably.'

'What's the message?'

'It's more of a question.'

'OK, what's the question?'

'The question is, how do *you* like it?' Reacher hit him, a straight right to the nose, a big vicious blow, his knuckles driving through cartilage and bone and crushing it all flat. Duncan went over backward and landed on the table. He bounced once and plates broke and glasses tipped over and knives skittered away and fell to the floor.

Duncan made no attempt to get up.

Reacher walked away, down the corridor, past the lectern, back to the lot.

The key the red-headed guy had given him was marked with a big figure six, so Reacher parked next to the sixth cabin and went inside and found a miniature version of the lounge, a purely circular space except for a straight section boxed off for a bathroom and a closet. The ceiling was domed and washed with light. The bed was against the wall, on a platform that had been custom built to fit the curve. There was a tub-shaped armchair and a small round table next to it, with an old-fashioned glass television on a larger table nearby. There was an old-fashioned telephone next to the bed. It had a rotary dial. The bathroom was small but adequate, with a shower head over a tub, and the closet was about the same size as the bathroom.

Everything he needed, and nothing he didn't.

He undressed and left his clothes on the bed and took a shower. He ran the water as hot as he could stand and let it play over his neck, his shoulders, his arms, his ribs. He raised one arm, then the other, then both of them together. They moved, but they moved like a newly constructed machine in need of some further development. The good news was that his knuckles didn't hurt at all.

Seth Duncan's doctor was more than two hundred miles away in Denver, Colorado. A first-class medical man, no question, but obviously impractical for emergency services. And the nearest ER was an hour away. And no one in his right mind would go near the local quack. So Duncan had a friend drive him to his uncle Jasper Duncan's place. Because his uncle Jasper Duncan was the kind of guy who could handle odd things at odd hours. He lived five miles south of the motel crossroads, in the northernmost of the three old houses that stood all alone at the end of their long shared driveway. The house was a warren, filled with all kinds of things saved against the day they might be useful. Uncle Jasper himself was more than sixty years old, built like the bole of an oak, a man of various arcane skills, a reservoir of folk wisdom and backwoods knowledge.

Jasper sat Seth Duncan in a kitchen chair and took a look at the injury. Then he went away and rooted around and came back with a syringe and some local anaesthetic. It was a veterinary product, designed for hogs, but mammals were mammals, and it worked. When the site was properly numb, Jasper used a strong thumb and a strong forefinger to set the bone and then went away again and rooted around and came back with an old aluminium facial splint. It was the kind of thing he could be counted on to have at hand. He worked at it and reshaped it to fit and taped it over his nephew's nose. He stopped up the nostrils with wads of gauze and used warm water to sponge away the blood.

Then he got on the phone and called his neighbours.

Next to him lived his brother Jonas Duncan, and next to Jonas lived their brother Jacob Duncan, who was Seth Duncan's father. Five minutes later all four men were sitting around Jasper's kitchen table, and a council of war had started.

Jacob Duncan said, 'First things first, son. Who was the guy?'

Seth Duncan said, 'I never saw him before.'

Jonas said, 'No, first things first, where the hell was your boy Brett?'

'The guy jumped him in the parking lot. Brett was escorting him out. The guy kicked him in the balls and then kicked him in the head. Just left him lying there.'

'Is he OK?'

'He's got a concussion. Doesn't know what day it is. Useless piece of shit. I want him replaced.'

'Plenty more where he came from,' Jonas said.

Jasper asked, 'So who was this guy?'

'He was a big man in a brown coat. With a watch cap

on his head. That's all I saw. That's all I remember. He just came in and hit me.'

'Why would he?'

'I don't know.'

'Didn't he say anything?'

'Just some bullshit. But Brett said he was driving the doctor's car.'

'He doesn't know what day it is but he remembers what car the guy was in?'

'I guess concussions are unpredictable.'

'And you're sure it wasn't the doctor who hit you?'

'I told you, I never saw the guy before. I know the doctor. And the damn doctor wouldn't hit me, anyway. He wouldn't dare.'

Jacob Duncan said, 'What aren't you telling us, son?'

'I have a bad headache.'

'I'm sure you do. But you know that's not what I mean.'

'I don't want to talk.'

'But you know you have to. We can't let a thing like this go by.'

Seth Duncan looked left, looked right. He said, 'OK, I had a dispute with Eleanor tonight. Before I went out. No big deal. But I had to slap her.'

'How hard?'

'I might have made her nose bleed.'

'How bad?'

'You know she's delicate.'

The kitchen went quiet for a moment. Jonas Duncan said, 'So let's try to piece it together. Your wife called the doctor.'

'She's been told not to do that.'

'But maybe she did anyway. Because she's delicate. And maybe the doctor wasn't home. Maybe he was in the motel lounge, like he usually is, halfway through a bottle of Jim Beam, like he usually is. Maybe Eleanor reached him there.'

'He's been told to stay away from her.'

'But maybe he didn't obey. Sometimes doctors have strange notions. And perhaps he was too drunk to drive. He usually is. Because of the bourbon. So perhaps he asked someone else to drive him. Because of his level of concern.'

'Who else?'

'Another guy in the lounge.'

'Nobody would dare do that.'

'Nobody who lives here, I agree. Nobody who knows not to. But a stranger might do it. And it's a motel, after all. That's what motels are for. Strangers, passing through.'

'OK, so then what?'

'Maybe the stranger didn't like what he saw at your house, and he came to find you.'

'Eleanor gave me up?'

'She must have. How else would the guy have known where to look? He can't know his way around, if he's a stranger.'

Jacob Duncan asked, 'What exactly did he say to you?'

'Some bullshit about marriage counselling.'

Jonas Duncan nodded and said, 'There you go. That's how it played out. We've got a passer-by full of moral outrage. A guest in the motel.'

Seth Duncan said, 'I want him hurt bad.'

His father said, 'He will be, son. He'll be hurt bad and sent on his way. Who have we got?'

Jasper said, 'Not Brett, I guess.'

Jonas said, 'Plenty more where he came from.'

Jacob Duncan said, 'Send two of them. Have them call me for orders before they deploy.'

SEVEN

Reacher dressed again after his shower, coat and all because the room was cold, and then he turned the lights off and sat in the tub armchair and waited. He didn't expect Seth Duncan to call the cops. Apparently the cops were a county department, sixty miles away. No local ties. No local loyalties. And calling the cops would require a story, and a story would unravel straight to a confession about beating his wife. No smug guy would head down that route.

But a smug guy who had just lost a bodyguard might have access to a replacement, or two or three. And whereas bodyguarding was generally a reactive profession, those two or three substitutes might be persuaded to go proactive for one night only, especially if they were Brett's friends. And Reacher knew it wouldn't be hard to track him down. The Apollo Inn was probably the only public accommodation in two hundred square miles. And if the doctor's drinking habits were well known in the neighbourhood, it wouldn't be difficult to puzzle out the chain of causation. The phone call, the treatment, the intervention.

So Reacher dressed again and laced his boots and sat in the dark and kept his ears open for tyres on gravel.

More than four hundred and fifty miles due north of where Reacher was sitting, the United States finished and Canada began. The world's longest land border followed the 49th Parallel, over mountains and roads and rivers and streams, and through towns and fields and woods, its western portion running perfectly straight for nearly nineteen hundred miles, all the way from Washington State to Minnesota, every inch of it undefended in the military sense, most of it unfenced and unmarked, but much of it surveilled more closely than people knew. Between Washington State and Minnesota there were fifty-four official crossings, seventeen manned around the clock, thirty-six manned through daylight hours only, and one entirely unstaffed but equipped with telephones connected to remote customs offices. Elsewhere the line was randomly patrolled by a classified number of agents, and more isolated spots had cameras, and great lengths of it had motion sensors buried in the earth. The governments on both sides of the line had a pretty good idea of what was happening along its length.

A pretty good idea, but not perfect knowledge. In the state of Montana, east of the Rockies, below the tree line, the land spent a hundred miles flattening from jagged peaks to gentle plains, most of it thickly forested with conifers, the woods interrupted only by sparkling streams and freshwater lakes and occasional sandy needle-strewn paths. One of those paths connected through labyrinthine miles of twists and turns to a dirt fire road, which ran south and in turn connected to a wandering gravel road, which many miles later ended as an inconspicuous left-hand turn off a minor county two-lane far to the north of a small no-account town called Hogg Parish.

A grey panel truck made that left-hand turn. It rolled slowly along the gravel, crunching quietly, getting bounced left and right by the ruts and the bad camber, its springs creaking, its headlights off and its parking lights on. It burrowed ever deeper into the bitter cold and the darkness, endlessly. Then eventually it turned on to the fire road, beaten dirt now under its wheels, bare frozen trunks to the left and right, a narrow slice of night sky visible overhead, plenty of stars, no moon, the GPS satellites thousands of miles up connecting perfectly, guiding it, showing it the limits of safety.

It crawled onward, many miles, and then the fire road petered out and the sandy track began. The truck slowed to a walk and locked into the ruts it had made on its many previous trips. It followed them left and right through arbitrary turns and curves, between scarred trees where the clearance was tight, with stubs of low branches scraping the sides. It drove for more than an hour and then came to a stop in a location chosen long before, exactly two miles south of the border. No one was certain where the motion sensors had been buried, but most assumed that a belt a mile either side of the line was the practical limit. Like a minefield. Another mile had been added as a safety margin, and a small area of underbrush had been hacked out to allow the truck to turn.

The truck backed up and turned and stopped astride the sandy track, facing south, in position, ready. It shut down and settled and its lights went off.

It waited.

Reacher waited in the dark in his tub armchair, forty minutes, an hour, tracing the next day's intended route in his head. South to the Interstate, and then east. The Interstate would be easy. He had hitchhiked most of the network before. There were on-ramps and rest areas and a vast travelling population, some of it commercial, some of it private, a fair proportion of it lonely and ready for company. The problem would come before the Interstate, on the middle-of-nowhere trek down to it. Since climbing out of the car that had dumped him at the crossroads he had heard no traffic at all. Night-time was always worse than daytime, but even so it was rare in America to be close to a road and hear nothing go by. In fact he had heard nothing at all, no wind, no night sounds, and he had been listening hard, for tyres on gravel. It was like he had gone deaf. He raised his hand awkwardly and clicked his fingers near his ear, just to be sure. He wasn't deaf. It was just the middle of the night, in the countryside. That was all. He got up and used the bathroom and sat back down.

Then he heard something.

Not a passing vehicle, not wind, not night sounds.

Not tyres on gravel.

Footsteps on gravel.

EIGHT

Footsteps on gravel. One pair. A light, hesitant tread, approaching. Reacher watched the window and saw a shape flit across it. Small, slight, head ducked down into the collar of a coat.

A woman.

There was a knock at the door, soft and tentative and padded. A small nervous hand, wearing a glove. A decoy, possibly. Not beyond the wit of man to send someone on ahead, all innocent and unthreatening, to get the door open and lull the target into a sense of false security. Not unlikely that such a person would be nervous and hesitant about her role.

Reacher crossed the floor silently and headed back to the bathroom. He eased the window up and clipped out the screen and rested it in the bathtub. Then he ducked his head and climbed out, scissoring his legs over the sill, stepping down to the gravel. He walked one of the silver timbers that boxed the path, like a tightrope, silently. He went counterclockwise around the circular cabin and came up on the woman from behind.

She was alone.

No cars on the road, nobody in the lot, nobody flattened either side of his door, nobody crouched under his window. Just the woman, standing there on her own. She looked cold. She was wearing a wool coat and a scarf. No hat. She was maybe forty, small, dark, and worried. She raised her hand and knocked again.

Reacher said, 'I'm here.'

She gasped and spun around and put her hand on her chest. Her mouth stayed open and made a tiny O. He said, 'I'm sorry if I startled you, but I wasn't expecting visitors.'

She said, 'Perhaps you should have been.'

'Well, in fact, perhaps I was. But not you.'

'Can we go inside?'

'Who are you?'

'I'm sorry,' she said. 'I'm the doctor's wife.'

'I'm pleased to meet you,' Reacher said.

'Can we go inside?'

Reacher found the key in his pocket and unlocked the door from the outside. The doctor's wife stepped in and he followed her and locked the door again behind them. He crossed the room and closed the bathroom door against the night air coming in through the open window. He turned back to find her standing in the middle of the space. He indicated the armchair and said, 'Please.'

She sat down. Didn't unbutton her coat. She was still nervous. If she had been carrying a purse, she would have had it clamped hard on her knees, defensively. She said, 'I walked all the way over here.'

'To pick up the car? You should have let your husband

do that, in the morning. That's what I arranged with him.'

'He's too drunk to drive.'

'He'll be OK by morning, surely.'

'Morning's too late. You have to get going. Right now. You're not safe here.'

'You think?'

'My husband said you're heading south to the Interstate. I'll drive you there.'

'Now? It's got to be a hundred miles.'

'A hundred and twenty.'

'It's the middle of the night.'

'You're not safe here. My husband told me what happened. You interfered with the Duncans. You *saw*. They'll punish him for sure, and we think they'll come after you too.'

'They?'

'The Duncans. There are four of them.'

'Punish him how?'

'Oh, I don't know. Last time they wouldn't let him come here for a month.'

'Here? To the lounge?'

'It's his favourite place.'

'How could they stop him coming here?'

'They told Mr Vincent not to serve him. The owner.'

'Why would the owner of this place do what the Duncans tell him?'

'The Duncans run a trucking business. All of Mr Vincent's supplies come through them. He signed a contract. He kind of had to. That's how the Duncans work. So if Mr Vincent doesn't play ball, a couple of deliveries will be late, a couple lost, a couple damaged. He knows that. He'll go out of business.'

Reacher asked, 'What will they figure to do to me?'

The woman said, 'They hire football players right out of college. Cornhuskers. The ones who were good enough to get scholarships, but not good enough to go to the NFL. Guards and tackles. Big guys.'

Brett, Reacher thought.

The woman said, 'They'll connect the dots and figure out where you are. I mean, where else could you be? They'll pay you a visit. Maybe they're already on their way.'

'From where?'

'The Duncan depot is twenty miles from here. Most of their people live close to it.'

'How many football players have they got?'

'Ten.'

Reacher said nothing.

The woman said, 'My husband heard you say you're headed for Virginia.'

'That's the plan.'

'Is that where you live?'

'As much as anywhere else.'

'We should get going. You're in big trouble.'

'Not unless they send all nine at once,' Reacher said.

'All nine what?'

'Football players.'

'I said there were ten.'

'I already met one of them. He's currently indisposed. They're one short, as of tonight.'

'What?'

'He got between me and Seth Duncan.'

'What did you do to Seth Duncan?'

'I broke his nose.'

'Oh, sweet Jesus. Why?'

'Why not?'

'Oh sweet, sweet Jesus. Where are the car keys?'

'What will happen to Mrs Duncan?'

'We need to get going. Right this minute.'

'First answer the question.'

'Mrs Duncan will be punished too. For calling my husband. She's been told not to do that. Just like he's been told not to go treat her.'

'He's a doctor. He doesn't get a choice. They take an oath, don't they?'

'What's your name?'

'Jack Reacher.'

'We have to go, Mr Reacher. Right now.'

'What will they do to Mrs Duncan?'

'This isn't your business,' the woman said. Which, strictly speaking, was fairly close to Reacher's own opinion at that point. His business was to get himself to Virginia, and he was being offered a ride through the hardest part of the journey, fast and free. 1-80 awaited, two hours away. An on-ramp, the last of the night drivers, the first stirrings of morning traffic. Maybe breakfast. Maybe there was a rest area or a truck stop with a greasy spoon café. Bacon, eggs, coffee.

'What will they do to her?' he asked again.

The woman said, 'Probably nothing much.'

'What kind of nothing much?'

'Well, they might put her on a coagulant. One of the

uncles seems to have medical supplies. Or maybe they'll just stop her taking so much aspirin. So she doesn't bleed so bad next time. And they'll probably ground her for a month. That's all. Nothing too serious. Nothing for you to worry about. They've been married ten years, after all. She's not a prisoner. She could leave if she wanted to.'

'Except this time she inadvertently got her husband's nose broken. He might take that out on her, if he can't take it out on me.'

The doctor's wife said nothing. But it sounded like she was agreeing. The strange round room went quiet. Then Reacher heard tyres on gravel.

NINE

Reacher checked the window. There were four tyres in total, big knobbly off-road things, all of them on a Ford pick-up truck. The truck had a jacked suspension and lights on a roof bar and a snorkel air intake and a winch on the front. There were two large shapes in the gloom inside. The shapes had thick necks and huge shoulders. The truck nosed slowly down the row of cabins and stopped twenty feet behind the parked Subaru. The headlights stayed on. The engine idled. The doors opened. Two guys climbed out.

They both looked like Brett, only bigger. Late twenties, easily six-six or six-seven, probably close to three hundred pounds each, big waists made tiny by huge chests and arms and shoulders. They had cropped hair and small eyes and fleshy faces. They were the kind of guys who ate two dinners and were still hungry afterwards. They were wearing red Cornhuskers football jackets made grey by the blue light from the cabin's eaves.

The doctor's wife joined Reacher at the window.

'Sweet Jesus,' she said.

Reacher said nothing.

The two guys closed the truck's doors and stepped back in unison to the load bed and unlatched a tool locker bolted across its width behind the cab. They lifted the lid and one took out an engineer's ball-peen hammer and the other took out a two-headed wrench at least a foot and a half long. They left the lid open and walked forward into the truck's headlight wash and their shadows jumped ahead of them. They were light on their feet and nimble for their size, like football players usually were. They paused for a moment and looked at the cabin's door, and then they turned away.

Towards the Subaru.

They attacked it in a violent frenzy, an absolute blitzkrieg, two or three minutes of uncontrolled smashing and pounding. The noise was deafening. They smashed every shard of glass out of the windshield, they smashed the side windows, the back window, the headlights, the tail lights. They hammered jagged dents into the hood, into the doors, into the roof, into the fenders, into the tailgate. They put their arms through the absent glass and smashed up the dials and the switches and the radio.

Shit, Reacher thought. *There goes my ride.*

'My husband's punishment,' the doctor's wife whispered. 'Worse this time.'

The two guys stopped as suddenly as they had started. They stood there, one each side of the wrecked wagon, and they breathed hard and rolled their shoulders and let their weapons hang down by their sides. Pebbles of broken automotive glass glittered in the neon and the boom and clang of battered sheet metal echoed away to absolute silence.

Reacher took off his coat and dumped it on the bed.

The two guys formed up shoulder to shoulder and headed for the cabin's door. Reacher opened it up and stepped out to meet them head on. Win or lose, fighting inside would bust up the room, and Vincent the motel owner had enough problems already.

The two guys stopped ten feet away and stood there, side by side, symmetrical, their weapons in their outside hands, four cubic yards of bone and muscle, six hundred pounds of beef, all flushed and sweating in the chill.

Reacher said, 'Pop quiz, guys. You spent four years in college learning how to play a game. I spent thirteen years in the army learning how to kill people. So how scared am I?'

No answer.

'And you were so bad at it you couldn't even get drafted afterwards. I was so good at it I got all kinds of medals and promotions. So how scared are you?'

'Not very,' said the guy with the wrench.

Wrong answer. But understandable. Being a good enough guard or tackle in high school to get a full-boat free ride to the big school in Lincoln was no mean achievement. Playing even a cameo role on the field in Memorial Stadium made a guy close to the best of the best. And failing to make the National Football League was no kind of real disgrace. The dividing line between success and failure in the world of sports was often very narrow, and the reasons for falling on one side or the other were often very arbitrary. These guys had been

61

the elite for most of twenty years, the greatest thing their neighbourhood had ever seen, then their town, then their county, maybe their state. They had been popular, they had been feted, they had gotten the girls. And they probably hadn't lost a fight since they were eight years old.

Except they had never had a fight. Not in the sense meant by people paid to fight or die. Pushing and shoving at the schoolyard gate or on the sidewalk outside the soda shop or late at night after a start-of-summer keg party was as far from fighting as two fat guys tossing lame spirals in the park were from the Superbowl. These guys were amateurs, and worse, they were complacent amateurs, accustomed to getting by on bulk and reputation alone. In the real world, they would be dead before they even landed a blow.

Case in point: bad choice of weapons. Best are shooting weapons, second best are stabbing weapons, third best are slashing weapons. Blunt instruments are way down the list. They slow hand speed. Their uncontrolled momentum is disadvantageous after a miss. And: if you have to use them, the backhand is the only way to go, so that you accelerate and strike in the same sudden fluid motion. But these guys were shoulder to shoulder with their weapons in their outer hands, which promised forehand swings, which meant that the hammer or the wrench would have to be swung backward first, then stopped, then brought forward again. The first part of the move would be a clear telegraph. All the warning in the world. No surprise. They might as well put a notice in the newspaper, or send a cable by Western Union.

Reacher smiled. He had been raised on military bases all around the world, battling hardcore Marine progeny, honing his skills against gangs of resentful native youths in dusty Pacific streets and damp European alleys. Whatever hardscrabble town in Texas or Arkansas or Nebraska these guys had come up in had been a feather bed by comparison. And while they had been studying the playbook and learning to run and jump and catch, he had been broken down and built back up by the kind of experts who could snap your neck so fast you never knew it had happened until you went to nod your head and it rolled away down the street without you.

The guy with the wrench said, 'We've got a message for you, pal.'

Reacher said, 'Really?'

'Actually it's more of a question.'

'Any difficult words? You need more time?' Reacher stepped forward and a little to his right. He put himself directly in front of the two guys, equidistant, seven feet away, so that if he was six on a clock face, they were eleven and one. The guy with the wrench was on his left, and the guy with the hammer was on his right.

The guy with the wrench moved first. He dumped his weight on his right foot and started a short, compact backswing with the heavy metal tool, a backswing that looked designed to bounce off tensed muscles after perhaps forty degrees or a couple of feet, and then snap forward again through a low horizontal arc, aiming to break Reacher's left arm between the shoulder and the elbow. The guy wasn't a total idiot. It was a decent first try.

But it was uncompleted.

Reacher had his weight on his left foot, and he had his right foot moving a split second after the wrench, driving the same way at the same speed, maybe even a little faster, and before the wrench stopped moving backward and started moving forward the heel of Reacher's boot met the big guy's knee and drove right through it, smashing the kneecap deep into the joint, bursting it, rupturing ligaments, tearing tendons, dislocating the joint, turning it inside out, making it fold forward the way no knee is designed to go. The guy started to drop and before he was past the first vertical inch and before the first howl was starting in his throat Reacher was stepping past him, on the outside, shouldering him aside, deleting him from memory, forgetting all about him. He was now essentially an unarmed one-legged man, and one-legged men had never featured near the top of Reacher's concerns.

The guy with the hammer had a split-second choice to make. He could spin on the forehand, but that would give him almost a full circle to move through, because Reacher was now almost behind him, and anyway his crippled buddy was in the way of the spin, just waiting helplessly for a face to face collision. Or the guy could flail on the backhand, a Hail Mary blind swing into the void behind him, hoping for surprise, hoping for a lucky contact.

He chose to flail behind him.

Which Reacher was half expecting and wholly rooting for. He watched the lunge, the arm moving, the wrist flicking back, the elbow turning inside out, and he planted his feet and jerked from the waist and drove the heel of his hand into the knob of the guy's elbow, that huge force jabbing one way, the weight of the swinging hammer pulling the other way, the elbow joint cracking, the wrist overextending, the hammer falling, the guy instantly crumpling and dancing and hopping and trying to force his body to a place where his elbow stayed bent the right way around, which pulled him through a tight counterclockwise circle and left him unsteady and unbalanced and face to face with Reacher, who paused less time than it took for the hammer to hit the floor and then head-butted him hard in the face, a savage, snapping movement, solid bone-to-bone contact, and then Reacher danced away towards the wrecked Subaru and turned and planned the next second and a half.

The guy who had held the wrench was down, rolling around, in Reacher's judgement stunned not so much by the pain, most of which would be still to come, but by the awful dawning knowledge that life as he knew it was over, the momentary fears he might have experienced as an athlete after a bad on-field collision finally come true, his future now holding nothing but canes and braces and limps and pain and frustration and unemployment. The guy who had held the hammer was still on his feet, back on his heels, blinking, his nose pouring blood, one arm limp and numb, his eyes unfocused, not a whole lot going on in his head.

Enough, a person might say, if that person lived in the civilized world, the world of movies and television and fair play and decent restraint. But Reacher didn't live there. He lived in a world where you don't start fights but you sure as hell finish them, and you don't lose them either, and he was the inheritor of generations of hard-won wisdom that said the best way to lose them was to assume they were over when they weren't yet. So he stepped back to the guy who had held the hammer and risked his hands and his arms and crashed a low right hook into the skinny triangle below the guy's pectorals and above his six-pack abdominals, a huge blow, timed and jerked and delivered to perfection, straight into the solar plexus, hitting it like a switch, and the guy went into all kinds of temporary distress and sagged forward and down. Reacher waited until he was bent low enough for the finishing kick to the face, delivered hard but with a degree of mercy, in that smashed teeth and a busted jaw were better than out-and-out brain damage.

Then he turned to the guy who had held the wrench and waited until he rolled the right way and put him to sleep with a kick to the forehead. He picked up the wrench and broke the guy's wrist with it, *one*, and then the other wrist, *two*, and turned back and did the same to the guy who had held the hammer, *three*, *four*. The two men were somebody's weapons, consciously deployed, and no soldier left an enemy's abandoned ordnance on the field in working order.

The doctor's wife was watching from the cabin door, all kinds of terror in her face.

'What?' Reacher asked her.

TEN

The Ford pick-up truck was still idling patiently. Its headlights were still on. The two guys lay slack and heaped in the gloom beyond the bright beams, steaming slightly, four cubic yards of bone and muscle, six hundred pounds of beef, now horizontal, not vertical. They were going to be very hard to move. The doctor's wife said, 'Now what the hell are we going to do?'

Reacher said, 'About what?'

'I wish you hadn't done that.'

'Why?'

'Because nothing good can possibly come of it.'

'Why not? What the hell is going on here? Who are these people?'

'I told you. Football players.'

'Not them,' Reacher said. 'The Duncans. The people who sent them.'

'Did they see me?'

'These two? I doubt it.'

'That's good. I really can't get involved in this.'

'Why not? What's going on here?'

'This isn't your business.'

'Tell that to them.'

'You seemed so angry.'

'Me?' Reacher said. 'I wasn't angry. I was barely interested. If I had been angry, we'd be cleaning up with a fire hose. As it is we're going to need a forklift truck.'

'What are you going to do with them?'

'Tell me about the Duncans.'

'They're a family. That's all. Seth, and his father, and two uncles. They used to farm. Now they run a trucking business.'

'Which one of them hires the football players?'

'I don't know who makes the decisions. Maybe it's a majority thing. Or maybe they all have to agree.'

'Where do they live?'

'You know where Seth lives.'

'What about the other three? The old guys?'

'Just south of here. Three houses all alone. One each.'

'I saw them. Your husband was staring at them.'

'Did you see his hands?'

'Why?'

'He was probably crossing his fingers for luck. Whistling past the graveyard.'

'Why? Who the hell are they?'

'They're a hornets' nest, that's what. And you just poked it with a stick and now you're going to leave.'

'What was I supposed to do? Let them hit me with shop tools?'

'That's what we do. We take our punishments and we keep smiles on our faces and our heads down. We go along to get along.'

'What the hell are you talking about?'

She paused. Shook her head.

'It's not a big deal,' she said. 'Not really. So we tell ourselves. If you throw a frog in hot water, he'll jump right out again. Put him in cold water and heat it up slowly, he'll let himself get boiled to death without ever noticing.'

'And that's you?'

'Yes,' she said. 'That's us.'

'Give me the details.'

She paused again. She shook her head again.

'No,' she said. 'No, no, no. You won't hear anything bad about the Duncans from me. I want that on the record. I'm a local girl, and I've known them all my life. They're a fine family. There's nothing wrong with them. Nothing at all.'

The doctor's wife took a long hard look at the wrecked Subaru and then she set off walking home. Reacher offered her a ride in the pick-up truck, but she wouldn't hear of it. He watched her out of the motel lot until she was swallowed by the dark and lost to sight. Then he turned back to the two guys on the gravel outside his door. No way could he lift an unconscious human weighing three hundred pounds. Three hundred pounds of free weights on a bar, maybe. But not three hundred pounds of inert flesh and blood the size of a refrigerator.

He opened the pick-up's door and climbed into the cab. It smelled of pine disinfectant and hot oil. He found the gearshift and took off forward on a curve and then stopped and backed up until the tailgate was in line with where the two guys lay. He got out again and stepped around the hood and looked at the winch that was bolted to the frame at the front. It was electric. It had a motor connected to a drum wrapped with thin steel cable. The cable had a snap hook on the end. There was a release ratchet and a winding button.

He hit the ratchet and unwound the cable, ten feet, twenty, thirty. He flipped it up over the hood, over the roof of the cab, between two lights on the light bar, over the load bed, and down to where the guys were lying behind the truck. He dropped the tailgate flat and bent and fastened the hook on to the front of the first guy's belt. He walked back to the front of the truck and found the winding button and pressed.

The motor started and the drum turned and the slack pulled out of the cable. Then the cable went tight and quivered like a bowstring and burred a groove into the front edge of the hood and pulled a crease into the light bar on the roof. The drum slowed, and then it dug in and kept on turning. The truck squatted low on its springs. Reacher walked back and saw the first guy getting dragged by his belt towards the load bed, scuffling along the ground, waist first, arms and legs trailing. The guy dragged all the way to the edge of the tailgate. Then the cable came up vertically and shrieked against the sheet metal and the guy's belt stretched oval and he started up into the air, spinning a little, his back arched, his head and legs and arms hanging down. Reacher waited and timed it and pulled and pushed and shoved and got him up over the angle and watched as he dragged onward into the load bed. Reacher stepped back to the front and waited a beat and then stopped the winch. He came back and leaned into the load bed and released the hook, and then he did the same things all over again for the second guy, like a veterinarian called out to a couple of dead heifers.

Reacher drove five miles south and slowed and stopped just before the shared driveway that ran west towards the three houses huddled together. They had been painted white a generation ago and still managed a grey gleam in the moonlight. They were substantial buildings, arranged along a short arc without much space between them. There was no landscaping. Just threadbare gravel and weeds and three parked cars, and then a heavy post-and-rail fence, and then flat empty fields running away into the darkness.

There was a light behind a ground floor window in the house on the right. No other signs of activity.

Reacher pulled thirty feet ahead and then backed up and turned and reversed into the driveway. Gravel crunched and scrabbled under his tyres. A noisy approach. He risked fifty yards, which was about halfway. Then he stopped and slid out and unlatched the tailgate. He climbed up into the load bed and grabbed the first guy by the belt and the collar and heaved and hauled and half dragged and half rolled him to the edge and then put the sole of his boot against the guy's hip and shoved him over. The guy fell three feet and thumped down on his side and settled on his back.

Return to sender.

Reacher went back for the second guy and pushed and pulled and hauled and rolled him out of the truck right on top of his buddy. Then he latched the tailgate again and vaulted over the side to the ground and got behind the wheel and took off fast.

The four Duncans were still around the table in Jasper's kitchen. Not a planned meeting, but they had a permanently long agenda and they were taking advantage of circumstances. Foremost in their minds was an emerging delay on the Canadian border. Jacob said, 'We're getting pressure from our friend to the south.'

Jonas said, 'We can't control what we can't control.'

'Try telling that to him.'

'He'll get his shipment.'

'When?'

'Whenever.'

'He paid upfront.'

'He always does.'

'A lot of money.'

'It always is.'

'But this time he's agitated. He wants action. And here's the thing. It was very strange. He called me, and it was like jumping into the conversation halfway through.'

'What?'

'He was frustrated, obviously. But also a little surly, like we weren't taking him seriously. Like he had made prior communications that had gone unheeded. Like we had ignored warnings. I felt like he was on page three and I was on page one.'

'He's losing his mind.'

'Unless.'

'Unless what?'

'Unless one of us took a couple of his calls already.'

Jonas Duncan said, 'Well, I didn't.'

'Me either,' Jasper Duncan said.

'You sure?'

'Of course.'

'Because there's really no other explanation here. And remember, this is a guy we can't afford to mess with. This is a deeply unpleasant person.'

Jacob's brothers both shrugged. Two men in their sixties, gnarled, battered, built like fireplugs. Jonas said, 'Don't look at me.'

'Me either,' Jasper said again.

Only Seth Duncan hadn't spoken. Not a word. Jacob's son.

His father asked, 'What aren't you telling us, boy?'

Seth looked down at the table. Then he looked up, awkwardly, the aluminium plate huge on his face. His father and his two uncles stared right back at him. He said, 'It wasn't me who broke Eleanor's nose tonight.'

ELEVEN

Jasper Duncan took a part-used bottle of Knob Creek whiskey from his kitchen cabinet and stuck three gnarled fingers and a blunt thumb in four chipped glasses. He put them on the table and pulled the cork from the bottle and poured four generous measures. He slid the glasses across the scarred wood, a little ceremony, focused and precise. He sat down again and each man took an initial sip, and then the four glasses went back to the table, a ragged little volley of four separate thumps in the quiet of the night.

Jacob Duncan said, 'From the beginning, son.'

Seth Duncan said, 'I'm dealing with it.'

'But not very well, by the sound of it.'

'He's my customer.'

Jacob shook his head. 'He was your contact, back in the day, but we're a family. We do everything together, and nothing apart. There's no such thing as a side deal.'

'We were leaving money on the table.'

'You don't need to go over ancient history. You found a guy willing to pay more for the same merchandise, and we surely appreciate that. But rewards bring risks.

There's no such thing as something for nothing. No free lunch. So what happened?'

'We're a week late.'

'We aren't. We don't specify dates.'

Seth Duncan said nothing.

Jacob said, 'What? You guaranteed a date?'

Seth Duncan nodded.

Jacob said, 'That was dumb, son. We never specify dates. You know we can't afford to. There are a hundred factors outside of our control. The weather, for one.'

'I used a worst-case analysis.'

'You think too much. There's always something worse than the worst. Count on it. So what happened?'

'Two guys showed up. At my house. Two days ago. His people. Tough guys.'

'Where was Brett?'

'I had to tell him I was expecting them.'

'Were you?'

'More or less.'

'Why didn't you tell us?'

'Because I'm dealing with it.'

'Not very well, son. Apparently. What did they do?'

'They said they were there to deliver a message from their boss. An expression of displeasure. I said I understood. I explained. I apologized. They said that wasn't good enough. They said they had been told to leave marks. I said they couldn't. I said I have to be out and about. I have a business to run. So they hit Eleanor instead. To make their point.'

'Just like that?'

'They asked first. They made me agree. They made

her agree, too. They made me hold her. They took turns. I told her sorry afterwards. She said, what's the difference? Them then or you later? Because she knew I was agitated.'

'And then what?'

'I asked for another week. They gave me forty-eight hours.'

'So they came back again? Tonight?'

'Yes. They did it all over again.'

'So who was the guy in the restaurant? One of them?'

'No, he wasn't one of them. I told you, I never saw him before.'

Jonas Duncan said, 'He was a passer-by. Like we figured. From what he said at the time, to the boy. A passer-by full of the wrong end of the stick on this occasion.'

Jacob said, 'Well, at least *he's* out of our hair.'

Then they heard faint sounds outside. Tyres on gravel. A vehicle, on their driveway. It came slow, whining in a low gear. It seemed to stop halfway. The engine kept on running. There was a pause, and then a ragged thump, dull, percussive, somehow mixed with the sound of breath expelled, and then another pause, and another sound. Then the vehicle drove away, faster this time, with acceleration and gear changes, and the world went quiet again.

Jonas Duncan was first out the door. From fifty yards he could see strange humped shapes in the moonlight. From twenty he saw what they were. From five he saw

76

what condition they were in. He said, 'Not out of our hair. Not exactly. Not yet.'

Jacob Duncan said, 'Who the hell *is* this guy?'

Seth Duncan and his uncle Jasper didn't speak.

Reacher parked the pick-up truck next to the wrecked Subaru and found the motel owner waiting at his door. Mr Vincent. His hair looked black in the light.

'Changing the locks?' Reacher asked him.

The guy said, 'I hope I won't have to.'

'But?'

'I can't let you stay here.'

Reacher said, 'I paid thirty dollars.'

'I'll refund it, of course.'

'That's not the point. A deal is a deal. I didn't damage anything.'

Vincent said nothing.

Reacher said, 'They already know I'm here. Where else could I be?'

'It was OK before.'

'Before what?'

'Before they told me not to let you stay here. Ignorance of the law is no offence. But I can't defy them now. Not after they informed me.'

'When did they inform you?'

'Two minutes ago. By phone.'

'You always do what they tell you?'

Vincent didn't answer.

'Dumb question, I suppose,' Reacher said.

'I'd lose everything I've worked for. And my family before me. All those years.'

'Since 1969?' Reacher asked.

'How did you know that?'

'Just a lucky guess. The moon landing and all. The Apollo programme.'

'Do you remember 1969?'

'Vaguely.'

'I loved it. So many things were going on. I don't know what happened afterwards. It really seemed like the start of a new era.'

'It was,' Reacher said. 'Just not the era you expected.'

'I'm sorry about this.'

'You going to offer to drive me down to the Interstate now?'

'I can't do that either. We're not supposed to help you in any way at all.'

'We?'

'Any of us. They're putting the word out.'

'Well, I seem to have inherited a truck,' Reacher said. 'I can drive myself.'

'Don't,' Vincent said. 'They'll report it stolen. The county police will stop you. You won't get halfway there.'

'The Duncans control the cops too?'

'No, not really. But a stolen truck is a stolen truck, isn't it?'

'They *want* me to stay here?'

'They do now. You started a war. They want to finish it.'

TWELVE

Reacher stood in the cold between the truck and the motel cabin and looked all around. There was nothing much to see. The blue glow of the neon reached only as far as the dead Subaru, and then it faded away. Overhead was a moon and a billion chilly stars.

Reacher said, 'You still got coffee in the pot?'

Vincent said, 'I can't serve you.'

'I won't rat you out.'

'They might be watching.'

'They're driving two guys sixty miles to the hospital.'

'Not all of them.'

'This is the last place they'll look. They told you to move me on. They'll assume you obeyed.'

'I don't know.'

'Let's make a deal,' Reacher said. 'I'll move on, to spare you the embarrassment. You can keep the thirty bucks, because this isn't your fault. In return I want a cup of coffee and some answers.'

The lounge was dark, except for a lone work light behind the bar. No more soft reds and pinks. Just a harsh fluorescent tube, with a pronounced flicker and a green colour cast and a noisy component. The music was off and the room was silent, apart from the buzz of the light and the rush of air in the heating system. Vincent filled the Bunn machine with water and spooned ground coffee from a can the size of a drum into a paper filter the size of a hat. He set it going and Reacher listened to the water gulping and hissing and watched the precious brown liquid streaming down into the flask.

Reacher said, 'Start at the beginning.'

Vincent said, 'The beginning is a long time ago.'

'It always is.'

'They're an old family.'

'They always are.'

'The first one I knew was old man Duncan. He was a farmer, from a long line of farmers. I guess the first one came here on a land grant. Maybe after the Civil War. They grew corn and beans and built up a big acreage. The old man inherited it all. He had three sons, Jacob, Jasper, and Jonas. It was an open secret that the boys hated farming. But they kept the place going until the old man died. So as not to break his heart. Then they sold up. They went into the trucking business. Much less work. They split up their place and sold it off to their neighbours. Which made sense all around. What was a big spread back in the days of horses and mules wasn't so big any more, with tractors and all, and economies of scale. Land prices were high back then, but the boys sweetened the deals. They gave discounts, if their neighbours signed up to use Duncan Transportation to haul away their harvests.

Which again made sense all around. Everyone was getting what they wanted. Everyone was happy.'

'Until?'

'Things went sour kind of slowly. There was a dispute with one of the neighbours. Ancient history now. This was twenty-five years ago, probably. But it was an acrimonious situation. It festered all one summer, and then that guy didn't get his crop hauled away. The Duncans just wouldn't do it. It rotted on the ground. The guy didn't get paid that year.'

'He couldn't find someone else to haul it?'

'By then the Duncans had the county all sewn up. Not worth it for some other outfit to come all the way here just for one load.'

'The guy couldn't haul it himself?'

'They had all sold their trucks. No need for them, as far as they could see, because of the contracts, and they needed the money for mortgages anyway.'

'The guy could have rented. One time only.'

'He wouldn't have gotten out of his gate. The fine print said only a Duncan truck could haul anything off a farm. No way to contest it, not in court, and definitely not on the ground, because the football players were on the scene by then. The first generation. They must be old men themselves by now.'

'Total control,' Reacher said.

Vincent nodded.

'And very simple,' he said. 'You can work all year, but you need your harvest trucked away, or it's the same thing as sitting on your butt and growing nothing. Farmers live season to season. They can't afford to lose a whole crop. The Duncans found the perfect pinch-point. Whether by accident or design, I don't really know. But as soon as they realized what they had, they sure started enjoying it.'

'How?'

'Nothing real bad. People pay a little over the odds, and they mind their manners. That's about all, really.'

'You too, right?'

Vincent nodded again. 'This place needed some fixing, ten years ago. The Duncans loaned me the money, interest free, if I signed up with them for my deliveries.'

'And you're still paying.'

'We're all still paying.'

'Why sit still and take it?'

'You want a revolution? That's not going to happen. People have got to eat. And the Duncans are smart. No one thing is really that bad. You understand?'

'Like a frog in warm water,' Reacher said. 'That's how the doctor's wife described it to me.'

'That's how we all describe it.'

'You still get boiled to death in the end.'

'Long time coming.' Vincent turned away and filled a mug with coffee. Another NASA logo. He pushed it across the bar. He said, 'My mother was related to Neil Armstrong. The first man on the moon. Fifteenth cousin or something.'

Reacher sniffed the steam and tried the coffee. It was excellent. It was fresh, hot, and strong. Vincent said, 'President Nixon had a speech prepared, you know, just in case they got stuck up there. In case they couldn't lift off the surface. Can you imagine? Just sitting there, looking up at Earth in the sky, waiting for the air to run out?'

Reacher said, 'Aren't there laws? Monopolies, or restraint of trade or something?'

Vincent said, 'Going to a lawyer is the same thing as going bankrupt. A lawsuit takes what? Two, three years? Two or three years without your crop getting hauled is suicide. And have you ever worked on a farm? Or run a motel? Believe me, at the end of the day you don't feel like cracking the law books. You feel like getting some sleep.'

Reacher said, 'Wrecking the doctor's car wasn't a small thing.'

Vincent said, 'I agree. It was worse than usual. We're all a little unsettled by that.'

'All?'

'We all talk to each other. There's a phone tree. You know, for when something happens. We share information.'

'And what are people saying?'

'The feeling is maybe the doctor deserved it. He was way out of line.'

'For treating his patient?'

'She wasn't sick. It was an intervention.'

'I think you're all sick,' Reacher said. 'I think you're all a bunch of spineless cowards. How hard would it be to do something? One guy on his own, I agree, that's difficult. But if everyone banded together and called another trucker, they'd come. Why wouldn't they? If there's enough business here for the Duncans, there's enough for someone else.'

'The Duncans might sue.'

'Let them. Then they've got three years of legal bills and no income. The shoe would be on the other foot.'

'I don't think another trucker would take the business. They carve things up. They don't poach, in a place like this.'

'You could try.'

Vincent didn't answer.

'Whatever,' Reacher said. 'I really don't care who gets an ear of corn hauled away, or how, or if, or when. Or a bushel of beans. Or a peck or a quart or however the hell you measure beans. You can sort it out for yourselves. Or not. It's up to you. I'm on my way to Virginia.'

'It's not that easy,' Vincent said. 'Not here. People have been scared so long they can't even remember what it's like not to be scared any more.'

Reacher said nothing.

Vincent asked, 'What are you going to do?'

Reacher said, 'That depends on the Duncans. Plan A is to hitch a ride out of here. But if they want a war, then plan B is to win it. I'll keep on dumping football players on their driveway until they got none left. Then I'll walk on up and pay them a visit. Their choice.'

'Stick to plan A. Just go. That's my advice.'

'Show me some traffic and I might.'

'I need something from you.'

'Like what?'

'Your room key. I'm sorry.'

Reacher dug it out of his pocket and placed it on the bar. A big brass item, marked with a figure six.

Vincent said, 'Where are you going to sleep tonight?'

'Better that you don't know,' Reacher said. 'The Duncans might ask you. And you'd tell them, wouldn't you?'

'I'd have to,' Vincent said.

There was no more conversation. Reacher finished his coffee and walked out of the lounge, back to the truck. The winch cable had bent the light bar on the roof, so that from the front the whole thing looked a little cross-eyed. But the key turned and the engine started. Reacher drove out of the motel lot. If in doubt, turn left, was his motto. So he headed south, rolling slow, lights off, letting his eyes adjust to the night-time gloom, looking for a direction to follow.

THIRTEEN

The road was a narrow straight ribbon, with dark empty fields to the right, and dark empty fields to the left. There was enough moonlight and enough starlight to make out shapes, but there weren't many shapes to make out. There was an occasional tree here and there, but mostly the land had been ploughed flat all the way to the horizon. Then three miles out Reacher saw two buildings far to the west, one large, one small, both standing alone in a field. Even at a distance and even in the dark he could tell both buildings were old and made of wood. They were no longer quite square, no longer quite upright, as if the earth was sucking them back down into itself, an inch a time, a corner at a time.

Reacher slowed and turned into a track that was nothing more than a pair of deep parallel ruts put there by the passage of tractor tyres. There was a raised hump of grass between them. The grass was frozen solid, like wire. The pick-up truck lurched and bounced and pattered. Small stones scrabbled under the wheels and skittered away. The track ran straight, then turned, then turned again, following the chequerboard pattern of the fields. The ground was bone hard. No dust came up. The two old buildings got nearer, and larger. One was a barn. The other was a smaller structure. They were about a hundred yards apart. Maybe a hundred and twenty. They were both fringed with dormant vegetation, where errant seeds had blown against their sides, and then fallen and taken root. In the winter the vegetation was nothing more than dry tangled sticks. In the summer it might be a riot of colourful vines.

Reacher looked at the barn first. It stood alone, surrounded by worn-out blacktop. It was built of timbers that looked as hard as iron, but it was rotting and leaning. The door was a slider big enough to admit some serious farm machinery. But the tilt of the building had jammed it in its tracks. The lower right-hand corner was wedged deep in the earth. The iron wheel on the rail above it had lifted off its seat.

There was a judas hole in the slider. A small regular door, inset. It was locked. There were no windows.

Reacher got back in the truck and headed for the smaller shed. It was three-sided, open at the narrow end that faced away from the barn. The tractor ruts ran all the way inside. It was for storage of some kind. Or it had been, once upon a time, long ago. It was about twice as long and a little wider than the truck.

Perfect.

Reacher drove in, all the way, and stopped with the hood of the truck under a kind of mezzanine half-loft built like a shelf under the peak of the roof. He shut the engine down and climbed out and walked back the way he had come, out of the shed, then twenty yards more.

He turned and checked. The truck was completely hidden.

He smiled.

He thought: time for bed.

He set out walking.

He walked in the tractor ruts. The ground under his feet was uneven and hard, and progress was slower than it would have been on the grassy hump in the centre of the track, but even frozen grass can bruise and show footsteps, and Reacher always preferred to leave no trail. He made it back to the road and turned north and walked where the centre line would have been, if anyone had ever painted one. The night was still and quiet, the air frigid, the stars still bright overhead. Nothing else was moving. Up ahead there was no blue glow. The motel's lights had been turned off for the night.

He walked three fast road miles, less than an hour, and came up on the crossroads from the south. He stopped a hundred yards out and checked. On his left, the abandoned mall foundation. Beyond it, the abandoned gas station. On his right, nothing, and beyond that, the motel, dark and silent, just shapes and shadows.

No parked cars.

No parked trucks.

No watchers.

No ambush.

Reacher moved on. He came up on the motel from the rear, at the end of the curl of cabins, behind the smallest of them. All was quiet. He stayed off the gravel and minced along the silver timbers to his bathroom window. It was still open. The screen was still in the bath-tub. He sat on the sill and ducked his head and swivelled his legs up and slid inside. He closed the window against the cold and turned and looked around.

His towels were where he had left them after his shower. Vincent hadn't made up the room. Reacher guessed that was tomorrow's task. No great urgency. No one was expecting a sudden demand for accommodation. Not in the wilds of Nebraska, not in the depths of winter.

Reacher stepped through to the main room and found an undisturbed situation. All was exactly as he had left it. He kept the lights off and the drapes open. He untucked the bed all around and slid in, fully dressed, boots and all. Not the first time he had slept that way. Sometimes it paid to be ready. Hence the boots, and the untucked bedding. He rolled left, rolled right, got as comfortable as he could, and a minute later he was fast asleep.

He woke up five hours later and found out he had been wrong. Vincent was not pulling quintuple duty. Only quadruple. He employed a maid. A housekeeper. Reacher was woken by the sound of her feet on the gravel. He saw her through the window. She was heading for his door, getting ready to make up his room. He threw aside the covers and sat up, feet on the floor, blinking. His arms felt a little better. Or maybe they were still numb from sleep. There was mist and cold grey light outside, a bitter winter morning, not long after dawn.

People see what they expect to see. The housekeeper

used a pass key and pushed the door wide open and stepped into what she thought was a vacant room. Her eyes passed over Reacher's shape on the bed and moved on and it was a whole long second before they came back again. She didn't really react. She showed no big surprise. No yelp, no scream. She looked like a solid, capable woman. She was about sixty years old, maybe more, white, blunt and square, with blond hair fading slowly to yellow and grey. Plenty of old German genes in there, or Scandinavian.

'Excuse me,' she said. 'But Mr Vincent believed this room to be empty.'

'That was the plan,' Reacher said. 'Better for him that way. What you don't know can't hurt you.'

'You're the fellow the Duncans told him to turn out,' she said. Not a question. Just a statement, a conclusion derived from shared intelligence on the phone tree.

'I'll move on today,' Reacher said. 'I don't want to cause him any trouble.'

'I'm afraid it's you that will have the trouble. How do you plan to move on?'

'I'll hitch a ride. I'll set up south of the crossroads. I've done it before.'

'Will the first car you see stop?'

'It might.'

'What are the chances?'

'Low.'

'The first car you see won't stop. Because almost certainly the first car you see will be a local resident, and that person will get straight on the phone and tell the Duncans exactly where you are. We've had our

90

instructions. The word is out. So the second car you see will be full of the Duncans' people. And the third, and the fourth. You're in trouble, sir. The land is flat here and it's wintertime. There's nowhere to hide.'

FOURTEEN

The housekeeper moved through the room in an orderly, preprogrammed way, following a set routine, ignoring the anomaly represented by an illicit guest seated on the bed. She checked the bathroom, as if assessing the size of the task ahead of her, and then she butted the tub armchair with her thigh, moving it back an inch to the position decreed for it by the dents in the carpet.

Reacher asked, 'You got a cell phone?'

The woman said, 'Sure. Some minutes on it, too.'

'You going to rat me out?'

'Rat who out? This is an empty room.'

Reacher asked, 'What's to the east of here?'

'Nothing worth a lick to you,' the woman said. 'The road goes to gravel after a mile, and doesn't really take you anywhere.'

'West?'

'Same thing.'

'Why have a crossroads that doesn't lead anywhere, east or west?'

'Some crazy plan,' the woman said. 'About fifty years ago. There was supposed to be a strip right here, all commercial, a mile long, with houses east and west. A couple of farms were sold for the land, but that's about all that happened. Even the gas station went out of business, which is pretty much the kiss of death, wouldn't you say?'

'This motel is still here.'

'By the skin of its teeth. Most of what Mr Vincent earns comes from feeding whiskey to the doctor.'

'Big cash flow right there, from what I saw last night.'

'A bar needs more than one customer.'

'He's paying you.'

The woman nodded. 'Mr Vincent is a good man. He helps where he can. I'm a farmer, really. I work the winters here, because I need the money. To pay the Duncans, basically.'

'Haulage fees?'

'Mine are higher than most.'

'Why?'

'Ancient history. I wouldn't give up.'

'On what?'

'I can't talk about it,' the woman said. 'It's a forbidden subject. It was the start of everything bad. And I was wrong, anyway. It was a false allegation.'

Reacher got up off the bed. He headed for the bathroom and rinsed his face with cold water and brushed his teeth. Behind him the woman stripped the bed with fast practised movements of her wrists, sheets going one way, blankets the other. She said, 'You're heading for Virginia.'

Reacher said, 'You know my Social Security number too?'

'The doctor told his wife you were a military cop.'

'Were, as in used to be. Not any more.'

'So what are you now?'

'Hungry.'

'No breakfast here.'

'So where?'

'There's a diner an hour or so south. In town. Where the county cops get their morning coffee and doughnuts.'

'Terrific.'

The housekeeper stepped out to the path and took fresh linens from a cart. Bottom sheet, top sheet, pillowcases. Reacher asked her, 'What does Vincent pay you?'

'Minimum wage,' she said. 'That's all he can afford.'

'I could pay you more than that to cook me breakfast.'

'Where?'

'Your place.'

'Risky.'

'Why? You a terrible cook?'

She smiled, briefly. 'Do you tip well?'

'If the coffee's good.'

'I use my mother's percolator.'

'Was her coffee good?'

'The best.'

'So we're in business.'

'I don't know,' the woman said.

'They're not going to be conducting house-to-house searches. They expect to find me out in the open.'

'And when they don't?'

'Nothing for you to worry about. I'll be long gone. I like breakfast as much as the next guy, but I don't take hours to eat it.'

The woman stood there for a minute, unsure, a crisp white pillowcase held flat across her chest like a sign, or a flag, or a defence. Then she said, 'OK.'

Four hundred and fifty miles due north, because of the latitude, dawn came a little later. The grey panel truck sat astride the sandy path, hidden, inert, dewed over with cold. Its driver woke up in the dark and climbed down and took a leak against a tree, and then he drank some water and ate a candy bar and got back in his sleeping bag and watched the pale morning light filter down through the needles. He knew at best he would be there most of the day, or most of two days, and at worst most of three or four days. But then would come his share, of money and fun, and both things were worth waiting for.

He was patient by nature.

And obedient.

Reacher stood still in the middle of the room and the housekeeper finished up around him. She made the bed tight enough to bounce a dime, she changed the towels, she replaced a tiny vial of shampoo, she put out a new morsel of paper-wrapped soap, she folded an arrowhead into the toilet roll. Then she went to get her truck. It was a pick-up, a battered old item, very plain, with rust and skinny tyres and a sagging suspension. She looped around the wrecked Subaru and parked with the passenger door next to the cabin door. She checked front and rear, long and hard, and then she paused. Reacher could see she wanted to forget the whole thing and take off without him. It was right there in her face. But she didn't. She leaned across the width of the cab and opened the door and flapped her hand. *Hurry up.*

Reacher stepped out of the cabin and into the truck. The woman said, 'If we see anyone, you have to duck down and hide, OK?'

Reacher agreed, although it would be hard to do. It was a small truck. A Chevrolet, grimy and dusty inside, all worn plastic and vinyl, with the dash tight against his knees and the window into the load bed tight against the back of his seat.

'Got a bag?' he asked.

'Why?'

'I could put it on my head.'

'This isn't funny,' she said. She drove off, the worn old transmission taking a second to process her foot's command, something rattling under the hood, a holed muffler banging away like a motorcycle. She turned left out of the lot and drove through the crossroads and headed south. There was no other traffic. In the daylight the land all around looked flat and featureless and immense. It was all dusted white with frost. The sky was high and blank. After five minutes Reacher saw the two old buildings in the west, the sagging barn and the smaller shed with the captured pick-up in it. Then three minutes later they passed the Duncans' three houses standing alone at the end of their long shared driveway. The woman's hands went tight on the wheel and Reacher saw she had crossed her fingers. The truck rattled onward and she watched the mirror more than the road ahead and then a mile later she breathed out and relaxed.

Reacher said, 'They're only people. Three old guys and a skinny kid. They don't have magic powers.'

'They're evil,' the woman said.

They were in Jonas Duncan's kitchen, eating breakfast, biding their time, waiting for Jacob to come out with it. He had a pronouncement to make. A decision. They all knew the signs. Many times Jacob had sat quiet and distracted and contemplative, and then eventually he had delivered a nugget of wisdom, or an analysis that had cut to the heart of the matter, or a proposal that had killed three or four birds with one stone. So they waited for it, Jonas and Jasper patiently enjoying their meal, Seth struggling with it a little because chewing had become painful for him. Bruising was spreading out from under his aluminium mask. He had woken up with two black eyes the size and colour of rotting pears.

Jacob put down his knife and his fork. He dabbed his lips with his cuff. He folded his hands in front of him. He said, 'We have to ask ourselves something.'

Jonas was hosting, so he was entitled to the first response.

'What something?' he asked.

'We have to consider whether it might be worth trading a little dignity and self-respect for a useful outcome.'

'In what way?'

'We have a provocation and a threat. The provocation

comes from the stranger in the motel throwing his weight around in matters that don't concern him. The threat comes from our friend to the south getting impatient. The first thing must be punished, and the second thing shouldn't have happened at all. No date should have been guaranteed. But it was, so we have to deal with it, and without judgement either. No doubt Seth was doing what he thought was best for all of us.'

Jonas asked, 'How do we deal with it?'

'Let's think about the other thing first. The stranger from the motel.'

Seth said, 'I want him hurt bad.'

'We all do, son. And we tried, didn't we? Didn't work out so well.'

'What, now we're afraid of him?'

'We are, a little bit, son. We lost three guys. We'd be stupid not to be at least a little concerned. And we're not stupid, are we? That's one thing a Duncan will never be accused of. Hence my question about self-respect.'

'You want to let him walk?'

'No, I want to tell our friend to the south that the stranger is the problem. That he's somehow the reason for the delay. Then we point out to our friend that he's already got two of his boys up here, and if he wants a bit of giddy-up in the shipment process, then maybe those two boys could be turned against the stranger. That's a win all around, isn't it? Three separate ways. First, those two boys are off Seth's back, as of right now, and second, the stranger gets hurt or killed, and third, some of the sting goes out of our friend's recent attitude, because he comes to see that the delay isn't really our fault at all. He comes to see that we're beleaguered, by outside forces, in ways that he'll readily understand, because no doubt he's beleaguered too, from time to time, in similar ways. In other words, we make common cause.'

Silence for a moment.

Then Jasper Duncan said, 'I like it.'

Jacob said, 'I like it too. Otherwise I wouldn't be proposing it. The only downside is a slight blow to our self-respect and dignity, in that it won't be our own hands on the man who transgressed against us, and we'll be admitting to our friend to the south that there are problems in this world that we can't solve all by ourselves.'

'No shame in that,' Jonas said. 'This is a very complicated business.'

Seth asked, 'You figure his boys are better than our boys?'

'Of course they are, son,' Jacob said. 'As good as our boys are, his are in a different league. There's no comparison. Which we need to bear in mind. Our friend to the south needs to remain our friend, because he would make a very unpleasant enemy.'

'But suppose the delay doesn't go away?' Jasper asked. 'Suppose nothing changes? Suppose the stranger gets nailed today and we still can't deliver for a week? Then our friend to the south knows we were lying to him.'

'I don't think the stranger will get nailed in one day,' Jacob said.

'Why not?'

'Because he seems to be a very capable person. All the evidence so far points in that direction. It could take a few days, by which time our truck could well be on its way. And even if it isn't, we could say that we thought it prudent to keep the merchandise out of the country until the matter was finally resolved. Our friend might believe that. Or, of course, he might not.'

'It's a gamble, then.'

'Indeed it is. But it's probably the best we can do. Are we in or out?'

'We should offer assistance,' Jasper said. 'And information. We should require compliance from the population.'

Jacob said, 'Naturally. Our friend would expect nothing less. Instructions will be issued, and sanctions will be advertised.'

'And our boys should be out there too. Ears and eyes open. We need to feel we made some contribution, at least.'

'Naturally,' Jacob said again. 'So are we in or out?'

No one spoke for a long moment. Then Jasper said, 'I'm in.'

'Me too,' Jonas said.

Jacob Duncan nodded and unfolded his hands.

'That's a majority, then,' he said. 'Which I'm mighty relieved to have, because I took the liberty of calling our friend to the south two hours ago. Our boys and his are already on the hunt.'

'I want to be there,' Seth said. 'When the stranger gets it.'

FIFTEEN

Reacher was half expecting something nailed together from sod and rotten boards, like a Dust Bowl photograph, but the woman drove him down a long gravel farm track to a neat two-storey dwelling standing alone in the corner of a spread that might have covered a thousand acres. The woman parked behind the house, next to a line of old tumbledown barns and sheds. Reacher could hear chickens in a coop, and he could smell pigs in a sty. And earth, and air, and weather. The countryside, in all its winter glory. The woman said, 'I don't mean to be rude, but how much are you planning to pay me?'

Reacher smiled. 'Deciding how much food to give me?'

'Something like that.'

'My breakfast average west of the Mississippi is about fifteen bucks with tip.'

The woman looked surprised. And satisfied.

'That's a lot of money,' she said. 'That's two hours' wages. That's like having a nine-day work week.'

'Not all profit,' Reacher said. 'I'm hungry, don't forget.'

She led him inside through a door to a back hallway. The house was what Seth Duncan's place might have been before the expensive renovations. Low ceilings overhead, small panes of wavy glass in the windows, uneven floors underfoot, the whole place old and antique and outdated in every possible way, but cleaned and tidied and well maintained for a hundred consecutive years. The kitchen was immaculate. The stove was cold.

'You didn't eat yet?' Reacher asked.

'I don't eat,' the woman said. 'Not breakfast, at least.'

'Dieting?'

The woman didn't answer, and Reacher immediately felt stupid.

'I'm buying,' he said. 'Thirty bucks. Let's both have some fun.'

'I don't want charity.'

'It isn't charity. I'm returning a favour, that's all. You stuck your neck out bringing me here.'

'I was just trying to be a decent person.'

'Me too,' Reacher said. 'Take it or leave it.'

She said, 'I'll take it.'

He said, 'What's your name? Most times when I have breakfast with a lady, I know her name at least.'

'My name is Dorothy.'

'I'm pleased to meet you, Dorothy. You married?'

'I was. Now I'm not.'

'You know my name?'

'Your name is Jack Reacher. We've all been informed. The word is out.'

'I told the doctor's wife.'

'And she told the Duncans. Don't blame her for it. It's automatic. She's trying to pay down her debt, like all of us.'

'What does she owe them?'

'She sided with me, twenty-five years ago.'

Roberto Cassano and Angelo Mancini were driving north in a rented Impala. They were based in a Courtyard Marriott, which was the only hotel in the county seat, which was nothing more than a token grid of streets set in the middle of what felt like a billion square miles of absolutely nothing at all. They had learned to watch their fuel gauge. Nebraska was that kind of place. It paid to fill up at every gas station you saw. The next one could be a million miles away.

They were from Vegas, which as always meant they were really from somewhere else. New York, in Cassano's case, and Philadelphia, in Mancini's. They had paid their dues in their home towns, and then they had gotten hired together in Miami, like playing triple-A ball, and then they had moved up to the big show out in the Nevada desert. Tourists were told that what happens in Vegas stays in Vegas, but that wasn't true as far as Cassano and Mancini were concerned. They were travelling men, always on the move, tasked to roam around and deal with the first faint pre-echoes of trouble long before it rolled in and hit their boss where he lived.

Hence the trip to the vast agricultural wastelands, nearly eight hundred miles north and east of the glitter and the glamour. There was a snafu in the supply chain, and it was a day or two away from getting extremely

103

embarrassing. Their boss had promised certain specific things to certain specific people, and it would do him no good at all if he couldn't deliver. So Cassano and Mancini had so far been on the scene for seventy-two hours straight, and they had smacked some beanpole yokel's wife around, just to make their point. Then some other related yokel had called with a claim that the snafu was being caused by a stranger poking his nose in where it didn't belong. Bullshit, possibly. Quite probably entirely unconnected. Just an excuse. But Cassano and Mancini were only sixty miles away, so their boss was sending them north to help, because if the yokel's statement was indeed a lie, then it indicated vulnerability, and therefore minor assistance rendered now would leverage a better deal later. An obvious move. This was American business, after all. Forcing down the wholesale price was the name of the game.

They came up the crappy two-lane and rolled through the crappy crossroads and pulled in at the motel. They had seen it before. It looked OK at night. Not so good in the daylight. In the daylight it looked sad and botched and half-hearted. They saw a damaged Subaru standing near one of the cabins. It was all smashed up. There was nothing else to see. They parked in the lot outside the lounge and got out of the rental car and stood and stretched. Two city boys, yawning, scoured by the endless wind. Cassano was medium height, dark, muscled, blank-eyed. Mancini was pretty much the same. They both wore good shoes and dark suits and coloured shirts and no ties and wool overcoats. They were often mistaken for each other.

They went inside, to find the motel owner. Which they did, immediately. They found him behind the bar, using a rag, wiping a bunch of sticky overlapping rings off the wood. Some kind of a sadsack loser, with dyed red hair.

Cassano said, 'We represent the Duncan family,' which he had been promised would produce results. And it did. The guy with the hair dropped the rag and stepped back and almost came to attention and saluted, like he was in the army, like a superior officer had just yelled at him.

Cassano said, 'You sheltered a guy here last night.'

The guy with the hair said, 'No, sir, I did not. I tossed him out.'

Mancini said, 'It's cold.'

The guy behind the bar said nothing, not following.

Cassano said, 'If he didn't sleep here, where the hell did he sleep? You got no local competition. And he didn't sleep out under a hedge. For one thing, there don't seem to be any hedges in Nebraska. For another, he'd have frozen his ass off.'

'I don't know where he went.'

'You sure?'

'He wouldn't tell me.'

'Any kindly souls here, who would take a stranger in?'

'Not if the Duncans told them not to.'

'Then he must have stayed here.'

'Sir, I told you, he didn't.'

'You checked his room?'

'He returned the key before he left.'

'More than one way into a room, asshole. Did you check it?'

'The housekeeper already made it up.'

'She say anything?'

'No.'

'Where is she?'

'She finished. She left. She went home.'

'What's her name?'

'Dorothy.'

Mancini said, 'Tell us where Dorothy lives.'

SIXTEEN

Dorothy's idea of a fifteen-dollar breakfast turned out to be a regular feast. Coffee first, while the rest of it was cooking, which was oatmeal, and bacon, and eggs, and toast, big heaping portions, lots of everything, all the food groups, all piping hot, served on thick china plates that must have been fifty years old, and eaten with ancient silverware that had heavy square Georgian handles.

'Fabulous,' Reacher said. 'Thank you very much.'

'You're welcome. Thank you for mine.'

'It isn't right, you know. People not eating because of the Duncans.'

'People do all kinds of things because of the Duncans.'

'I know what I'd do.'

She smiled. 'We all talked like that, once upon a time, long ago. But they kept us poor and tired, and then we got old.'

'What do the young people do here?'

'They leave, just as soon as they can. The adventurous

ones go all over the place. It's a big country. The others stay closer to home, in Lincoln or Omaha.'

'Doing what?'

'There are jobs there. Some boys join the State Police. That's always popular.'

'Someone should call those boys.'

She didn't answer.

He asked, 'What happened twenty-five years ago?'

'I can't talk about it.'

'You can, to me. No one will know. If I ever meet the Duncans, we'll be discussing the present day, not ancient history.'

'I was wrong anyway.'

'About what?'

She wouldn't answer.

He asked, 'Were you the neighbour with the dispute?'

She wouldn't answer.

He asked, 'You want help cleaning up?'

She shook her head. 'You don't wash the dishes in a restaurant, do you?'

'Not so far.'

'Where were you, twenty-five years ago?'

'I don't remember,' he said. 'Somewhere in the world.'

'Were you in the army then?'

'Probably.'

'People say you beat up three Cornhuskers yesterday.'

'Not all at once,' he said.

'You want more coffee?'

'Sure,' he said, and she recharged the percolator and set it going again. He asked, 'How many farms contracted with the Duncans?'

'All of us,' she said. 'This whole corner of the county. Forty farms.'

'That's a lot of corn.'

'And soybeans and alfalfa. We rotate the crops.'

'Did you buy part of the old Duncan place?'

'A hundred acres. A nice little parcel. It squared off a corner. It made sense.'

'How long ago was that?'

'It must be thirty years.'

'So things were good for the first five years?'

'I'm not going to tell you what happened.'

'I think you should,' he said. 'I think you want to.'

'Why do you want to know?'

'Like you said, I had three football players sent after me. I'd like to understand why, at least.'

'It was because you busted Seth Duncan's nose.'

'I've busted lots of noses. Nobody ever retaliated with retired athletes before.'

She poured the coffee. She placed his mug in front of him. The kitchen was warm from the stove. It felt like it would stay warm all day long. She said, 'Twenty-five years ago Seth Duncan was eight years old.'

'And?'

'This corner of the county was like a little community. We were all spread out and isolated, of course, but the school bus kind of defined it. Everybody knew everybody else. Children would play together, big groups of them, at one house, then another.'

109

'And?'

'No one liked going to Seth Duncan's place. Girls especially. And Seth played with girls a lot. More so than with boys.'

'Why didn't they like it?'

'No one spelled it out. A place like this, a time like that, such things were not discussed. But something unpleasant was going on. Or nearly going on. Or in the air. My daughter was eight years old at the time. Same age as Seth. Almost the same birthday, as a matter of fact. She didn't want to play there. She made that clear.'

'What was going on?'

'I told you, no one said.'

'But you knew,' Reacher said. 'Didn't you? You had a daughter. Maybe you couldn't prove anything, but you knew.'

'Have you got kids?'

'None that I know about. But I was a cop of sorts for thirteen years. And I've been human all my life. Sometimes people just know things.'

The woman nodded. Sixty years old, blunt and square, her face flushed from the heat and the food. She said, 'I suppose today they would call it inappropriate touching.'

'On Seth's part?'

She nodded again. 'And his father's, and both his uncles'.'

'That's awful.'

'Yes, it was.'

'What did you do?'

'My daughter never went there again.'

'Did you talk to people?'

'Not at first,' she said. 'Then it all came out in a rush. Everyone was talking to everyone else. Nobody's girl wanted to go there.'

'Did anyone talk to Seth's mother?'

'Seth didn't have a mother.'

Reacher said, 'Why not? Had she left?'

'No.'

'Had she died?'

'She never existed.'

'She must have.'

'Biologically, I suppose. But Jacob Duncan was never married. He was never seen with a woman. No woman was ever seen with any of them. Their own mother had passed on years before. It was just old man Duncan and the three of them. Then the three of them on their own. Then all of a sudden Jacob was bringing a little boy to kindergarten.'

'Didn't anyone ask where the kid came from?'

'People talked a little, but they didn't ask. Too polite. Too inhibited. I suppose we all thought Seth was a relative. You know, maybe orphaned or something.'

'So what happened next? You all stopped your kids from going there to play, and that's what caused the trouble?'

'That's how it started. There was a lot of talk and whispers. The Duncans were all alone in their little compound. They were shunned. They resented it.'

'So they retaliated?'

'Not at first.'

111

'So when?'

'After a little girl went missing.'

Roberto Cassano and Angelo Mancini got back in their rented Impala and fired up the engine. The car had a bolt-on navigation system, a couple of extra dollars a day, but it was useless. The screen came up with nothing more than a few thin red lines, like doodles on a pad. None of the roads had names. Just numbers, or else nothing at all. Most of the map was blank. And it was either inaccurate or incomplete, anyway. The crossroads wasn't even marked. Just like Vegas, to be honest. Vegas was growing so fast no GPS company could keep up with it. So Cassano and Mancini were used to navigating the old-fashioned way, which was to scribble down turn-by-turn directions freely given by a source who was anxious to be accurate, in order to avoid a worse beating than he was getting along with the initial questions. And the motel guy had been more anxious than most, right after the first two smacks. He was no kind of hero. That was for sure.

'Left out of the lot,' Mancini read out loud.

Cassano turned left out of the lot.

Dorothy the housekeeper made a third pot of coffee. She rinsed the percolator and filled it again and set it going. She said, 'Seth Duncan had a hard time in school. He got bullied. Eight-year-old boys can be very tribal. I guess they felt they had permission to go after him, because of the whispers at home. And none of the girls stuck with him. They wouldn't go to his house, and they wouldn't even talk to him. That's how children are. That's how it was. All except one girl. Her parents had raised her to be decent and compassionate. She wouldn't go to his house, but she still talked to him. Then one day that little girl just disappeared.'

Reacher said, 'And?'

'It's a horrible thing, when that happens. You have no idea. There's a kind of crazy period at first, when everyone is mad and worried but can't bring themselves to believe the worst. You know, a couple of hours, maybe three or four, you think she's playing somewhere, maybe out picking flowers, she's lost track of the time, she'll be home soon, right as rain. No one had cell phones back then, of course. Some people didn't even have regular phones. Then you think the girl has gotten lost, and everyone starts driving around, looking for her. Then it goes dark, and then you call the cops.'

Reacher asked, 'What did the cops do?'

'Everything they could. They did a fine job. They went house to house, they used flashlights, they used loudhailers to tell everyone to search their barns and outbuildings, they drove around all night, then at first light they got dogs and called in the State Police and the State Police called in the National Guard and they got a helicopter.'

'Nothing?'

The woman nodded.

'Nothing,' she said. 'Then I told them about the Duncans.'

'You did?'

'Someone had to. As soon as I spoke up, others joined in. We were all pointing our fingers. The State Police took us very seriously. I guess they couldn't afford not to. They took the Duncans to a barracks over near Lincoln and questioned them for days. They searched their houses. They got help from the FBI. All kinds of laboratory people were there.'

'Did they find anything?'

'Not a trace.'

'Nothing at all?'

'Every test was negative. They said the child hadn't been there.'

'So what happened next?'

'Nothing. It all fizzled out. The Duncans came home. The little girl was never seen again. The case was never solved. The Duncans were very bitter. They asked me to apologize, for naming names, but I wouldn't. I couldn't give it up. My husband, neither. Some folks were on our side, like the doctor's wife. But most weren't, really. They saw which way the wind was blowing. The Duncans withdrew into themselves. Then they started punishing us. Like revenge. We didn't get our crop hauled that year. We lost it all. My husband killed himself. He sat right in that chair where you're sitting and he put his shotgun under his chin.'

'I'm sorry.'

The woman said nothing.

Reacher asked, 'Who was the girl?'

No reply.

'Yours, right?'

'Yes,' the woman said. 'It was my daughter. She was eight years old. She'll always be eight years old.'

She started to cry, and then her phone started to ring.

SEVENTEEN

The phone was a clunky old Nokia. It was on the kitchen counter. It hopped and buzzed and trilled the old Nokia tune that Reacher had heard a thousand times before, in bars, on buses, on the street. Dorothy snatched it up and answered. She said hello and then she listened, to what sounded like a fast slurred message of some kind, maybe a warning, and then she clicked off and dropped the phone like it was scalding hot.

'That was Mr Vincent,' she said. 'Over at the motel.'

Reacher said, 'And?'

'Two men were there. They're coming here. Right now.'

'Who?'

'We don't know. Men we've never seen before.' She opened the kitchen door and glanced down a hallway towards the front of the house. There was silence for a second and then Reacher heard the distant hiss of tyres on blacktop, the moan of a slowing engine, the sound of

116

brakes, and then the crunch of a wheel on gravel, then another, then two more together, as a car turned in and bumped on to the track.

The woman said, 'Get out of here. Please. They can't know you're here.'

'We don't know who they are.'

'They're Duncan people. Who else would they be? I can't let them find you here. It's more than my life is worth.'

Reacher said, 'I can't get out of here. They're already on the track.'

'Hide out back. Please. I'm begging you. They can't find you here. I mean it.' She stepped out to the hallway, ready to meet them head on at the front door. They were close, and moving fast. The gravel was loud. She said, 'They might search. If they find you, tell them you snuck in the yard. Over the fields. Please. Tell them I didn't know. Make them believe you. Tell them you're nothing to do with me.' Then she closed the door on him and was gone.

Angelo Mancini folded the sheet of handwritten directions and put it in his pocket. They were on some lumpy, bumpy, piece-of-shit farm track, heading for some broken-down old woebegone piece-of-shit farmhouse that belonged in a museum or a history book. The navigation screen showed nothing at all. Just white space. Roberto Cassano was at the wheel, hitting every pothole. What did he care? They were Hertz's tyres, not his. Up ahead the front door opened and an old woman appeared on the step, clutching the jamb, like she would fall over if she let go.

Mancini said, 'That's a woman with a guilty secret, right there. Count on it.'

'Looks that way,' Cassano said.

Reacher checked the view across the yard at the back. Maybe sixty feet to the parked pick-up, maybe sixty more to the line of barns and sheds and coops and sties. He eased the door open. He turned back and checked the door to the front hallway. It was closed, but he could hear the car. It was crunching to a stop. Its doors were opening. He sensed the woman out there, staring at it, fearful and panicking. He shrugged and turned again to leave. His gaze passed over the kitchen table.

Not good.

They might search.

Tell them I didn't know.

The table held the remains of two breakfasts.

Two oatmeal bowls, two plates all smeared with egg, two plates all full of toast crumbs, two spoons, two knives, two forks, two coffee mugs.

He put his toast plate on his egg plate, and he put his oatmeal bowl on his toast plate, and he put his coffee mug in his oatmeal bowl, and he put his knife and fork and spoon in his pocket. He picked up the teetering stack of china and carried it with him, across the kitchen, out the door. He held the stack one-handed and pulled the door shut after him and set off across the yard. The ground was beaten dirt mixed with crushed stone and matted with winter weeds. It was reasonably quiet underfoot.

But the shakes in his arm were rattling the mug in the bowl. He was making a tinkling noise with every step he took. It sounded as loud as a fire alarm. He passed the pick-up truck. Headed onward to a barn. It was an old swaybacked thing made from thin tarred boards. It was in poor condition. It had twin doors. Hinged in the conventional way, not sliders. The hinges were shot and the doors were warped. He hooked a heel behind one of them and forced his butt into the gap and pushed with his hip and scraped his way inside, back first, then his shoulders, then the stack of crockery.

It was dark inside. No light in there, except blinding sparkles from chinks between the boards. They threw thin lines and spots of illumination across the floor. The floor was earth, soaked in old oil, matted with flakes of rust. The air smelled of creosote. He put the stack of china down. All around him was old machinery, uniformly brown and scaly with decay. He didn't know what any of it was. There were tines and blades and wheels and metal all bent and welded into fantastical shapes. Farm stuff. Not his area of expertise. Not even close.

He stepped back to the leaning doors and peered through a crack and looked and listened, and drew up rules of engagement in his head. He couldn't touch these guys, not unless he was prepared to go all the way and make them disappear for ever, and their car, and then force Vincent at the motel to hold his tongue, also for ever. Anything less than that, and it would all come back to Dorothy sooner or later. So prudence dictated he should stay quiet and out of sight, which he was prepared to do, maybe, just possibly, depending on what he heard from the house. One scream might be nerves or fright. Two screams, and he was going in there, come what may.

He heard nothing.

And he saw nothing, for ten long minutes. Then a guy stepped out the back door, into the yard, and another came out behind him. They walked ten paces and stopped and stood there side by side like they owned the place. They gazed left, gazed ahead, gazed right. City boys. They had shined shoes and wool pants and wool overcoats. They were both on the short side of six feet, both heavy in the chest and shoulders, both dark. Both regular little tough guys, like something out of a television show.

They tracked left a little, towards the pick-up truck. They checked the load bed. They opened a door and checked the cab. They moved on, towards the line of barns and sheds and coops and sties.

Directly towards Reacher.

They came pretty close.

Reacher rolled his shoulders and snapped his elbows and flapped his wrists and tried to work some feeling into his arms. He made a fist with his right hand, and then his left.

The two guys walked on, closer still.

They looked left. They looked right. They sniffed the air.

They stopped.

Shiny shoes, wool coats. City boys. They didn't want to be wading through pigshit and chicken feathers and turning over piles of old crap. They looked at each other and then the one on the right turned back to the house and called out, 'Hey, old lady, get your fat ass out here right now.'

Forty yards away, Dorothy stepped out the door. She paused a beat and then walked towards the two guys, slow and hesitant. The two guys walked back towards her, just as slow. They all met near the pick-up truck. The guy on the left stood still. The guy on the right caught Dorothy by the upper arm with one hand and used the other to take a pistol out from under his coat. A shoulder holster. The gun was some kind of a nickel-plated semi-automatic. Or stainless steel. Reacher was too far away to make out the brand. Maybe a Colt. Or maybe a copy. The guy raised it across his body and laid its muzzle against Dorothy's temple. He held the gun flat, like a punk in a movie. His thumb and three fingers were wrapped tight around the grip. The fourth finger was on the trigger. Dorothy flinched away. The guy hauled on her arm and pulled her back.

He called out, 'Reacher? Is that your name? You there? You hiding somewhere? You listening to me? I'm going to count to three. Then you come on out. If you don't, I'm going to shoot the old cow. I've got a gun to her head. Tell him, grandma.'

Dorothy said, 'There's no one here.'

The yard went quiet. Three people, all alone in a thousand acres.

Reacher stood still, right where he was, on his own in the dark.

He saw Dorothy close her eyes.

The guy with the gun said, 'One.'

Reacher stood still.

The guy said, 'Two.'

Reacher stood still.

The guy said, 'Three.'

EIGHTEEN

Reacher stood still and watched through the crack. There was a long second's pause. Then the guy who had been counting dropped his hand and stuffed the gun back under his coat. He let go of the woman's arm. She staggered away a step. The two guys looked left, looked right, looked at each other. They shrugged. A test, passed. A precaution, properly explored. They turned and headed away around the side of the house and disappeared from sight. A minute later Reacher heard doors slam and an engine start and the crunch and whine of a car backing down the track. He heard it make the blacktop, he heard it change gear, he heard it drive away.

The world went quiet again.

Reacher stayed right where he was, on his own in the dark. He wasn't dumb. Easiest thing in the world for one of the guys to be hiding behind the corner of the house, while his buddy drove away like a big loud decoy. Reacher knew all the tricks. He had used most of them. He had invented some of them himself.

Dorothy stood in the yard with one hand on the side

of her truck, steadying herself. Reacher watched her. He guessed she was about thirty seconds away from gathering her wits and taking a breath and shouting that the guys were gone and he could come out now. Then he saw twenty-five years of habitual caution get the better of her. She pushed off the truck and walked the same path the two guys had taken. She was gone a whole minute. Then she came back, around the other side of the house. A full circle. Flat land all around. Wintertime. No place to hide.

She called, 'They're gone.'

He picked up the stack of plates and shouldered his way out between the barn's warped doors. He blinked in the light and shivered in the cold. He walked on and met her near the pick-up truck. She took the plates from him. He said, 'You OK?'

She said, 'I was a little worried there for a minute.'

'The safety catch was on. The guy never moved his thumb. I was watching. It was a bluff.'

'Suppose it hadn't been a bluff? Would you have come out?'

'Probably,' Reacher said.

'You did good with these plates. I suddenly remembered them, and thought I was a goner for sure. Those guys looked like they wouldn't miss much.'

'What else did they look like?'

'Rough,' she said. 'Menacing. They said they were here representing the Duncans. Representing them, not working for them. That's something new. The Duncans never used outsiders before.'

'Where will they go next?'

'I don't know. I don't think they know, either. Nowhere to hide is pretty much the same as nowhere to look, isn't it?'

'The doctor's, maybe?'

'They might. The Duncans know you had contact.'

'Maybe I should head over there.'

'And maybe I should get back to the motel. I think they hurt Mr Vincent. He didn't sound too good on the phone.'

'There's an old barn and an old shed south of the motel. Off the road, to the west. Made of wood. All alone in a field. Whose are they?'

'They're nobody's. They were on one of the farms that got sold for the development that never happened. Fifty years ago.'

'I have a truck in there. I took it from the football players last night. Give me a ride?'

'No,' she said. 'I'm not driving you past the Duncan place again.'

'They don't have X-ray vision.'

'They do. They have a hundred pairs of eyes.'

'So you want me to *walk* past their place?'

'You don't have to. Head west across the fields until you see a cell tower. One of my neighbours leases half an acre to the phone company. That's how he pays his haulage. Turn north there and skirt the Duncan place on the blind side and then you'll see the barns.'

'How far is it?'

'It's a morning's walk.'

'I'll burn up all that breakfast.'

'That's what breakfast is for. Make sure you turn

north, OK? South takes you near Seth Duncan's house, and you really don't want to go there. You know the difference between north and south?'

'I walk south, I get warmer. North, I get colder. I should be able to figure it out.'

'I'm serious.'

'What was your daughter's name?'

'Margaret,' the woman said. 'Her name was Margaret.'

So Reacher walked around the back of the barns and the sheds and the coops and the sties and struck out across the fields. The sun was nothing more than a bright patch of luminescence in the high grey sky, but it was enough to navigate by. After ten o'clock in the morning in Nebraska in the wintertime, and it was solidly east of south, behind his left shoulder. He kept it there for forty minutes, and then he saw a cell phone tower looming insubstantial in the mist. It was tall and skeletal, with a microwave receptor the shape of a bass drum, and cell antennas the shape of fungo bats. It had a tangle of dead brown weeds at its base, and it was surrounded by a token barbed wire fence. In the far distance beyond it was a farmhouse similar to Dorothy's. The neighbour's, presumably. The ground underfoot was hard and lumpy, all softball-sized clods and clarts of frozen earth, the wreckage from the last year's harvest. They rolled away either left or right or crushed under his heels as he walked.

He turned north at the tower. The sun had moved on. Now it was high and almost behind him, an hour before the season's drab version of noon. There was no warmth in it. Just light, a little brighter than the rest of the day. Far ahead, to the right, he could see a smudge on the horizon. The three Duncan houses, he guessed, grouped together at the end of their long shared driveway. He couldn't make out any detail. Certainly nothing man-sized. Which meant no one there could make out any man-sized detail either, in reverse. Same number of miles east to west as west to east, same grey gloom, same mist. But even so, he tracked left a little, following a curve, maintaining his distance, making sure.

Dorothy the housekeeper sat Mr Vincent down in a red velvet chair and sponged the blood off his face. He had a split lip and a cut brow and a lump the size of an egg under his eye. He had apologized for being so slow with his warning call. He had passed out, he said, and had scrambled for the phone as soon as he came around.

Dorothy told him to hush up.

On the other side of the circular room one of the bar stools was lying on its side and a mirrored panel on the bar back had been shattered. Shards of silvered glass had fallen among the bottles like daggers. One of the NASA mugs was broken. Its handle had come right off.

Angelo Mancini had the doctor's shirt collar bunched in his left hand and he had his right hand bunched into a fist. The doctor's wife was sitting in Roberto Cassano's lap. She had been ordered to, and she had refused. So Mancini had hit her husband, hard, in the face. She had refused again. Mancini had hit her husband again, harder. She had complied. Cassano had his hand on her thigh, his thumb an inch under the hem of her skirt. She was rigid with fear and shuddering with revulsion.

'Talk to me, baby,' Cassano whispered, in her ear. 'Tell me where you told Jack Reacher to hide.'

'I didn't tell him anything.'

'You were with him twenty minutes. Last night. The weirdo at the motel told us so.'

'I didn't tell him anything.'

'So what were you doing there for twenty minutes? Did you have sex with him?'

'No.'

'You want to have sex with me?'

She didn't answer.

'Shy?' Cassano asked. 'Bashful? Cat got your tongue?'

He moved his hand another inch, upward. He licked the woman's ear. She ducked away. Just twisted at the waist and leaned right over, away from him.

He said, 'Come back, baby.'

She didn't move.

He said, 'Come *back*,' a little louder.

She straightened up. He got the impression she was about to puke. He didn't want that. Not all over his good clothes. But he licked her ear one more time anyway, just to show her who was boss. Mancini hit the doctor one more time, just for fun. Travelling men, roaming around, getting the job done. But wasting their time in Nebraska, that was for sure. No one knew a damn thing. The whole place was as barren as the surface of the moon, with much less to do. Who would stay? This guy

128

Reacher was long gone, obviously, totally in the wind, probably halfway to Omaha by the time the sun came up, rumbling along in the stolen truck, completely unnoticed by the county cops, who clearly sat around all night with their thumbs up their butts, because hadn't they missed every single one of the deliveries roaring through from Canada to Vegas? For months? Hadn't they? Every single one?

Assholes.

Yokels.

Retards.

All of them.

Cassano jerked upright and spilled the doctor's wife off his lap. She sprawled on the floor. Mancini punched the doctor one more time, and then they left, back to the rented Impala parked outside.

Reacher kept the three smudged shapes far to his right and tracked onward. He was used to walking. All soldiers were. Sometimes there was no alternative to a long fast advance on foot, so soldiers trained for it. It had been that way since the Romans, and it was still that way, and it would stay that way for ever. So he kept on going, satisfied with his progress, enjoying the small compensations that fresh air and country smells brought with them.

Then he smelled something else.

Up ahead was a tangle of low bushes, like a miniature grove. Wild raspberries or wild roses, maybe, a remnant, somehow spared by the ploughs, now bare and dormant but still thick and dense with thorns. There was a thin plume of smoke coming from them, from right in the middle, horizontal and almost invisible on the wind. It smelled distinctive. Not a wood fire. Not a cigarette.

Marijuana.

Reacher was familiar with the smell. All cops are, even military cops. Grunts get high like anyone else, off duty. Sometimes even on duty. Reacher guessed what he was smelling was a fine sativa, probably not imported junk from Mexico, probably a good home-grown strain. And why not, in Nebraska? Corn country was ideal for a little clandestine farming. Corn grew as high as an elephant's eye, and dense, and a twenty-foot clearing carved out a hundred yards from the edge of a field was as secret a garden as could be planted anywhere. More profitable than corn, too, even with all the federal subsidies. And these people had their haulage fees to meet. Maybe someone was sampling his recent harvest, judging its quality, setting its price in his mind.

It was a kid. A boy. Maybe fifteen years old, maybe sixteen. Reacher walked on and looked down into the chest-high thicket and found him there. He was quite tall, quite thin, with the kind of long centre-parted hair Reacher hadn't seen on a boy for a long time. He was wearing thick pants and a surplus parka from the old West German army. He was sitting on a spread-out plastic grocery bag, his knees drawn up, his back against a large granite rock that jutted up from the ground. The rock was wedge-shaped, as if it had been broken out of a bigger boulder and rolled into a different position far from its source. And the rock was why the ploughs had spared the thicket. Big tractors with vague steering had given it a wide berth, and nature had taken advantage. Now the boy was taking advantage in turn, hiding from the world, getting through his day. Maybe not a semi-commercial grower after all. Maybe just an amateur enthusiast, with mail-order seeds from Boulder or San Francisco.

'Hello,' Reacher said.

'Dude,' the boy said. He sounded mellow. Not high as a kite. Just cruising gently a couple of feet off the ground. An experienced user, probably, who knew how much was too much and how little was too little. His thought processes were slow, and right there in his face. First: *Am I busted?* Then: *No way.*

'Dude,' he said again. 'You're the man. You're the guy the Duncans are looking for.'

Reacher said, 'Am I?'

The kid nodded. 'You're Jack Reacher. Six-five, two-fifty, brown coat. They want you, man. They want you real bad.'

'Do they?'

'We had Cornhuskers at the house this morning. We're supposed to keep our eyes peeled. And here you are, man. You snuck right up on me. I guess your eyes were peeled, not mine. Am I right?' Then he lapsed into a fit of helpless giggles. He was maybe a little higher than Reacher had thought.

Reacher said, 'You got a cell phone?'

'Hell yes. I'm going to text my buddies. I'm going to tell them I've seen the man, large as life, twice as natural. Hey, maybe I could put you on the line with them. That would be a kick, wouldn't it? Would you do that? Would you talk to my buds? So they know I'm not shitting them?'

'No,' Reacher said.

The kid went instantly serious. 'Hey, I'm with you, man. You got to lie low. I can dig that. But dude, don't worry. We're not going to rat you out. Me and my buds, I mean. We're on your side. You're putting it to the Duncans, we're with you all the way.'

Reacher said nothing. The kid concentrated hard and lifted his arm high out of the brambles and held out his joint.

'Share?' he said. 'That would be a kick too. Smoking with the man.'

The joint was fat and well rolled, in yellow paper. It was about half gone.

'No, thanks,' Reacher said.

'Everyone hates them,' the kid said. 'The Duncans, I mean. They've got this whole county by the balls.'

'Show me a county where someone doesn't.'

'Dude, I hear you. The system stinks. No argument from me on that score. But the Duncans are worse than usual. They killed a kid. Did you know that? A little girl. Eight years old. They took her and messed her up real bad and killed her.'

'Did they?'

'Hell yes. Definitely.'

'You sure?'

'No question, my friend.'

'It was twenty-five years ago. You're what, fifteen?'

'It happened.'

'The FBI said different.'

'You believe them?'

'As opposed to who? A stoner who wasn't even born yet?'

'The FBI didn't hear what I hear, man.'

'What do you hear?'

'Her ghost, man. Still here, after twenty-five years. Sometimes I sit out here at night and I hear that poor ghost screaming, man, screaming and wailing and moaning and crying, right here in the dark.'

NINETEEN

Our ship has come in. An old, old phrase, from old sea-faring days, full of hope and wonder. An investor could spend all he had, building a ship, fitting it out, hiring a crew, or more than all he had, if he was borrowing. Then the ship would sail into a years-long void, unimaginable distances, unfathomable depths, incalculable dangers. There was no communication with it. No radio, no phone, no telegraph, no mail. No news at all. Then, maybe, just maybe, one chance day the ship would come back, weather-beaten, its sails heaving into view, its hull riding low in the channel waters, loaded with spices from India, or silks from China, or tea, or coffee, or rum, or sugar. Enough profit to repay the costs and the loans in one fell swoop, with enough left over to live generously for a decade. Subsequent voyages were all profit, enough to make a man rich beyond his dreams. *Our ship has come in.*

Jacob Duncan used that phrase, at eleven-thirty that morning. He was with his brothers, in a small dark room at the back of his house. His son Seth had gone home.

Just the three elders were there, stoic, patient, and reflective.

'I got the call from Vancouver,' Jacob said. 'Our man in the port. Our ship has come in. The delay was about weather in the Luzon Strait.'

'Where's that?' Jasper asked.

'Where the South China Sea meets the Pacific Ocean. But now our goods have arrived. They're here. Our truck could be rolling tonight. Tomorrow morning, at the very latest.'

'That's good,' Jasper said.

'Is it?'

'Why wouldn't it be?'

'You were worried before, in case the stranger got nailed before the delay went away. You said that would prove us liars.'

'True. But now that problem is gone.'

'Is it? Seems to me that problem has merely turned itself inside out. Suppose the truck gets here before the stranger gets nailed? That would prove us liars, too.'

'We could hold the truck up there.'

'We couldn't. We're a transportation company, not a storage company. We have no facilities.'

'So what do we do?'

'We think. That's what we do. Where is that guy?'

'We don't know.'

'We know he hasn't slept or eaten since yesterday. We know we've had our boys out driving the roads all morning and they haven't seen a damn thing. So where is he?'

Jonas Duncan said, 'Either he's snuck in a chicken coop somewhere, or he's out walking the fields.'

'Exactly,' Jacob said. 'I think it's time to turn our boys off the nice smooth roads. I think it's time they drove out across the land, big circles, sweeping and beating.'

'We only have seven of them left.'

'They all have cell phones. First sight of the guy, they can call the boys from the south and turn the problem over to the professionals. If they need to, that is. Or at least they can get some coordinated action going. Let's turn them loose.'

By that point Reacher was starting to hurry. He was about four hundred yards due west of the three Duncan houses, which was about as close as he intended to get. He was walking parallel to the road. He could already see the wooden buildings ahead. They were tiny brown pinpricks on the far horizon. Nothing between him and them. Flat land. He was watching for trucks. He knew they would be coming. By now his hunters would have checked the roads, and found nothing. Therefore they would have concluded he was travelling cross-country. They would be putting trucks in the fields, and soon, if they hadn't already. It was predictable. Fast, mobile patrols, cell phone communications, maybe even radios, the whole nine yards. Not good.

He slogged onward, another five minutes, then ten, then twenty. The three Duncan houses fell away behind his shoulder. The wooden buildings up ahead stayed resolutely on the horizon, but they got a little larger, because they were getting a little closer. Four hundred yards away was another bramble thicket, spreading wide and chest-high, but apart from that there was nothing in sight taller than an inch. Reacher was dangerously exposed, and he knew it.

In Las Vegas a Lebanese man named Safir took out his phone and dialled a number. The call was answered six blocks away by an Italian man named Rossi. There were no pleasantries. No time for any. The first thing Safir said was, 'You're making me angry.'

Rossi said nothing in reply. He couldn't really afford to. It was a question of protocol. He was absolutely at the top of his own particular tree, and it was a big tree, high, wide, and handsome, with roots and branches spreading everywhere, but there were bigger trees in the forest, and Safir's was one of them.

Safir said, 'I favoured you with my business.'

Rossi said, 'And I'm grateful for that.'

'But now you're embarrassing me,' Safir said. Which, Rossi thought, was a mistake. It was an admission of weakness. It made it clear that however big Safir was, he was worried about someone bigger still. A food chain thing. At the bottom were the Duncans, then came Rossi, then came Safir, and at the top came someone else. It didn't matter who. The mere existence of such a person put Safir and Rossi in the same boat. For all their graduated wealth and power and glory, they were both intermediaries. Both scufflers. Common cause.

Rossi said, 'You know that merchandise of this quality is hard to source.'

Safir said, 'I expect promises to be kept.'

'So do I. We're both victims here. The difference between us is that I'm doing something about it. I've got boots on the ground up in Nebraska.'

'What's the problem there?'

'They claim a guy is poking around.'

'What, a cop?'

'No,' Rossi said. 'Absolutely not a cop. The chain is as secure as ever. Just a passer-by, that's all. A stranger.'

'Who?'

'Nobody. Just a busybody.'

'So how is this nobody busybody stranger holding things up?'

'I don't think he is, really. I think they're lying to me. I think they're just making excuses. They're late, that's all.'

'Unsatisfactory.'

'I agree. But this is a sellers' market.'

'Who have you got up there?'

'Two of my boys.'

'I'm going to send two of mine.'

'No point,' Rossi said. 'I'm already taking care of it.'

'Not to Nebraska, you idiot,' Safir said. 'I'm going to send two of my boys across town to babysit you. To keep the pressure on. I want you to be very aware of what happens to people who let me down.'

The Port of Vancouver had been combined with the Fraser River Port Authority and the North Fraser Port Authority and the shiny new three-in-one business had been renamed Port Metro Vancouver. It was the largest port in Canada, the largest port in the Pacific

Northwest, the fourth largest port on the west coast of North America, and the fifth largest port in North America overall. It occupied 375 miles of coastline, and had twenty-five separate terminals, and handled three thousand vessel arrivals every year, for a total annual cargo throughput of a hundred million tons, which averaged out to considerably more than a quarter-million tons every day. Almost all of those tons were packed into intermodal shipping containers, which, like a lot of things, traced their origins all the way back to United States Department of Defense drawings made in the 1950s, because in the 1950s the U.S. DoD had been one of the few agencies in the world with the will and the energy to make drawings at all, and the only one with the power to make them stick.

Intermodal shipping containers were corrugated metal boxes. They could be easily swapped between different modes of transport, like ships, or railroad flatcars, or semi trucks. Hence, intermodal. They were all a little more than eight feet high and eight feet wide. The shortest and rarest were twenty feet long. Most were forty feet long, or forty-five, or forty eight, or fifty-three. But traffic was always measured by reference to the basic minimum length, in multiples called twenty-foot-equivalent-units, or TEUs. A twenty-foot container was scored as a one, and a forty-foot as a two, and so on. Port Metro Vancouver handled two million TEUs a year.

The Duncans' shipment came in a twenty-foot container. The smallest available. One TEU. Gross weight was 6,110 pounds, and net weight was 4,850 pounds, which meant that there were 1,260 pounds of cargo inside, in a space designed to handle more than sixty thousand. In other words, the box was about 98 per cent empty. But that proposition was not as wasteful or as inefficient as it first appeared. Each of the pounds that the container carried was worth more than gold.

It was lifted off a South Korean ship by a gantry crane, and it was placed gently on Canadian soil, and then it was immediately picked up again by another crane, which shuttled it to an inspection site where a camera read its BIC code. BIC was the Bureau International des Containers, which was headquartered in Paris, France, and the code was a combination of four letters from the Latin alphabet and seven numbers. Together they told Port Metro Vancouver's computers who owned the container, and where it had come from, and what was in it, and that those contents had been pre-cleared by Canadian customs, none of which information was in the least little bit true. The code also told the computers where the container was going, and when, which was true, to a limited extent. It was going onward into the interior of Canada, and it was to be loaded immediately, without delay, on to a semi truck that was already waiting for it. So it was shuttled on ahead, through a sniffer designed to detect smuggled nuclear material, a test that it passed very easily, and then out to the marshalling yard. At that point the port computers generated an automatic text message to the waiting driver, who fired up his truck and swung into position. The container was lowered on to his flatbed and clamped down. A minute later it was rolling, and ten minutes after that it was through the port gates, heading east, sitting high and proud and alone on a trailer more than twice its length, its minimal weight barely noticed by the roaring diesel.

Reacher walked on through the dirt, another hundred yards, and then he stopped and turned a full circle and checked all around. There was no activity ahead of him. Nothing to the west. Nothing to the east. Just flat, empty land. But behind him, way far to the south, there was a truck. Maybe a mile away, maybe more. It was driving across the fields, bumping and lurching and pattering across the rough ground, faint light glinting off its dull chrome bumper.

TWENTY

Reacher dropped into a crouch. He was dressed in olive and brown and tan, and the acres of winter dirt all around him were olive and brown and tan, too. Decomposing stalks and leaves, lumps of fertile earth, some of them cracked and powdered by frosts and winds. There was still mist in the air. It hung motionless and invisible, an atmospheric layer like the finest gauze.

The truck a mile to the south kept on moving. The field was immense and rectangular and the truck was roughly in the middle of it. It was following an endless series of S-shaped curves, steering sequentially half-left, then straight ahead, then half-right, then straight ahead, then half-left. Rhythmic and regular and relentless, the driver's view sweeping the horizon like a searchlight beam.

Reacher stayed down in his crouch. Static targets attract the eye much less than moving targets. But he knew that sooner or later the truck was going to get close to him. That was inevitable. At some point he was going to have to move on. But where? There was no natural cover. No hills, no woods, no streams, no rivers.

Nothing at all. And he was a slow runner, and not very agile. Not that anyone was fast enough or agile enough to win a game of man-versus-truck on flat and infinitely spacious land.

The truck kept on coming, tiny in the distance, slow and patient and methodical. Half-left, straight ahead, half-right. Its half-right turns aimed it directly at him. Now it was about a thousand yards away. He couldn't make out the driver. Therefore in return the driver couldn't make him out. Not yet, anyway. But it was only a matter of time. It would be at a distance of about two hundred yards, he figured, when his vague crouching shape resolved itself. Maybe a hundred and fifty, if the windshield was grimy. Maybe a hundred, if the driver was shortsighted or bored or lazy. Then there would be a blank moment of dawning realization, and then there would be acceleration. Maximum speed over the rough ground would be about thirty miles an hour. Somewhere between seven and fifteen seconds, he figured, between launch and arrival.

Not enough.

Better to go sooner than later.

But where?

He turned around, slow and cautious. Nothing to the east. Nothing to the west. But three hundred yards due north was the bramble thicket he had noted before. The second such thing he had seen within a two-mile span. A tangle of chest-high bushes, a miniature grove, wild raspberries or wild roses, bare and dormant, thick and dense with thorns. Spared by the ploughs. The first had been spared because of a large rock in its centre.

There was no possible reason for the second to be any different. No farmer on earth would spare wild flowers year after year through a hundred seasons just for sentiment alone.

The thicket was the place to go.

Three hundred yards for Reacher. Slow as he was, maybe sixty seconds.

A thousand yards for the truck. Fast as it was, maybe seventy seconds.

A ten-second margin.

No brainer.

Reacher ran.

He came up out of his crouch and started pounding away, stiff clumsy strides, arms pumping, mouth open, breathing hard. Ten yards, twenty, then thirty. Then forty, then fifty. Far behind him he heard the sudden muffled roar of an engine. He didn't look back. Just kept on going, slipping and sliding, feeling painfully slow.

Two hundred yards to go.

He kept on running, maximum speed. He heard the truck behind him all the way. Still muffled. Still comfortably distant. But moving fast. Revving motor, whistling belts, sucking air, juddering springs, pattering tyres.

A hundred yards to go.

He risked a glance back. Clearly the truck had gotten a late jump. It was still further away than it might have been. But even so it was gaining handily. It was coming on fast. It was an SUV, not a pick-up. Domestic, not foreign. GMC, maybe. Dark red. Not new. A high blunt snout and a chrome bumper the size of a bathtub.

Fifty yards to go. Ten seconds. He stopped twenty yards out and turned in place. Faced south. He stood still, panting hard. He raised his arms level with his shoulders.

Come and get me.

The truck hammered on. Straight at him. He sidestepped right, one long pace, two, three. He lined it up perfectly. The truck directly ahead of him, the hidden rock directly behind him. The truck kept on coming. He walked backward, then ran backward, up on his toes, dainty, watching all the way. The truck kept on coming, lurching, hopping, bouncing, roaring. Twenty yards away, then ten, then five. Reacher moved with it. Then when he felt the first brambles against the backs of his legs he jerked sideways and flung himself out of the truck's path and rolled away and waited for the truck to smash through the thicket and wreck itself on the rock.

Didn't happen.

The guy at the wheel braked hard and slewed to a stop with his front bumper a yard into the brush. A local boy. He knew what was in there. Reacher heard the gearbox smack into reverse and the truck backed up and the front wheels turned and the gear changed again and the truck came straight at him, fast and enormous. The tyres were big off-road items with dirty white letters and savage tread. They were squirming and churning and clods of earth were spattering up off all of them equally. Four-wheel-drive. The motor was roaring. A big V-8. Reacher was on the ground and he could see suspension members and shock absorbers and exhaust headers and differential casings the size of soccer balls. He got up

145

and feinted right and flung himself left. He rolled away and the truck turned tight but missed him, crunching over the clods of earth a foot from his face. He could smell hot oil and gasoline and exhaust fumes. There was a cacophony of sound. The motor, grinding gears, yelping springs. The truck slammed into reverse again and came at Reacher backwards. By that point he was up on his knees, deciding. Where next? In or out? In the thicket, or out in the open?

No choice at all.

Out in the open was suicide. At close quarters the truck was relatively clumsy, but he couldn't run and jink and dodge for ever. No one could. Exhaustion would tell in the end. So he got to his feet and waded into the brambles. The thorns tore at his pants. The truck came after him, driving backwards, narrowing its radius. The driver was staring over his shoulder. A big guy. Big neck. Big shoulders. Short hair. Reacher headed straight for the centre of the thicket. Long thorny tendrils latched together and tugged at his ankles. He ripped his way onward. The driver turned the wheel as far as it would go. The truck's radius tightened, but not enough. Reacher ducked inside its turn and barged on.

He made it to the rock.

It was a hell of a rock. Much bigger than the first one he had seen. Maybe the parent of the first one he had seen. The first one had been wedge-shaped, as if it had been busted out of a larger boulder. This second rock looked like that larger boulder. It was shaped like a pie with a broad piece broken out of it, but not flat like a pie. It was humped and round. Like an orange, with three or

146

four segments missing, half buried in the earth. Maybe fifty thousand years ago an Ice Age glacier had rolled it all the way down from Canada, and the weight of a billion tons of frozen snow had cracked it apart, and the smaller fragment had been pushed onward two more miles before grinding to a stop and weathering gently over the next countless centuries. The larger fragment had stayed right in place, and it was still there, waist-deep in the rich dirt, itself gently weathered, a huge granite ball with a worn and shallow triangular notch in it, like a bite, like an open mouth, facing south towards its smaller relation. The bite was maybe ten feet wide at the opening, and it narrowed down to a point maybe five feet later.

Reacher came to rest with his back against the boulder, on the east side, the bite a quarter-circle away, behind his right shoulder. The truck turned and drove out of the thicket and for a crazy moment Reacher thought the guy was giving up and going home, but then the truck turned again, a wide lazy circle out on the dirt, and it came back, slow and menacing, head-on, straight at him. The driver was smiling behind the windshield glass, a wide feral grin of triumph. The first of the brambles collapsed under the chrome bumper. The driver was holding the wheel carefully, two-handed, aiming precisely.

Aiming to pin Reacher by the legs against the rock.

Reacher scrambled up on to the granite slope, backward, palms and soles, like a crab. He worked and scuffled and stood upright on the top of the dome, balanced uneasily maybe five feet in the air. The truck came to rest with its front bumper an inch from the rock, its hood a little below the level of Reacher's feet, its roof a little above. The motor calmed to an idle and Reacher heard four ragged thumps as the doors locked from the inside. The driver was worried. Didn't want to be dragged out of his seat for a fistfight. Smart guy. Now Reacher's options were reduced. He could step down on the hood and try to kick the windshield in, but automotive glass was tougher than it looked, and all the guy had to do was take off suddenly and Reacher would be thrown clear, unless he grabbed the roof bars, but his arms were hurting too much to survive a wild-ass ride all the way across Nebraska, clinging to the top of a bouncing truck at thirty or more miles an hour.

Impasse.

Or maybe not. The guy had laid out his tactics for all to see. He hadn't used his phone. He wanted to capture Reacher all by himself, for the glory of it. He intended to do it by using his truck like a hammer and the rock like an anvil. But he wouldn't wait for ever. He would dial his buddies just as soon as frustration got the better of him.

Time to go.

Reacher scrambled down the far side of the rock and waded into the thorny growth. He heard the truck back up and swing around after him. It appeared on his right, crunching through the brambles, holding a tight curve as if it was rounding a traffic circle, driving slow, staying deliberate. Reacher faked a break for the open land and the driver bought it and steered maybe ten degrees out of the circle, and then Reacher ducked back towards the rock and slid around the granite circumference and tucked himself into the shallow triangular bite, right at the point of the V, shoulders tight against the converging walls. The truck paused a second and then leapt ahead and steered a tight loop out on the dirt and came right back at him, head-on again, the same low gear, the same low menacing speed, closer and closer, ten feet, five feet, three feet, then two feet.

Then simultaneously the left end and the right end of the truck's front bumper jammed hard against the narrowing walls of rock, and the truck came to a stop, immobile, right where Reacher wanted it, the big chrome bumper making a new boundary, closing off the shallow triangle a foot from Reacher's thighs. He could feel the heat from the radiator, and the idling beat of the motor resonated in his chest. He could smell oil and gas and rubber and exhaust fumes. He put his hands on the bulbous chrome and started easing down towards a sitting position, intending to slide feet-first underneath the vehicle and wriggle away on his back.

Didn't work.

The driver wanted Reacher more than he wanted an undamaged front bumper.

Reacher got halfway to the ground and then he heard a snick and a crunch as the transfer box changed down to low-range gearing. Ideal for pulling stumps. Or for crushing chrome. The engine roared and all four tyres bit down hard and the truck pushed forward against nothing except the resistance of its own sheet metal. Both ends of the bumper shrieked and deformed and then crumpled and flattened and the truck kept on coming, one inch, then two, then three. The tyres turned slowly but relentlessly, one knob of tread at a time. The bumper crushed from the outside in, grinding and scraping, as the massive V-8 torque turned the bulbous cosmetic panel into a piece of flattened junk.

Now the centre of the bumper was six inches from Reacher's chest.

And it kept on coming. The bumper flattened all the way to where the steel brackets bolted it to the frame. Sterner stuff. The engine roared louder and the truck dug in hard and squatted and strained on its suspension. One front tyre lost traction for a second and spun wildly and spattered dirt and stones and shredded pieces of bramble into the wheel well. The whole truck rocked and bucked and danced in place and then the tyre bit again and the tailpipes bellowed and the steel brackets collapsed and gave an inch and the truck lurched forward.

Four inches from Reacher's chest.

Then three.

Then the brackets gave a little more and the hot metal touched Reacher's coat.

Time to go.

He turned his head sideways and pushed up on the chrome with his hands and forced himself downward, like immersing himself in water. He got halfway there, and then the sheet metal itself behind the bumper started giving way, shrieking and bending and crushing, the curves inverting, the contours flattening. The engine roared and the pipes bellowed louder and the truck lurched forward another inch and the centre of the bumper tapped Reacher on the side of his face. He scraped on down, one ear on the hot chrome and the other on the cold granite. He kicked and scrabbled with his heels and got his feet out from under him and he forced his butt through the brambles and got down on his back. Right above his face the last tiny triangle of clear air disappeared as the fenders gave way and what was left of the bumper folded violently into a forward-facing point and hit the granite.

The driver didn't let up.

The guy kept his foot down hard. Clearly he didn't know exactly where Reacher was. Because he couldn't see. Clearly he hoped he had him pinned by the chest. The truck bucked and squatted and pushed. Reacher was flat on his back underneath it, straining tyres to his left, straining tyres to his right, throbbing exhaust pipes above him, all kinds of ribbed and dirty metal components inches from his face. Things were racing and whirring and turning. There were nuts and bolts and tubes and belts. Reacher didn't know much about cars. Didn't know how to fix them, didn't know how to break them. And he had no tools, anyway.

Or did he?

He patted his pockets, habit and desperation, and felt hard metal inside. Dorothy's silverware. From breakfast. The knife, the fork, the spoon. Heavy old items, hastily concealed, never returned. He pulled them out. They had long thick handles, some kind of early stainless steel.

Right above his nose was a broad flat pan, on the bottom of the engine block. Like a shallow square container, seen from below. Black and dirty. The sump, he figured. For the engine oil. He saw a hexagonal bolt head right in the centre of it. For changing the oil. The guy at the service station would undo the bolt, and the oil would come out. The new oil would go in the top.

The guy at the service station would have a wrench.

Reacher didn't.

The engine roared and strained. The truck shook and juddered. Reacher scuttled backward a yard and got his hands way up above his head and he clamped the knife handle on one side of the hex bolt and the fork handle on the other. He held them tight with thumbs and forefingers and used half his strength to keep them hard together and the other half to turn them counterclockwise.

Nothing.

He took a breath and clamped his teeth and ignored the pain in his arms and tried again. Still nothing. He changed his technique. He clamped the bolt with the very ends of the silverware handles held between his right thumb and forefingers, and he used his left hand to rotate the whole assembly.

The bolt moved.

Just a little. He took another breath and held it and clamped hard until the flesh on his fingers was crushed white and flat and he eased the knife and the fork around. The bolt was set very tight and it turned and grated reluctantly, and grit and dirt in the threads threatened to stick it fast, but he kept on going, smooth and steady, breathing hard, concentrating, and after two and a half turns the oil inside must have started seeping out and flushing the threads, because all of a sudden resistance gave way and the bolt started moving fast and smooth and easy. Reacher dropped the silverware and scooted further out of the way and used his fingertips high above his head to spin the bolt right out. The engine was still revving hard and as soon as the bolt was out of the hole the enormous pressure inside just dumped the oil out on the ground in a half-inch jet. It hissed and hosed and splattered on the frozen dirt and bounced back up and coated the nearby brambles slick and black, hot and smoking.

Reacher got his arms back down by his sides and wriggled out under the rear of the truck, feet first, on his back, the undergrowth impeding him, tearing at him, scratching him. He grasped the rear bumper and hauled and pulled and twisted himself up in a crouch. He wanted a fist-sized rock to bust the rear window, but he couldn't find one, so he contented himself with banging on it with his hand, once, twice, hard, and harder, and then he turned and ran.

TWENTY-ONE

Reacher ran thirty yards across the winter dirt and stopped. Inside the truck the driver was twisted around in his seat, staring back at him, pawing and fumbling blindly at the wheel and the gearshift. The truck backed up, straining, still locked in low-range, the engine revving fast and the ground speed grinding slow. Reacher had no idea how long it would take for a hard-worked engine with no oil in it to seize up and die.

Not long, he hoped.

He danced sideways, left, and left, and left, and the truck tracked him all the way, coming on slow, the crushed bumper plastered across the front like an ugly afterthought, the axles locked up for maximum traction, the tyres squirming and hopping and grinding out new ruts all their own. The driver hit the gas and jerked the wheel to his left, aiming to decode Reacher's decoy dance and hit him after the inevitable sudden change of direction at its end, but Reacher double-bluffed him and jumped to his own left, and the truck missed him by ten whole feet.

The truck stopped dead and Reacher saw the guy tugging on levers and heard the transmission change back to normal-speed road duty. The truck made a big forty-foot loop out on the dirt and headed back in. Reacher stood still and watched it and sidestepped right, and right, and right, and then he triple-bluffed and jumped right again while the truck slammed left and missed him again. The truck ended up with its battered nose deep in the thicket. All kinds of unpleasant noises were coming out of it. Deep banging sounds, like tuneless church bells. Bearings, Reacher thought. The big ends. He knew some terminology. He had heard car guys talking, on military bases. He saw the driver glance down in alarm, as if red warning lights were blazing on the dash. There was steam in the air. And blue smoke.

The truck backed up, one more time.

Then it died.

It swung through a short backward arc and stopped, ready for a change of gear, which happened, but it didn't move on again. It just bounced forward a foot against the slack in its suspension and seized up solid. The engine noise shut off and Reacher heard wheezing and hissing and ticking and saw steam jetting out and a final fine black spray from underneath, like a cough, like a death rattle.

The driver stayed where he was, in his seat, behind locked doors.

Reacher looked again for a rock, and couldn't find one.

Impasse.

But not for long.

Reacher saw them first. He had a better vantage point.

Flames, coming out of the seams between the hood and the fenders, low down at the front of the vehicle. The flames were small and colourless at first, boiling the air above them, spreading fast, blistering the paint around them. Then they got bigger and turned blue and yellow and started spilling black smoke from their edges. The hood was a big square pressing and within a minute all four seams surrounding it were alive with flame and the paint all over it was cooking and bubbling and splitting from the heat underneath.

The driver just sat there.

Reacher ran over and tried his door. Still locked. He banged on the window glass, dull padded thumps from his fist, and he pointed urgently at the hood. But it was impossible that the guy didn't already know he was on fire. His wiper blades were alight. Black smoke was rolling off them and swirling up the windshield in coils. The guy was looking right at them, then looking at Reacher, back and forth, panic in his eyes.

He was as worried about Reacher as he was about the fire.

So Reacher backed off ten feet and the door opened up and the guy jumped out, a big slabby white boy, very young, maybe six-six, close to three hundred pounds. He ran five feet and stopped dead. His hands bunched into fists. Behind him the flames started shooting out of the wheel wells at the front of the truck, starting downward, curling back up around the sheet metal, burning hard. The front tyres were smoking. The guy just stood there, rooted. So Reacher ran in again, and the guy swung at him, and missed. Reacher ducked under the blow and popped the guy in the gut and then grabbed him by the collar. The guy went straight down in a crouch and cradled his head, defensively. Reacher pulled him back to his feet and hauled him away across the field, fast, thirty feet, forty, then fifty. He stopped and the guy swung again and missed again. Reacher feinted with a left jab and threw in a huge right hook that caught the guy on the ear. The guy wobbled for a second and then went down on his butt. Just sat there, blinking, in the middle of a field in the middle of nowhere. Twenty yards away the truck was burning fiercely, all the way back to the windshield pillars. The front tyres were alight and the hood was buckled.

Reacher asked, 'How much gas is in the tank?'

The guy said, 'Don't hit me again.'

'Answer my question.'

'I filled it this morning.'

So Reacher grabbed him again and pulled him up and hauled him further away, another thirty feet, then ten more. The guy stumbled all the way and eventually resisted and said, 'Please don't hit me again.'

'Why shouldn't I? You just tried to kill me with a truck.'

'I'm sorry about that.'

'You're *sorry* about that?'

'I had to do it.'

'Just following orders?'

'I'm surrendering, OK? I'm out of the fight now. Like a POW.'

'You're bigger than me. And younger.'

'But you're a crazy man.'

'Says who?'

'We were told. About last night. You put three of us in the hospital.'

Reacher asked, 'What's your name?'

The guy said, 'Brett.'

'What is this, the Twilight Zone? You've all got the same name?'

'Only three of us.'

'Out of ten, right?'

'Yes.'

'Thirty per cent. What are the odds?'

The guy didn't answer.

Reacher asked, 'Who's in charge here?'

'I don't know what you mean.'

'Who told you to come out this morning and kill me with a truck?'

'Jacob Duncan.'

'Seth Duncan's father?'

'Yes.'

'You know where he lives?'

The guy nodded and pointed into the distance, south and east, beyond the burning vehicle. The flames had moved inside it. The glass had shattered and the seats were on fire. There was a column of black smoke in the air, thick and dirty. It was going straight up and then hitting a low atmospheric layer and spreading sideways. Like a miniature mushroom cloud.

Then the gas tank exploded.

An orange fireball kicked the rear of the truck clear off the ground and a split second later a dull boom rolled across the dirt on a pressure wave hard enough

158

to make Reacher stagger a step and hot enough to make him flinch away. Flames leapt fifty feet in the air and died instantly and the truck crashed back to earth, now all black and skeletal inside a hot new fire that roiled the air a hundred feet above it.

Reacher watched for a second. Then he said, 'OK, Brett, this is what you're going to do. You're going to jog over to Jacob Duncan's place, and you're going to tell him three things. You listening to me?'

The big guy looked away from the fire and said, 'Yes.'

'OK, first, if Duncan wants to, he can send his six remaining boys after me, and each one will delay me a couple of minutes, but then I'll come right over and kick his ass. Got that?'

'Yes.'

'Second, if he prefers, he can skip getting the six boys hurt, and he can come out and meet with me face to face, right away. Got that?'

'Yes.'

'And third, if I see those two out-of-towners again, they'll be going home in a bucket. Is that clear? Got all that?'

'Yes.'

'You got a cell phone?'

'Yes,' the guy said.

'Give it to me.'

The guy dug in a pocket and came back with a phone, black and tiny in his giant red paw. He handed it over and Reacher pulled it apart. He had seen cell phones dropped on sidewalks, and he knew what was in there.

A battery, and a SIM card. He pulled off the cover and clipped out the battery and tossed it twenty feet in one direction, and he took out the SIM card and threw the rest of the phone twenty feet in the other direction. He balanced the SIM card on his palm and held it out, a tiny silicon wafer with gold tracks on it.

'Eat it,' he said.

The guy said, 'What?'

'Eat it. That's your forfeit. For being a useless tub of lard.'

The guy paused a second and then he took it, delicately, finger and thumb, and he opened his mouth and placed it on his tongue. He closed his mouth and worked up some saliva and swallowed.

'Show me,' Reacher said.

The guy opened his mouth again and stuck out his tongue. Like a kid at the clinic. The card was gone.

'Now sit down,' Reacher said.

'What?'

'Like you were before.'

'I thought you wanted me to head for the Duncans' place.'

'I do,' Reacher said. 'But not yet. Not while I'm still in the neighbourhood.'

The guy sat down, a little worried, facing south, his legs straight out and his hands on his knees and his upper body curled forward a little.

'Arms behind you,' Reacher said. 'Lean back on your hands.'

'Why?'

Enemy ordnance.

'Just do it,' Reacher said.

The guy got his arms behind him and put his weight on his hands. Reacher stepped behind him and crashed the sole of his boot through the guy's right elbow. The guy went down flat and shrieked and rolled and whimpered. Then he sat up again and cradled his broken arm and stared at Reacher accusingly. Reacher stepped around behind him again and kicked him hard in the back of the head. The guy toppled slowly, forward at first, and then he twisted sideways as his gut got in the way of further progress. He sprawled out and landed softly on one shoulder and lay still, like a large letter L on a dirty brown page. Reacher turned away and slogged on north, towards the two wooden buildings on the horizon.

TWENTY-TWO

The Canadian semi truck with the Duncans' shipment aboard was making good time, heading due east on Route 3 in British Columbia, driving mostly parallel to the die-straight international border, with Alberta up ahead. Route 3 was a lonely road, mountainous, with steep grades and tight turns. Not ideal for a large vehicle. Most drivers took Route 1, which looped north out of Vancouver before turning east later. A better road, all things considered. Route 3 was quiet by comparison. It had long stretches of nothing but asphalt ribbon and wild scenery. And very little traffic. And occasional gravel turn-outs, for rest and recuperation.

One of the gravel turn-outs was located a mile or so before the Waterton Lakes National Park. In U.S. terms it was directly above the Washington–Idaho state line, about halfway between Spokane and Coeur d'Alene, about a hundred miles north of both. The turn-out had an amazing view. Endless forest to the south, the snowy bulk of the Rockies to the east, magnificent lakes to the north. The truck driver pulled off and parked there, but not for the view. He parked there because it was a prearranged location, and because a white panel van was waiting there for him. The Duncans had been in business a long time, because of luck and caution, and one of their cautionary principles was to transfer their cargo between vehicles as soon as possible after import. Shipping containers could be tracked. Indeed they were designed to be tracked, by the BIC code. Better not to risk a delayed alert from a suspicious Customs agent. Better to move the goods within hours, into something anonymous and forgettable and untraceable, and white panel vans were the most anonymous and forgettable and untraceable vehicles on earth.

The semi truck parked and the panel van K-turned on the gravel and backed up to it and stopped rear to rear with it. Both drivers got out. They didn't speak. They just stepped out into the roadway and craned their necks and checked what was coming, one east, one west. Nothing was coming, which was not unusual for Route 3, so they jogged back to their vehicles and got to work. The van driver opened his rear doors, and the truck driver climbed up on his flatbed and cut the plastic security seal and smacked the bolts and levers out of their brackets and opened the container's doors.

One minute later the cargo was transferred, all 1,260 pounds of it, and another minute after that the white van had K-turned again and was heading east, and the semi truck was trailing behind it for a spell, its driver intending to turn north on 95 and then loop back west on Route 1, a better road, back to Vancouver for his next job, which was likely to be legitimate, and therefore better for his blood pressure but worse for his wallet.

*　　*　　*

In Las Vegas the Lebanese man named Safir selected his two best guys and dispatched them to babysit the Italian man named Rossi. An unwise decision, as it turned out. Its unwisdom was made clear within the hour. Safir's phone rang and he answered it, and found himself talking to an Iranian man named Mahmeini. Mahmeini was Safir's customer, but there was no transactional equality in their business relationship. Mahmeini was Safir's customer in the same way a king might have been a boot maker's customer. Much more powerful, imperious, superior, dismissive, and likely to be lethally angry if the boots were defective.

Or late.

Mahmeini said, 'I should have received my items a week ago.'

Safir couldn't speak. His mouth was dry.

Mahmeini said, 'Please look at it from my point of view. Those items are already allocated, to certain people in certain places, for certain date-specific uses. If they are not delivered in time, I'll take a loss.'

'I'll make good,' Safir said.

'I know you will. That's the purpose of my call. We have much to discuss. Because my loss won't be a one-time thing. It will be ongoing. My reputation will be ruined. Why would my contacts trust me again? I'll lose their business for ever. Which means you'll have to compensate me for ever. In effect I will own you for the rest of your life. Do you see my point?'

All Safir could say was, 'I believe the shipment is actually on its way, as of right now.'

'A week late.'

'I'm suffering too. And I'm trying to do something about it. I made my contact send two of his men up there. And then I sent two of my men over to him, to make sure he concentrates.'

'Men?' Mahmeini said. 'You employ men? Or boys?'

'They're good people.'

'You're about to find out what men are. I'm sending two of mine. To you. To make sure *you* concentrate.'

Then the phone went dead, and Safir was left sitting there, awaiting the arrival of two Iranian tough guys in an office that had, just an hour ago, been stripped of the better half of its security.

Reacher made it to the two wooden buildings without further trouble, which was no big surprise to him. Six remaining football players and two out-of-towners made a total of just eight warm bodies, and he guessed the out-of-towners would be riding together, which made a total of just seven roving vehicles loose in a county that must have covered many hundreds of square miles. One random encounter had been fortuitous in the extreme. Two would be incalculably unlikely.

The old barn was still locked and listing, and the pick-up truck was still hidden in the smaller shelter. Undiscovered and undisturbed, as far as Reacher could tell. It was cold and inert. The air in the shelter was dry, and it smelled of dust and mouse droppings. The countryside all around was empty and silent.

Reacher opened up the tool locker in the pick-up's load bed and took a look at the contents. The biggest thing left in there was an adjustable wrench about a foot long. Some kind of polished steel alloy. It weighed about a pound and a half. Made in the U.S.A. Not the greatest weapon in the world, but better than nothing. Reacher put it in his coat pocket and rooted around for more. He came up with two screwdrivers, one a stubby Phillips cross-head design with a rubber handle, and one a long slender thing with a regular blade for a regular slotted screw. He put them in his other pocket and closed the locker and climbed in the cab. He started up and backed out and then he followed the deep tractor ruts all the way east to the road, where he turned north and headed for the motel.

Safir's two tough guys arrived in Rossi's office carrying guns in shoulder holsters and black nylon bags in their hands. They unpacked the bags on Rossi's desk, right in front of him. The first bag carried just one item, and the second bag carried two items. From the first bag came a belt sander, already loaded with a fresh loop of coarse-grain abrasive. From the second bag came a propane blowtorch and a roll of duct tape.

Tools of the trade.

And therefore an unmistakable message, to a guy in Rossi's world. In Rossi's world victims were taped naked to chairs, and belt sanders were fired up and applied to tender areas like knees or elbows or chests. Or faces, even. Then blowtorches were sparked to life for a little extra fun.

Nobody spoke.

Rossi dialled his phone. Three rings, and Roberto

166

Cassano answered, in Nebraska. Rossi said, 'What the hell is happening up there? This thing really can't wait.'

Cassano said, 'We're chasing shadows.'

'Chase them harder.'

'What's the point? Who knows whether this guy has anything to do with anything? You told us you figure he's an excuse. So whatever happens to him isn't going to make the shipment show up any faster.'

'Have you ever told a lie?'

'Not to you, boss.'

'To anyone else?'

'Sure.'

'Then you know how it goes. You arrange things to make sure you don't get caught out. And I think that's what those Duncan bastards are going to do. They're going to hold the shipment somewhere until the guy gets caught. To make it look like they were telling the truth all along. Like cause and effect. So whether we want to or not, we're going to have to play their game their way. So find this asshole, will you? And fast. This thing can't wait.'

Rossi clicked off the call. One of the Lebanese guys had been unrolling the belt sander's cord. Now he bent down and plugged it in. He flicked the switch, just a blip, just a second, and the machine started and whirred and stopped.

A test.

A message.

Reacher drove to the motel and parked next to the doctor's wrecked Subaru. It was still there, outside cabin six. He got out and squatted down front and rear and used the smaller screwdriver from his pocket to take the plates off the pick-up truck. Then he took the plates off the Subaru and put them on the pick-up. He tossed the pick-up's plates into the load bed and put the screwdriver back in his pocket and headed for the lounge.

Vincent was in there, behind the bar, wiping it with a rag. He had a black eye and a thick lip and a swelling the size of a mouse's back on his cheek. One of the mirrors behind him was broken. Pieces of glass the shape of lightning bolts had fallen out. Old wallboard was exposed, taped and yellowing, earthbound and prosaic. The room's cheerful illusion was diminished.

Reacher said, 'I'm sorry I got you in trouble.'

Vincent asked, 'Did you spend the night here?'

'Do you really want to know?'

'No, I guess I don't.'

Reacher checked himself in the broken mirror. One ear was scabbing over, where he had scraped it on the rock. His face had scratches from the thorns. His hands, too, and his back, where his coat and shirt and sweater had ridden up. He asked, 'Did those guys have a list of places they were looking?'

Vincent said, 'I imagine they'll go house to house.'

'What are they driving?'

'A rental.'

'Colour?'

'It was something dark. Dark blue, maybe? A Chevrolet, I think.'

'Did they say who they were?'

'Just that they were representing the Duncans. That's

how they put it. I'm sorry I told them about Dorothy.'

'She did OK,' Reacher said. 'Don't worry about it. She's had bigger troubles in her life.'

'I know.'

'You think the Duncans killed her kid?'

'I would like to. It would fit with what we think we know about them.'

'But?'

'There was no evidence. Absolutely none at all. And it was a very thorough investigation. Lots of different agencies. Very professional. I doubt if they missed anything.'

'So it was just a coincidence?'

'It must have been.'

Reacher said nothing.

Vincent asked, 'What are you going to do now?'

'A couple of things,' Reacher said. 'Maybe three. Then I'm out of here. I'm going to Virginia.'

He walked back out to the lot and climbed into the pick-up truck. He fired it up and took off, out to the road, towards the doctor's house.

TWENTY-THREE

Mahmeini's two tough guys arrived in Safir's Las Vegas office about an hour after Safir's own two tough guys had left it. Mahmeini's men were not physically impressive. No straining shirt collars, no bulging muscles. They were small and wiry, dark and dead-eyed, rumpled, and not very clean. Safir was Lebanese and he knew plenty of Iranians. Most of them were the nicest people in the world, especially when they lived somewhere else. But some of them were the worst. These two had brought nothing with them. No bags, no tools, no equipment. They didn't need any. Safir knew they would have guns under their arms and knives in their pockets. It was the knives he was worried about. Guns were fast. Knives were slow. And these two Iranians could be very slow with knives. And very inventive. Safir knew that for a fact. He had seen one of their victims, out in the desert. A little decomposed, but even so the cops had taken longer than they should even to determine the sex of the corpse. Which was no surprise. There had been no external evidence of gender. None at all.

Safir dialled his phone. Three rings, and one of his

guys answered, six blocks away. Safir said, 'Give me a progress report.'

His guy said, 'It's all messed up.'

'Evidently. But I need more than that.'

'OK, it turns out Rossi's contacts are a bunch of Nebraska people called Duncan. They're all in an uproar over some guy poking around. Nothing to do with anything, probably, but Rossi thinks the Duncans are going to stall until the guy is down, to save face, because they've been claiming the guy is the cause of the delay. Which Rossi thinks is most likely bullshit, but the whole thing has gone completely circular. Rossi thinks nothing is going to happen now until the guy is captured. He's got boys up there, working on it.'

'How hard?'

'As hard as they can, I guess.'

'Tell Rossi to tell them to work harder. Much, much harder. And make sure he knows I'm serious, OK? Tell him I've got people in my office too, and if I'm going to get hurt over this, then he's going to get hurt first, and twice as bad.'

Reacher remembered the way to the doctor's house from the night before. In daylight the roads looked different. More open, less secret. More exposed. They were just narrow ribbons of blacktop, built up a little higher than the surrounding dirt, unprotected by hedgerows, unshaded by trees. The morning mist had risen up and was now a layer of low cloud at about five hundred feet. The whole sky was like a flat lit panel, casting baleful illumination everywhere. No glare, no shadows.

But Reacher arrived OK. The plain ranch house, the couple of flat acres, the post-and-rail fence. In the daylight the house looked raw and new. There was a satellite dish on the roof. There were no cars on the driveway. No dark blue Chevrolet. No neighbours, either. The nearest house might have been a mile away. On three sides there was nothing beyond the doctor's fence except dirt, tired and hibernating, waiting for ploughing and seeding in the spring. On the fourth side was the road, and then more dirt, flat and featureless all the way to the horizon. The doctor and his wife were not gardeners. That was clear. Their lot was all grass, from the base of the fence posts to the foundation of the house. No bushes, no evergreens, no flowerbeds.

Reacher parked on the driveway and walked to the door. It had a spy hole. A little glass lens, like a fat drop of water. Common in a city. Unusual in a rural area. He rang the bell. There was a long delay. He guessed he wasn't the first visitor of the day. More likely the third. Hence the reluctance on the part of the doctor and his wife to open up. But open up they did, eventually. The spy hole darkened and then lightened again and the door swung back slowly and Reacher saw the woman he had met the night before, standing there in the hallway, looking a little surprised but plenty relieved.

'You,' she said.

'Yes, me,' Reacher said. 'Not them.'

'Thank God.'

'When were they here?'

'This morning.'

'What happened?'

172

The woman didn't answer. She just stepped back. A mute invitation. Reacher stepped in and walked down the hallway and found out pretty much what had happened when he came face to face with the doctor. The guy was a little damaged, in much the same way that Vincent was, over at the motel. Bruising around the eyes, swellings, blood in the nostrils, splits in the lips. Loose teeth too, probably, judging by the way the guy was pursing his mouth and moving his tongue, as if he was pressing them home, or counting how many were left. Four blows, Reacher figured, each one hard but subtly different in placement. Expert blows.

Reacher asked, 'Do you know who they are?'

The doctor said, 'No. They're not from around here.' His words were thick and indistinct and hard to decipher. Loose teeth, split lips. And a hangover, presumably. 'They said they were representing the Duncans. Not working for them. So they're not hired hands. We don't know who they are or what their connection is.'

'What did they want?'

'You, of course.'

Reacher said, 'I'm very sorry for your trouble.'

The doctor said, 'It is what it is.'

Reacher turned back to the doctor's wife. 'Are you OK?'

She said, 'They didn't hit me.'

'But?'

'I don't want to talk about it. Why are you here?'

'I need medical treatment,' Reacher said.

'What kind?'

'I got scratched by thorns. I want to get the cuts cleaned.'

'Really?'

'No, not really,' Reacher said. 'I need some pain-killers, that's all. I haven't been able to rest my arms like I hoped.'

'What do you really want?'

'I want to talk,' Reacher said.

They started in the kitchen. They cleaned his cuts, purely as a way of occupying themselves. The doctor's wife said she had trained as a nurse. She poured some thin stinging liquid into a bowl and used cotton balls. She started on his face and neck and then did his hands. She made him take off his shirt. His back was all ripped up by the long scrabbling escape from under the truck. He said, 'I had breakfast with Dorothy this morning. At her place.'

The doctor's wife said, 'You shouldn't be telling us that. It could get her in trouble.'

'Only if you rat her out to the Duncans.'

'We might have to.'

'She said she's a friend of yours.'

'Not really a friend. She's much older.'

'She said you stood by her, twenty-five years ago.'

The woman said nothing. Just continued her careful ministrations behind his back. She was thorough. She was opening each scratch with thumb and forefinger, and swabbing extensively. The doctor said, 'Would you like a drink?'

'Too early for me,' Reacher said.

'I meant coffee,' the doctor said. 'You were drinking coffee last night.'

Reacher smiled. The guy was trying to prove he could remember something. Trying to prove he hadn't been really drunk, trying to prove he wasn't really hung over.

'A cup of coffee is always welcome,' Reacher said.

The doctor stepped away to the sink and got a drip machine going. Then he came back and took Reacher's arm, like doctors do, his fingertips in Reacher's palm, lifting, turning, manipulating. The doctor was small and Reacher's arm was big. The guy was struggling like a butcher with a side of beef. He dug the fingers of his other hand deep into Reacher's shoulder joint, poking, feeling, probing.

'I could give you cortisone,' he said.

'Do I need it?'

'It would help.'

'How much?'

'A little. Maybe more than a little. You should think about it. It would ease the discomfort. Right now it's nagging at you. Probably making you tired.'

'OK,' Reacher said. 'Go for it.'

'I will,' the doctor said. 'In exchange for some information.'

'Like what?'

'How did you hurt yourself?'

'Why do you want to know?'

'Call it professional interest.'

The doctor's wife finished her work. She tossed the last cotton ball on the table and handed Reacher his

175

shirt. He shrugged it on and started buttoning it. He said, 'It was like you figured. I was caught in a hurricane.'

The doctor said, 'I don't believe you.'

'Not a natural weather event. I was in an underground chamber. It caught on fire. There was a stair shaft and two ventilation shafts. I was lucky. The flames went up the ventilation shafts. I was on the stairs. So I wasn't burned. But air to feed the fire was coming down the stair shaft just as hard as the flames were going back up the ventilation shafts. So it was like climbing through a hurricane. It blew me back down twice. I couldn't keep my feet. In the end I had to haul myself up by the arms.'

'How far?'

'Two hundred and eighty steps.'

'Wow. That would do it. Where was this?'

'That's outside of your professional interest.'

'Then what happened?'

'That's outside of your professional interest, too.'

'Recent event, yes?'

'Feels like yesterday,' Reacher said. 'Now go get the needle.'

It was a long needle. The doctor went away and came back with a stainless steel syringe that looked big enough for a horse. He made Reacher take his shirt off again and sit forward with his elbow on the table. He eased the sharp point deep into the joint, from the back. Reacher felt it pushing and popping through all kinds of tendons and muscles. The doctor pressed the plunger, slow and steady. Reacher felt the fluid flood the joint.

Felt the joint loosen and relax, in real time, immediately, like healing insanely accelerated. Then the doctor did the other shoulder. Same procedure. Same result.

'Wonderful,' Reacher said.

The doctor asked, 'What did you want to talk about?'

'A time long ago,' Reacher said. 'When your wife was a kid.'

TWENTY-FOUR

Reacher dressed again and all three of them took mugs of fresh coffee to the living room, which was a narrow rectangular space with furniture arranged in an L-shape along two walls, and a huge flat screen television on a third wall. Under the screen was a rack loaded with audio-visual components all interconnected with thick wires. Flanking the screen were two serious loudspeakers. Set into the fourth wall was an undraped picture window that gave a great view of a thousand acres of absolutely nothing at all. Dormant lawn, the post-and-rail fence, then dirt all the way to the horizon. No hills, no dales, no trees, no streams. But no trucks or patrols, either. No activity of any kind. Reacher took an armchair where he could see the door and the view both at the same time. The doctor sat on a sofa. His wife sat next to him. She didn't look enthusiastic about talking.

Reacher asked her, 'How old were you when Dorothy's kid went missing?'

She said, 'I was fourteen.'

'Six years older than Seth Duncan.'

'About.'

'Not quite in his generation.'

'No.'

'Do you remember when he first showed up?'

'Not really. I was ten or eleven. There was some talk. I'm probably remembering the talk, rather than the event.'

'What did people say?'

'What could they say? No one knew anything. There was no information. People assumed he was a relative. Maybe orphaned. Maybe there had been a car wreck in another state.'

'And the Duncans never explained?'

'Why would they? It was nobody's business but theirs.'

'What happened when Dorothy's little girl went missing?'

'It was awful. Almost like a betrayal. It changed people. A thing like that, OK, it puts a scare in you, but it's supposed to have a happy ending. It's supposed to turn out right. But it didn't.'

'Dorothy thought the Duncans did it.'

'I know.'

'She said you stood by her.'

'I did.'

'Why?'

'Why not?'

Reacher said, 'You were fourteen. She was what? Thirty? Thirty-five? More than twice your age. So it wasn't about solidarity between two women or two mothers or two neighbours. Not in the normal sense. It was because you knew something, wasn't it?'

179

'Why are you asking?'

'Call it professional interest.'

'It was a quarter of a century ago.'

'It was yesterday, as far as Dorothy is concerned.'

'You're not from here.'

'I know,' Reacher said. 'I'm on my way to Virginia.'

'So go there.'

'I can't. Not yet. Not if I think the Duncans did it and got away with it.'

'Why does it matter to you?'

'I don't know. I can't explain it. But it does.'

'The Duncans get away with plenty, believe me. Every single day.'

'But I don't care about that other stuff. I don't care who gets their harvest hauled or when or how much they pay for it. You all can take care of that for yourselves. It's not rocket science.'

The doctor's wife said, 'I was the Duncans' babysitter that year.'

'And?'

'They didn't really need one. They rarely went out. Or actually they went out a lot, but then they came right back. Like a trick or a subterfuge. Then they would be real slow about driving me home. It was like they were paying me to be there with them. With all four of them, I mean, not just with Seth.'

'How often did you work for them?'

'About six times.'

'And what happened?'

'In what way?'

'Anything bad?'

She looked straight at him. 'You mean, was I inter-fered with?'

He asked, 'Were you?'

'No.'

'Did you feel in any danger?'

'A little.'

'Was there any inappropriate behaviour at all?'

'Not really.'

'So what was it made you stand by Dorothy when the kid went missing?'

'Just a feeling.'

'What kind of a feeling?'

'I was fourteen, OK? I didn't really understand any-thing. But I knew I felt uncomfortable.'

'Did you know why?'

'It dawned on me slowly.'

'What was it?'

'They were disappointed that I wasn't younger. They made me feel I was too old for them. It creeped me out.'

'You felt too old for them at fourteen?'

'Yes. And I wasn't, you know, very mature. I was a small girl.'

'What did you feel would have happened if you had been younger?'

'I really don't want to think about it.'

'And you told the cops about how you felt?'

'Sure. We all told them everything. The cops were great. It was twenty-five years ago, but they were very modern. They took us very seriously, even the kids. They listened to everybody. They told us we could say anything, big or small, important or not, truth or rumour. So it all came out.'

'But nothing was proved.'

The doctor's wife shook her head. 'The Duncans were clean as a whistle. Pure as the driven snow. I'm surprised they didn't get the Nobel prize.'

'But still you stood by Dorothy.'

'I knew what I felt.'

'Did you think the investigation was OK?'

'I was fourteen. What did I know? I saw dogs and guys in FBI jackets. It was like a television show. So yes, I thought it was OK.'

'And now? Looking back?'

'They never found her bike.'

The doctor's wife said that most farm kids started driving their parents' beat-up pick-up trucks around the age of fifteen, or even a little earlier, if they were tall enough. Younger or shorter than that, they rode bikes. Big old Schwinn cruisers, baseball cards in the spokes, tassels on the handlebars. It was a big county. Walking was too slow. The eight-year-old Margaret had ridden away from the house Reacher had seen, down the track Reacher had seen, all knees and elbows and excitement, on a pink bicycle bigger than she was. Neither she nor the bike was ever seen again.

The doctor's wife said, 'I kept on expecting them to find the bike. You know, maybe on the side of a road somewhere. In the tall grass. Just lying there. That's what happens on the television shows. Like a clue. With a footprint, or maybe the guy had dropped a piece of paper or something. But it didn't happen that way. Everything was a dead end.'

'So what was your bottom line at the time?' Reacher asked. 'On the Duncans? Guilty or not guilty?'

'Not guilty,' the woman said. 'Because facts are facts, aren't they?'

'Yet you still stood by Dorothy.'

'Partly because of the way I felt. Feelings are different than facts. And partly because of the aftermath. It was horrible for her. The Duncans were very self-righteous. And people were starting to wake up to the power they had over them. It was like the thought police. First Dorothy was supposed to apologize, which she wouldn't, and then she was supposed to just shut up and carry on like nothing had ever happened. She couldn't even grieve, because somehow that would have been like accusing the Duncans all over again. The whole county was uneasy about it. It was like Dorothy was supposed to take one for the team. Like one of those old legends, where she had to sacrifice her child to the monster, for the good of the village.'

There was no more talk. Reacher collected the three empty coffee cups and carried them out to the kitchen, partly to be polite, partly because he wanted to check the view through a different window. The landscape was still clear. Nothing coming. Nothing happening. After a minute the doctor joined him in the room, and asked, 'So what are you going to do now?'

Reacher said, 'I'm going to Virginia.'

'OK.'

'With two stops along the way.'

'Where?'

'I'm going to drop in on the county cops. Sixty miles south of here. I want to see their paperwork.'

'Will they still have it?'

Reacher nodded. 'A thing like that, lots of different departments cooperating, everyone on best behaviour, they'll have built a pretty big file. And they won't have junked it yet. Because technically it's still an open case. Their notes will be in storage somewhere. Probably a whole cubic yard of them.'

'Will they let you see them? Just like that?'

'I was a cop of sorts myself, thirteen years. I can usually talk my way past file clerks.'

'Why do you want to see it?'

'To check it for holes. If it's OK, I'll keep on running. If it's not, I might come back.'

'To do what?'

'To fill in the holes.'

'How will you get down there?'

'Drive.'

'Showing up in a stolen truck won't help your cause.'

'It's got your plates on it now. They won't know.'

'My plates?'

'Don't worry, I'll swap them back again. If the paperwork's OK, then I'll leave the truck right there near the police station with the proper plates on it, and sooner or later someone will figure out whose it is, and word will get back to the Duncans, and they'll know I'm gone for good, and they'll start leaving you people alone again.'

'That would be nice. What's your second stop?'

'The cops are the second stop. First stop is closer to home.'

'Where?'

'We're going to drop in on Seth Duncan's wife. You and me. A house call. To make sure she's healing right.'

TWENTY-FIVE

The doctor was immediately dead set against the idea. It was a house call he didn't want to make. He looked away and paced the kitchen and traced his facial injuries with his fingertips and pursed his lips and ran his tongue over his teeth. Then eventually he said, 'But Seth might be there.'

Reacher said, 'I hope he is. We can check he's healing right, too. And if he is, I can hit him again.'

'He'll have Cornhuskers with him.'

'He won't. They're all out in the fields, looking for me. The few that remain, that is.'

'I don't know about this.'

'You're a doctor. You took an oath. You have obligations.'

'It's dangerous.'

'Getting out of bed in the morning is dangerous.'

'You're a crazy man, you know that?'

'I prefer to think of myself as conscientious.'

Reacher and the doctor climbed into the pick-up truck and headed back to the county two-lane and turned right. They came out on the road a couple of miles south of the motel and a couple of miles north of the three Duncan houses. Two minutes later the doctor stared at them as they passed by. Reacher took a look, too. Enemy territory. Three white houses, three parked vehicles, no obvious activity. By that point Reacher assumed the second Brett had delivered his messages. He assumed they had been heard and then immediately dismissed as bravado. Although the burned-out truck should have counted for something. The Duncans were losing, steadily and badly, and they had to know it.

Reacher made the left where he had the night before in the Subaru wagon, and then he threaded through the turns until Seth Duncan's house appeared ahead on his right. It looked much the same lit by daylight as it had by electricity. The white mailbox with *Duncan* on it, the hibernating lawn, the antique horse buggy. The long straight driveway, the outbuilding, the three sets of doors. This time two of them were standing open. The back ends of two cars were visible in the gloom inside. One was a small red sports car, maybe a Mazda, very feminine, and the other was a big black Cadillac sedan, very masculine.

The doctor said, 'That's Seth's car.'

Reacher smiled. 'Which one?'

'The Cadillac.'

'Nice car,' Reacher said. 'Maybe I should go smash it up. I've got a wrench of my own now. Want me to do that?'

'No,' the doctor said. 'For God's sake.'

Reacher smiled again and parked where he had the

night before and they climbed out together and stood for a moment in the chill. The cloud was still low and flat, and mist was peeling off the underside of it and drifting back down to earth, ready for afternoon, ready for evening. The mist made the air itself look visible, grey and pearlescent, shimmering like a fluid.

'Show time,' Reacher said, and headed for the door. The doctor trailed him by a yard or two. Reacher knocked and waited and a long minute later he heard feet on the boards inside. A light tread, slow and a little hesitant. Eleanor.

She opened up and stood there, with her left hand cupping the edge of the door and her right-hand fingers spidered against the opposite wall, as if she needed help with stability, or as if she thought her horizontal arm was protecting the inside of the house from the outside. She was wearing a black skirt and a black sweater. No necklace. Her lips had scabbed over, dark and thick, and her nose was swollen, the white skin tight over yellow contusions that were not quite hidden by her make-up.

'You,' she said.

'I brought the doctor,' Reacher said. 'To check on how you're doing.'

Eleanor Duncan glanced at the doctor's face and said, 'He looks as bad as I do. Was that Seth? Or one of the Cornhuskers? Either way, I apologize.'

'None of the above,' Reacher said. 'It seems we have a couple of tough guys in town.'

Eleanor Duncan didn't answer that. She just took her right hand off the wall and trailed it through a courtly

188

gesture and invited them in. Reacher asked, 'Is Seth home?'

'No, thank goodness,' Eleanor said.

'His car is here,' the doctor said.

'His father picked him up.'

Reacher asked, 'How long will he be gone?'

'I don't know,' Eleanor said. 'But it seems they have much to discuss.' She led the way to the kitchen, where she had been treated the night before, and maybe on many previous occasions. She sat down in a chair and tilted her face to the light. The doctor stepped up and took a look. He touched the wounds very lightly and asked questions about pain and headaches and teeth. She gave the kinds of answers Reacher had heard from many people in her situation. She was brave and somewhat self-deprecating. She said yes, her nose and mouth still hurt a little, and yes, she had a slight headache, and no, her teeth didn't feel entirely OK. But her diction was reasonably clear and she had no loss of memory and her pupils were reacting properly to light, so the doctor was satisfied. He said she would be OK.

'And how is Seth?' Reacher asked.

'Very angry at you,' Eleanor said.

'What goes around comes around.'

'You're much bigger than him.'

'He's much bigger than you.'

She didn't answer. She just looked at Reacher for another long second, and then she looked away, seemingly very unsure of herself, an expression of complete uncertainty on her face, its extent limited only by the immobility caused by the stiff scabs on her lips and the frozen ache in her nose. She was hurting bad, Reacher thought. She had taken two blows, he figured, probably the first to her nose and the second aimed lower, at her mouth. The first had been hard enough to do damage without breaking the bone, and the second had been hard enough to draw blood without smashing her teeth.

Two blows, carefully aimed, carefully calculated, carefully delivered.

Expert blows.

Reacher said, 'It wasn't Seth, was it?'

She said, 'No, it wasn't.'

'So who was it?'

'I'll quote your earlier conclusion. It seems we have a couple of tough guys in town.'

'They were here?'

'Twice.'

'Why?'

'I don't know.'

'Who are they?'

'I don't know.'

'They've been saying they represent the Duncans.'

'Well, they don't. The Duncans don't need to hire people to beat me. They're perfectly capable of doing that themselves.'

'How many times has Seth hit you?'

'A thousand, maybe.'

'That's good. Not from your point of view, of course.'

'But good from the point of view of your own clear conscience?'

'Something like that.'

She said, 'Have at Seth all you like. All day, every day.

Beat him to a pulp. Break every bone in his body. Be my guest. I mean it.'

'Why do you stay?'

'I don't know,' she said. 'Whole books have been written on that subject. I've read most of them. Ultimately, where else would I go?'

'Anywhere else.'

'It's not that simple. It never is.'

'Why not?'

'Trust me, OK?'

'So what happened?'

She said, 'Four days ago two men showed up here. They had East Coast accents. They were kind of Italian. They were wearing expensive suits and cashmere overcoats. Seth took them into his den. I didn't hear any of the discussion. But I knew we were in trouble. There was a real animal stink in the house. After twenty minutes they all trooped out. Seth was looking sheepish. One of the men said their instructions were to hurt Seth, but Seth had bargained it down to hurting me. At first I thought I was going to be raped in front of my husband. That was what the atmosphere was like. The animal stink. But, no. Seth held me in front of him and they took turns hitting me. Once each. Nose, and then mouth. Then yesterday evening they came back and did all the same things over again. Then Seth went out for a steak. That's what happened.'

'I'm very sorry,' Reacher said.

'So am I.'

'Seth didn't tell you who they were? Or what they wanted?'

'No. Seth tells me nothing.'

'Any ideas?'

'They were investors,' she said. 'I mean, they were here on behalf of investors. That's the only sense I can make out of it.'

'Duncan Transportation has investors?'

'I suppose so. I imagine it's not a wonderfully profitable business. Gas is very expensive right now, isn't it? Or diesel, or whatever it is they use. And it's wintertime, which must hurt their cash flow. There's nothing to haul. Although, really, what do I know? Except that they're always complaining about something. And I see on the news that apparently ordinary banks are difficult right now, for small businesses. So maybe they had to find a loan through unconventional sources.'

'Very unconventional,' Reacher said. 'But if this is all about some financial issue with Duncan Transportation, why are those guys looking for me?'

'Are they looking for you?'

'Yes,' the doctor said. 'They are. They were at my house this morning. They hit me four times and threatened to do much worse to my wife. And all they ever asked was where Reacher was. It was the same at the motel, apparently. Mr Vincent was visited. And Dorothy, the woman who works for him. His housekeeper.'

'That's awful,' Eleanor said. 'Is she OK?'

'She survived.'

'Is your wife OK?'

'A little shaken.'

'I can't explain it,' Eleanor said. 'I know nothing about Seth's business.'

Reacher asked, 'Do you know anything about Seth himself?'

'Like what?'

'Like who he is, and where he came from.'

'Do you guys want a drink?'

'No, thank you,' Reacher said. 'Tell me where Seth came from.'

'That old question? He's adopted, like a lot of people.'

'Where from?'

'He doesn't know, and I don't think his father knows for sure, either. It was some kind of charity network. There was a degree of anonymity involved.'

'No stories at all?'

'None.'

'Doesn't Seth remember anything? People say he was ready for kindergarten when he got here. He should have some memories of where he was before.'

'He won't talk about it.'

'What about the missing girl?'

'That other old question? Lord knows I'm not blind to Seth's faults, or his family's, but as I understand it they were cleared after an investigation by a federal agency. Isn't that good enough for people?'

'You weren't here at the time?'

'No, I grew up in Illinois. Just outside of Chicago. Seth was twenty-two when I met him. I was trying to be a journalist. The only job I could find was at a paper out of Lincoln. I was doing a story about corn prices, of course. That's all that was in that paper, that and college sports. Seth was the new CEO of Duncan

Transportation. I interviewed him for the story. Then we had a cocktail. At first, I was bowled over. Later, not so much.'

'Are you going to be OK?'

'Are you? With two tough guys looking for you?'

'I'm leaving,' Reacher said. 'Heading south and then east, to Virginia. You want to ride along? You could hit the Interstate and never come back.'

Eleanor Duncan said, 'No.'

'You sure?'

'I am.'

'Then I can't help you.'

'You helped me already. More than I can say. You broke his nose. I was so happy.'

Reacher said, 'You should come with me. You should get the hell out. It's crazy to stay, talking like that. Feeling like that.'

'I'll outlast him,' the woman said. 'That's my mission, I think, to outlast them all.'

Reacher said nothing more. He just looked around the kitchen, at the stuff she would inherit if she succeeded in outlasting them all. There was a lot of stuff, all of it expensive and high quality, a lot of it Italian, some of it German, some of it American. Including a Cadillac key in a glass bowl.

'Is that Seth's key?' Reacher asked.

Eleanor said, 'Yes, it is.'

'Does he keep his car gassed up?'

'Usually. Why?'

'I'm going to steal it,' Reacher said.

TWENTY-SIX

Reacher said, 'I've got at least an hour's drive ahead of me. I could use something more comfortable than a truck. And the doctor should keep the truck, anyway. He might need it around here. For his job.'

Eleanor Duncan said, 'You won't get away with it. You'll be driving a stolen car straight through where the county police are based.'

'They won't know it's stolen. Not if Seth doesn't tell them.'

'But he will.'

'Tell him not to. Tell him if he does, I'll come back here and break his arms. Tell him to keep quiet and pick it up tomorrow. I'll leave it somewhere along the way.'

'He won't listen.'

'He will.'

'He doesn't listen to anyone.'

'He listens to those two out-of-towners.'

'Because he's scared of them.'

'He's scared of me, too. He's scared of everybody. Believe me, that's how Seth is.'

Nobody spoke. Reacher took the Cadillac key from

the bowl, and gave the pick-up key to the doctor, and headed for the door.

Seth Duncan was at his father's kitchen table, opposite the old man himself, elbow to elbow with his uncle Jonas on one side and his uncle Jasper on the other. The four men were still and subdued, because they weren't alone in the room. Roberto Cassano was there, leaning on the sink, and Angelo Mancini was there, leaning on the door. Cassano had made a point of smoothing his shirt into the waistband of his pants, even though it was already immaculate, and Mancini had opened his coat and pressed the heels of his hands into the small of his back, as if it was aching from driving, but really both men's gestures had been designed to show off their pistols in their shoulder holsters. The pistols were Colt Double Eagles. Stainless steel semi-automatics. A matched pair. The Duncans had seen the weapons and gotten the point, and so they were sitting quiet and saying nothing.

Cassano said, 'Tell me again. Explain it to me. Convince me. How is this stranger disrupting the shipment?'

Jacob Duncan said, 'Do I tell your boss how to run his business?'

'I guess not.'

'Because it's his business. Presumably it has a thousand subtleties that I don't fully understand. So I stay well out of it.'

'And Mr Rossi stays well out of your business. Until he gets inconvenienced.'

196

'He's welcome to find an alternative source.'

'I'm sure he will. But right now there's a live contract.'

'We'll deliver.'

'When?'

'As soon as this stranger is out of our hair.'

Cassano just shook his head in frustration.

Mancini said, 'You guys need to change your tactics. The stranger was in the fields, OK, no question, but now he's not any more. He's back in the truck he took from those two donkeys last night. He had it stashed somewhere. You should be looking for it. You should be checking the roads again.'

Seth Duncan's Cadillac was new enough to have all the bells and whistles, but old enough to be a straight-up turnpike cruiscr. It wasn't competing against BMW and Mercedes Benz for yuppie money, like the current models were. It was competing against planes and trains for long-distance comfort, like traditional full-boat Caddies always had. Reacher liked it a lot. It was a fine automobile. It was long and wide and weighed about two tons. It was smooth and silent. It was rclaxcd. It was a one-finger, one-toe kind of car, designed for sprawling. It had black paint and black leather and black glass. And a warm-toned radio and a three-quarters-full tank of gas.

Reacher had got in it and racked its seat back and eased it out of the garage and K-turned it behind the house and nosed it cautiously back to the two-lane. He had turned left, south, and wafted on down the road in a rolling cocoon of calm and quiet. The landscape didn't change at all. Straight road ahead, dirt to the right, dirt to the left, clouds overhead. He saw no other traffic. Ten miles south of where he started there was an old roadhouse standing alone in the weedy remnant of a beaten-earth parking lot. It was closed down and boarded up, with a bad roof and ancient Pabst Blue Ribbon and Miller High Life signs on the walls, barely visible behind layers of mud. After that there was nothing, all the way to the horizon.

Roberto Cassano stepped out of Jacob Duncan's back door and walked across weedy gravel to where he couldn't be overheard. A thin plume of black smoke rose far to the north. The burned-out truck, still smouldering. The stranger's work.

Cassano dialled his cell and got Rossi after three rings. He said, 'They're sticking to their story, boss. We're not going to get the shipment until they get the stranger.'

Rossi said, 'That makes no sense.'

'Tell me about it. It's Alice in Wonderland.'

'How much pressure have you applied?'

'To the Duncans themselves? That's my next question. How much pressure do you want us to apply?'

There was a long pause, with a breath, like a sigh, resigned. Rossi said, 'The problem is, they sell great stuff. I won't find better. I won't find anything half as good. So I can't burn them. Because I'm going to need them again, in the future. Over and over. No question about that.'

'So?'

'So play their game. Find the damn stranger.'

The doctor stepped out of Eleanor Duncan's door and stared hard at the pick-up truck. He didn't want to get in it. Didn't want to drive it. Didn't want to be seen with it. Didn't want to be anywhere near it. It was a Duncan vehicle. It had been misappropriated, and the manner of its misappropriation had been a major humiliation for the Duncans. Two Cornhuskers, tossed aside, contemptuously. Therefore to be involved with the truck in any way at all would be an outrageous provocation. Insane. He would be punished, severely and for ever.

But he was a doctor.

And sober, unfortunately.

Therefore clear-headed.

He had patients. He had responsibilities. To Vincent at the motel, for one. To Dorothy the housekeeper, for another. Both were shaken up. And he was a married man. His wife was eight miles away, scared and alone.

He looked at the key in his hand and the truck on the driveway. He mapped out a route in his head. He could park behind Dorothy's house and keep the truck out of sight. He could park on the wrong side of the motel office and achieve the same result. Then he could dump the truck to the north and hike across the fields to home.

Total exposure, maybe two miles on minor tracks, and four on the two-lane road.

Ten minutes.

That was all.

Safe enough.

Maybe.

He climbed in the cab and started the engine.

The anonymous white van was still on Route 3, still in Canada, but it had left British Columbia behind and had entered Alberta. It was making steady progress, heading east, completely unnoticed. Its driver was making no calls. His phone was switched off. The assumption was that cell towers close to the 49th Parallel were monitored for activity. Perhaps conversations were recorded and analysed. Homeland Security departments on both sides of the border had computer programs with sophisticated software. Individual words could trigger alerts. And even without compromising language, an electronic record of where a guy had been, and when, was always best avoided. For the same reason, all gas purchases were made with cash, in the local currency, and at every stop the driver turned his collar up and pulled his hat down low, in case there were cameras connected to digital recorders or distant control rooms.

The van rolled on, making steady progress, heading east.

Rossi clicked off the call with Cassano and thought hard for five minutes, and then he dialled Safir, six blocks away. He took a breath and held it and asked, 'Have you ever seen better merchandise?'

Safir said, 'You don't have to play the salesman. I already fell for your pitch.'

'And you've always been satisfied, right?'

'I'm not satisfied now.'

'I understand,' Rossi said. 'But I want to discuss something with you.'

'Equals discuss,' Safir said. 'We're not equals. I tell, you ask.'

'OK, I want to ask you something. I want to ask you to take a step back and consider something.'

'For example?'

'I need this shipment, you need this shipment, everyone needs this shipment. So I want to ask you to put our differences aside and make common cause. Just for a day or two.'

'How?'

'My contacts in Nebraska have a bug up their ass.'

'I know all about that,' Safir said. 'My men gave me a full report.'

'I want you to send them up there to help.'

'Send who? Up where?'

'Your men. To Nebraska. There's no point in having them here in my office. Your interests are my interests, and I'm already working as hard as I can on this. So I'm thinking your guys could go help my guys and between us we could solve this problem.'

The doctor made it to Dorothy's farmhouse unobserved and parked in the yard behind it, nose to tail with Dorothy's own pick-up. He found her in her kitchen, washing dishes. Breakfast dishes, presumably. Hers and Reacher's. Which had been a crazy risk.

He asked, 'How are you holding up?'

She said, 'I'm OK. You look worse than me.'

'I'll survive.'

'You're in a Duncan truck.'

'I know.'

'That's dumb.'

'Like cooking breakfast for the guy was dumb.'

'He was hungry.'

The doctor asked, 'You need anything?'

'I need to know how this is going to end.'

'Not well, probably. He's one guy, on his own. And there's no guarantee he'll even stick around.'

'You know where he is right now?'

'Yes. More or less.'

'Don't tell me.'

'I won't.'

Dorothy said, 'You should go check on Mr Vincent. He was hurt pretty bad.'

'That's where I'm headed next,' the doctor said.

Safir clicked off the call with Rossi and thought hard for ten long minutes, and then he dialled his customer Mahmeini, eight blocks across town. He took a breath and held it and asked, 'Have you ever seen better merchandise?'

Mahmeini said, 'Get to the damn point.'

'There's a kink in the chain.'

'Chains don't have kinks. Hoses have kinks. Chains have weak links. Are you confessing? You're the weak link?'

'I'm just saying. There's a speed bump. A Catch-22. It's crazy, but it's there.'

'And?'

'We all have a common goal. We all want that shipment. And we're not going to get it until the speed bump disappears. That's a fact, unfortunately. There's nothing any of us can do about it. We're all victims here. So I'm asking you to put our differences aside and make common cause, just for a day or two.'

'How?'

'I want you to take your guys out of my office and send them up to Nebraska. I'm sending my guys. We could all work together and solve this problem.'

Mahmeini went quiet. Truth was, he was nothing more than a link in a chain, too, the same as Safir, the same as Rossi, who he knew all about, the same as the Duncans, who he knew all about too, and Vancouver. He knew the lie of the land. He had exercised due diligence. He had done the research. They were all links in a chain, except that he was the penultimate link, the second to last, and therefore he was under the greatest strain. Because right next to him at the top were Saudis, unbelievably rich and beyond vicious. A bad combination.

Mahmeini said, 'Ten per cent discount.'

Safir said, 'Of course.'

Mahmeini said, 'Call me back with the arrangements.'

The doctor parked to the rear of the motel lounge, between its curved wall and a circular stockade that hid the trash cans and the propane tanks, nose to tail with Vincent's own car, which was an old Pontiac sedan. Not a perfect spot. The truck would be clearly visible from certain angles, both north and south. But it was the best he could do. He got out and paused in the chill and checked the road. Nothing coming.

He found Vincent in the lounge, just sitting there in one of his red velvet armchairs, doing absolutely nothing at all. He had a black eye and a split lip and a swelling the size of a hen's egg on his cheek. Exactly like the doctor himself, in fact. They were a matched pair. Like looking in a mirror.

The doctor asked, 'You need anything?'

Vincent said, 'I have a terrible headache.'

'Want painkillers?'

'Painkillers won't help. I want this to be over. That's what I want. I want that guy to finish what he started.'

'He's on his way to Virginia.'

'Great.'

'He said he's going to check in with the county cops along the way. He said he's going to come back if there's something wrong with the case file from twenty-five years ago.'

'Ancient history. They'll have junked the file.'

'He says not.'

'Then they won't let him see it.'

'He says they will.'

'But what can he find now, that they didn't find then? Saying all that just means he's never coming back. He's softening the blow, that's all he's doing. He's slipping away, with an excuse. He's leaving us in the lurch.'

The strange round room went quiet.

'You need anything?' the doctor asked again.

'Do you?' Vincent asked back. 'You want a drink?'

'Are you allowed to serve me?'

'It's a little late to worry about that kind of thing, don't you think? You want one?'

'No,' the doctor said. 'I better not.' Then he paused and said, 'Well, maybe just one, for the road.'

Safir called Rossi back and said, 'I want a twenty per cent discount.'

Rossi said, 'In exchange for what?'

'Helping you. Sending my boys up there.'

'Fifteen per cent. Because you'll be helping yourself too.'

'Twenty,' Safir said. 'Because I'm talking about sending more boys than just mine.'

'How so?'

'I've got guys babysitting me too. Two of them. Right here, right now. I told you that, didn't I? So you think I'm taking my guys out of your office while I've still got guys in my own office? Well, dream on. That's not going to happen any time soon, believe me. So I got my customer to agree to send his guys, too. Like a shared sacrifice. And anyway, a thing like this, we'll all want our fingers in the pie.'

Rossi paused.

'OK,' he said. 'That's good. That's real good. Between us we'll have six men up there. We can take care of this thing real fast. We'll be out of the woods in no time at all.'

'Arrangements?'

Rossi said, 'The nearest civilization is sixty miles south. Where the county offices are. The only accommodation is a Courtyard Marriott. My guys are based

205

there. I'll tell them to pull back there right now and I'll book a couple more rooms. Then everyone can meet up as soon as possible, and then they can all get going.'

The two-lane road stayed arrow-straight the whole way. Reacher kept the Cadillac rolling along at a steady sixty per, covering a mile a minute, no stress at all. Fifty minutes from where he started he passed a lonely bar on the right shoulder. It was a small hunched building made of wood, with dirty windows with beer signs in them, and three cars in its lot, and a name board that said Cell Block. Which was marginally appropriate. Reacher figured that if he squinted the place might look like a jail from an old Western movie. He blew past it and a mile later the far horizon changed. A water tower and a Texaco sign loomed up out of the afternoon gloom. Civilization. But not much of it. The place looked small. It was just a chequerboard of a dozen low-rise blocks dumped down on the dirt in the middle of nowhere.

Eight hundred yards out there was a Chamber of Commerce billboard that listed five different ways a traveller could spend his money. If he wanted to eat, there were two restaurants. One was a diner, and one wasn't. Reacher recognized neither name. Not chains. If a traveller needed to fix his car, there was a service station and a tyre shop. If he wanted to sleep, the only choice was a Courtyard Marriott.

TWENTY-SEVEN

Reacher blew straight past the billboard and then slowed and checked ahead. In his experience most places reserved the main drag for profit-and-loss businesses. Municipal enterprises like cops and county offices would be a block or two over. Maybe more. Something to do with tax revenues. A town couldn't charge as much for a lot on a back street.

He slowed a little more and passed the first building. It was on the left. It was an aluminium coach diner, as advertised on the billboard, as mentioned by Dorothy the housekeeper. It was the place where the county cops got their morning coffee and doughnuts. And their afternoon snacks, apparently. There was a black-and-white Dodge police cruiser parked outside. Plus two working pick-up trucks, both of them farm vehicles, both of them dented and dirty. Next up in terms of infrastructure was a gas station across the street, Texaco, with three service bays attached. Then came a long sequence of miscellaneous enterprises, on the left and the right, a hardware store, a liquor store, a bank, tyre bays, a John Deere dealership, a grocery, a pharmacy. The street was broad and muddy and had diagonal parking on both sides.

Reacher drove all the way through town. At the end of it was a genuine crossroads, signposted left to an ethanol plant and right to a hospital and straight ahead to I-80, another sixty miles farther on. He U-turned shoulder-to-shoulder and came back again, north on the main drag. There were three side streets on the right, and three on the left. They all had names that sounded like people. Maybe original Nebraska settlers, or famous football players, or coaches, or champion corn growers. He made the first right, on a street named McNally, and saw the Marriott hotel up ahead. It was four o'clock in the afternoon, which was awkward. The old files would be in the police station or a county storeroom, and either way the file clerks would be quitting at five. He had one hour. That was all. Access alone might take thirty minutes to arrange, and there was probably plenty of paper, which would take much more than the other thirty to read. He was going to have to wait for the morning.

Or, maybe not.

Worth a try.

He rolled ahead and took a look at the hotel on the way. He wasn't sure what the difference was between a regular Marriott and a Courtyard Marriott. Maybe one was high-rise and the other was low-rise. This was a low-rise, just two storeys, H-shaped, a lobby flanked by two modest wings of bedrooms. There was a parking lot out front with marked spaces for about twenty cars, only two of them occupied. Same again at the rear of the building.

Twenty spaces, only two of them occupied. Plenty of vacancies. Wintertime, in the middle of nowhere.

He made a left and came back north again, parallel to the main drag, three blocks over. He saw the second restaurant. It was a rib shack. It boasted a dry rub recipe direct from Kansas. He turned left again just beyond it and came back to the main street and pulled in at the diner. The cop car was still there. Still parked. The diner wasn't busy. Reacher could see in through the windows. Two cops, three civilians, a waitress, and a cook behind a hatch.

Reacher locked the Cadillac and walked in. The cops were face to face in a booth, each of them wide and bulky, each of them taking up most of a two-person bench. One of them was about Reacher's age, and one of them was younger. They had grey uniforms, with badges and insignia, and nameplates. The older cop was called Hoag. Reacher walked past him and stopped and panto-mimed a big double take and said, 'You're Hoag, right? I don't believe it.'

The cop said, 'Excuse me?'

'I remember you from Desert Storm. Don't I? The Gulf, in 1991? Am I right?'

The cop said, 'I'm sorry, my friend, but you'll have to help me out here. There's been a lot of water over the dam since 1991.'

Reacher offered his hand. He said, 'Reacher, 110th MP.'

The cop wiped his hand on his pants and shook. He said, 'I'm not sure I was ever in contact with you guys.'

'Really? I could have sworn. Saudi, maybe? Just before? During Desert Shield?'

'I was in Germany just before.'

'I don't think it was Germany. But I remember the name. And the face, kind of. Did you have a brother in the Gulf? Or a cousin or something?'

'A cousin, sure.'

'Looks just like you?'

'Back then, I guess. A little.'

'There you go. Nice guy, right?'

'Nice enough.'

'And a fine soldier, as I recall.'

'He came home with a Bronze Star.'

'I knew it. VII Corps, right?'

'Second Armored Cavalry.'

'Third Squadron?'

'That's the one.'

'I knew it,' Reacher said again. An old, old process, exploited by fortune tellers everywhere. Steer a guy through an endless series of yes-no, right-wrong questions, and in no time at all a convincing illusion of intimacy built itself up. A simple psychological trick, sharpened by listening carefully to answers, feeling the way, and playing the odds. Most people who wore name tags every day forgot they had them on, at least initially. And a lot of heartland cops were ex-military. Way more than the average. And even if they weren't, most of them had big families. Lots of brothers and cousins. Virtually certain that at least one of them would have been in the army. And Desert Storm had been the main engagement for that whole generation, and VII Corps had been by far its largest component, and a Bronze Star winner from the Second Armored Cavalry was almost certainly from the Third Squadron, which had been the tip of the spear. An algorithm. Playing the odds. No-brainers all the way.

Reacher asked, 'So what's your cousin doing now?'

'Tony? He's back in Lincoln. He got out before the second go-round, thank God. He's working for the railroad. Two kids, one in junior high and one in college.'

'That's terrific. You see him much?'

'Now and then.'

'Be sure to remember me to him, OK? Jack Reacher, 110th MP. One desert rat to another.'

'So what are you doing now? He's bound to ask.'

'Me? Oh, the same old, same old.'

'What, you're still in?'

'No, I mean I was an investigator, and I'm still an investigator. But private now. My own man, not Uncle Sam's.'

'Here in Nebraska?'

'Just temporarily,' Reacher said. Then he paused. 'You know what? Maybe you could help me out. If you don't mind me asking.'

'What do you need?'

'You guys going on duty or going off?'

'We're coming on. We got the night shift ahead of us.'

'Mind if I sit down?'

The cop called Hoag scooted over, all swishing vinyl and creaking leather. Reacher perched on the part of the bench he had vacated. It was warm. He said, 'I knew this other guy, name of McNally. Another Second Armored guy, as a matter of fact. Turns out he has a friend of a friend who has an aunt in this county. She's a farmer. Her daughter disappeared twenty-five years ago. Eight years old, never seen again. The woman never really got over it. Your department handled it, with the FBI as the icing on the cake. McNally's friend of a friend thinks the FBI screwed up. So McNally hired me to review the paperwork.'

'Twenty-five years ago?' Hoag said. 'Before my time.'

'Right,' Reacher said. 'I guess we were both in basic back then.'

'And the kid was never seen again? That means it's an open case. Cold, but open. Which means the paperwork should still exist. And someone should remember it.'

'That's exactly what McNally was hoping.'

'And he's looking to screw the FBI? Not us?'

'The story is you guys did a fine job.'

'And what did the FBI do wrong?'

'They didn't find the kid.'

'What good will all this do?'

'I don't know,' Reacher said. 'You tell me. You know how it is with people. It might put some minds at rest, I guess.'

'OK,' Hoag said. 'I'll put the word out at the station house. Someone will get you in, first thing tomorrow morning.'

'Any chance of doing something tonight? If I could get this done by midnight, it would cut McNally's bill by one day. He doesn't have much money.'

'You turning down a bigger pay cheque?'

'One veteran to another. You know how it is. Plus I've got business elsewhere. I need to get to Virginia as soon as I can.'

Hoag checked his watch. Twenty minutes past four. He said, 'All that old stuff is in the basement under the county clerk's office. You can't be in there after five o'clock.'

'Any way of getting it out?'

'Oh, man, that's asking a lot.'

'I don't need court exhibits. I don't want the physical evidence, assuming there is any. I just want the paperwork.'

'I could get my ass kicked real bad.'

'I just want to read it. Where's the harm in that? In and out in one night, who's even going to know?'

'There's probably a lot of it. Boxes and boxes.'

'I'll help with the grunt work.'

'McNally was Second Armored? Same as Tony?'

Reacher nodded. 'But Second Squadron, not Third. Not quite in Tony's class.'

'Where are you staying?'

'The Marriott. Where else?'

There was a long pause. The younger cop looked on. Hoag was well aware of his scrutiny. Reacher watched the dynamic unfold. Hoag cycled through proper civil caution to a kind of nostalgic old-school can-do soldier-to-soldier recklessness. He looked at Reacher and said, 'OK, I know a guy. We'll get this done. But it's better that you're not there. So go wait for us. We'll deliver.'

So Reacher drove back to the Courtyard Marriott

213

and put the Cadillac way in the rear, behind the building itself, where it couldn't be seen from the front. Safer that way, in case Seth Duncan couldn't be stopped from getting on the horn and spreading the word. Then he walked back and waited at the lobby desk for the clerk to finish on the phone. He seemed to be taking a couple of bookings from someone. When he was done Reacher bought a night in a ground floor room, which turned out to be way in the back of the H, very quiet and very adequate, very clean and very well equipped, all green and tan colours and brass accents and pale wood. Then forty minutes later Hoag and his partner showed up in a borrowed K-9 van loaded with eleven cardboard cartons of files. Five minutes after that, all eleven cartons were in Reacher's room.

And five minutes after that, but sixty miles to the north, the doctor left the motel lounge. He had talked with Vincent a bit, just shooting the shit, but mostly he had drunk three triples of Jim Beam. Nine measures of bourbon, in a little more than an hour. And it was cloudy and going dark, which meant that his glance up and down the road didn't reveal what it would have if the sun had been brighter. He climbed into the pick-up truck and started the motor and backed out from his place of concealment. He swung the wheel and crossed the lot and turned right on the two-lane.

TWENTY-EIGHT

The six remaining Cornhuskers had split up and were operating solo. Two were parked north on the two-lane, two were parked south, one was out cruising the tangle of lanes to the southeast, and the sixth was out cruising the tangle of lanes to the southwest.

The doctor ran into the two to the north.

Almost literally. His plan was to dump the truck as soon as he found some neutral no-man's-land and then walk home cross-country. He was getting his bearings and looking around as he drove, staring left and right, the bourbon making him slow and numb. His gaze came back to the traffic lane and he saw he was about one second away from colliding head-on with another truck parked half on and half off the shoulder. It was just sitting there, facing the wrong way, with its lights off. Eyes to brain to hands, everything buffered by the bourbon fog, a split second of delay, a wrench of the wheel, and suddenly he was heading diagonally for another truck parked on the other shoulder, thirty yards farther on. He stamped on the brake and all four wheels locked up and he skidded and came to a stop more or less sideways.

The second truck pulled out and blocked the road ahead of him.

The first truck pulled out and blocked the road behind him.

In Las Vegas Mahmeini dialled his phone. His main guy answered, eight blocks away, in Safir's office. Mahmeini said, 'Change of plan. You two are going to Nebraska, right now. Use the company plane. The pilot will have the details.'

His guy said, 'OK.'

Mahmeini said, 'It's a two-part mission. First, find this stranger everybody is talking about and take him out. Second, get close to the Duncans. Build up some trust. Then take out Safir's guys, and Rossi's too, so that from this point onward we're bypassing two links in the chain. In future we can deal direct. Much more profit that way. Much more control, too.'

His guy said, 'OK.'

The doctor sat still behind the wheel, shaking with shock and fear and adrenalin. The Cornhuskers climbed out of their vehicles. Big guys. Red jackets. They walked towards the doctor's stalled truck, taking it slow and easy, one from the left, one from the right. They stood for a second, one each side of the pick-up's cab, still and quiet in the afternoon gloom. Then the first guy opened the passenger door, and the second guy opened the driver's door. The guy at the passenger door stood ready to block an escape, and the guy at the driver's door reached inside and hauled the doctor out by the collar of his coat. The doctor went down like a dead weight, straight to the blacktop, and the guy hauled him up again and hit him hard in the gut and then turned him around and hit him twice more, low in the back, right over his kidneys. The doctor fell to his knees and puked bourbon on the road.

The guy who had been waiting at the passenger door walked back to his vehicle and parked it where it had been before. Then he put the doctor's truck right behind it. He rejoined his buddy and between them they wrestled the doctor up into the cab of the first guy's truck. Then they drove away, one on the right, one on the left, with the doctor jammed between them on the three-person bench, shaking and shivering, his chin on his chest.

In Las Vegas Safir dialled his phone, and his guy answered, in Rossi's office, six blocks away. Safir said, 'New developments. I'm sending you two to Nebraska. I'll fax the details to the airport.'

His guy said, 'OK.'

Safir said, 'Rossi's guys will meet you at the hotel. Mahmeini is sending guys too. The six of you will work together until the stranger is down. In the meantime try and get something going with the Duncans. Build a relationship. Then take Rossi's guys out. That way we're one step closer to the motherlode. We can double our margin.'

His guy said, 'OK.'

'And if you get the chance, take Mahmeini's guys out too. I think I can get next to his customer. I mean, where else can he get stuff like this? We could maybe quadruple our margin.'

His guy said, 'OK, boss.'

The Cornhuskers drove south, five fast miles, and then they slowed and turned in on the Duncans' shared driveway. The doctor looked up at the change of speed and direction and moaned a strangled inarticulate sigh and closed his eyes and dropped his head again. The guy on his right smacked an elbow in his ribs. He said, 'You need to get that voice working better, my friend. Because you've got some explaining to do.'

They took it slow all the way up to the houses, formal and ceremonial, mission accomplished, and they parked out front and got out and hauled their prize out after them. They marched him to Jacob Duncan's door and knocked. A minute later Jacob Duncan opened it up and one of the Cornhuskers put his hand flat on the doctor's back and shoved him inside, and said, 'We found this guy using the truck we lost. He put his own damn plates on it.'

Jacob Duncan looked at the doctor for ten long seconds. He raised his hand and patted him gently on the cheek. Pale skin, damp and clammy, lumps and bruises. Then he bunched the front of the doctor's shirt in his fist and dragged him farther into the hallway. He turned and pushed him onward, through the dark depths of the house, towards the kitchen in back. Their prisoner, in the system.

Jacob Duncan turned back to the Cornhuskers.

'Good work, boys,' he said. 'Now go finish the job. Find Reacher. He's on foot again, clearly. If the doctor knows where he is, he's sure to tell us soon, and we'll let you know. But in the meantime, keep looking.'

Roberto Cassano was still in Jacob Duncan's kitchen. Angelo Mancini was still in there with him. They saw the sadsack doctor stumble in from the hallway, all drunk and raggedy and terrified, with Mancini's earlier handiwork still clearly visible all over his face. Then Cassano's phone rang. He checked the screen and saw that it was Rossi calling and he stepped out the back door and walked across the weedy gravel. He hit the button and raised the phone and Rossi said, 'Complications.'

Cassano said, 'Such as?'

'I had to calm things down at this end. It was getting out of control. I had to talk to people, change a few perceptions. Long story short, you're getting reinforcements. Two of Safir's guys, and two of Mahmeini's.'

'That should shorten the process.'

'Initially,' Rossi said. 'But then it's going to get very difficult. A buck gets ten they're coming with instructions to cut us out of the chain. Mahmeini is probably looking to cut Safir out too. So don't let any of them get close to the Duncans. Not for a minute. Don't let the Duncans make any new friends. And watch your step as soon as the stranger is down. You're going to have four guys gunning for you.'

'What do you want us to do?'

'I want you to stay alive. And in control.'

219

'Rules of engagement?'

'Put Safir's guys down for sure. That way we remove the link above us. We can sell direct to Mahmeini, at Safir's prices.'

'OK.'

'And put Mahmeini's guys down too, if you have to, for self-defence. But make sure to make it look like Safir's guys or the Duncans did it. I still need Mahmeini himself. There's no wiggle room there. I have no access to the ultimate buyer without him.'

'OK.'

'So leave right now. Pull back to the hotel and lie low. You'll meet the others there, probably very soon. Make contact and make a plan.'

'Who's in charge?'

'The Iranians will claim they are. But they can stick that where the sun don't shine. You know the people and the terrain. Keep on top of it and be very careful.'

'OK, boss,' Cassano said. And two minutes later he and Mancini were back in their rented blue Impala, heading south on the arrow-straight two-lane, sixty miles to go.

The white van was still on Route 3, still in Canada, still heading east, more than halfway across Alberta, with Saskatchewan up ahead. It had just skipped a right turn on Route 4, which led south to the border, where the modest Canadian blacktop ribbon changed to the full-blown majesty of U.S. Interstate 15, which ran all the way to Las Vegas and then Los Angeles. The change of status in what had once been the same horse trail was emblematic of the two nations' sense of self, and as well as that it was taken to be a very dangerous road. It was an obvious artery, with two big prizes at the end of it, and so it was assumed to be monitored very carefully. Which was why the white van had passed up the chance of its speed and convenience and was still labouring east on the minor thoroughfare, towards a small town called Medicine Hat, where it intended to finally turn south and lose itself in the wild country around Pakowki Lake, before finding a nameless rutted track that ran deep into the woods, and all the way to America.

The Duncans made the doctor stand upright at the head of the table. They sat and looked at him and said nothing for a minute, Jacob and Seth on one side, Jasper and Jonas on the other. Finally Jacob asked, 'Was it an act of deliberate rebellion?'

The doctor didn't answer. His throat was swollen and painful from vomiting, and he didn't understand the question anyway.

Jacob asked, 'Or was it some imagined sense of entitlement?'

The doctor didn't answer.

'We need to know,' Jacob said. 'You must tell us. This is a fascinating subject. It needs to be thoroughly explored.'

The doctor said, 'I don't know what you're talking about.'

'But perhaps your wife does,' Jacob said. 'Should we go pick her up and bring her here and ask her?'

'Leave her out of it.'

221

'I'm sorry?'

'Please. Please leave her alone.'

'She could entertain us. She used to, you know. We knew her long before you did. She came here half a dozen times. To this very house. She was happy to. Of course, we were paying her, which might have influenced her attitude. You should ask her, about what she used to do for money.'

'She babysat.'

'Is that what she says? I suppose she would, now.'

'That's what she did.'

'Ask her again sometime. Catch her in an unguarded moment. She was a girl of many talents, your wife, once upon a time. She might tell you all about it. You might enjoy it.'

'What do you want?'

Jacob Duncan said, 'We want to know the psychology behind what you did.'

'What did I do?'

'You put your licence plates on our truck.'

The doctor said nothing.

Jacob Duncan said, 'We want to know why. That's all. It's not much to ask. Was it just impertinence? Or was it a message? Were you retaliating for our having disabled your own vehicle? Were you claiming a right? Were you making a point? Were you scolding us for having gone too far?'

'I don't know,' the doctor said.

'Or did someone else change the plates?'

'I don't know who changed them.'

'But it wasn't you?'

'No.'

'Where did you find the truck?'

'At the motel. This afternoon. It was next to my car. With my plates on it.'

'Why didn't you change them back?'

'I don't know.'

'To drive with phoney plates is a criminal offence, isn't it? A misdemeanour at best. Should medical practitioners indulge in criminal behaviour?'

'I guess not.'

'But you did.'

'I'm sorry.'

'Don't apologize to us. We're not a court of law. Or a state board. But you should rehearse an excuse. You might lose your job. Then what would your wife do for money? She might have to return to her old ways. A comeback tour, of sorts. Not that we would have her back. I mean, who would? A raddled old bitch like that?'

The doctor said nothing.

'And you treated my daughter-in-law,' Jacob Duncan said. 'After being told not to.'

'I'm a doctor. I had to.'

'The Hippocratic oath?'

'Exactly.'

'Which says, first, do no harm.'

'I didn't do any harm.'

'Look at my son's face.'

The doctor looked.

'You did that,' Jacob said.

'I didn't.'

'You caused it to be done. Which is the same thing. You did harm.'

'That wasn't me.'

'So who was it?'

'I don't know.'

'I think you do. The word is out. Surely you've heard it? We know you people talk about us all the time. On the phone tree. Did you think it was a secret?'

'It was Reacher.'

'Finally,' Jacob said. 'We get to the point. You were his co-conspirator.'

'I wasn't.'

'You asked him to drive you to my son's house.'

'I didn't. He made me go.'

'Whatever,' Jacob said. 'There's no use crying over spilt milk. But we have a question for you.'

'What is it?'

'Where is Reacher now?'

TWENTY-NINE

Reacher was in his ground floor room at the Courtyard Marriott, knee deep in old police reports. He had used the flat-bladed screwdriver from his pocket to slit the tape on all eleven cartons, and he had sampled the first page out of every box to establish the correct date order. He had shuffled the cartons into a line, and then he had started a quick-and-dirty overview of the records, right from the very beginning.

As expected, the notes were comprehensive. It had been a high-profile case with many sensitivities, and there had been three other agencies on the job, the State Police, the National Guard, and the FBI. The county PD had taken pains to be very professional. Multi-agency cases were essentially competitions, and the county PD hadn't wanted to lose. The department had recorded every move and covered every base and covered every ass. In some ways the files were slices of history. They had been nowhere near a computer. They were old-fashioned, human, and basic. They were typewritten, probably on old IBM electric machines. They had misaligned lines and corrections made with white fluid.

The paper itself was foxed and brown, thin and brittle, and musty. There were no reams of cell phone records, because no one had had cell phones back then, not even the cops. No DNA samples had been taken. There were no GPS coordinates.

The files were exactly like the files Reacher himself had created, way back at the start of his army career.

Dorothy had called the cops from a neighbour's house, at eight in the evening on an early summer Sunday. Not 911, but the local switchboard number. There was a transcript of the call, by the look of it probably not from a recording. Probably reconstructed from the desk sergeant's memory. Dorothy's last name was Coe. Her only child Margaret had last been seen more than six hours previously. She was a good girl. No problems. No troubles. No reasons. She had been wearing a green dress and had ridden away on a pink bicycle.

The desk sergeant had called the captain and the captain had called a detective who had just gotten off the day shift. The detective was called Miles Carson. Carson had sent squad cars north and the hunt had begun. The weather had been good and there had been an hour of twilight and then darkness had fallen. Carson himself had arrived on scene within forty minutes. The next twelve hours had unfolded pretty much the way Dorothy had described over breakfast, the house to house canvass, the flashlight searches, the loudhailer appeals to check every barn and outbuilding, the all-night motor patrols, the arrival of the dogs at first light, the State Police contribution, the National Guard's loan of a helicopter.

Miles Carson was a thorough man, but he had gotten no result.

In principle Reacher might have criticized a couple of things. No reason to wait until dawn to call in the dogs, for instance. Dogs could work in the dark. But it was a moot point anyway, because as soon as Margaret had gotten on her bicycle, her scent had disappeared, suspended in the air, whisked away by the breeze, insulated by rubber tyres. The dogs tracked her to her own driveway, and that was all. The loudhailer appeals for folks to search their own property were curiously circular too, because what was a guilty party going to do? Turn himself in? Although in Carson's defence, foul play was not yet suspected. The first Carson had heard about local suspicions had come at nine the next morning, when Dorothy Coe had broken down and spilled the beans about the Duncans. That interview had lasted an hour and filled nine pages of notes. Then Carson had gotten right on it.

But from the start, the Duncans had looked innocent.

They even had an alibi. Five years earlier they had sold the family farm, retaining only a T-shaped acre that encompassed their driveway and their three houses, and in the country way of things they had never gotten around to marking off their new boundaries. Their neighbours' last ploughed furrows were their property line. But eventually they decided to put up a post-and-rail fence. It was a big production, much heavier and sturdier than was standard. They hired four local teenagers to come do the work. The four boys had been there all day on that Sunday, dawn to dusk, measuring, sawing, digging deep holes for the posts. The three Duncans and the eight-year-old Seth had been right there with them, all day, dawn to dusk, supervising, directing, checking up, helping out. The four boys confirmed that the Duncans had never left the property, and no one had stopped by, least of all a little girl in a green dress on a pink bicycle.

Even so, Carson had hauled the Duncans in for questioning. By that point a hint of foul play was definitely in the air, so the State Police had to be involved, because of jurisdiction issues, so the Duncans were taken to a State barracks over near Lincoln. Seth went with them and was questioned by female officers, but had nothing to say. The three adults were grilled for days. Nebraska, in the 1980s. Rules and procedures were pretty loose where child kidnapping was suspected. But the Duncans admitted nothing. They allowed their property to be searched, voluntarily. Carson's people did the job thoroughly, which wasn't hard because there wasn't much property. Just the T-shaped acre of land, bounded by the unfinished post-and-rail fence, and the three houses themselves. Carson's people found nothing. Carson called the FBI, who sent a team equipped with the latest 1980s technology. The FBI found nothing. The Duncans were released, driven home, and the case went cold.

Reacher crawled across the room, back to the first carton, hands and knees, overview completed, ready to start in on the fine details.

*   *   *

The doctor didn't answer. He just stood there, bruised, sore, shaking, sweating. Jacob Duncan repeated the question: 'Where is Reacher now?'

The doctor said, 'I would like to sit down.'

'Have you been drinking?'

'A little.'

'At the motel?'

'No,' the doctor said. 'I figured Mr Vincent wouldn't serve me.'

'So where were you drinking?'

'At home.'

'And then you walked to the motel?'

'Yes.'

'Why?'

'I needed something from my car. Some medical equipment.'

'So you were already drunk when you stole our truck?'

'Yes. I wouldn't have done it if I was sober.'

'Where is Reacher now?'

'I don't know.'

'Would you like a drink?'

The doctor said, 'A drink?'

'You're familiar with the concept, I think.'

'Yes, I would like a drink.'

Jacob Duncan got up and stepped across his kitchen to a cabinet on the wall. He opened it up and took out a bottle of Wild Turkey, almost full. From another cabinet he took a glass. He carried both back to the table and set them down. He took stuff off a chair in the corner, a pair of boots, old mail, a ball of string, and he carried the chair across the room and placed it behind the doctor.

He said, 'Sit down, please. And help yourself.'

The doctor sat down and shuffled the chair closer to the table and uncorked the bottle. He poured himself a generous measure and drank it all in one go. He poured a second glass.

Jacob Duncan asked, 'Where is Reacher now?'

The doctor said, 'I don't know.'

'I think you do. And it's time to make your choice. You can sit here with us and drink my fine bourbon and pass the time of day in pleasant conversation. Or we could do it another way. We could have Seth break your nose, for instance. I'm pretty certain he would like to. Or we could have your wife join us, and we could subject her to petty humiliations. My guess is she wouldn't put up much of a fight, having known us all these years. No marks, no overt damage. But the shared experience might have an effect on your marriage, in the years to come, you having shown yourself unable to defend her. Because she'll see it as unwilling, not unable. You should think about it.'

'Reacher's gone,' the doctor said.

'Gone?'

'He left this afternoon.'

'How?'

'He got a ride.'

'Impossible,' Jacob said. 'We blocked the road, north and south.'

'Not in time.'

'Did you see him go?'

'He was at the motel. I think he changed the plates because he was going to use your truck. But someone else came along and he hitched a ride, which was better.'

'Who came along?'

'Not one of us. Just someone driving through.'

'What kind of car?'

'I'm not good with cars. I think it was white.'

'Did he say where he was going?'

The doctor drank most of his second glass. Gulp, swallow, gulp, swallow. He said, 'He's going to Virginia.'

'Why?'

'I don't know,' the doctor said. He filled his glass again. 'But that's all he's ever talked about, right from the first moment he got here. He's on his way to Virginia, and always was.'

'What's in Virginia?'

'He didn't say. A woman, perhaps. That's the impression I got.'

'From what?'

'Just a feeling.'

Jacob Duncan said, 'You're nervous.'

The doctor said, 'Of course I am.'

'Why? You're just sharing a drink with your neighbours.'

The doctor said nothing.

Jacob Duncan said, 'You think he's coming back.'

'I don't.'

'Is he coming back?'

The doctor said nothing.

'Tell us.'

The doctor said, 'He was a military cop. He knows how to do things.'

'What things?'

'He said he's going to visit with the county police. Tomorrow morning, I suppose. He said he's going to look at the file from twenty-five years ago. If it's OK, he's going to Virginia. If it's not, he's coming back here.'

'Why would he?'

'To get you, that's why.'

Up in Canada, the white van had made the right turn just shy of the town called Medicine Hat, and was heading south on the lonely road that led down towards Pakowki Lake. It was already full dark up there. No lights at all, and no moon or stars either, because of the cloud. The road was bad. It was pitted with potholes. It twisted and it wandered, and it rose and it fell. It was hard going, and not entirely safe. It was dangerous, even, because at that stage a broken axle or a busted half-shaft would ruin everything. So the driver turned left, on a rough grassy track he had used before, and bumped and bounced two hundred yards to a picnic spot provided for summer visitors. In winter it was always deserted. The driver had seen bears there, and coyotes, and red foxes, and moose, and twice he thought he had seen elk, although they might have been shadows, and once he thought he had seen a wolf, but it might have been just another coyote. But he had never seen people. Not in winter. Not even once.

He parked under a towering pine and shut down for the night.

*　　*　　*

Roberto Cassano and Angelo Mancini pulled their rented Impala around the back of the Marriott and slotted it next to a black Cadillac that was standing alone in the rear of the lot. They got out and stretched and checked their watches. They figured they had time for a quick dinner before their reinforcements arrived. The diner or the rib shack? They liked neither one. Why would they? They had taste, and the retard local yokels sure as hell didn't. But they were hungry, and they had to eat somewhere.

They pondered for a second and decided on the diner. They turned away from the hotel lobby and headed for the main drag.

The Duncans let the doctor finish a third glass of Wild Turkey, and then they sent him on his way. They pushed him out the door and told him to walk home. They watched him down the driveway, and then they turned and strolled back and regrouped in Jacob's kitchen. Jacob put the bottle back in the cupboard, and put the glass in the sink, and returned the chair to the corner of the room. His brother Jasper asked, 'So what do you think?'

Jacob said, 'About what?'

'Should we call the county and stop them showing Reacher the files?'

'I don't see how we could do that.'

'We could try.'

'It would draw attention.'

Jonas asked, 'Should we call Eldridge Tyler? Strictly as a back-up?'

'Then we would owe him something.'

'It would be a wise investment, if Reacher is coming back.'

'I don't think he's coming back,' Jacob said. 'That's my first thought, certainly.'

'But?'

'Ultimately I guess it depends on what he finds, and what he doesn't find.'

THIRTY

Reacher found a statement from the little girl's father. It was long and detailed. Cops weren't dumb. Fathers were automatic suspects when little girls disappeared. Margaret's father had been Arthur Coe, universally known as Artie. At the time of his daughter's disappearance he was thirty-seven years old. Relatively ancient for a father of an eight-year-old, back in the 1980s. He was a local man. He was a Vietnam veteran. He had refused an offer from the local Selective Service board to classify his farm work as an essential occupation. He had served, and he had come back. A brave man. A patriot. He had been fixing machinery in an outbuilding when Margaret had ridden away, and he had still been fixing it four hours later, when his wife came to tell him that the kid was still out. He had dropped everything and started the search. His statement was full of the same kinds of feelings Dorothy had described over breakfast, the unreality, the hope against hope, the belief that the kid was just out playing somewhere, surely to God, maybe picking flowers, that she had lost track of time, that she would be home soon, right as rain. Even after twenty-five years the typewritten words still reeked of shock and pain and misery.

Arthur Coe was an innocent man, Reacher thought.

He moved on, to a packet marked by hand *Margaret Coe Biography*. Just a regular manila envelope, quite thin, as would befit an eight-year-old's short life story. The gummed flap had never been licked, but it was stuck down anyway, from dampness in the storage facility. Reacher eased it open. There were sheets of paper inside, plus a photograph in a yellowed glassine jacket. Reacher eased it out. And was surprised.

Margaret Coe was Asian.

Vietnamese, possibly, or Thai, or Cambodian, or Chinese, or Japanese, or Korean. Dorothy wasn't. Arthur probably hadn't been, either. Not a native Nebraskan farm worker. Therefore Margaret was adopted. She had been a sweet little thing. The photograph was dated on the back, in a woman's handwriting, with an added note: *Nearly eight! Beautiful as ever!* It was a colour picture, probably amateur, but proficient. Better than a snapshot. It had been thought about and composed, and taken with a decent camera. A good likeness, obviously, to have been given to the police. It showed a little Asian girl, standing still, posing, smiling. She was small and slight and slender. She had trust and merriment in her eyes. She was wearing a plaid skirt and a white blouse.

She was a lovely child.

Reacher heard the stoner's voice in his mind, from earlier in the day: *I hear that poor ghost screaming, man, screaming and wailing and moaning and crying, right here in the dark.*

And at that point Reacher took a break.

Sixty miles north Dorothy Coe took a pork chop from her refrigerator. The chop was part of a pig a friend had slaughtered a mile away, part of a loose cooperative designed to get people through tough times. Dorothy trimmed the fat, and put a little pepper on the meat, and a little mustard, and a little brown sugar. She put the chop in an open dish and put the dish in the oven. She set her table, one place, a knife, a fork, and a plate. She took a glass and filled it with water and put it next to the plate. She folded a square of paper towel for a napkin. Dinner, for one.

Reacher was hungry. He had eaten no lunch. He called the desk and asked for room service and the guy who had booked him in told him there was no room service. He apologized for the lack. Then he went ahead and mentioned the two restaurants named on the billboard Reacher had already seen. The guy promised a really excellent meal could be gotten at either one of them. Maybe he was on a retainer from the Chamber of Commerce.

Reacher put his coat on and headed down the hallway to the lobby. Two more guests were checking in. Both men. They looked Middle Eastern. Iranian, possibly. They were small and rumpled and unshaven and not very clean. One of them glanced at Reacher and Reacher nodded politely and headed for the door. It was dark outside, and cold. Reacher figured he would use the diner for breakfast, and therefore the rib shack for dinner. So he turned right on the back street and hustled.

The doctor walked fast to beat the cold and made it home inside an hour. His wife was waiting for him. She was worried. He had some explaining to do. He started talking and got through the whole story before she spoke a word. At the end he went quiet and she said, 'So it's a gamble, isn't it? Is that what you're saying? Like a horse race. Will Reacher come back before Seth gets home and finds out that you just sat there and watched his car get stolen?'

The doctor said, 'Will Reacher come back at all?'

'I think he will.'

'Why would he?'

'Because the Duncans took that kid. Who else do you think did it?'

'I don't know. I wasn't here. I was in Idaho. I was a kid myself. So were you.'

'Believe me.'

'I do. But I wish you would tell me exactly why I should.'

She said nothing.

The doctor said, 'Maybe Seth won't go home. Maybe he'll spend the night at his father's place.'

'That's possible. People say he often does. But we shouldn't assume.' She started moving around the house, checking the window locks, checking the door locks, front and back. She said, 'We should wedge the doors with furniture.'

'Then they'll come in the window.'

'Tornado glass. It's pretty strong.'

'Those guys weigh three hundred pounds. You saw what they did to my car.'

'We have to do something.'

'They'll burn us out. Or they'll just stand on the step and tell us to open up. Then what are we going to do? Disobey them?'

'We could hold out a day or two. We have food and water.'

'Might be longer than a day or two. Might be for ever. Even if you're right, there's no guarantee Reacher will find the proof. There probably isn't any proof. How can there be? The FBI would have found it at the time.'

'We have to hope.'

Reacher ordered baby back ribs with coleslaw and a cup of coffee. The place was dim and dirty and the walls were covered with old signs and advertisements. Probably all fake. Probably all ordered in bulk from a restaurant supplier, probably all painted in a Taiwanese factory and then scuffed and scratched and battered by the next guy along on the production line. But the ribs turned out to be good. The rub was subtle and the meat was tender. The coleslaw was crisp. The coffee was hot. And the check was tiny. Tip money, any place east of the Mississippi or south of Sacramento.

Reacher paid and left and walked back to the hotel. Two guys were in the lot, hauling bags out of the trunk of a red Ford Taurus. More guests. The Marriott was experiencing a regular wintertime bonanza. The Taurus was new and plain. Probably a rental. The guys were big. Arabs of some kind. Syrians, maybe, or Lebanese. Reacher was familiar with that part of the world. The two guys looked at him as he passed and he nodded politely and walked on. A minute later he was back in his room, with faded and brittle paper in his hands.

That night the Duncans ate lamb, in Jonas Duncan's kitchen. Jonas fancied himself a hell of a cook. And in truth he wasn't too bad. His roast usually came in on the right side of OK, and he served it with potatoes and vegetables and a lot of gravy, which helped. And a lot of liquor, which helped even more. All four Duncans ate and drank together, two facing two across the table, and then they cleaned up together, and then Jasper looked at his brother Jacob and said, 'We still have six boys capable of walking and talking. We need to decide how to deploy them tonight.'

Jacob said, 'Reacher won't come back tonight.'

'Can we guarantee that?'

'We can't really guarantee anything at all, except that the sun will rise in the east and set in the west.'

'Therefore it's better to err on the side of caution.'

'OK,' Jacob said. 'Put one to the south and tell the other five to get some rest.'

Jasper got on the phone and issued the instructions. Then he hung up and the room went quiet and Seth Duncan looked at his father and said, 'Drive me home?'

His father said, 'No, stay a little longer, son. We have things to talk about. Our shipment could be here this

240

time tomorrow. Which means we have preparations to make.'

Cassano and Mancini got back from the diner and went straight to Cassano's room. Cassano called the desk and asked if any pairs of guests had just checked in. He was told yes, two pairs had just arrived, separately, one after the other. Cassano asked to be connected with their rooms. He spoke first to Mahmeini's men, and then to Safir's, and he set up an immediate rendezvous in his own room. He figured he could establish some dominance by keeping the others off balance, by denying them any kind of thinking time, and by bringing them to his own turf, not that he would want anyone to think that a shitty flophouse room in Nebraska was his kind of place. But he knew psychology, and he knew no one gets the upper hand without working on the details.

The Iranians arrived first. Mahmeini's men. Only one of them spoke, which Cassano thought was OK, given that he spoke for Rossi, and Mancini didn't. No names were exchanged. Again, OK. It was that kind of business. The Iranians were not physically impressive. They were small and ragged and rumpled, and they seemed quiet and furtive and secretive. And strange. Cassano opened the minibar door and told them to help themselves. Whatever they wanted. But neither man took a thing.

The Lebanese arrived five minutes later. Safir's men. Arabs, for sure, but they were big, and they looked plenty tough. Again, only one of them spoke, and he gave no names. Cassano indicated that they should sit on the bed, but they didn't. They leaned on the wall

241

instead. They were trying for menace, Cassano figured. And nearly succeeding. A little psychology of their own. Cassano let the room go quiet and he looked at them all for a minute, one after the other, four men he had only just met, and who would soon be trying to kill him.

He said, 'It's a fairly simple job. Sixty miles north of here there's a corner of the county with forty farms. There's a guy running around causing trouble. Truth is, it's not really very important, but our supplier is taking it personally. Business is on hold until the guy goes down.'

Mahmeini's man said, 'We know all that. Next?'

'OK,' Cassano said. 'Next is we all move up there and work together and take care of the problem.'

'Starting when?'

'Let's say tomorrow morning, first light.'

'Have you seen the guy?'

'Not yet.'

'Got a name?'

'Reacher.'

'What kind of name is that?'

'It's an American name. What's yours?'

'My name doesn't matter. Got a description?'

'Big guy, blue eyes, white, six-five, two-fifty, brown coat.'

Mahmeini's man said, 'That's worthless. This is America. This is farm country. It's full of settlers and peasants. They all look like that. I mean, we just saw a guy exactly like that.'

Safir's guy said, 'He's right. We saw one too. We're going to need a much better description.'

Cassano said, 'We don't have one. But it will be easier when we get up there. He stands out, apparently. And the local population is prepared to help us. They've been told to phone in with sightings. And there's no cover up there.'

Mahmeini's man said, 'So where is he hiding out?'

'We don't know. There's a motel, but he's not in it. Maybe he's sleeping rough.'

'In this weather? Is that likely?'

'There are sheds and barns. I'm sure we'll find him.'

'And then what?'

'We put him down.'

'Risky.'

'I know. He's tough. So far he's taken out four of the local people.'

Mahmeini's man said, 'I don't care how tough he thinks he is. And I don't care how many local people he's taken out either. Because I'm sure they're all idiots up there. I mean it's risky because this isn't the Wild West any more. Do we have a safe exit strategy?'

Cassano said, 'They tell me he's a kind of hobo. So nobody is going to miss him. There's not going to be an investigation. There aren't even any cops up there.'

'That helps.'

'And it's farm country. Like you said. There must be backhoes all over the place. We'll bury him. Alive, preferably, the way our supplier is talking.'

THIRTY-ONE

The physical search of the area was described four separate ways, in four separate files, the first from the county PD, the second from the State Police, the third from the National Guard's helicopter unit, and the fourth from the FBI. The helicopter report was thin and useless. Margaret Coe had been wearing a green dress, which didn't help in corn country in early summer. And the pilot had stayed above a thousand feet, to stop his downdraught damaging the young plants. Priorities had to be observed in a farm state, even when a kid was missing. Nothing significant had been seen from the air. No freshly turned earth, no flash of pink or chrome from the bike, no flattened stalks in any of the fields. Nothing at all, in fact, except an ocean of corn.

A waste of time and aviation fuel.

Both the county PD and the State Police had covered the forty farms at ground level. First had come the loudhailer appeals in the dark, and the next day every house had been visited and every occupant had been asked to verify that they hadn't seen the kid and that they had searched their outbuildings thoroughly. There was near-universal cooperation. Only one old couple confessed they hadn't checked properly, so the cops searched their place for themselves. Nothing was found. The motel had been visited, every cabin checked, the Dumpster emptied, the lot searched for evidence. Nothing was found.

The Duncan compound showed up in three files. Everyone except the helicopter unit had been there. First the county PD had gone in, then the county PD and the State Police together, then the State Police on its own, and then finally the FBI, which had been a lot of visits and a lot of people for such a small place. The searches had been intense, because the smallness of the place had struck people as somehow sinister in itself. Reacher could sense it between the lines, quite clearly, even a quarter-century later. Rural cops. They had been confused and disconcerted. It was almost like the Duncans hated the land. They had stripped away every inch of it they could. They had kept a single track driveway, plus token shoulders, plus a grudging five or ten yards beyond the foundations of their three houses. That was all. That was the whole extent of the place.

But the smallness had made it easy to search. The reports were meticulous. The piles of heavy lumber for the half-built fence had been taken apart and examined. Gravel had been raked up, and lines of men had walked slow and bent over, staring at the ground, and the dogs had covered literally every square inch ten times each.

Nothing was found.

The search moved indoors. As intense as it had been outside, it was twice as thorough inside. Absolutely painstaking. Reacher had searched a lot of places, a lot of times, and he knew how hard it was. But four times in quick succession not a single corner had been cut, and not a single effort had been spared. Stuff had been taken apart, and voids in walls had been opened up, and floors had been lifted. Reacher knew why. Nothing was stated on paper, and nothing was admitted, but again, he could read it right there between the lines. They were looking for a kid, certainly, but by that point they were also looking for parts of a kid.

Nothing was found.

The FBI contribution was a full-on forensics sweep, 1980s style. It was documented and described at meticulous length on sheets of Bureau paper that had been photocopied and collated and stapled and passed on as a courtesy. Hairs and fibres had been collected, every flat surface had been fingerprinted, all kinds of magic lights and devices and gadgets had been deployed. A corpse-sniffing dog had been flown in from Denver and then sent back again after producing a null result. Technicians with a dozen different specialist expertises had been in and out for twelve solid hours.

Nothing was found.

Reacher closed the file. He could hear it in his head right then, the same way they must have heard it all those years ago: the sound of a case going cold.

Sixty miles north Dorothy Coe was standing at her sink, washing her plate and her knife and her fork and her glass, and scrubbing the oven dish that her chop had cooked in. She dried it all with a thin linen towel and put it all away, the plate and the glass in a cupboard, the silverware in a drawer, the oven dish in another cupboard. She put her napkin in the trash and wiped her table with a rag and pushed her chair in neatly. Then she stepped out to her front parlour. She intended to sit a spell, and then go to bed, and then get up early and drive to the motel. Maybe she could help Mr Vincent fix the mirror behind his bar. Maybe she could even glue the handle back on his NASA mug.

Reacher sat a spell on the floor in his Marriott room, thinking. It was ten o'clock in the evening. His job was done, two hours ahead of his pretended midnight schedule. He got to his feet and packed up all eleven cartons and folded their flaps into place. He stacked them neatly in the centre of the floor, two piles of four and one of three. He dialled nine for a line, from the bedside table, and then he dialled the switchboard number he remembered from the transcript of Dorothy Coe's original panic call, twenty-five years earlier. It was still an active number. It was answered. Reacher asked for Hoag, not really expecting to get him, but there was a click and a second of dead air and then the guy himself came on.

'I'm done,' Reacher told him.

'Find anything?'

'You guys did a fine job. Nothing for you to worry about. So I'm moving out.'

'So soon? You're not staying for the nightlife?'

'I'm a simple soul. I like peace and quiet.'

'OK, leave the stuff right there. We'll swing by and

pick it up. We'll have it back in the basement before the file jockeys even get in tomorrow. They'll never know a thing. Mission accomplished.'

'I owe you,' Reacher said.

'Forget it,' Hoag said. 'Be all you can be, and all that shit.'

'The chance would be a fine thing,' Reacher said. He hung up and grabbed his coat and headed for the door. He was way in the back of the H-shaped layout, and he had to walk all the way forward to the lobby before getting outside and looping back around to where his car was parked. The stairs came down from the second floor just before the lobby, in a space that would have been another room in the wing, if it had been a one-storey structure. Just as Reacher got to them, a guy stepped off the last stair and fell in alongside him, heading the same way, to the lobby, to the door. He was one of the guys Reacher had seen checking in at the desk. Small and rumpled. Unshaven. Iranian, possibly. The guy glanced across. Reacher nodded politely. The guy nodded back. They walked on together. The guy had car keys swinging from his finger. A red tag. Avis. The guy glanced at Reacher again, up and across. Reacher glanced back. He held the door. The guy stepped out. Reacher followed. The guy looked at him again. Some kind of speculation in his eyes. Some kind of intense curiosity.

Reacher stepped left, to loop around the length of the H on the outside. The Iranian guy stayed with him. Which made some kind of possible sense, after Reacher glanced ahead and saw two cars parked back there. Seth

Duncan's Cadillac, and a dark blue Chevrolet. Prime rental material. Avis probably had thousands of them.

A dark blue Chevrolet.

Reacher stopped.

The other guy stopped.

THIRTY-TWO

Nobody knows how long it takes for thoughts to form. People talk about electrical impulses racing through nerves at a substantial fraction of the speed of light, but that's mere transmission. That's mail delivery. The letter is written in the brain, sparked to life by some sudden damp chemical reaction, two compounds arcing across synapses and reacting like lead and acid in an automobile battery, but instead of sending twelve dumb volts to a turn signal the brain floods the body with all kinds of subtle adjustments all at once, because thoughts don't necessarily happen one at a time. They come in starbursts and waterfalls and explosions and they race away on parallel tracks, jostling, competing, fighting for supremacy.

Reacher saw the dark blue Chevrolet and instantly linked it through Vincent's testimony back at the motel to the two men he had seen from Dorothy Coe's barn, while simultaneously critiquing the connection, in that Chevrolets were very common cars and dark blue was a very common colour, while simultaneously recalling the two matched Iranians and the two matched Arabs he had seen, and asking himself whether the rendezvous of two separate pairs of strange men in winter in a Nebraska hotel could be just a coincidence, and if indeed it wasn't, whether it might then reasonably imply the presence of a third pair of men, which might or might not be the two tough guys from Dorothy's farm, however inexplicable those six men's association might be, however mysterious their purpose, while simultaneously watching the man in front of him dropping his car key, and moving his arm, and putting his hand in his coat pocket, while simultaneously realizing that the guys he had seen on Dorothy's farm had not been staying at Vincent's motel, and that there was nowhere else to stay except right there, sixty miles south at the Marriott, which meant that the Chevrolet was likely theirs, at least within the bounds of reasonable possibility, which meant that the Iranian with the moving arm was likely connected with them in some way, which made the guy an enemy, although Reacher had no idea how or why, while simultaneously knowing that *likely* didn't mean shit in terms of civilian jurisprudence, while simultaneously recalling years of hard-won experience that told him men like this Iranian went for their pockets in dark parking lots for one of only four reasons, either to pull out a cell phone to call for help, or to pull out a wallet or a passport or an ID to prove their innocence or their authority, or to pull out a knife, or to pull out a gun. Reacher knew all that, while also knowing that violent reaction ahead of the first two reasons would be inexcusable, but that violent reaction ahead of the latter two reasons would be the only way to save his life.

Starbursts and waterfalls and explosions of thoughts, all jostling and competing and fighting for supremacy.

Better safe than sorry.

Reacher reacted.

He twisted from the waist in a violent spasm and started a low sidearm punch aimed at the centre of the Iranian's chest. Chemical reaction in his brain, instantaneous transmission of the impulse, chemical reaction in every muscle system from his left foot to his right fist, total elapsed time a small fraction of a second, total distance to target less than a yard, total time to target another small fraction of a second, which was good to know right then, because the guy's hand was all the way in his pocket by that point, his own nervous system reacting just as fast as Reacher's, his elbow jerking up and back and trying to free whatever the hell it was he wanted, be it a knife, or a gun, or a phone, or a driver's licence, or a passport, or a government ID, or a perfectly innocent letter from the University of Tehran proving he was a world expert on plant genetics and an honoured guest in Nebraska just days away from increasing local profits a hundredfold and eliminating world hunger at one fell swoop. But right or wrong Reacher's fist was homing in regardless and the guy's eyes were going wide and panicked in the gloom and his arm was jerking harder and the brown skin and the black hair on the back of his moving hand was showing above the hem of his pocket, and then came his knuckles, all five of them bunched and knotted because his fingers were clamping hard around something big and black.

Then Reacher's blow landed.

Two hundred and fifty pounds of moving mass, a huge fist, a huge impact, the zipper of the guy's coat driving backward into his breastbone, his breastbone driving backward into his chest cavity, the natural elasticity of his ribcage letting it yield whole inches, the resulting violent compression driving the air from his lungs, the hydrostatic shock driving blood back into his heart, his head snapping forward like a crash test dummy, his shoulders driving backward, his weight coming up off the ground, his head whipping backward again and hitting a plate glass window behind him with a dull boom like a kettle drum, his arms and legs and torso all going down like a rag doll, his body falling, sprawling, the hard polycarbonate click and clatter of something black skittering away on the ground, Reacher tracking it all the way in the corner of his eye, not a wallet, not a phone, not a knife, but a Glock 17 semi-automatic pistol, all dark and boxy and wicked. It ended up six or eight feet away from the guy, completely out of his reach, safe, not retrievable, partly because of the distance itself and partly because the guy was down and he wasn't moving at all.

In fact he was looking like he might never move again.

Something Reacher had heard about, but never actually seen.

His army medic friends had called it *commotio cordis*, their name for low-energy trauma to the chest wall. Low energy only in the sense that the damage wasn't done by a car wreck or a shotgun blast, but by a line drive in baseball or a football collision or a punch in a fight or a bad fall on to a blunt object. Gruesome research on laboratory animals proved it was all about luck and timing. Electrocardiograms showed waveforms associated with the beating of the heart, one of which was called the T-wave, and the experiments showed that if the blow landed when the T-wave was between fifteen and thirty milliseconds short of its peak, then lethal cardiac dysrhythmia could occur, stopping the heart just like a regular heart attack. And in a high-stress environment like a confrontation in a parking lot, a guy's heart was pounding away much harder than normal and therefore it was bringing those T-wave peaks around much faster than usual, as many as two or possibly three times a second, thereby dramatically increasing the odds that the luck and the timing would be bad, not good.

The Iranian lay completely still.

Not breathing.

No visible pulse.

No signs of life.

The standard first-aid remedies taught by the army medics were artificial respiration and external chest compressions, eighty beats a minute, as long as it took, but Reacher's personal rule of thumb was never to revive a guy who had just pulled a gun on him. He was fairly inflexible on the matter. So he let nature take its course for a minute, and then he helped it along a little with heavy pressure from his finger and thumb on the big arteries in the guy's neck. Four minutes without oxygen to the brain was reckoned to be the practical limit. Reacher gave it five, just to be certain, squatting there, looking around, listening hard. No one reacted.

No one came. The Iranian died, the slack tensions of deep unconsciousness fading away, the absolute soft limpness of recent death replacing them. Reacher stood up and found the car key and picked up the Glock. The key was marked with the Chevrolet stove bolt logo, but it wasn't for the blue car. Reacher stabbed the unlock button and nothing happened. The Glock was close to new and fully loaded, seventeen bright nine-millimetre Parabellums in the magazine and one in the chamber. Reacher put it in his pocket with his screwdrivers.

He walked back to the front lot and tried again with the key. A yellow Chevy Malibu answered him. It flashed all four of its turn signals and unlocked all four of its doors. It was new and plain and clean. An obvious rental. He got in and pushed the seat back and started it up. The tank was close to full. There were rental papers in the door pocket, dated that day and made out to a Las Vegas corporation under a name that communicated nothing. There were bottles of water in the cup holders, one part-used, one unopened. Reacher backed out of the slot and drove around to the back of the H and stopped with the dead guy between the wall and the car. He found the remote button and popped the trunk. He got out and checked the space. It was not a very big opening and not a very big trunk, but then, the Iranian was not a very big guy.

Reacher bent down and went through the Iranian's pockets. He found a phone and a knife and a wallet and a handkerchief and about a dollar in coins. He left the coins and stripped the battery out of the phone and put the battery back in one of the dead guy's pockets and the rest of the phone in another. The knife was a switchblade with a pearl handle. Heavy, solid, and sharp. A decent implement. He put it in his own pocket, with his adjustable wrench. He checked the wallet. It held close to four hundred bucks in cash, plus three credit cards, plus a driver's licence from the state of Nevada made out to a guy named Asghar Arad Sepehr at a Las Vegas address. The photograph was plausible. The credit cards were in the same name. The cash was mostly twenties, crisp and fresh and fragrant, straight from an ATM. Reacher kept the cash and wiped the wallet with the handkerchief and put it back in the dead guy's pocket. Then he hoisted him up, two hands, collar and belt, and turned and made ready to fold him into the yellow Malibu's trunk.

Then he stopped.

He got a better idea.

He carried the guy over to Seth Duncan's Cadillac and laid him gently on the ground. He found the Cadillac key in his pocket and opened the trunk and picked the guy up again and put him inside. An old-fashioned turnpike cruiser. A big trunk. Plenty of space. He closed the lid on the guy. He opened the driver's door and used the handkerchief to wipe everything he had touched that day, the wheel, the gearshift, the mirror, the radio knobs, the door handles inside and out. Then he blipped the remote and locked up again and walked away, back to the Malibu. It was yellow, but apart from that it was fairly anonymous. Domestic brand, local plates, conventional shape. Probably less conspicuous out on the open road than the Cadillac, despite the garish colour. And probably less likely to be reported stolen. Out-of-state guys with guns and knives in their pockets generally kept a lot quieter than outraged local citizens.

He checked left, checked right, checked behind, checked ahead. All quiet. Just cold air and silence and stillness and a night mist falling. He got back in the Malibu and kept the headlights off and turned around and nosed slowly out of the lot. He drove the length of McNally Street and paused. To the left was I-80, sixty miles south, a fast six-lane highway, a straight shot east all the way to Virginia. To the right were the forty farms, and the Duncans, and the Apollo Inn, and Eleanor, and the doctor and his wife, and Dorothy Coe, all of them sixty miles north.

Decision time.

Left or right? South or north?

He flicked the headlights on and turned right and headed back north.

THIRTY-THREE

The Duncans had moved from Jonas Duncan's kitchen to Jasper's, because Jasper still had a mostly full bottle of Knob Creek in his cupboard. All four men were around the table, elbow to elbow, amber half-inches of bourbon in thick chipped glasses set out in front of them. They were sipping slow and talking low. Their latest shipment was somewhere between twelve and twenty-four hours away. Usually a time for celebration. Like the night before Christmas. But this time they were a little subdued.

Jonas asked, 'Where do you suppose it is right now?'

'Parked up for the night,' Jacob said. 'At least I hope so. Close to the border, but waiting for daylight. Prudence is the key now.'

'Five hundred miles,' Jonas said. 'Crossing time plus ten hours, maybe. Plus contingencies.'

Jasper asked, 'How long do you suppose it takes to read a police file?'

'Good question,' Jacob said. 'I've been giving it a little thought, naturally. It must be a very big file. And it must be stored away somewhere. Let's say government workers start at nine in the morning. Let's say they quit at five. Let's say there's some measure of bureaucracy involved in gaining access to the file. So let's say noon tomorrow would be a practical starting point. That would give him five hours tomorrow, and maybe the full eight on the day after. That might be enough.'

'So he won't come back for forty-eight hours at least.'

'I'm only guessing. I can't be sure.'

'Even so. We'll have plenty of margin.'

Seth Duncan said, 'He won't come back at all. Why would he? A hundred people read that file and said there was nothing wrong with it. And this guy isn't a hundred times smarter than anyone else. He can't be.'

Nobody spoke.

Seth said, 'What?'

His father said, 'He doesn't have to be smarter than anyone else, son. Certainly not a hundred times smarter. He just has to be smart in a different way. Lateral, is what they call it.'

'But there's no evidence. We all know that.'

'I agree,' Jacob said. 'But that's the damn point. It's not about what's in the file. It's about what isn't in the file.'

The Malibu was like half a Cadillac. Four cylinders instead of eight, one ton instead of two, and about half as long. But it worked OK. It was cruising nicely. Not that Reacher was paying much attention to it. He was thinking about the dead Iranian, and the odds against hitting a T-wave window. The guy had been small, built like a bird, and Reacher tended to assume that people opposite him on the physical spectrum were also opposite him on the personality spectrum, so that in place of his own placid nature he imagined the guy was all strung out and nervous, which might have meant that back there in the parking lot the guy's heart was going as fast as 180 beats a minute, which meant those T-waves were coming around fast and furious, three times a second, which meant that the odds of hitting one of those crucial fifteen-millisecond windows ahead of a peak were about forty-five in a thousand, or a little better than one in twenty.

Unlucky. For the Iranian, certainly. But no cause for major regret. Most likely Reacher would have had to put him down anyway, one way or another, sooner or later, probably within just a few more heartbeats. It would have been practically inevitable. Once a gun was pulled, there were very few other available options. But still, it had been a first. And a last, probably, at least for a spell. Because Reacher was pretty sure the next guy he met would be a football player. He figured the Duncans knew he had gone out of town, possibly for a day, possibly for ever. He figured they would have gotten hold of the doctor long ago and squeezed that news out of him. And they were realistic but cautious people. They would have stood down five of their boys for the night, and left just one lone sentry to the south. And that one lone sentry would have to be dealt with. But not via *commotio cordis*. Reacher wasn't about to aim a wild punch at a Cornhusker's centre mass. Not in this lifetime. He would break his hand.

He kept the Malibu humming along, eight miles,

nine, and then he started looking ahead for the bar he had seen on the shoulder. The small wooden building. The Cell Block. Maybe just outside the city limit. Unincorporated land. Maybe a question of licensing or regulation. There was mist in the air and the Malibu's headlights made crisp little tunnels. Then they were answered by a glow in the air. A halo, far ahead on the left. Neon, in kelly green, and red, and blue. Beer signs. Plus yellow tungsten from a couple of token spots in the parking lot.

Reacher slowed and pulled in and parked his yellow car next to a pick-up that was mostly brown with corrosion. He got out and locked up and headed for the door. From close up the place looked nothing at all like a prison. It was just a shack. It could once have been a house or a store. Even the sign was written wrong. The words Cell Block were stencilled like a notation on an electrician's blueprint. Like something technological. There was noise inside, the warm low hubbub and hoo-hah of a half-empty late-evening bar in full swing, plus a little music under it, probably from a jukebox, a tune Reacher didn't recognize but was prepared to like.

He went in. The door opened directly in the left front corner of the main public room. The bar ran front to back on the right, and there were tables and chairs on the left. There were maybe twenty people in the room, mostly men. The decoration scheme was really no scheme at all. Wooden tables, wheelback chairs, bar stools, board floor. There was no prison theme. In fact the electronic visuals from outside were continued in-side. The stencilled words Cell Block were repeated on the bar back, flanked by foil-covered cut-outs of radio towers with lightning bolts coming out of them.

Reacher threaded sideways between tables and caught the barman's eye and the barman shuffled left to meet him. The guy was young, and his face was open and friendly. He said, 'You look confused.'

Reacher said, 'I guess I was expecting bars on the windows, maybe booths in the old cells. I thought maybe you would be wearing a suit with arrows all over it.'

The guy didn't answer.

'Like an old prison,' Reacher said. 'Like a cell block.'

The guy stayed blank for a second, and then he smiled.

'Not that kind of cell block,' he said. 'Take out your phone.'

'I don't have a phone.'

'Well, if you did, you'd find it wouldn't work here. No signal. There's a null zone about a mile wide. That's why people come here. For a little undisturbed peace and quiet.'

'They can't just not answer?'

'Human nature doesn't really work that way, does it? People can't ignore a ringing phone. It's about guilty consciences. You know, wives or bosses. All kinds of hassle. Better that their phones don't ring at all.'

'So do you have a pay phone here? Strictly for emergencies?'

The guy pointed. 'Back corridor.'

'Thanks,' Reacher said. 'That's why I came in.'

He threaded down the line of stools, some of them occupied, some of them not, and he found an opening that led to the restrooms and a rear door. There was a pay phone on the wall opposite the ladies' room. It was mounted on a cork rectangle that was dark and stained with age and marked with scribbled numbers in faded ink. He checked his pockets for quarters and found five. He wished he had kept the Iranian's coins. He dialled the same number he had used a quarter of an hour ago, and Dorothy Coe had used a quarter of a century ago. The call was answered and he asked for Hoag, and he was connected inside ten short seconds.

'One more favour,' he said. 'You got phone books for the whole county, right?'

Hoag said, 'Yes.'

'I need a number for a guy called Seth Duncan, about sixty miles north of you.'

'Wait one,' Hoag said. Reacher heard the click and patter of a keyboard. A computer database, not a paper book. Hoag said, 'That's an unlisted number.'

'Unlisted as in you don't have it, or as in you can see it but you won't tell me?'

'Unlisted as in please don't ask me, because you'll be putting me on the spot.'

'OK, I won't ask you. Anything under Eleanor Duncan?'

'No. There are four Duncans, all male names. All un-listed.'

'So give me the doctor instead.'

'What doctor?'

'The local guy up there.'

'What's his name?'

'I don't know,' Reacher said. 'I don't have his name.'

263

'Then I can't help you. This thing is purely alphabetical by last name. It's going to say Smith, Dr Bill, or whatever. Something like that. In very small letters.'

'Got to be a contact number for a doctor. There might be an emergency. Got to be some way of getting hold of the guy.'

'I don't see anything.'

'Wait,' Reacher said. 'I know how. Give me the Apollo Inn.'

'Apollo like the space rocket?'

'Exactly like the space rocket.'

The keyboard pattered and Hoag read out a number, a 308 area code for the western part of the state, and then seven more digits. Reacher repeated them once in his head and said, 'Thanks,' and hung up and redialled.

Ten miles south, Mahmeini's man was dialling too, calling home. He got Mahmeini on his cell, and said, 'We have a problem.'

Mahmeini said, 'Specifically?'

'Asghar has run out on us.'

'Impossible.'

'Well, he has. I sent him down to the car to get me a bottle of water. He didn't come back, so I checked. The car is gone, and he's gone too.'

'Call him.'

'I tried ten times. His phone is off.'

'I don't believe it.'

'What do you want me to do?'

'I want you to find him.'

'I have no idea where to look.'

Mahmeini said, 'He drinks, you know.'

'I know. But there's no bar in town. Just a liquor store. And it will be closed by now. And he wouldn't have driven to the liquor store anyway. He would have walked. It's only about three blocks away.'

'There must be a bar. This is America. Ask the concierge.'

'There is no concierge. This isn't the Bellagio. They don't even put water in the rooms.'

'There must be someone at the desk. Ask him.'

'I can't go anywhere. I don't have a car. And I can't ask the others for help. Not now. That would be an admission of weakness.'

'Find a way,' Mahmeini said. 'Find a bar, and find a way of getting there. That's an order.'

Reacher listened to the ring tone. It was loud and sonorous and resonant in his ear, the product of a big old-fashioned earpiece maybe an inch and a half across, buried deep inside a big old-fashioned plastic handset that probably weighed a pound. He pictured the two phones ringing in the motel, fifty miles north, one at the desk, one behind the bar. Or maybe there were more than two phones. Maybe there was a third extension in a back office, and a fourth in Vincent's private quarters. Maybe the whole place was a regular rats' nest of wiring, just like the inside of a lunar module. But however many phones there were, they all rang for a long period, and then one of them was answered. Vincent came on and said, 'This is the Apollo Inn,' just like Reacher had heard him say it before, very brightly and enthusiastically, like

265

it was a brand new establishment taking its first-ever call on its first-ever night in business.

Reacher said, 'I need Eleanor Duncan's phone number.'

Vincent said, 'Reacher? Where are you?'

'Still out of town. I need Eleanor's number.'

'Are you coming back?'

'What could possibly keep me away?'

'Are you not going to Virginia?'

'Eventually, I hope.'

'I don't have Eleanor's number.'

'Isn't she on the phone tree?'

'No, how could she be? Seth might answer.'

'OK, is the doctor there?'

'Not right now.'

'Slow night, then.'

'Unfortunately.'

'Do you have his number?'

'Hold the line,' Vincent said. There was a thump as he put the handset down, maybe on the bar, and then a pause, just about long enough for him to walk across the lounge, and then the sound of a second handset being raised, maybe at the desk. The two open lines picked up on each other and Reacher heard the room's slow echo hissing and bouncing off the round domed ceiling. Vincent read out a number, the area code and seven more digits, and Reacher repeated them once in his head and said, 'Thanks,' and hung up and redialled.

The guy at the Marriott's desk told Mahmeini's man that yes, there was a bar, not exactly in town but ten miles

266

north, just outside the city limit, on the left shoulder of the two-lane, called the Cell Block, a pleasant place, reasonably priced, and that yes, it was usually open late, and that yes, there was a taxi service in town, and that yes, he would be happy to call a cab immediately.

And so less than five minutes later Mahmeini's man was sliding across stained vinyl into the rear seat of an ancient Chevy Caprice, and the driver was pulling out of the lot, and heading down McNally Street, and making the right at the end.

The doctor answered a lot faster than Vincent had. Reacher said, 'I need Eleanor Duncan's phone number.'

The doctor said, 'Reacher? Where are you?'

'Still out of town.'

'Are you coming back?'

'What, are you missing me?'

'I didn't tell the Duncans about the Cadillac.'

'Good man. Has Seth gone home yet?'

'He was still with his father when I left.'

'Will he stay?'

'People say he often does.'

'You OK?'

'Not too bad. I was in the truck. The Cornhuskers got me.'

'And?'

'Nothing much. Just words, really.'

Reacher pictured the guy, maybe standing in his hallway or his kitchen, quaking, shaking, watching the windows, checking the doors. He asked, 'Are you sober?'

The doctor said, 'A little.'

'A little?'

'That's about as good as it gets these days, I'm afraid.'

'I need Eleanor Duncan's number.'

'She's not listed.'

'I know that.'

'She's not on the phone tree.'

'But she's your patient.'

'I can't.'

'How much more trouble could you be in?'

'It's not just that. There are confidentiality issues too. I'm a doctor. Like you said, I took an oath.'

'We're making an omelette here,' Reacher said. 'We're going to have to break some eggs.'

'They'll know it came from me.'

'If it comes to it I'll tell them different.'

The doctor went quiet, and then he sighed, and then he recited a number.

'Thanks,' Reacher said. 'Take care. Best to your wife.' He hung up and redialled and listened to yet more ring tone, the same languid electronic purr, but this time from a different place, from somewhere inside the restored farmhouse, among the pastel colours and the fancy rugs and the oil paintings. He figured that if Seth was home, then Seth would answer. It seemed to be that kind of a relationship. But he bet himself a buck Seth wasn't home. The Duncans were in two kinds of trouble, and Reacher's experience told him they would huddle together until it passed. So Eleanor was probably home alone, and would pick up. Or not. Maybe she would just

268

ignore the bell, whatever the barman thirty feet away thought about human nature.

She picked up.

'Hello?' she said.

Reacher asked, 'Is Seth there?'

'Reacher? Where are you?'

'Doesn't matter where I am. Where's Seth?'

'He's at his father's. I don't expect him home to-night.'

'That's good. You still up and dressed?'

'Why?'

'I want you to do something for me.'

THIRTY-FOUR

The old Caprice's rear bench was contoured like two separate bucket seats, not by design but by age and relentless wear and tear. Mahmeini's man settled into the right-hand pit, behind the front passenger seat, and cocked his head to the left so he could see out the windshield. He saw the blank back of a billboard in the headlight beams, and then he saw nothing. The road ahead was straight and empty. No oncoming lights, which was a disappointment. One drink on Asghar's part might be overlooked. Or even two. Or three, followed by a prompt return. But a night of it would be considered desertion.

The wheezing old motor had the needle trembling over the sixty mark. A mile a minute. Nine more miles to go. Nine minutes.

Reacher said, 'Exactly one hour and ten minutes from now, I want you to take a drive. In your little red sports car.'

Eleanor Duncan said, 'A drive? Where?'

'South on the two-lane,' Reacher said. 'Just drive. Eleven miles. As fast as you want. Then turn around and go home again.'

'Eleven miles?'

'Or twelve. Or more. But not less than ten.'

'Why?'

'Doesn't matter why. Will you do it?'

'Are you going to do something to the house? You want me out of the way?'

'I won't come near the house. I promise. No one will ever know. Will you do it?'

'I can't. Seth took my car key. I'm grounded.'

'Is there a spare?'

'He took that too.'

Reacher said, 'He's not carrying them around in his pocket. Not if he keeps his own key in a bowl in the kitchen.'

Eleanor said nothing.

Reacher asked, 'Do you know where they are?'

'Yes. They're on his desk.'

'On or in?'

'On. Just sitting there. Like a test for me. He says obedience without temptation is meaningless.'

'Why the hell are you still there?'

'Where else could I go?'

'Just take the damn keys, will you? Stand up for yourself.'

'Will this hurt Seth?'

'I don't know how you want me to answer that question.'

'I want you to answer it honestly.'

'It might hurt him indirectly. And eventually. Possibly.'

There was a long pause. Then Eleanor said, 'OK, I'll do it. I'll drive south eleven miles on the two-lane and come back again. An hour and ten minutes from now.'

'No,' Reacher said. 'An hour and six minutes from now. We've just been talking for four minutes.'

He hung up and stepped back to the main public room. The barman was working like a good barman should, using fast efficient movements, thinking ahead, watching the room. He caught Reacher's eye and Reacher detoured towards him and the guy said, 'I should get you to sign a napkin or something. Like a memento. You're the only guy who ever came in here to use a phone, not avoid one. You want a drink?'

Reacher scanned what the guy had to offer. Liquor of all kinds, beer on tap, beer in bottles, sodas. No sign of coffee. He said, 'No thanks, I'm good. I should hit the road.' He moved on, shuffling sideways between the tables, and he pushed out the door and walked back to his car. He got in, started up, backed out and drove away north.

Mahmeini's man saw a glow in the air, far ahead on the left. Neon, green and red and blue. The driver kept his foot down for a minute more, and then he lifted off and coasted. The engine coughed and the exhaust popped and sputtered and the taxi slowed. Way far up the road in the distance were a pair of red tail lights. Very faint and far away. Almost not there at all. The taxi braked. Mahmeini's man saw the bar. Just a simple wooden building. There were two weak spotlights under the eaves at the front. They threw two pools of token light into the lot. There were plenty of parked vehicles. But no yellow rental.

The taxi pulled in and stopped. The driver looked back over his shoulder. Mahmeini's man said, 'Wait for me.'

The driver said, 'How long?'

'A minute.' Mahmeini's man got out and stood still. The tail lights in the north had disappeared. Mahmeini's man watched the darkness where they had been, just for a second. Then he walked to the wooden building's door. He entered. He saw a large room, with chairs and tables on the left and a bar on the right. There were about twenty customers in the room, mostly men, none of them Asghar Arad Sepehr. There was a barman behind the bar, serving a customer, lining up the next, glancing over at the new arrival. Mahmeini's man threaded between the tables towards him. He felt that everyone was watching him. A small man, foreign, unshaven, rumpled, and not very clean. The barman's customer peeled away, holding two foaming glasses of beer. The barman moved on, to the next customer, serving him, but glancing beyond him for the next in line, as if he was planning two moves ahead.

Mahmeini's man said, 'I'm looking for someone.'

The barman said, 'I guess we all are, sir. That's the very essence of human nature, isn't it? It's an eternal quest.'

'No, I'm looking for someone I know. A friend of mine.'

'A lady or a gentleman?'

'He looks like me.'

'Then I haven't seen him. I'm sorry.'

'He has a yellow car.'

'Cars are outside. I'm inside.'

Mahmeini's man turned and scanned the room, and thought about the red tail lights in the north, and turned back and asked, 'Are you sure?'

The barman said, 'I don't want to be rude, sir, but really, if two of you had been in here tonight, someone would have called Homeland Security already. Don't you think?'

Mahmeini's man said nothing.

'Just saying,' the barman said. 'This is Nebraska. There are military installations here.'

Mahmeini's man asked, 'Then was someone else just here?'

'This is a bar, my friend. People are in and out all night long. That's kind of the point of the place.'

The barman turned back to his current customer. Interaction over. Mahmeini's man turned and scanned the room, one more time. Then he gave it up and moved away, between the tables, back to the door. He stepped into the lot and took out his phone. No signal. He stood still for a second and glanced north at where the red lights had gone, and then he climbed back into the taxi. He closed the door against a yowling hinge and said, 'Thank you for waiting.'

The driver looked back over his shoulder and asked, 'Where to now?'

Mahmeini's man said, 'Let me think about that for a minute.'

Reacher kept the Malibu at a steady sixty. A mile a minute. Hypnotic. Power line poles flashed past, the tyres sang, the motor hummed. Reacher took the fresh bottle of water from the cup holder and opened it and drank from it one-handed. He switched his headlights to bright. Nothing to see ahead of him. A straight road, then mist, then darkness. He checked the mirror. Nothing to see behind him. He checked the dials and the gauges. All good.

Eleanor Duncan checked her watch. It was a small Rolex, a present from Seth, but probably real. She had counted ahead an hour and six minutes from when she had hung up the phone, and she had forty-five minutes still to go. She stepped out of the living room into the hallway, and stepped out of the hallway into her husband's den. It was a small square space. She had no idea of its original purpose. Maybe a gun room. Now it was set up as a home office, but with an emphasis on gentlemanly style, not clerical function. There was a club chair made of leather. The desk was yew. It had a light with a green glass shade. There were bookshelves. There was a rug. The air in the room smelled like Seth.

There was a shallow glass bowl on the desk. From Murano, near Venice, in Italy. It was green. A souvenir.

It had paperclips in it. And her car keys, just sitting there, two small serrated lances with big black heads. For her Mazda Miata. A tiny red two-seat convertible. A fun car. Carefree. Like the old British MGs and Lotuses used to be, but reliable.

She took one of the keys.

She stepped back to the hallway. Eleven miles. She thought she knew what Reacher had in mind. So she opened the coat closet and took out a silk headscarf. Pure white. She folded it into a triangle and tied it over her hair. She checked the mirror. Just like an old-fashioned movie star. Or an old-fashioned movie star after a knockout round with an old-fashioned heavyweight champion.

She left by the back door and walked through the cold to the garage, Seth's empty bay to the right, hers in the middle, the doors all open. She got in her car and unlatched the clips above the windshield and dropped the top. She started up and backed out and turned and waited on the driveway, the motor running, the heater warming, her heart beating hard. She checked her watch. Twenty-nine minutes to go.

Reacher cruised onward, sixty miles an hour, three more minutes, and then he slowed down and put his lights back on bright. He watched the right shoulder. The old abandoned roadhouse loomed up at him, right on cue, pinned and stark in his headlight beams. The bad roof, the beer signs on the walls behind the mud, the bruised earth all around where cars had once parked. He pulled off the road and into the lot. Loose stones popped and crunched and slithered under his tyres. He drove a full circuit.

The building was long and low and plain, like a barn cut off at the knees. Rectangular, except for two separate square bump-outs added at the back, one at each end of the structure, the first for restrooms, probably, and the second for a kitchen. Efficient, in terms of plumbing lines. Between the bump-outs was a shallow U-shaped space, like a bay, empty apart from a little windblown trash, enclosed on three sides, open only to the dark empty fields to the east. It was maybe thirty feet long and twelve feet deep.

Perfect, for later.

Reacher came back around to the south gable wall and parked thirty feet from it, out of sight from the north, facing the road at a slight diagonal angle, like a cop on speed trap duty. He killed the lights and kept the motor running. He got out into the cold and looped around the hood and walked to the corner of the building. He leaned on the old boards. They felt thin and veined, frozen by a hundred winters, baked by a hundred summers. They smelled of dust and age. He watched the darkness in the north, where he knew the road must be.

He waited.

THIRTY-FIVE

Reacher waited twenty long minutes, and then he saw light in the north. Very faint, maybe five or six miles away, really just a high hemispherical glow in the mist, trembling a little, bouncing, weakening and strengthening and weakening again. A moving bubble of light. Very white. Almost blue. A car, coming south towards him, pretty fast.

Eleanor Duncan, presumably, right on time.

Reacher waited.

Two minutes later she was two miles closer, and the high hemispherical glow was bigger, and stronger, still bouncing, still trembling, but now it had a strange asynchronous pulse inside it, the bouncing now going two ways at once, the strengthening and the weakening now random and out of phase.

There were two cars on the road, not one.

Reacher smiled. The sentry. The football player, posted to the south. A college graduate. Not a dumb guy. He knew his five buddies had been sent home to bed because absolutely nothing was going to happen. He knew he had been posted as a precaution only, just for the sake of it. He knew he was facing a long night of boredom, staring into the dark, no chance of glory. So what's a guy going to do, when Eleanor Duncan suddenly blasts past him from behind, in her little red sports car? He's going to see major brownie points on the table, that's what. He's going to give up on the blank hours ahead, and he's going to pull out and follow her, and he's going to dream of a promotion to the inner circle, and he's going to imagine a scene and he's going to rehearse a speech, because he's going to pull Seth Duncan aside tomorrow, first thing in the morning, very discreetly, like an old friend or a trusted aide, and he's going to whisper, *Yes, sir, I followed her all the way and I can show you exactly where she went.* Then he's going to add, *No, sir, I told no one else, but I thought you should know.* Then he's going to hop and shuffle in a modest and self-deprecating way and he's going to say, *Well yes, sir, I thought it was much more important than sentry duty, and I'm glad you agree I did the right thing.*

Reacher smiled again.

Human nature.

Reacher waited.

Two more minutes, and the travelling bubble of light was another two miles closer, now much flatter and more elongated. Two cars, with some little distance between them. Predator and prey, some hundreds of yards apart. There was no red glow in the bubble. The football player's headlights were falling short of the Mazda's paint. The guy was maybe a quarter of a mile back, following the Mazda's tail lights, no doubt thinking he was doing a hell of a job of staying inconspicuous.

Maybe not such a smart guy. The Mazda had a mirror, and halogen headlights on a Nebraska winter night were probably visible from outer space.

Reacher moved.

He pushed off the corner of the building and looped around the Malibu's hood and got in the driver's seat. He locked the selector in first gear and put his left foot hard on the brake and his right foot on the gas. He goosed the pedal until the transmission was straining against the brake and the whole car was wound up tight and ready to launch. He kept one hand on the wheel and the other on the headlight switch.

He waited.

Sixty seconds.

Ninety seconds.

Then the Mazda flashed past, right to left, instantaneously, a tiny dark shape chasing a huge pool of bright light, its top down, a woman in a headscarf at the wheel, all chased in turn by tyre roar and engine noise and the red flare of tail lights. Then it was gone. Reacher counted *one* and flicked his headlights on and took his foot off the brake and stamped on the gas and shot forward and braked hard and stopped again sideways across the crown of the road. He wrenched open the door and spilled out and danced back towards the Malibu's trunk, towards the shoulder he had just left. Two hundred yards to his right a big SUV was starting a panic stop. Its headlights flared yellow against the Malibu's paint and then they nosedived into the blacktop as the truck's front suspension crushed under the force of violent braking. Huge tyres howled and the truck lost its line and slewed to its right and went into a four-wheel slide and its nearside wheels tucked under and its high centre of gravity tipped over and its offside wheels came up in the air. Then they crashed back to earth and the rear end fishtailed violently a full ninety degrees and the truck snapped around and came to rest parallel with the Malibu, less than ten feet away, stalled out and silent, the scream of stressed rubber dying away, thin drifts of moving blue smoke following it and catching it and stopping and rising all around it and billowing away into the cold night air.

Reacher pulled the Iranian's Glock from his pocket and stormed the driver's door and wrenched it open and danced back and pointed the gun. In general he was not a big fan of dramatic arrests, but he knew from long experience what worked and what didn't with shocked and unpredictable subjects, so he screamed GET OUT OF THE CAR GET OUT OF THE CAR GET OUT OF THE CAR as loud as he could, which was plenty loud, and the guy behind the wheel more or less tumbled out, and then Reacher was on him, forcing him down, flipping him, jamming him face down into the blacktop, his knee in the small of the guy's back, the Glock's muzzle hard in the back of the guy's neck, all the time screaming STAY DOWN STAY DOWN STAY DOWN, all the while watching the sky over his shoulder for more lights.

There were no more lights. No one else was coming. No back-up. The guy hadn't called it in. He was planning a solo enterprise. All the glory for himself. As expected.

Reacher smiled.

Human nature.

The scene went quiet. Nothing to hear, except the Malibu's patient idle. Nothing to see, except four high beams stabbing the far shoulder. The air was full of the smell of burned rubber and hot brakes, and gas, and oil. The Cornhusker lay completely still. Hard not to, with 250 pounds on his back, and a gun to his head, and television images of SWAT arrests in his mind. Maybe real images. Country boys get arrested from time to time, the same as anyone else. And things had happened fast, all dark and noise and blur and panic, enough that maybe the guy hadn't really seen Reacher's face yet, or recognized his description from the Duncans' warnings. Maybe the guy hadn't put two and two together. Maybe he was waiting it out like a civilian, waiting to explain to a cop that he was innocent, like people do. Which gave Reacher a minor problem. He was about to transition away from what the guy might have taken to be a legitimate law enforcement takedown, straight to what the guy was going to know for sure was a wholly illegitimate kidnap attempt. And the guy was big. Six-six or a little more, two-ninety or a little more. He had on a large red football jacket and baggy jeans. His feet were the size of boats.

Reacher said, 'Tell me your name.'

The guy's chin and his lips and his nose were all jammed hard down on the blacktop. He said, 'John,' like a gasp, like a grunt, just a soft expulsion of breath, quiet and indistinct.

'Not Brett?' Reacher asked.

'No.'

'That's good.' Reacher shifted his weight, turned the guy's head, jammed the Glock in his ear, saw the whites of his eyes. 'Do you know who I am?'

The guy on the ground said, 'I do now.'

'You know the two things you really need to understand?'

'What are they?'

'Whoever you think you are, I'm tougher than you, and I'm more ruthless than you. You have absolutely no idea. I'm worse than your worst nightmare. Do you believe that?'

'Yes.'

'Really believe it? Like you believe in mom and apple pie?'

'Yes.'

'You know what I did to your buddies?'

'Yes.'

'What did I do?'

'You finished them.'

'Correct. But here's the thing, John. I'm prepared to work with you, to save your life. We can do this, if we try. But if you step half an inch out of line, I'll kill you and walk away and I'll never think about you again and I'll sleep like a baby the whole rest of my life. We clear on that?'

'Yes.'

'So you want to try?'

'Yes.'

'Are you thinking about some stupid move? Are you quarterbacking it right now? You planning to wait until my attention wanders?'

'No.'

'Good answer, John. Because my attention never wanders. You ever seen someone get shot?'

'No.'

'It's not like the movies, John. Big chunks of disgusting stuff come flying out. Even a flesh wound, you never really recover. Not a hundred per cent. You get infections. You're weak and hurting, for ever.'

'OK.'

'So stand up now.' Reacher got up out of his crouch and moved away, pointing the gun, aiming it two-handed at arm's length for theatrical effect, tracking the guy's head, a big pale target. First the guy went foetal for a second, and then he gathered himself and got his hands under him and jacked himself to his knees. Reacher said, 'See the yellow car? You're going to go stand next to the driver's door.'

The guy said, 'OK,' and got to his feet, a little unsteady at first, then firmer, taller, squarer. Reacher said, 'Feeling good now, John? Feeling brave? Getting ready? Going to rush over and get me?'

The guy said, 'No.'

'Good answer, John. I'll put a double tap in you before you move the first muscle. Believe me, I've done it before. I used to get paid to do it. I'm very good at it. So move over to the yellow car and stand next to the driver's door.' Reacher tracked him all the way around the Malibu's hood. The driver's door was still open. Reacher had left it that way, for the sake of a speedy exit. The guy stood in its angle. Reacher aimed the gun across the roof of the car and opened the passenger door. The two men stood there, one on each side, both doors open like little wings.

Reacher said, 'Now get in.'

The guy ducked and bent and slid into the seat. Reacher backed off a step and aimed the gun down inside the car, a low trajectory, straight at the guy's hips and thighs. He said, 'Don't touch the wheel. Don't touch the pedals. Don't put your seat belt on.'

The guy sat still, with his hands in his lap.

Reacher said, 'Now close your door.'

The guy closed his door.

Reacher asked, 'Feeling heroic yet, John?'

The guy said, 'No.'

'Good answer, my friend. We can do this. Just remember, the Chevrolet Malibu is an OK mid-range product, especially for Detroit, but it doesn't accelerate for shit. Not like a bullet, anyway. This gun of mine is full of nine-millimetre Parabellums. They come out of the barrel doing nine hundred miles an hour. Think a four-cylinder GM motor can outrun that?'

'No.'

'Good, John,' Reacher said. 'I'm glad to see all that education didn't go to waste.'

Then he looked up across the roof of the car, and he saw light in the mist to the south. A high hemispherical glow, trembling a little, bouncing, weakening and strengthening and weakening again. Very white. Almost blue.

A car, coming north towards him, pretty fast.

THIRTY-SIX

The oncoming car was about two miles away. Doing about sixty, Reacher figured. Sixty was about all the road was good for. Two minutes. He said, 'Sit tight, John. Stop thinking. This is your time of maximum danger. I'm going to play it very safe. I'll shoot first and ask questions later. Don't think I won't.'

The guy sat still behind the Malibu's wheel. Reacher watched across the roof of the car. The bubble of light in the south was still moving, still bouncing and trembling and strengthening and weakening, but coherently this time, naturally, in phase. Just one car. Now about a mile away. One minute.

Reacher waited. The glow resolved itself to a fierce source low down above the blacktop, then twin fierce sources spaced feet apart, both of them oval in shape, both of them low to the ground, both of them blue-white and intense. They kept on coming, flickering and floating and jittering ahead of a firm front suspension and fast go-kart steering, at first small because of the distance, and then small because they *were* small, because they were mounted low down on a small low car, because the car was a Mazda Miata, tiny, red in colour, slowing now, coming to a stop, its headlights unbearably bright against the Malibu's yellow paint.

Then Eleanor Duncan killed her lights and manoeuvred around the Malibu's trunk, half on the road and half on the shoulder, and came to a stop with her elbow on the door and her head turned towards Reacher. She asked, 'Did I do it right?'

Reacher said, 'You did it perfectly. The headscarf was a great touch.'

'I decided against sunglasses. Too much of a risk at night.'

'Probably.'

'But you took a risk. That's for sure. You could have gotten creamed here.'

'He's an athlete. And young. Good eyesight, good hand-eye coordination, lots of fast-twitch muscles. I figured I'd have time to jump clear.'

'Even so. He could have wrecked both vehicles. Then what would you have done?'

'Plan B was shoot him and ride back with you.'

She was quiet for a second. Then she said, 'Need anything else?'

'No, thanks. Go on home now.'

'This guy will tell Seth, you know. About what I did.'

'He won't,' Reacher said. 'He and I are going to work something out.'

Eleanor Duncan said nothing more. She just put her lights back on and her car in gear and drove away, fast and crisp, the sound of her exhaust ripping the night air behind her. Reacher glanced back twice, once when she was half a mile away and again when she was gone altogether. Then he slid into the Malibu's passenger seat, alongside the guy called John, and closed his door. He held the Glock right-handed across his body. He said, 'Now you're going to park this car around the back of this old roadhouse. If the speedo gets above five miles an hour, I'm going to shoot you in the side. Without immediate medical attention you'll live about twenty minutes. Then you'll die, in hideous agony. Believe me, I've seen it happen. Truth is, John, I've made it happen, more than once. We clear?'

'Yes.'

'Say it, John. Say we're clear.'

'We're clear.'

'How clear are we?'

'I don't know what you want me to say.'

'I want you to say we're crystal clear.'

'You got it. Crystal.'

'OK, so let's do it.'

The guy fumbled the lever into gear and turned the wheel and drove a wide circle, painfully slow, bumping up on the far shoulder, coming around to the near shoulder, bumping down on to the beaten earth of the old lot, passing the south gable wall, turning sharply behind the building. Reacher said, 'Pull ahead and then back in, between the two bump-outs, like parallel parking. Do they ask for that in the Nebraska test?'

The guy said, 'I passed in Kentucky. In high school.'

'Does that mean you need me to explain it to you?'

'I know how to do it.'

'OK, show me.'

The guy pulled ahead of the second square bump-out and lined up and backed into the shallow U-shaped bay. Reacher said, 'All the way, now. I want the back bumper hard against the wood and I want your side of the car hard against the building. I want you to trash your door mirror, John. Totally trash it. Can you do that for me?'

The guy paused and then turned the wheel harder. He did pretty well. He got the rear bumper hard against the bump-out and he trashed his door mirror good, but he left about an inch between his flank of the car and the back of the building. He checked behind him, checked left, and then looked at Reacher like he was expecting praise.

'Close enough,' Reacher said. 'Now shut it down.'

The guy killed the lights and turned off the motor.

Reacher said, 'Leave the key.'

The guy said, 'I can't get out. I can't open my door.'

Reacher said, 'Crawl out after me.' He opened his own door and slid out and backed off and stood tall and aimed the gun two-handed. The guy came out after him, hands and knees, huge and awkward, feet first, butt high up in the air. He got straight and turned around and said, 'Want me to close the door?'

Reacher said, 'You're thinking again, aren't you, John? You're thinking it's dark out here, now the lights are off, and maybe I can't see too well. You're figuring maybe this would be a good time. But it isn't. I can see just fine. An owl has got nothing on me in the eyesight department, John. An owl with night-vision goggles sees worse. Believe it, kid. Just hang in there. You can get through this.'

'I'm not thinking anything,' the guy said.

'So close the door.'

The guy closed the door.

'Now step away from the car.'

The guy stepped away. The car was crammed tight in the back southwest quarter of the shallow bay, occupying a fifteen-by-six footprint within the total thirty-by-twelve space. It would be invisible from the road, either north or south, and no one was going to be in the fields to the east until spring ploughing. Safe enough.

Reacher said, 'Now move to your right.'

'Where?'

'So when I aim the gun at you I'm aiming parallel with the road.'

The guy moved, two steps, three, and then he stopped and turned and faced front, with his back to the forty empty miles between him and the Cell Block bar.

Reacher asked him, 'How close is the nearest house?'

He said, 'Miles away.'

'Close enough to hear a gunshot in the night?'

'Maybe.'

'What would they think if they did?'

'Varmint. This is farm country.'

Reacher said, 'I'd be happier if you heard the gun go off, John. At least once. I'd be happier if you knew what it was like to have a bullet coming your way. It might help you with all that thinking. It might help you reach sensible conclusions.'

'I won't try anything.'

'Do I have your word on that?'

290

'Absolutely.'

'So we're bonded now, John. I'm trusting you. Am I wise to do that?'

'Absolutely.'

'OK, turn around and walk back to your truck.' Reacher kept ten feet behind the guy all the way, around the back corner of the building, along the face of the south gable wall, across the old lot, back to the two-lane. Reacher said, 'Now get in the truck the same way you got out of the car.'

The guy closed the driver's door and tracked around the hood and opened the passenger door. Reacher watched him all the way. The guy climbed into the passenger seat and lifted his feet one at a time into the driver's foot well, and then he jacked himself up and over the console between the seats, on the heels of his hands, squirming, scraping, ducking his head. Reacher watched him all the way. When he was settled Reacher climbed into the passenger seat and closed the door. He swapped the gun into his left hand for a second and put his seat belt on. Then he swapped the gun back to his right and said, 'I've got my seat belt on, John, but you're not going to put yours on, OK? Just in case you're getting ideas. Just in case you're thinking about driving into a telephone pole. See the point? You do that, and I'll be fine, but you'll be hurt bad, and then I'll shoot you anyway. We clear on that?'

The guy said, 'Yes.'

'Say it, John.'

'I'm clear on that.'

'How clear?'

'Crystal.'

'And we're bonded, right? I have your word, don't I?'

'Yes.'

'Promise?'

'Yes.'

'Where do you live?'

'At the Duncan Transportation depot.'

'Where is that?'

'From here? About thirty miles, give or take, north and then west.'

'OK, John,' Reacher said. 'Take me there.'

THIRTY-SEVEN

Mahmeini's man was in his room at the Courtyard Marriott. He was on the phone with Mahmeini himself. The conversation had not started well. Mahmeini had been reluctant to accept that Sepehr had lit out. It was inconceivable to him. It was like being told the guy had grown a third arm. Just not humanly possible.

Mahmeini's man said, 'He definitely wasn't in the bar.'

'By the time you got there.'

'He was never there. It was a most unpleasant place. I didn't like it at all. They looked at me like I was dirt. Like I was a terrorist. I doubt if they would even have served me. Asghar wouldn't have lasted five minutes without getting in a fight. And there was no sign of trouble. There was no blood on the floor. Which there would have been. Asghar is armed, and he's fast, and he doesn't suffer fools gladly.'

Mahmeini said, 'Then he went somewhere else.'

'I checked all over town. Which didn't take long. The sidewalks roll up when it gets dark. There's nowhere to hide. He isn't here.'

'Women?'

'Are you kidding me? Here?'

'Did you try his phone again?'

'Over and over.'

There was a long, long pause. Mahmeini, in his Las Vegas office, processing data, changing gears, improvising. He said, 'OK, let's move on. This business is important. It has to be taken care of tomorrow. So you'll have to manage on your own. You can do that. You're good enough.'

'But I don't have a car.'

'Get a ride from Safir's boys.'

'I thought of that. But the dynamic would be weird. I wouldn't be in charge. I would be a passenger, literally. And how would I explain why I let Asghar take off somewhere and leave me high and dry? We can't afford to look like idiots here. Or weak. Not in front of these people.'

'So get another car. Tell the others you told Asghar to go on ahead, or somewhere else entirely, for some other purpose.'

'Get another car? From where?'

Mahmeini said, 'Rent one.'

'Boss, this isn't Vegas. They don't even have room service here. The nearest Hertz is back at the airport. I'm sure it's closed until the morning. And I can't get there anyway.'

Another long, long pause. Mahmeini, recalibrating, re-evaluating, reassessing, planning on the fly. He asked, 'Did the others see the first car you were in?'

His guy said, 'No. I'm sure they didn't. We all arrived separately, at different times.'

Mahmeini said, 'OK. You're right about the dynamic. We need to be visibly in charge. And we need to keep the others off balance. So here's what you're going to do. Find a suitable car, within the hour. Steal one, if you have to. Then call the others, in their rooms. I don't care what time it is. Midnight, one o'clock, whatever. Tell them we've decided to start the party early. Tell them you're leaving for the north immediately. Give them five minutes, or you're going without them. They'll be in disarray, packing up and running down to the parking lot. You'll be waiting in your new car. But they won't know it's new. And they won't even notice that Asghar isn't with you. Not in the dark. Not in all the confusion. Then drive fast. Like a bat out of hell. Be the first one up there. When the others get there, tell them you turned Asghar loose, on foot, behind the lines. That will worry them. It will keep them even more off balance. They'll be looking over their shoulders all the time. That's it. That's what you're going to do. That's pretty much a silk purse out of a sow's ear, wouldn't you say?'

Mahmeini's man put his coat on and carried his bag down to the lobby. The desk guy had gone off duty. Presumably there was an all-purpose night porter holed up in a back room somewhere, but Mahmeini's man didn't see any sign of him. He just walked out, bag in hand, looking for a car to steal. Which in many ways was a backward step and an affront to his dignity. Guys in his position had left car theft behind a long time ago.

But, needs must. And he still remembered how. There would be no technical difficulty. He would perform with his usual precision. The difficulty would come from being forced to work with such a meagre pool of potential targets.

He had two requirements. First, he needed a vehicle with a degree of prestige. Not necessarily much, but at least some. He couldn't be seen in a rusted and listing pick-up truck, for instance. That would not be remotely appropriate or plausible for a Mahmeini operative, especially one tasked to impress the Duncans. Image was by no means everything, but it greased the skids. Perception was reality, at least half the time.

Second, he needed a car that wasn't brand new. Late-model cars had too much security built in. Computers, microchips in the keys, matching microchips in the keyholes. Nothing was unbeatable, of course, but a quick-and-dirty street job had its practical limits. Newer cars were best tackled with tow trucks or flatbeds, and then patient hours hidden away with ethernet cables and laptop computers. Lone men in the dark needed something easier.

So, a clean sedan from a mainstream manufacturer, not new, but not too old either. Easy to find in Vegas. Five minutes, tops. But not in rural Nebraska. Not in farm country. He had just walked all over town looking for Asghar, and 90 per cent of what he had seen had been utilitarian, either pick-up trucks or ancient four-wheel-drives, and 99 per cent of those had been worn out, all battered and corroded and failing. Apparently Nebraskans didn't have much money, and even if they did they seemed to favour an ostentatiously blue-collar lifestyle.

He stood in the cold and reviewed his options. He mapped out the blocks he had quartered before, and he tried to identify the kind of density he needed, and he came up with nothing. He had seen a sign to a hospital, and hospital parking lots were often good, because doctors bought new cars and sold their lightly used cast-offs to nurses and medical students, but for all he knew the hospital was miles away, certainly too far to walk without a guarantee of success.

So he started in the Marriott lot.

And finished there.

He walked all around the H-shaped hotel and saw three pick-up trucks, two with fitted camper beds, and an old Chrysler sedan with Arizona plates and a dented fender and sun-rotted paint, and a blue Chevrolet Impala, and a red Ford Taurus, and a black Cadillac. The pick-ups and the old Chrysler were out of the question for obvious reasons. The Impala and the Taurus were out of the question because they were too new, and they were obviously rentals, because they had barcode stickers in the rear side windows, which meant that almost certainly they belonged to Safir's guys and Rossi's guys, and he couldn't call them down to the lot and have them find him sitting in one of their own cars.

Which left the Cadillac. Right age, right style. Local plates, neat, discreet, well looked after, clean and polished. Black glass. Practically perfect. A no-brainer. He put his bag on the ground right next to it and dropped flat and shuffled on his back until his head was underneath the engine. He had a tiny LED Maglite on his key chain, and he fumbled it out and lit it up and went hunting. Cars of that generation had a module bolted to the frame designed to detect a frontal impact. A simple accelerometer, with a two-stage function. Worst case, it would trigger the airbags. Short of that, it would unlock the doors, so that first responders could drag dazed drivers to safety. A gift to car thieves everywhere, therefore not much publicized, and replaced almost immediately with more sophisticated systems.

He found the module. It was a simple tin can, square and small, cheap and basic, all caked in dry dirt, with wires coming out of it. He took out his knife and used the butt end of the handle and banged hard on the module. Dirt flaked off, but nothing else happened. He thought the dirt was maybe insulating the force of the blow, so he popped the blade on his knife and scraped the front of the module clean. Then he closed the blade and tried again. Nothing happened. He tried a third time, hard enough to worry about the noise he was making, *bang*, and the message got through. The Cadillac's dim electronic brain thought it had just suffered a minor frontal impact, not serious enough for the airbags, but serious enough to consider the first responders. There were four ragged thumps from above, and the doors unlocked.

Technology. A wonderful thing.

Mahmeini's man scrambled out and stood up. A minute later his bag was on the back seat and he was in the driver's seat. It was set way back. There was enough leg room for a giant. More proof, as if he needed any.

Like he had told Rossi's guy, American peasants were all huge. He found the button and buzzed the cushion forward, on and on, about a foot, and then he jacked the seat back upright and got to work.

He used the tip of his blade to force the steering lock, and then he pulled off the column shroud and stripped the wires he needed with the knife and touched them together. The engine started and a chime told him he didn't have his seat belt on. He buckled up and backed out and turned around and waited in the narrow lane parallel to the long side of the H, the engine idling silently, the climate control already warming.

Then he pulled out his phone and went through the Marriott switchboard, first to Safir's guys, then to Rossi's, in both cases following Mahmeini's script exactly, telling them that plans had changed, that the party was starting early, that he and Asghar were leaving for the north immediately, and that they had five minutes to get their asses in gear, no more, or they would be left behind.

The SUV was a GMC Yukon, metallic gold in colour, equipped to a high standard with a couple of option packs. It had beige leather inside. It was a nice truck. Certainly the kid called John seemed proud of it, and Reacher could see why. He was looking forward to owning it for the next twelve hours, or however long his remaining business in Nebraska might take.

He said, 'Got a cell phone, John?'

The guy paused a fatal beat and said, 'No.'

Reacher said, 'And you were doing so well. But now

you're screwing up. Of course you've got a cell phone. You're part of an organization. You were on sentry duty. And you're under thirty, which means you were probably born with a minutes plan.'

The guy said, 'You're going to do to me what you did to the others.'

'What did I do?'

'You crippled them.'

'What were they going to do to me?'

The guy didn't answer that. They were on the two-lane road, north of the motel, well out in featureless farm country, rolling steadily along, nothing to see beyond the headlight beams. Reacher was half turned in his seat, his left hand on his knee, his right wrist resting on his left forearm, the Glock held easy in his right hand.

Reacher said, 'Give me your cell phone, John.' He saw movement in the guy's eyes, a flash of speculation, a narrowing of the lids. Fair warning. The guy jacked his butt off the seat and took one hand off the wheel and dug in his pants pocket. He came out with a phone, slim and black, like a candy bar. He went to hand it over, but he lost his grip on it for a moment and juggled it and dropped it in the passenger foot well.

'Shit,' he said. 'I'm sorry.'

Reacher smiled. 'Good try, John,' he said. 'Now I bend over to pick it up, right? And you cave the back of my skull in with your right fist. I wasn't born yesterday, you know.'

The guy said nothing.

Reacher said, 'So I guess we'll leave it right where it is. If it rings, we'll let it go to voice mail.'

'I had to try.'

'Is that an apology? You promised me.'

'You're going to break my legs and dump me on the side of the road.'

'That's a little pessimistic. Why would I break both of them?'

'It's not a joke. Those four guys you hurt will never work again.'

'They'll never work for the Duncans again. But there are other things to do in life. Better things.'

'Like what?'

'You could shovel shit on a chicken farm. You could whore yourself out in Tijuana. With a donkey. Either thing would be better than working for the Duncans.'

The guy said nothing. Just drove.

Reacher asked, 'How much do the Duncans pay you?'

'More than I could get back in Kentucky.'

'In exchange for what, precisely?'

'Just being around, mostly.'

Reacher asked, 'Who are those Italian guys in the overcoats?'

'I don't know.'

'What do they want?'

'I don't know.'

'Where are they now?'

'I don't know.'

They were in the blue Impala, already ten miles north of the Marriott, Roberto Cassano at the wheel, Angelo Mancini sitting right beside him. Cassano was working hard to stay behind Safir's boys in their red Ford, and both drivers were working hard to keep Mahmeini's guys in sight. The big black Cadillac was really hustling. It was doing more than eighty miles an hour. It was way far outside of its comfort zone. It was bouncing and wallowing and floating. It was quite a sight. Angelo Mancini was staring ahead at it. He was obsessed with it.

He asked, 'Is it a rental?'

Cassano was much quieter. Occupied by driving, certainly, concentrating on the crazy high-speed dash up the road, definitely, but thinking, too. Thinking hard.

He said, 'I don't think it's a rental.'

'So what is it? I mean, what? Those guys have their own cars standing by in every state? Just in case? How is that possible?'

'I don't know,' Cassano said.

'I thought at first maybe it's a limo. You know, like a car service. But it isn't. I saw the little squirt driving it himself. Not a car service driver. Just a glimpse, but it was him. The one who mouthed off at you.'

Cassano said, 'I didn't like him.'

'Me either. And even less now. They're way bigger than we are. Way bigger than we thought. I mean, they have their own cars on standby in every state? They fly in on the casino plane, and there's a car there for them, wherever? What's that about?'

'I don't know,' Cassano said again.

'Is it a funeral car? Do the Iranians run funeral parlours now? That could work, right? Mahmeini could call the nearest parlour and say, send us one of your cars.'

'I don't think the Iranians took over the funeral business.'

'So what else? I mean, how many states are there? Fifty, right? That's at least fifty cars standing by.'

'Not even Mahmeini can be active in all fifty states.'

'Maybe not Alaska and Hawaii. But he's got cars in Nebraska, apparently. How far up the list is Nebraska likely to be?'

'I don't know,' Cassano said again.

'OK,' Mancini said. 'You're right. It has to be a rental.'

'I told you it's not a rental,' Cassano said. 'It can't be. It's not a current model.'

'Times are tough. Maybe they rent older cars now.'

'It's not even last year's model. Or the year before. That's practically an antique. That's an old-guy car. That's your neighbour's granddad's Cadillac.'

'Maybe they have rent-a-wreck here.'

'Why would Mahmeini need that?'

'So what is it?'

'It doesn't really matter what it is. You're not looking at the big picture. You're missing the point.'

'Which is what?'

'That car was already at the hotel. We parked right next to it, remember? Late afternoon, when we got back. Those guys were there before us. And you know what that means? It means they were on their way before Mahmeini was even asked to send them. Something really weird is going on here.'

The metallic gold GMC Yukon turned left off the north-south two-lane and headed west towards Wyoming on another two-lane that was just as straight and featureless as the first. Reacher pictured planners and engineers a century before, hard at work, leaning over parchment maps and charts with long rulers and sharp pencils, drawing roads, dispatching crews, opening up the interior. He asked, 'How far now, John?'

The kid said, 'We're real close,' which as always turned out to be a relative statement. *Real close* in some places meant fifty yards, or a hundred. In Nebraska it meant ten miles and fifteen minutes. Then Reacher saw a group of dim lights, off to the right, seemingly in the middle of nowhere. The truck slowed and turned, another precise ninety-degree right angle, and headed north on a blacktop strip engineered in a different way from the standard county product. A private approach road, leading towards what looked like a half-built or half-demolished industrial facility of some kind. There was a concrete rectangle the size of a football field, possibly an old parking lot but more likely the floor slab of a factory that had either never been completed or had been later dismantled. It was enclosed on all four sides by a head-high hurricane fence that was topped by a mean and token allocation of razor wire. Here and there the fence posts carried lights, like domestic backyard fixtures, containing what must have been regular sixty- or hundred-watt bulbs. The whole enormous space was empty, apart from two grey panel vans in a marked-off bay big enough to handle three.

The approach road was scalloped out at one point to allow access in and out of the concrete rectangle through a pair of gates. Then it ran onward towards a long low one-storey building built of brick in an unmistakable style. Classic 1940s industrial architecture. The building was an office block, built to serve the factory it once stood next to. The factory would have been a defence plant, almost certainly. Give a government a choice of where to build in wartime, and it will seek the safe centre of a land mass, away from coastal shelling and marauding aircraft and potential invasion sites. Nebraska and other heartland states had been full of such places. The ones lucky enough to be engaged on fantasy Cold War systems were probably still in business. The ones built to produce basic war-fighting items like boots and bullets and bandages had perished before the ink was dry on the armistice papers.

The kid called John said, 'This is it. We live in the office building.'

The building had a flat roof with a brick parapet, and a long line of identical windows, small panes framed with white-painted steel. In the centre was an unimpressive double door with a lobby behind it and dim bulkhead lights either side of it. In front of the doors was a short concrete path that led from an empty rectangle made of cracked and weedy paving stones, the size of two tennis courts laid end to end. Managerial parking, presumably, back in the day. There were no lights on inside the building. It just stood there, dead to the world.

Reacher asked, 'Where are the bedrooms?'

John said, 'To the right.'

'And your buddies are in there now?'

'Yes. Five of them.'

'Plus you, that's six legs to break. Let's go do it.'

THIRTY-EIGHT

Reacher made the guy get out of the truck the same way he had before, through the passenger door, awkward and unbalanced and unable to spring any surprises. He tracked him with the Glock and glanced beyond the wire and asked, 'Where are all the harvest trucks?'

The guy said, 'They're in Ohio. Back at the factory, for refurbishment. They're specialist vehicles, and some of them are thirty years old.'

'What are the two grey vans for?'

'This and that. Service and repairs, tyres, things like that.'

'Are there supposed to be three?'

'One is out. It's been gone a few days.'

'Doing what?'

'I don't know.'

Reacher asked, 'When do the big trucks get back?'

The guy said, 'Spring.'

'What's this place like in the early summer?'

'Pretty busy. The first alfalfa crop gets harvested early. There's a lot of preparation ahead of time and a lot of maintenance afterwards. This place is humming.'

'Five days a week?'

'Seven, usually. We're talking forty thousand acres here. That's a lot of output.' The guy closed the passenger door and took a step. Then he stopped dead, because Reacher had stopped dead. Reacher was staring ahead at the empty rectangle in front of the building. The cracked stones. The managerial parking lot. Nothing in it.

Reacher asked, 'Where do you normally park your truck, John?'

'Right out front there, by the doors.'

'Where do your buddies park?'

'Same place.'

'So where are they?'

The night-time silence clamped down and the young man's mouth came open a little, and he whirled around as if he was expecting his friends to be hiding somewhere behind him. Like a practical joke. But they weren't. He turned back and said, 'I guess they're out. They must have gotten a call.'

'From you?' Reacher asked. 'When you saw Mrs Duncan?'

'No, I swear. I didn't call. You can check my phone.'

'So who called them?'

'Mr Duncan, I guess. Mr Jacob, I mean.'

'Why would he?'

'I don't know. Nothing was supposed to happen tonight.'

'He called them but he didn't call you?'

'No, he didn't call me. I swear. Check my phone. He

wouldn't call me anyway. I'm on sentry duty. I was supposed to stay put.'

'So what's going on, John?'

'I don't know.'

'Best guess?'

'The doctor. Or his wife. Or both of them together. They're always seen as the weakest link. Because of the drinking. Maybe the Duncans think they have information.'

'About what?'

'You, of course. About where you are and what you're doing and whether you're coming back. That's what's on their minds.'

'It takes five guys to ask those questions?'

'Show of force,' the kid said. 'That's what we're here for. A surprise raid in the middle of the night can shake people up.'

'OK, John,' Reacher said. 'You stay here.'

'Here?'

'Go to bed.'

'You're not going to hurt me?'

'You already hurt yourself. You showed no fight at all against a smaller, older man. You're a coward. You know that now. That's as good to me as a dislocated elbow.'

'Easy for you to say. You've got a gun.'

Reacher put the Glock back in his pocket. He folded the flap down and stood with his arms out, hands empty, palms forward, fingers spread.

He said, 'Now I don't. So bring it on, fat boy.'

The guy didn't move.

'Go for it,' Reacher said. 'Show me what you've got.'

The guy didn't move.

'You're a coward,' Reacher said again. 'You're pathetic. You're a waste of good food. You're a useless three-hundred-pound sack of shit. And you're ugly, too.'

The guy said nothing.

'Last chance,' Reacher said. 'Step up and be a hero.'

The guy walked away, head down, shoulders slumped, towards the dark building. He stopped twenty feet later and looked back. Reacher looped around the rear of the Yukon, to the driver's door. He got in. The seat was too far back. The kid was huge. But Reacher wasn't about to adjust it in front of the guy. Some stupid male inhibition, way in the back of his brain. He just started up and turned and drove away, and fixed it on the fly.

The Yukon drove OK, but the brakes were a little spongy. The result of the panic stop, probably, back at the old roadhouse. Five years' wear and tear, all in one split second. But Reacher didn't care. He wasn't braking much. He was hustling hard, concentrating on speeding up, not slowing down. Twenty miles was a long distance, through the empty rural darkness.

He saw nothing the whole way. No lights, no other vehicles. No activity of any kind. He got back to the main two-lane north of the motel and five minutes later he passed the place. It was all closed up and dark. No blue neon. No activity. No cars, except the wrecked Subaru. It was still there, beaded over with dew, low down on slowly softening tyres, sad and inert, like road kill. Reacher charged onward past it, and then he made the right and the left and the right, along the boundaries of the dark empty fields, like twice before, to the plain ranch house with the post-and-rail fence and the flat, featureless yard.

There were lights on in the house. Plenty of them. Like a cruise ship at night on the open ocean. But there was no sign of uproar. There were no cars on the driveway. No pick-up trucks, no SUVs. No large figures in the shadows. No sound, no movement. Nothing. The front door was closed. The windows were intact.

Reacher turned in and parked on the driveway and walked to the door. He stood right in front of the spy hole and rang the bell. There was a whole minute's delay. Then the spy hole darkened and lightened and locks and chains rattled and the doctor opened up. He looked tired and battered and worried. His wife was standing behind him in the hallway, in the bright light, with the phone to her ear. The phone was the old-fashioned kind, big and black on a table, with a dial and a curly wire. The doctor's wife was not talking. She was just listening, concentrating hard, her eyes narrowing and widening.

The doctor said, 'You came back.'

Reacher said, 'Yes, I did.'

'Why?'

'Are you OK? The Cornhuskers are out and about.'

'We know,' the doctor said. 'We just heard. We're on the phone tree right now.'

'They didn't come here?'

'Not yet.'

'So where are they?'

'We're not sure.'

310

Reacher said, 'Can I come in?'

'Of course,' the doctor said. 'I'm sorry.' He stepped back and Reacher stepped in. The hallway was very warm. The whole house was warm, but it felt smaller than before, like a desperate little fortress. The doctor closed the door and turned two keys and put the chain back on. He asked, 'Did you see the police files?'

Reacher said, 'Yes.'

'And?'

'They're inconclusive,' Reacher said. He moved on into the kitchen. He heard the doctor's wife say, 'What?' She sounded puzzled. Maybe a little shocked. He glanced back at her. The doctor glanced back at her. She said nothing more. Just continued to listen, eyes moving, taking mental notes. The doctor followed Reacher into the kitchen.

'Want coffee?' he asked.

I'm not drunk, he meant.

Reacher said, 'Sure. Lots of it.'

The doctor set about filling the machine. The kitchen was even warmer than the hallway. Reacher took off his coat and hung it on the back of a chair.

The doctor asked, 'What do you mean, inconclusive?'

Reacher said, 'I mean I could make up a story about how the Duncans did it, but there's really no proof either way.'

'Can you find proof? Is that why you came back?'

Reacher said, 'I came back because those two Italian guys who were after me seem to have joined up with a regular United Nations of other guys. Not a

311

peacekeeping force, either. I think they're all coming here. I want to know why.'

'Pride,' the doctor said. 'You messed with the Duncans, and they won't tolerate that. Their people can't handle you, so they've called in reinforcements.'

'Doesn't make sense,' Reacher said. 'Those Italians were here before me. You know that. You heard what Eleanor Duncan said. So there's some other reason. They have some kind of a dispute with the Duncans.'

'Then why would they help the Duncans in their own dispute with you?'

'I don't know.'

'How many of them are coming?' the doctor asked.

From the hallway his wife said, 'Five of them.' She had just gotten off the phone. She stepped into the kitchen and said, 'And they're not coming. They're already here. That was the message on the phone tree. The Italians are back. With three other men. Three cars in total. The Italians in their blue Chevy, plus two guys in a red Ford, and one guy in a black car that everyone swears is Seth Duncan's Cadillac.'

THIRTY-NINE

Reacher poured himself a cup of coffee and thought for a long moment and said, 'I left Seth Duncan's Cadillac at the Marriott.'

The doctor's wife asked, 'So how did you get back here?'

'I took a Chevy Malibu from one of the bad guys.'

'That thing on the driveway?'

'No, that's a GMC Yukon I took from a football player.'

'So what happened with the Cadillac?'

'I left a guy stranded. I stole his car, and then I guess he stole mine. Probably not deliberate tit for tat. Probably just coincidental, because there wasn't really an infinite choice down there. He didn't want some piece-of-shit pick-up truck, obviously, and he didn't want anything with big-time security built in. The Cadillac fit the bill. Probably the only thing that did. Or else he was just plain lazy, and didn't want to look around too long. The Cadillac was right there. We were all in the same hotel.'

'Did you see the guys?'

313

'I didn't see the Italians. But I saw the other four.'

'That makes six, not five. Where's the other one?'

'I promise you something,' Reacher said. 'The guy who took the Cadillac put his bag on the back seat, not in the trunk.'

'How do you know?'

'Because that's where the sixth guy is. In the trunk. I put him there.'

'Does he have air?'

'He doesn't need air. Not any more.'

'Sweet Jesus. What happened?'

Reacher said, 'I think whatever else they're doing, they're coming here to get me first. Like a side issue of some kind. Like mission creep. I don't know why, but that's the only way I can explain it. The way I see it, they all assembled tonight in the Marriott and the Italians announced the mission and gave the others a description, probably vague and definitely secondhand, because they haven't actually laid eyes on me yet, and then I bumped into one of the others after that, in the lobby, and he was looking at me, like he was asking himself, is that the guy? Can it be? Can it? I could see him thinking. We got out to the lot and he put his hand in his pocket and I hit him. You ever heard of *commotio cordis*?'

'Chest wall trauma,' the doctor said. 'Causes fatal cardiac dysrhythmia.'

'Ever seen it?'

'No.'

'Neither had I. But I'm here to tell you, it works real good.'

'What was in his pocket?'

'A knife and a gun and an ID from Vegas.'

'Vegas?' the doctor said. 'Do the Duncans have gambling debts? Is that the dispute?'

'Possible,' Reacher said. 'No question the Duncans have been living beyond their means for a long time. They've been getting some extra income from somewhere.'

'Why say that? They've been extorting forty farms for thirty years. And a motel. That's a lot of money.'

'No, it isn't,' Reacher said. 'Not really. This isn't the wealthiest area in the world. They could be taking half of what everyone earns, and that wouldn't buy them a pot to piss in. But Seth lives like a king and they pay ten football players just to be here. They couldn't do all that on the back of a seasonal enterprise.'

The doctor's wife said, 'We should worry about that later. Right now the Cornhuskers are on the loose, and we don't know where or why. That's what's important tonight. Dorothy Coe might be coming over.'

'Here?' Reacher asked. 'Now?'

The doctor said, 'That's what happens sometimes. With the women, mostly. It's a support thing. Like a sisterhood. Whoever feels the most vulnerable clusters together.'

His wife said, 'Which is always Dorothy and me, and sometimes others too, depending on exactly what the panic is.'

'Not a good idea,' Reacher said. 'From a tactical point of view, I mean. It gives them one target instead of multiple targets.'

315

'It's strength in numbers. It works. Sometimes those boys can act a little inhibited. They don't necessarily like witnesses around, when they're sent after women.'

They took cups of coffee and waited in the dining room, which had a view of the road. The road was dark. There was nothing moving on it. It was indistinguishable from the rest of the night-time terrain. They sat quiet for a spell, on hard upright chairs, with the lights off to preserve their view out the window, and then the doctor said, 'Tell us about the files.'

'I saw a photograph,' Reacher said. 'Dorothy's kid was Asian.'

'Vietnamese,' the doctor's wife said. 'Artie Coe did a tour over there. Something about it affected him, I guess. When the boat people thing started, they stepped up and adopted.'

'Did many people from here go to Vietnam?'

'A fair number.'

'Did the Duncans go?'

'I don't think so. They were in an essential occupation.'

'So was Arthur Coe.'

'Different strokes for different folks.'

'Who was chairman of the local draft board?'

'Their father. Old man Duncan.'

'So the boys didn't keep on farming to please him. They kept on to keep their asses out of the war.'

'I suppose.'

'Good to know,' Reacher said. 'They're cowards, too, apart from anything else.'

316

The doctor said, 'Tell us about the investigation.'

'Long story,' Reacher said. 'There were eleven boxes of paper.'

'And?'

'The investigation had problems,' Reacher said.

'Like what?'

'One was a conceptual problem, and the others were details. The lead detective was a guy called Carson, and the ground kind of shifted under his feet over a twelve-hour period. It started out as a straightforward missing persons issue, and then it slowly changed to a potential homicide. And Carson didn't really revisit the early phase in the light of the later phase. The first night, he had people checking their own outbuildings. Which was reasonable, frankly, with a missing kid. But later he never really searched those outbuildings independently. Only one of them, basically, for an old couple who hadn't done it themselves. Everyone else self-certified, really. In effect they said no sir, the kid ain't here, and she never was, I promise. At some point Carson should have started over and treated everyone as a potential suspect. But he didn't. He focused on the Duncans only, based on information received. And the Duncans came out clean.'

'You think it was someone else?'

'Could have been anyone else in the world, just passing through. If not, it could have been any of the local residents. Probably not Dorothy or Arthur Coe themselves, but that still leaves thirty-nine possibilities.'

The doctor's wife said, 'I think it was the Duncans.'

'Three different agencies disagree with you.'

317

'They might be wrong.'

Reacher nodded in the dark, his gesture unobserved.

'They might be,' he said. 'There might have been another conceptual error. A failure of imagination, anyway. It's clear that the Duncans never left their compound, and it's clear that the kid never showed up there. There are reliable witnesses to both of those facts. Four boys were building a fence. And the science came up negative, too. But the Duncans could have had an accomplice. A fifth man, essentially. He could have scooped up the kid and taken her somewhere else. Carson never even thought about that. He never checked known associates. And he should have, probably. You wait five years to build a fence, and you happen to be doing it on the exact same day a kid disappears? Could have been a prefabricated alibi. Carson should have wondered, at least. I would have, for sure.'

'Who would the fifth man have been?'

'Anyone,' Reacher said. 'A friend, maybe. One of their drivers, perhaps. It's clear a vehicle was involved, otherwise why was the bike never found?'

'I always wondered about the bike.'

'Did they have a friend? Did you ever see one, when you were babysitting?'

'I saw a few people, I guess.'

'Anyone close? This would have been a very intimate type of relationship. Shared enthusiasms, shared passions, absolute trust. Someone into the same kind of thing they were into.'

'A man?'

'Almost certainly. The same kind of creep.'

318

'I'm not sure. I can't remember. Where would he have taken her?'

'Anywhere, theoretically. And that was another major mistake. Carson never really looked anywhere else, apart from the Duncans' compound. It was crazy not to search the transportation depot, for instance. As a matter of fact I don't think that was a real problem, because it seems like that place is real busy in the early part of the summer, seven days a week. Something to do with alfalfa, whatever that is. No one would take an abducted kid to a work site full of witnesses. But there was one other place Carson should have checked for sure. And he didn't. He ignored it completely. Possibly because of ignorance or confusion.'

'Which was where?'

But Reacher didn't get time to answer, because right then the window blazed bright and the room filled with moving lights and shadows. They played over the walls, the ceiling, their faces, alternately stark white and deep black.

Headlight beams, strobing through the posts of the fence.

A car, coming in fast from the east.

319

FORTY

It was Dorothy Coe coming in from the east, in her ratty old pick-up truck. Reacher knew it a second after he saw her lights. He could hear her holed muffler banging away like a motorcycle. Like a Harley Davidson moving away from a stoplight. She came on fast and then she braked hard and stopped dead and stood off just short of the house. She had seen the gold Yukon on the driveway. She had recognized it, presumably. A Cornhusker's car. She probably knew it well. The doctor's wife stepped out to the hallway and undid the locks and the chain and opened the front door and waved. Dorothy Coe didn't move an inch. Twenty-five years of habitual caution. She thought it could be a trick or a decoy. Reacher joined the doctor's wife on the step. He pointed to the Yukon and then to himself. Big gestures, like semaphore. *My truck*. Dorothy Coe moved on again and turned in. She shut down and got out and walked to the door. She had a wool hat pulled down over her ears and she was wearing a quilted coat open over a grey dress. She asked, 'Did the Cornhuskers come here?'

The doctor's wife said, 'Not yet.'

'What do you think they want?'

'We don't know.'

They all stepped back inside and the doctor closed up after them, locks and chain, and they went back to the dining room, now four of them. Dorothy Coe took off her coat, because of the heat. They sat in a line and watched the window like a movie screen. Dorothy Coe was next to Reacher. He asked her, 'They didn't go to your place?'

She said, 'No. But Mr Vincent saw one, passing the motel. About twenty minutes ago. He was watching out the window.'

Reacher said, 'That was me. I came in that way, in the truck I took. There are only five of them left now.'

'OK. I understand. But that concerns me a little.'

'Why?'

'I would expect at least one of us to have seen at least one of them, roaming around somewhere. But no one has. Which means they aren't all spread out. They're all bunched up. They're hunting in a pack.'

'Looking for me?'

'Possibly.'

'Then I don't want to bring them here. Want me to leave?'

'Maybe,' Dorothy said.

'Yes,' the doctor said.

'No,' his wife said.

Impasse. No decision. They all turned back to the window and watched the road. It stayed dark. The cloud was clearing a little. There was faint moonlight in the sky. It was almost one o'clock in the morning.

The motel was closed down for the night, but Vincent was still in the lounge. He was still watching out the window. He had seen the gold Yukon go by. He had recognized it. He had seen it before, many times. It belonged to a young man called John. A very unpleasant person. A bully, even by Duncan standards. Once he had made Vincent get down on his knees and beg not to be beaten. Beg, like a dog, with limp hands held up, pleading and howling, five whole minutes.

Vincent had called in the Yukon sighting, to the phone tree, and then he had gone back to the window and watched some more. Twenty minutes had gone by without incident. Then he saw the five men everyone was talking about. Their strange little convoy pulled into his lot. The blue Chevrolet, the red Ford, Seth Duncan's black Cadillac. He knew from the phone tree that someone else was using Seth's car. No one knew how or why. But he saw the guy. A small man slid out of the driver's seat, rumpled and unshaven, foreign, like people from the Middle East he had seen on the news. Then the two men who had roughed him up climbed out of the Chevrolet. Then two more got out of the Ford, tall, heavy, dark-skinned. Also foreign. They all stood together in the gloom.

Vincent didn't automatically think the five men were there for him. There could be other reasons. His lot was the only stopping place for miles. Plenty of drivers used it, for all kinds of purposes, passers-by checking their maps, taking off their coats, getting things from the trunk, sometimes just stretching their legs. It was private property, no question, properly deeded, but it was used almost like a public facility, like a regular roadside turnout.

He watched. The five men were talking. His windows were ordinary commercial items, chosen by his parents in 1969. They were screened on the inside and opened outward, with little winding handles. Vincent thought about opening the one he was standing behind. Just a crack. It was almost an obligation. He might hear what the five men were saying. He might get valuable information, for the phone tree. Everyone was expected to contribute. That was how the system worked. So he started to turn the handle, slowly, a little at a time. At first it went easily. But then it went stiff. The casement was stuck to the insulating strip. Paint and grime and long disuse. He used finger and thumb, and tried to ease some steady pressure into it. He wanted to pop it loose gently. He didn't want to make a loud plastic sound. The five men were still talking. Or rather, the man from the Cadillac was talking, and the other four were listening.

Mahmeini's man was saying, 'I let my partner out a mile back. He's going to work behind the lines. He's more use to me that way. Pincer movements are always best.'

Roberto Cassano said, 'Is he going to coordinate with the rest of us?'

'Of course he is. What else would he do? We're a team, aren't we?'

'You should have kept him around. We need to make a plan first.'

'For this? We don't need to make a plan. It's just

flushing a guy out. How hard can it be? You said it yourself, the locals will help.'

'They're all asleep.'

'We'll wake them up. With a bit of luck we'll get it done before morning.'

'And then what?'

'Then we'll spend the day leaning on the Duncans. We all need that delivery, and since we all had to drag ourselves up here, we might as well all spend our time on what's important.'

'So where do we start?'

'You tell me. You've spent time here.'

'The doctor,' Cassano said. 'He's the weakest link.'

Mahmeini's man said, 'So where's the doctor?'

'South and west of here.'

'OK, go talk to him. I'll go somewhere else.'

'Why?'

'Because if you know he's the weakest link, then so does Reacher. Dollars to doughnuts, he ain't there. So you go waste your time, and I'll go do some work.'

Vincent gave up on cracking the window. He could tell there was no way it would open without a ripping sound, and drawing attention right then would not be a good idea. And the impromptu conference in his lot was breaking up anyway. The small rumpled man slid back into Seth Duncan's Cadillac and the big black car crunched through a wide arc over the gravel. Its headlight beams swept across Vincent's window. He ducked just in time. Then the Cadillac turned left on the two-lane and took off south.

324

The other four men stayed right where they were. They watched until the Cadillac's tail lights were lost to sight, and then they turned back and started talking again, face to face in pairs, each one of them with his right hand in his right-hand coat pocket, for some strange reason, all four of them symmetrical, like a formal tableau.

Roberto Cassano watched the Cadillac go and said, 'He doesn't have a partner. There's nobody working behind the lines. What lines, anyway? It's all bullshit.'

Safir's main man said, 'Of course he has a partner. We all saw him, right there in your room.'

'He's gone. He ran out. He took whatever car they rented. That guy is on his own now. He stole that Cadillac from the lot. We saw it there earlier.'

No reply.

Cassano said, 'Unless one of you had a hand in it. Or both of you.'

'What are you saying?'

'We're all grown-ups here,' Cassano said. 'We know how the world works. So let's not pretend we don't. Mahmeini told his guys to take the rest of us out, and Safir told you guys to take the rest of us out, and Rossi sure as hell told us to take the rest of you out. I'm being honest here. Mahmeini and Safir and Rossi are all the same. They all want the whole pie. We all know that.'

Safir's guy said, 'We didn't do anything. We figured you did. We were talking about it all the way up here. It was obvious that Cadillac isn't a rental.'

'We didn't do anything to the guy. We were going to wait for later.'

'Us too.'

'You sure?'

'Yes.'

'Swear?'

'You swear first.'

Cassano said, 'On my mother's grave.'

Safir's guy said, 'On mine too. So what happened?'

'He ran out. Must have. Maybe chicken. Or short on discipline. Maybe Mahmeini isn't what we think he is. Which raises possibilities.'

Nobody spoke.

Cassano said, 'We have a vote here, don't you think? The four of us? We could take out Mahmeini's other boy, and leave each other alone. That way Rossi and Safir end up with fifty per cent more pie each. They could live with that. And we sure as hell could.'

'Like a truce?'

'Truces are temporary. Call it an alliance. That's permanent.'

Nobody spoke. Safir's guys glanced at each other. Not a difficult decision. A two-front war, or a one-front war? History was positively littered with examples of smart people choosing the latter over the former.

Vincent was still watching out the window. He saw quiet conversation, low tones, some major tension there, then some easing, the body language relaxing, some speculative looks, some tentative smiles. Then all four men took their hands out of their pockets and shook, four separate ways, wrists crossing, some pats on the back, some slaps on the shoulder. Four new friends, all suddenly getting along just great.

There was a little more talk after that, all of it fast and breezy, like simple obvious steps were being planned and confirmed, and then there were more pats on the back and slaps on the shoulder, all shuffling mobile *catch you later* kind of stuff, and then the two big dark-skinned men climbed back into their red Ford. They closed their doors and got set to go and then the Italian who had done all the talking suddenly remembered something and turned back and tapped on the driver's glass.

The window came down.

The Italian had a gun in his hand.

The Italian leaned in and there were two bright flashes, one hard after the other, like orange camera strobes right there inside the car, behind the glass, all six windows lighting up, and two loud explosions, then a pause, then two more, two more bright flashes, two more loud explosions, evenly spaced, carefully placed.

Then the Italian stepped away and Vincent saw the two dark-skinned men all slumped down in their seats, somehow suddenly much smaller, deflated, diminished, smeared with dark matter, their heads lolling down on their chests, their heads altered and misshapen, parts of their heads actually *missing*.

Vincent fell to the floor under the inside sill of his window and vomited in his throat. Then he ran for the phone.

Angelo Mancini opened the red Ford's trunk and found two nylon roll-aboard suitcases, which more or less confirmed a personal theory of his. Real men carried their bags. They didn't wheel them around like women. He unzipped one of the bags and rooted around and came up with a bunch of shirts on wire hangers, all folded together concertina-style. He took one and tore it off the hanger and crushed the hanger flat and opened the Ford's filler neck and used the hanger to poke the shirt down into the tube, one sleeve in, the body all bunched up, the other sleeve trailing out. He lit the trailing cuff with a paper match from a book he had taken from the diner near the Marriott. Then he walked away and got in the blue Chevrolet's passenger seat and Roberto Cassano drove him away.

The road beyond the post-and-rail fence outside the dining room window stayed dark. The doctor got up and left the room and came back with four mugs of fresh coffee on a plastic tray. His wife sat quiet. Next to her Dorothy Coe sat quiet. The sisterhood, enduring, waiting it out. Just one long night out of more than nine thousand in the last twenty-five years, most of them tranquil, presumably, but some of them not. Nine thousand separate sunsets, each one of them heralding who knew what.

Reacher was waiting it out, too. He knew that Dorothy wanted to ask what he had found in the county archive. But she was taking her time getting around to it, and that was OK with him. He wasn't about to bring it up unannounced. He had dealt with his fair share of other people's tragedy, all of it bad, none of it easy, but he figured there was nothing worse than the Coe family story. Nothing at all. So he waited, ten silent minutes, then fifteen, and finally she asked, 'Did they still have the files?'

He answered, 'Yes, they did.'

'Did you see them?'

'Yes, I did.'

'Did you see her photograph?'

'She was very beautiful.'

'Wasn't she?' Dorothy said, smiling, not with pride, because the kid's beauty was not her achievement, but with simple wonderment. She said, 'I still miss her. Which I think is strange, really, because the things I miss are the things I actually had, and they would be gone now anyway. The things I didn't get to see would have happened afterwards. She would be thirty-three now. All grown up. And I don't miss those things, because I don't have a clear picture of what they might have been. I don't know what she might have become. I don't know if she would have been a mother herself, and stayed around here, or if she would have been a career girl, maybe a lawyer or a scientist, living far away in a big city.'

'Did she do well in school?'

'Very well.'

'Any favourite subjects?'

'All of them.'

'Where was she going that day?'

'She loved flowers. I like to think she was going searching for some.'

'Did she roam around often?'

'Most days, when she wasn't in school. Sundays especially. She loved her bike. She was always going

329

somewhere. Those were innocent times. She did the same things I did, when I was eight.'

Reacher paused a beat and said, 'I was a cop of sorts for a long time. So may I ask you a serious question?'

She said, 'Yes.'

'Do you really want to know what happened to her?'

'Can't be worse than what I imagine.'

Reacher said, 'I'm afraid it can. And it sometimes is. That's why I asked. Sometimes it's better not to know.'

She didn't speak for a long moment.

Then she said, 'My neighbour's son hears her ghost screaming.'

'I met him,' Reacher said. 'He smokes a lot of weed.'

'I hear it too, sometimes. Or I think I do. It makes me wonder.'

'I don't believe in ghosts.'

'Neither do I, really. I mean, look at me.'

Reacher did. A solid, capable woman, about sixty years old, blunt and square, worn down by work, worn down by hardship, fading slowly to grey.

She said, 'Yes, I really want to know what happened to her.'

Reacher said, 'OK.'

Two minutes later the phone rang. An old-fashioned instrument. The slow peal of a mechanical bell, a low sonorous sound, doleful and not at all urgent. The doctor's wife jumped up and ran out to the hallway to answer. She said hello, but nothing more. She just listened. The phone tree again. The others heard the

330

thin distorted crackle of a loud panicked voice from the earpiece, and they sensed a gasping shuffle out there in the hallway. Some kind of surprising news. Dorothy Coe fidgeted in her chair. The doctor got to his feet. Reacher watched the window. The road stayed dark.

The doctor's wife came back in, more puzzled than worried, more amazed than frightened. She said, 'Mr Vincent just saw the Italians shoot the men from the red car. With a gun. They're dead. Then they set the car on fire. Right outside his window. In the motel lot.'

Nobody spoke, until Reacher said, 'Well, that changes things a little.'

'How?'

'I thought maybe we had six guys working for the same organization, with some kind of a two-way relationship, them and the Duncans. But we don't. They're three pairs. Three separate organizations, plus the Duncans make four. Which makes it a food chain. The Duncans owe somebody something, and that somebody owes somebody else, and so on, all the way up the line. They're all invested, and they're all here to safeguard their investment. And as long as they're all here, they're all trying to cut each other out. They're all trying to shorten the chain.'

'So we're caught in the middle of a gang war?'

'Look on the bright side. Six guys showed up this afternoon, and now there are only three of them left. Fifty per cent attrition. That works for me.'

The doctor said, 'We should call the police.'

His wife said, 'No, the police are sixty miles away. And the Cornhuskers are right here, right now. That's what we need to worry about tonight. We need to know what they're doing.'

Reacher asked, 'How do they normally communicate?'

'Cell phone.'

'I've got one,' Reacher said. 'In the truck I took. Maybe we could listen in. Then we'd know for sure what they're doing.'

The doctor undid the locks and unlatched the chain and they all crowded out to the driveway. Reacher opened the Yukon's passenger door and rooted around in the foot well and came out with the cell phone, slim and black, like a candy bar. He stood in the angle of the door and flipped it open and said, 'They'll use conference calls, right? This thing will ring and all five of them will be on?'

'More likely vibrate, not ring,' the doctor said. 'Check the settings and the call register and the address book. You should be able to find an access number.'

'You check,' Reacher said. 'I'm not familiar with cell phones.' He tracked around the back of the truck and handed the phone to the doctor. Then he looked to his left and saw light in the mist to the east. A high hemispherical glow, trembling, bouncing, weakening and strengthening and weakening, very white, almost blue.

A car, coming west towards them, pretty fast.

It was about half a mile away. Just like before, the misty glow resolved itself to a fierce source low down above the surface of the road, then to twin fierce sources, spaced just feet apart, oval in shape, low to the ground, blue-white and intense. And just like before, the ovals kept on coming, getting closer, flickering and jittering because of firm suspension and fast steering. They looked small at first, because of the distance, and they stayed small because they were small, because the car was a Mazda Miata, low and tiny and red. Reacher recognized it about two hundred feet out.

Eleanor Duncan.

The sisterhood, clustering together.

A hundred feet out the Mazda slowed a little. Its top was up this time, like a tight little hat. Cold weather, no further need for instant identification. No more sentries to distract.

Fifty feet out, it braked hard, ready for the turn in, and red light flared in the mist behind it.

Twenty feet out, it swung wide and started to turn.

Ten feet out, Reacher remembered three things.

First, Eleanor Duncan was not on the phone tree.

Second, his gun was in his coat.

Third, his coat was in the kitchen.

The Mazda swung in fast and crunched over the gravel and jammed to a stop right behind Dorothy Coe's pickup. The door opened wide and Seth Duncan unfolded his lanky frame and stepped out.

He was holding a shotgun.

FORTY-ONE

Seth Duncan had a huge aluminium splint on his face, like a dull metal patch taped to a large piece of rotten fruit. All kinds of sick moonlit colours were spreading out from under it. Yellows, and browns, and purples. He was wearing dark pants and a dark sweater with a new parka over it. The shotgun in his hands was an old Remington 870 pump. Probably a twelve-gauge, probably a twenty-inch barrel. A walnut stock, a seven-round tubular magazine, altogether a fine all-purpose weapon, well proven, more than four million built and sold, used by the Navy for shipboard security, used by the Marines for close-quarters combat, used by the army for heavy short-range firepower, used by civilians for hunting, used by cops as a riot gun, used by cranky homeowners as a get-off-my-lawn deterrent.

Nobody moved.

Reacher watched carefully and saw that Seth Duncan was holding the Remington pretty steady. His finger was on the trigger. He was aiming it from the hip, straight back at Reacher, which meant he was aiming it at Dorothy Coe and the doctor and his wife, too, because buckshot spreads a little, and all four of them were clustered tight together, on the driveway ten feet from the doctor's front door. All kinds of collateral damage, just waiting to happen.

Nobody spoke.

The Mazda idled. Its door was still open. Seth Duncan started to move up the driveway. He raised the Remington's stock to his shoulder and closed one eye and squinted along the barrel and walked forward, slow and steady. A useless manoeuvre on rough terrain. But feasible on smooth gravel. The Remington stayed dead on target.

He stopped thirty feet away. He said, 'All of you sit down. Right where you are. Cross-legged on the ground.'

Nobody moved.

Reacher asked, 'Is that thing loaded?'

Duncan said, 'You bet your ass it is.'

'Take care it doesn't go off by accident.'

'It won't,' Duncan said, all nasal and inarticulate, because of his injury, and because his cheek was pressed hard against the Remington's walnut stock.

Nobody moved. Reacher watched and thought. Behind him he heard the doctor stir and heard him ask, 'Can we talk?'

Duncan said, 'Sit down.'

The doctor said, 'We should discuss this. Like reasonable people.'

'Sit down.'

'No, tell us what you want.'

A brave try, but in Reacher's estimation the wrong

335

tactic. The doctor thought there was something to be gained by spinning things out, by using up the clock. Reacher thought the exact opposite was true. He thought there was no time to waste. None at all. He said, 'It's cold.'

Duncan said, 'So?'

'Too cold to sit down outside. Too cold to stand up outside. Let's go inside.'

'I want you outside.'

'Why?'

'Because I do.'

'Then let them go get their coats.'

'Why should I?'

'Self-respect,' Reacher said. 'You're wearing a coat. If it's warm enough not to need one, then you're a pussy. If it's cold enough to bundle up, then you're making innocent people suffer unnecessarily. If you think you've got a beef with me, OK, but these folks have never hurt you.'

Seth Duncan thought about it for a second, the gun still up at his shoulder, his head still bent down to it, one eye still closed. He said, 'OK, one at a time. The others stay here, like hostages. Mrs Coe goes first. Get your coat. Nothing else. Don't touch the phone.'

Nobody moved for a beat, and then Dorothy Coe peeled out of the cluster and walked to the door and stepped inside. She was gone a minute, and then she came back wearing her coat, this time buttoned over her dress. She resumed her position.

Duncan said, 'Sit down, Mrs Coe.'

Dorothy tugged her coat down and sat, not cross-legged, but with her knees drawn up to one side.

Reacher said, 'Now the doctor's wife.'

Duncan said, 'Don't tell me what to do.'

'I'm just saying. Ladies first, right?'

'OK, the doctor's wife. Go. Same rules. Just the coat. Don't touch the phone. Don't forget I have hostages here. Including your beloved husband.'

The doctor's wife peeled out of the cluster. A minute later she was back, wearing her wool coat, and a hat, and gloves, and a muffler.

'Sit down,' Duncan said.

She sat down, right next to Dorothy Coe, cross-legged, her back straight, her hands on her knees, her gaze level and aimed at a faraway spot in the fields. Nothing there, but Reacher guessed it was better than looking at her tormentor.

Reacher said, 'Now the doctor.'

'OK, go,' Duncan said.

The doctor peeled out and was gone a minute. He came back in a blue parka, all kinds of nylon and Goretex and zippered compartments. He sat down without waiting to be told.

Reacher said, 'Now me.'

Duncan said, 'No, not you. Not now, not ever. You stay right there. I don't trust you.'

'That's not very nice.'

'Sit down.'

'Make me.'

Duncan leaned into the gun, the final per cent, like he was ready to fire.

He said, 'Sit down.'

Reacher didn't move. Then he glanced to his right and saw lights in the mist, and he knew that his chance had gone.

The Cornhuskers came on fast, five of them in five separate vehicles, a tight little high-speed convoy, three pick-up trucks and two SUVs. They all jammed to a stop on the road in line with the fence, five vehicles all nose to tail, and five doors flung open, and five guys spilled out, all of them in red jackets, all of them moving fast, the smallest of them the size of a house. They swarmed straight in, climbing the fence in unison, moving across the dormant lawn on a broad front, coming in wide of the Remington's potential trajectory. The Remington stayed rock steady in Seth Duncan's hands. Reacher was watching its muzzle. It wasn't moving at all, its blued steel dark in the moonlight, trained dead on his chest from thirty feet, the smooth bore at its centre looking big enough to stick a thumb in.

Duncan said, 'Take the three others inside, and keep them there.'

Rough hands grabbed at the doctor, and his wife, and Dorothy Coe, hauling them back to their feet, by their arms and shoulders, pulling them away, hustling them across the last of the gravel, pushing them in through the door. Eight people went in, and a minute later four came out, all of them football players, all of them crunching back to where Reacher was standing.

Duncan said, 'Hold him.'

Reacher was spending no time on regret or recrimination. No time at all. The time for rueing mistakes and learning from them came later. As always he was focused in the present and the immediate future. People who wasted time and energy cursing recent errors were certain losers. Not that Reacher saw an easy path to certain victory. Not right then. Not in the short term. Right then he saw nothing ahead but a world of hurt.

The four big guys stepped up close. No opportunity. The Remington stayed trained on its target and two guys came in from wide positions, never getting between Reacher and the gun. They stepped alongside him and grabbed an arm each, big strong hands on his elbows from behind, on his wrists from in front, pushing one, pulling the other, straightening his arms, bending his elbows back, kicking his feet apart, hooking their ankles in front of his ankles, holding him immobile. A third guy came up behind him and stood between his spread feet and wrapped massive arms around his chest. The fourth backed off and stood ten feet from Duncan.

Reacher didn't struggle. No point. Absolutely no point at all. Each of the three men holding him was taller than him by inches and outweighed him by fifty pounds. No doubt they were all slow and stupid and untutored, but right then sheer dumb bulk was doing the job just fine. He could move his feet a little, and he could move his head a little, but that was all, and all he could do with his feet was move them backward, which would pitch him forward on his face, except that the guy who had him in the bear hug from behind would hold him upright. And all he could do with his head was duck his chin to his chest, or jerk it back a couple of inches. Not enough to hurt the guy behind him.

He was stuck, and he knew it.

Seth Duncan lowered the gun to his hip again. He walked forward with it and then handed it off to the fourth guy. He walked on without it and stopped face to face with Reacher, a yard away. His eyes were bloodshot and his breathing was low and shallow. He was quivering a little. Some kind of fury or excitement. He said, 'I have a message for you, pal.'

Reacher said, 'Who from? The National Association of Assholes?'

'No, from me personally.'

'What, you let your membership lapse?'

'Ten seconds from now we'll know who's a member of that club, and who isn't.'

'So what's the message?'

'It's more of a question.'

'OK, so what's the question?'

'The question is, how do *you* like it?'

Reacher had been fighting since he was five years old, and he had never had his nose broken. Not even once. Partly good luck, and partly good management. Plenty of people had tried, over the years, either deliberately or in a flurry of savage unaimed blows, but none had ever succeeded. Not one. Not ever. Not even close. It was a fact Reacher was proud of, in a peculiar way. It was a symbol. A talisman. A badge of honour. He had all kinds of nicks and cuts and scars on his face and his arms and his body, but he felt that the distinctive but intact bone in his nose made up for them.

It said: *I'm still standing.*

The blow came in exactly as he expected it to, a clenched fist, a straight right, hard and heavy, riding up a little, aiming high, as if Duncan subconsciously expected Reacher to flinch up and back, like his wife Eleanor probably did every single time. But Reacher didn't flinch up and back. He *started* with his head up and back, his eyes open, watching down his nose, timing it, then jerking forward from the neck, smashing a perfect improvised head-butt straight into Duncan's knuckles, an instant high-speed high-impact collision between the thick ridge in Reacher's brow and the delicate bones in Duncan's hand. No contest. No contest at all. Reacher had a skull like concrete, and an arch was the strongest structure known to man, and hands were the most fragile parts of the body. Duncan screamed and snatched his hand away and cradled it limp against his chest and hopped a whole yowling circle, looking up, looking down, stunned and whimpering. He had three or four busted phalanges, Reacher figured, certainly a couple of proximals, and maybe a couple of cracked distals too, from the fingers folding much tighter than nature intended, under the force of the sudden massive compression.

'Asshole,' Reacher said.

Duncan clamped his right wrist under his left armpit and huffed and blew and stomped around. He came to rest a whole minute later, a little cramped and crouched and bent, and he glowered up and out from either side of his splint, hurting and angry and humiliated, look-ing first at Reacher, and then at his fourth guy, who was standing there stock-still, holding the shotgun. Duncan jerked his head, from the guy to Reacher, a gesture full of silent fury and impatience.

Get him.

The fourth guy stepped up. Reacher was pretty sure he wasn't going to shoot. No one fires a shotgun at a group of four people, three of which are his friends.

Reacher was pretty sure it was going to be worse than shooting.

The guy reversed the gun. Right hand on the barrel, left hand on the stock.

The guy behind Reacher moved. He wrapped his left forearm tight around Reacher's throat, and he clamped his right palm tight on Reacher's forehead.

Immobile.

The fourth guy raised the gun horizontal, butt first, two-handed, and cocked it back over his right shoulder, ready to go, lining it up like a spear, and then he rocked forward and took a step and aimed carefully and jabbed the butt straight at the centre of Reacher's face and

CRACK

BLACK

FORTY-TWO

Jacob Duncan convened an unscheduled middle-of-the-night meeting with his brothers, in his own kitchen, not Jonas's or Jasper's, with Wild Turkey, not Knob Creek, and plenty of it, because his mood was celebratory.

'I just got off the phone,' he said. 'You'll be pleased to hear my boy has redeemed himself.'

Jasper asked, 'How?'

'He captured Jack Reacher.'

Jonas asked, 'How?'

Jacob Duncan leaned back in his chair and shot his feet straight out in front of him, relaxed, expansive, a man at ease, a man with a story to tell. He said, 'I drove Seth home, as you know, but I let him out at the end of his road, because he was a little down, and he wanted to walk a spell in the night air. He got within a hundred yards of his house, and he was nearly run over by a car. *His* car, as it happens. His own Cadillac, going like a bat out of hell. Naturally he hurried home. His wife was induced to reveal all the details. It turns out Reacher stole the Cadillac earlier in the afternoon. It turns out the doctor was with him. Misguided, of course, but it seems the poor fellow has formed an alliance of sorts with our Mr Reacher. So Seth took his old Remington pump and set off in Eleanor's car and sure enough, Reacher was indeed at the doctor's house, large as life and twice as natural.'

'Where is he now?'

'In a safe place. It seems like the capture was mostly uneventful.'

'Is he alive?'

'So far,' Jacob Duncan said. 'But how long he stays alive is what we need to discuss.'

The room went quiet. The others sat and waited, as they had so many times before, for their brother Jacob, the eldest, a contemplative man, always ready with a pronouncement, or a decision, or a nugget of wisdom, or an analysis, or a proposal.

Jacob said, 'Seth wants to finesse the whole thing, right down to the wire, and frankly I'm tempted to let him try. He wants to rebuild his credibility with us, which of course I told him isn't necessary, but it remains true that all of us need to pay some attention to our own credibility, in a collective sense, with Mr Rossi, our good friend to the south.'

Jasper asked, 'What does Seth want to do?'

'He wants to stage things so that our prior hedging is shown to have been entirely justified. He wants to wait until our shipment is about an hour away, whereupon he wants to unveil Reacher to Mr Rossi's boys, whereupon he wants to fake a phone call and have the truck arrive within the next sixty minutes, as if what we've been saying all along about the delay was indeed true and legitimate.'

'Too risky,' Jonas said. 'Reacher is a dangerous man. We shouldn't keep him around a minute longer than we have to. That's just asking for trouble.'

'As I said, he's in a safe place. Plus, in the end, if we do it Seth's way, we'll have been seen to have solved our own problems with our own hands, without any outside assistance at all, and therefore whatever small shred of vulnerability we displayed will evaporate completely.'

'Even so. It's still risky.'

'There are other factors,' Jacob said.

The room went quiet again.

Jacob said, 'We've never really known or cared what happens to our shipments once they're in Mr Rossi's hands, except that I imagine we always vaguely supposed they pass down a lengthy chain of commerce, sale and resale, to an ultimate destination. And now that chain, or at least a large part of it, has become visible. As of tonight, it seems that three separate participants have representation here. Probably they're all desperate. It's clear to me they have agreed to work together to break up the logjam. And once that is done, it's equally clear to me they will be under instructions to eliminate one another, so that the last man standing triples his profit.'

Jonas said, 'That's not relevant to us.'

'Except that Mr Rossi's boys seem to be jumping the gun. It was inevitable that one of them would seize the initiative. Our stooges on the phone tree tell me that two men are already dead. Mr Rossi's boys killed them outside Mr Vincent's motel. So my idea is to give Mr Rossi's boys enough time to shorten the chain a little more, so that by the end of tomorrow Mr Rossi himself will be the last man standing, whereupon he and we can have a little talk about splitting the extra profit equally. The way it works mathematically is that we'll all double our shares. Mr Rossi will be happy to live with that, I imagine, and so will we, I'm sure.'

'Still risky.'

'You don't like money, brother?'

'I don't like risk.'

'Everything's a risk. We know that, don't we? We've lived with risk for a long time. It's part of the thrill.'

A long silence.

Jonas said, 'The doctor lied to us. He told us Reacher hitched a ride in a white sedan.'

Jacob nodded. 'He has apologized for that, most sincerely. I'm told he's being a model of cooperation now. His wife is with him, of course. I'm sure that's a factor. He also claims Reacher left Seth's Cadillac sixty miles south of here, and that it was re-stolen quite independently by an operative from further up the chain. A small Middle Eastern person, according to reports on the phone tree. It appears he was the one who nearly ran Seth over.'

'Anything else?'

'The doctor says Reacher saw the police files.'

Silence in the room.

Then Jonas said, 'And?'

'Inconclusive, the doctor says.'

'Conclusive enough to come back.'

'The doctor says he came back because of the men in the cars.'

Nobody spoke.

Jacob said, 'But in the interests of full disclosure, the doctor also claims Reacher asked Mrs Coe if she really wants to be told what happened to her daughter.'

'Reacher can't possibly know. Not yet.'

'I agree. But he might be beginning to pull on threads.'

'Then we have to kill him now. We have to.'

'It's just one more day. He's locked up. Escape is impossible.'

More silence.

Nobody spoke.

Then Jonas asked, 'Anything else?'

'Eleanor helped Reacher get past the sentry,' Jacob said. 'She defied her husband and left his house, quite brazenly. She and Reacher conspired together to decoy the boy away from his post. He didn't perform well. We'll have to fire him, of course. We'll leave Seth to decide what happens to his wife. And it seems that Seth has broken his hand. He'll need some attention. It appears Reacher has a very hard head. And that's all the news I have.'

Nobody spoke.

Jacob said, 'We need to make a decision about the immediate matter at hand. Life or death. Always the ultimate choice.'

No reply.

Jacob asked, 'Who wants to go first?'

Nobody spoke.

Jacob said, 'Then I'll go first. I vote to let my boy do it his way. I vote to keep Reacher concealed until our truck is close by. It's a minor increase in risk. One more day, that's all. Overall, it's insignificant. And I like finesse. I like a measure of elegance in a solution.'

A long pause.

Then Jasper said, 'I'm in.'

And Jonas said, 'OK,' a little reluctantly.

Reacher woke up in a concrete room full of bright light. He was on his back on the floor, at the foot of a flight of steep stairs. He had been carried down, he figured, not thrown or fallen. Because the back of his skull was OK. He had no sprains or bruises. His limbs were intact, all four of them. He could see and hear and move. His face hurt like hell, but that was to be expected.

The lights were regular incandescent household bulbs, six or eight of them, randomly placed, maybe a hundred watts each. No shades. The concrete was smooth and pale grey. Very fine. Not dusty. It was like an engineering product. High strength. It had been poured with great precision. There were no seams. The angles where the walls met each other and the floor were chamfered and radiused, just slightly. Like a swimming pool, ready for tiling. Reacher had dug swimming pools once. Temporary employment, many years ago. He had seen them in all their different stages of completion.

His face hurt like hell.

Was he in a half-finished swimming pool? Unlikely. Unless it had a temporary roof. The roof was boards laid over heavy joists. The joists were made of multi-

348

ply wood. Manufactured articles. Very strong. Layers of exotic hardwoods, probably glued together with resins under enormous pressure in a giant press in a factory. Probably cut with computer-controlled saws. Delivered on a flat-bed truck. Craned into place. Each one probably weighed a lot.

His face hurt.

He felt confused. He had no idea what time it was. The clock in his head had stopped. He was breathing through his mouth. His nose was jammed solid with blood and swellings. He could feel blood on his lips and his chin. It was thick and almost dry. A nosebleed. Not surprising. Maybe thirty minutes old. Not like Eleanor Duncan's. His own blood clotted fast. It always had. He was the exact opposite of a haemophiliac. A good thing, from time to time. An evolutionary trait, no doubt bred into him through many generations of natural-born survivors.

His face hurt.

There were other things in the concrete room. There were pipes of all different diameters. There were green metal boxes a little crusted with mineral stains. Some wires, some in steel conduit, some loose. There were no windows. Just the walls. And the stairs, with a closed door at the top.

He was underground.

Was he in a bunker of some sort?

He didn't know.

His face hurt like hell. And it was getting worse. Much, much worse. Huge waves of pain were pulsing out between his eyes, behind his nose, boring straight

349

back into his head, one with every heartbeat, bumping and grinding, lapping out into his skull and bouncing around and then fading and receding just in time to be replaced by the next. Bad pain. But he could fight it. He could fight anything. He had been fighting since he was five years old. If there was nothing to fight, he would fight himself. Not that there had ever been a shortage of targets. He had fought his own battles, and his brother's. A family responsibility. Not that his brother had been a coward. Far from it. Nor weak. His brother had been big too. But he had been a rational boy. Gentle, even. Always a disadvantage. Someone would start something, and Joe would waste the first precious second thinking, *Why?* Reacher never did that. Never. He used the first precious second landing the first precious blow. Fight, and win. Fight, and win.

His face hurt like hell. He looked at the pain, and he set himself apart from it. He saw it, examined it, identified it, corralled it. He isolated it. He challenged it. *You against me? Dream on, pal.* He built borders for it. Then walls. He built walls and forced the pain behind them and then he moved the walls inward, compressing the pain, crushing it, boxing it in, limiting it, beating it.

Not beating it.

It was beating him.

It was exploding, like bombs on timers, one, two, three. Relentlessly. Everlastingly, with every beat of his heart. It was never going to stop, until his heart stopped. It was insane. In the past he had been wounded with shrapnel and shot in the chest and cut with knives. This was worse. Much worse. This was worse than all of his previous sufferings put together.

Which made no sense. No sense at all. Something was wrong. He had seen busted noses before. Many times. No fun, but nobody made a gigantic fuss about them. Nobody looked like grenades were going off in his head. Not even Seth Duncan. People got up, maybe spat a little, winced, walked it off.

He raised his hand to his face. Slowly. He knew it would be like shooting himself in the head. But he had to know. Because something was wrong. He touched his nose. He gasped, loud and sudden, like an explosive curse, pain and fury and disgust.

The ridge of bone on the front of his nose was broken clean off. It had been driven around under the tight web of skin and cartilage to the side. It was pinned there, like a mountaintop sliced off and reattached to a lower slope.

It hurt like hell.

Maybe the Remington's butt had a metal binding. Brass, or steel. Reinforcement against wear and tear. He hadn't noticed. He knew he had turned his head at the last split second, as much as he could against the resistance of the sweaty palm clamped on his forehead. He had wanted as much of a side-on impact as he could get. Better than head-on. A head-on impact could drive shards of loose bone into the brain.

He closed his eyes.

He opened them again.

He knew what he had to do.

He had to reset the break. He knew that. He knew the

costs and the benefits. The pain would lessen, and he would end up with a normal-looking nose. Almost. But he would pass out again. No question about that. Touching the injury with a gentle fingertip had nearly taken his head off at the neck. Like shooting himself. Fixing it would be like machine-gunning himself.

He closed his eyes. The pain battered at him. He laid his head gently on the concrete. No point in falling back and cracking his skull as well. He raised his hand. He grasped the knob of bone, finger and thumb. Atom bombs went off in his head. He pushed and pulled.

No result. The cartilage was clamping too hard. Like a web of miniature elastic straps, holding the damn thing in place. In completely the wrong place. He blinked water out of his eyes and tried again. He pushed and pulled. Thermonuclear devices exploded.

No result.

He knew what he had to do. Steady pressure was not working. He had to smack the knob of bone back into place with the heel of his hand. He had to think hard and set it up and be decisive. Like a chiropractor wrestling a spine, jerking suddenly, listening for the sudden click.

He rehearsed the move. He needed to hit low down on the angle of cheek and nose, with the side of his hand, the lower part, opposite the ball of his thumb, like a karate chop, a semi-glancing blow, upward and sideways and outward. He needed to drive the peak back up the mountainside. It would settle OK. Once it arrived, the skin and the cartilage would keep it in place.

He opened his eyes. He couldn't get an angle. Not down there on the floor. His elbow got in the way. He dragged himself across the smooth concrete, palms and heels pushing, five feet, ten, and he sat up against a wall, half reclining, his neck bent, space for his elbows in the void under his angled back. He squared his shoulders and his hips and he got as settled and as stable as he could, so that he wouldn't fall far, or even at all.

Show time.

He touched the heel of his hand to where it had to go. He let it feel what it had to do. He practised the move. The top of his palm would skim his eyebrow. Like a guide.

On three, he thought.

One.

Two.

CRACK

BLACK

FORTY-THREE

Mahmeini's man was afraid. He had driven around for twenty minutes and he had seen nothing at all, and then he had come to a house with a white mailbox with *Duncan* written on it, all proud and spotlit. The house was a decent place, expensively restored. Their HQ, he had assumed. But no. All it contained was a woman who claimed she knew nothing. She was relatively young. She had been beaten recently. She said there were four Duncans, a father and a son and two uncles. She was married to the son. They were all currently elsewhere. She gave directions to a cluster of three houses that Mahmeini's man had already seen and dismissed from his mind. They were unimpressive places, all meanly hemmed in by an old post-and-rail fence, unlikely homes for men of significance.

But he had set off back in that direction anyway, driving fast, almost running down some idiot pedestrian who loomed up at him out of the dark, and then from the two-lane he had seen a gasoline fire blazing to the north. He had ignored the three houses and hustled onward towards the fire and found it was in the motel lot. It was a car. Or, it had been a car. Now it was just a superheated cherry-red shell inside an inferno. Judging by the shape it had been the Ford that Safir's boys had been driving. They were still inside it. Or, what was left of them was still inside it. They were now just shrunken and hideous shapes, still burning and melting and peeling, their ligaments shrivelled, their hands forced up by the heat like ghastly claws, the furious roiled air in which they were sitting making it look like they were dancing and waving in their seats.

Rossi's boys had killed them, obviously. Which meant they had killed Asghar too, almost certainly, hours ago. Rossi's plan was clear. He already had a firm connection with the Duncans, at the bottom end of the chain. Now he intended to leapfrog both Safir and Mahmeini and sell to the Saudis direct, at the top end of the chain. An obvious move, displaying sound business sense, but Rossi had had his boys start early. They had seized the initiative. A real coup. Their timing was impressive. As were their skills. They had lain in wait for Asghar and taken him down and disposed of his car, all within thirty short minutes. Which was an excellent performance. Asghar was tough and wary, always thinking, not easy to beat. A good wingman. A good friend, too, now crying out for vengeance. Mahmeini's man could sense his presence, very strongly, like he was still close by. All of which made him feel alone and adrift in hostile territory, and very much on the defensive. All of which were unusual feelings for him, and all of which therefore made him a little afraid. And all of which made him change his plan. He had sudden new priorities. The

355

giant stranger could wait. His primary targets were now Rossi's boys.

Mahmeini's man started right there at the motel. He had seen someone earlier, lurking behind a window, watching. A man with strange hair. A local. Possibly the motel owner. At least he would know which way Rossi's boys had gone.

Roberto Cassano and Angelo Mancini were parked four miles north, with their lights off and their engine running. Cassano was on the phone with Rossi. Nearly two o'clock in the morning, but there were important matters to discuss.

Cassano asked, 'You and Seth Duncan made this deal, right?'

Rossi said, 'He was my initial contact, back in the day. It turned into a family affair pretty soon after that. It seems like nothing much happens up there without unanimous consent.'

'But as far as you know it's still your deal?'

'As opposed to what?'

'As opposed to someone else's deal.'

'Of course it's still my deal,' Rossi said. 'No question about that. It always was my deal, and it always will be my deal. Why are you even asking? What the hell is going on?'

'Seth Duncan lent his car to Mahmeini's guy, that's what.'

Silence on the line.

Cassano said, 'There was a Cadillac at the Marriott when we got down there this afternoon. Too old for a rental. Later we saw Mahmeini's guy using it. At first we thought he stole it, but no. The locals up here say it's Seth Duncan's personal ride. Therefore Seth Duncan must have provided him with it. He must have driven it down there and left it ready for him. And then after the initial contact we made, Mahmeini's guy seemed to start operating solo. At first we thought Safir's boys had taken out his partner, or maybe the guy just ran out, but now we think he must have come straight up here in their rental. He's probably hanging out with the Duncans right now. Maybe they both are, like best friends forever. We're getting royally screwed here, boss. We're getting squeezed out.'

'Can't be happening.'

'Boss, your contact lent his car to your rival. They're in bed together. How else do you want to interpret it?'

'I can't get close to the ultimate buyer.'

'You're going to have to try.'

More silence on the line. Then Rossi said, 'OK, I guess nothing is impossible. So go ahead and deal with Mahmeini's boys. Do that first. Make it like they were never born. Then show Seth Duncan the error of his ways. Find some way to get his attention. Through his wife, maybe. And then move in on the three old guys. Tell them if they step out of line again we'll take over the whole thing, all the way up to Vancouver. An hour from now I want them pissing in their pants.'

'What about Reacher?'

'Find him and cut his head off and put it in a box. Show the Duncans we can do anything we want. Show them we can reach out and touch anyone, anywhere, any time. Make sure they understand they could be next.'

Reacher woke up for the second time and knew instantly it was two in the morning. The clock in his head had started up again. And he knew instantly he was in the basement of a house. Not an unfinished swimming pool, not an underground bunker. The concrete was smooth and strong because Nebraska was tornado country, and either zoning laws or construction standards or insurance requirements or just a conscientious architect had demanded an adequate shelter. Which made it the basement of the doctor's house, almost certainly, partly because not enough time had elapsed for a move to another location, and partly because the doctor's house was the only house Reacher had seen that was new enough to be both designed by an architect and be subject to laws and standards and requirements. In the old days people just built things themselves and crossed their fingers and hoped for the best.

Therefore the pipes of various diameters were for water and the sewer and heating. The green metal boxes with the mineral stains were the furnace and the water heater. There was an electrical panel, presumably full of circuit breakers. The stairs came down and the door at the top would open outward into the hallway. Not inward. No one let doors open inward at the top of a staircase. Careless residents would go tumbling down like a slapstick movie. And tornadoes could blow at three hundred miles an hour. Better that a shelter door be pressed more firmly shut, not blown wide open.

Reacher sat up. Evidently he had come to rest in the angle of wall and floor, with his head bent. His neck was a little sore, which he took to be a very good sign. It meant the pain from his nose was relegated to background noise. He raised his hand and checked. His nose was still very tender, and there were open cuts on it, and big pillowy swellings, but the chip of bone was back in the right place. Basically. Almost. More or less. Not pretty, presumably, but then, he hadn't been pretty to start with. He spat in his palm and tried to wipe dried blood off his mouth and his chin.

Then he got to his feet. There was nothing stored in the basement. No crowded shelves, no piles of dusty boxes, no workbench, no peg boards full of tools. Reacher figured all that stuff was in the garage. It had to be somewhere. Every household had stuff like that. But the basement was a tornado shelter, pure and simple. Nothing else. Not even a rec room. There was no battered sofa, no last-generation TV, no old refrigerator, no pool table, no hidden bottles of bourbon. There was nothing down there at all, except the house's essential mechanical systems. The furnace was running hard, and it was making noise. It was a little too loud to hear anything else over. So Reacher crept up the stairs and put his ear to the door. He heard voices, low and indistinct, first one and then another, in a fixed and regular rhythm. Call and response. A man and a woman. Seth Duncan, he thought, asking questions, and either Dorothy Coe or the doctor's wife answering them, with short syllables and no sibilants. Negative answers. No real stress. No pain or panic. Just resignation. Either Dorothy Coe or the doctor's wife was saying *No*, quite calmly and patiently and resolutely, over and over again, to each new question. And whichever one of them it was, she had an audience. Reacher could sense the low physical vibe of other people in the house, breathing, stirring, moving their feet. The doctor himself, he thought, and two of the football players.

Reacher tried the door handle, slowly and carefully. It turned, but the door didn't open. It was locked, as expected. The door was a stout item, set tight and square in a wall that felt very firm and solid. Because of tornadoes, and laws and standards and requirements, and conscientious architects. He let go of the handle and crept back downstairs. For a moment he wondered if the laws and the standards and the requirements and the conscientious architects had mandated a second way in. Maybe a trapdoor, from the master bedroom. He figured such a thing would make a lot of sense. Storms moved fast, and a sleeping couple might not have time to get along the hallway to the stairs. So he walked the whole floor, looking up, his sore neck protesting, but he saw no trapdoors. No second way in, and therefore no second way out. Just solid unbroken floorboards, laid neatly over the strong multi-ply joists.

He came to rest in the middle of the space. He had a number of options, none of them guaranteed to succeed, some of them complete non-starters. He could turn off the hot water, but that would be a slow-motion provocation. Presumably no one was intending to take a shower in the next few hours. Equally he could turn off the heat, which would be more serious, given the season, but response time would still be slow, and he would be victimizing the innocent as well as the guilty. He could kill all the lights, at the electrical panel, one click of a circuit breaker, but there was at least one shotgun upstairs, and maybe flashlights too. He was on the wrong side of a locked door, unarmed, attacking from the low ground.

Not good.

Not good at all.

FORTY-FOUR

Seth Duncan had his right hand flat on the doctor's dining table, with a bag of peas from the freezer laid over it. The icy cold was numbing the pain, but not very effectively. He needed another shot of his uncle Jasper's pig anaesthetic, and he was about to go get one, but before he attended to himself he was determined to attend to his plan, which was working pretty well at that point. So well, in fact, that he had permitted himself to think ahead to the endgame. His long experience in the county had taught him that reality was whatever people said it was. If no one ever mentioned an event, then it had never happened. If no one ever mentioned a person, then that person had never existed.

Duncan was alone on one side of the table, with the dark window behind him and the doctor and his wife and Dorothy Coe opposite him, lined up on three hard chairs, upright and attentive. He was leading them one by one through a series of questions, listening to their answers, judging their sincerity, establishing the foundations of the story as it would be told in the future. He had finished with the doctor, and he had finished

362

with the doctor's wife, and he was about to start in on Dorothy Coe. He had a Cornhusker standing mute and menacing in the doorway, holding the old Remington pump, and he had another out in the hallway, leaning on the basement door. The other three were out somewhere in their cars, driving around in the dark, pretending to hunt for Reacher. The illusion had to be maintained, for the sake of Rossi's boys. Reacher's capture was scheduled for much later in the day. Reality was what people said it was.

Duncan asked, 'Did you ever meet a man named Reacher?'

Dorothy Coe didn't answer. She just glanced to her left, out to the hallway. A stubborn woman, hung up on quaint old notions of objectivity.

Duncan said, 'That's a very strong basement door. I know, because I installed the same one myself, when we remodelled. It has a steel core, and it fits into a steel frame, and it has oversized hinges and a burst-proof lock. It's rated for a category five storm. It can withstand a three-hundred-mile-an-hour gust. It carries a FEMA seal of approval. So if, just hypothetically, there was a person in the basement right now, you may rest assured that he's staying there. Such a person could not possibly escape. Such a person might as well not exist at all.'

Dorothy Coe asked, 'If the door is so good, why do you have a football player leaning on it?'

'He has to be somewhere,' Duncan said. Then he smiled. 'Would you prefer it if he was in the bedroom? Maybe he could kill some time in there, with your little friend, while you answer my questions.'

Dorothy Coe glanced the other way, at the doctor's wife.

Duncan asked, 'Did you ever meet a man named Reacher?'

Dorothy Coe didn't answer.

Duncan said, 'The calendar rolls on. It will be spring before you know it. You'll be ploughing and planting. With a bit of luck the rains will be right and you'll have a good harvest. But then what? Do you want it hauled? Or do you want to put a gun in your mouth, like your worthless husband?'

Dorothy Coe said nothing.

Duncan asked, 'Did you ever meet a man named Reacher?'

Dorothy Coe said, 'No.'

'Did you ever *hear* of a man named Reacher?'

'No.'

'Was he ever at your house?'

'No.'

'Did you ever give him breakfast?'

'No.'

'Was he here when you arrived tonight?'

'No.'

Out in the hallway, three inches from the second Cornhusker's hip, the handle on the basement door turned, a quarter circle, and paused a beat, and turned back.

No one noticed.

In the dining room, Duncan asked, 'Did any kind of stranger come here this winter?'

Dorothy Coe said, 'No.'

'Anyone at all?'

'No.'

'Any local troubles here?'

'No.'

'Did anything change?'

'No.'

'Do you want anything to change?'

'No.'

'That's good,' Duncan said. 'I like the status quo, very much, and I'm glad you do too. It benefits all of us. No reason why we can't all get along.' He got up, leaving the bag of peas on the table, a little meltwater beading on the wax. He said, 'You three stay here. My boys will look after you. Don't attempt to leave the house, and don't attempt to use the phone. Don't even answer it. The phone tree is off-limits tonight. You're out of the loop. Punishments for non-compliance will be swift and severe.'

Then Duncan put his parka on, awkwardly, leading with his left hand, and he stepped past the guy with the Remington and headed for the front door. The others heard it open and close and a minute later they heard the Mazda drive away, the sound of its exhaust ripping the night air behind it.

Mahmeini's man drove the Cadillac south on the two-lane, five gentle miles, and then he turned the lights off and slowed to a walk. The big engine whispered and the soft tyres rustled over the pavement. He saw the three old houses on his right. There was a light burning in one of the downstairs windows. Beyond that, there were no signs of life. There were three vehicles parked out front, vague moonlit shapes, all of them old, all of

365

them rustic and utilitarian pick-up trucks, none of them a new blue Chevrolet. But the Chevrolet would come. Mahmeini's man was absolutely sure of that. Half of Rossi's attention was fixed on leapfrogging Safir and Mahmeini himself, which meant the other half was fixed on securing his rear. His relationship with the Duncans had to be protected. Which meant his boys would be checking in with them often, calming them, stroking them, reassuring them, and above all making sure no one else was getting close to them. Standard commonsense precautions, straight out of the textbook.

Mahmeini's man rolled past the end of the Duncans' driveway and U-turned and parked a hundred yards south on the opposite shoulder, half on the blacktop, half on the dirt, his lights off, the big black car nestled in a slight natural dip, about as invisible as it was possible to get without a camouflage net. There would be a dull moonlit glow from some of the chrome, he figured, but there was mist in the air, and anyway Rossi's boys would be looking at the mouth of the driveway ahead of their turn, not at anything else. Drivers always did that. Human nature. Steering a car was as much a mental as a physical process. Heads turned, eyes sought their target, and the hands followed automatically.

Mahmeini's man waited. He was facing north, because on balance he expected Rossi's boys to come from the north, but it was always possible they would come from the south, so he adjusted his mirror to get a view in that direction. The mist that was helping to hide him was fogging his rear window a little. Nothing serious, but an approaching car with its lights off might be difficult to see. But then, why would Rossi's boys be driving with their lights off? They were three-for-three on the night, and therefore probably very confident.

Five miles north the orange glow of the gasoline fire was still visible, but it was dying back a little. Nothing burns for ever. Above the glow the moon was smudged with smoke. Apart from that the night-time landscape lay dark and quiet and still and uneventful, like it must have done for a century or more. Mahmeini's man stared at the road ahead, and saw nothing.

He waited.

Then he saw something.

Way ahead and off to his left he saw a blue glow in the mist, a high round bubble of light, moving fast from west to east. A car, coming in at him at a right angle, aiming to hit the two-lane a mile or two north of him, aiming to turn either left and away from him, or right and towards him. He took his gun from his pocket and laid it on the passenger seat next to him. The moving bubble of light slowed, and stopped, and started again, and flared bright. The car had turned right, towards him. Immediately he knew it was not the Chevrolet. The way the light moved told him it was too small, too low, too nimble. Porsches and Ferraris in Vegas moved the same way at night, their front ends rigidly connected to the pavement, their headlights jittering and hopping. Big dumb domestic sedans looked anaesthetized in comparison. They moved like lumps, swaying, dull and damped and padded and disconnected.

He watched and waited, and he saw the bubble of light resolve itself to twin nervous beams and then twin oval shapes close together and low to the ground. He saw the car slow two hundred yards away and then he saw it turn one hundred yards away, straight into the mouth of the driveway. It was the tiny red Mazda Miata he had seen parked at the restored Duncan farmhouse. The daughter-in-law's car. She was visiting. Not a social occasion, presumably. Not so late at night. She had called ahead on the phone, probably. She had reported the encounter with the strange Iranian man, and she had been told to come on in, for safety's sake. Probably the Duncans knew certain things were due to be settled before dawn, and they didn't want one of their own caught in the crossfire.

Mahmeini's man watched the Mazda bump and bounce down the driveway. He watched it park alongside the old pick-up trucks. He saw its lights go off. Ten seconds later he saw a doorway flare bright in the distance as a figure went inside, and then the scene went dark again.

Mahmeini's man watched the road, and waited. The night mist was getting worse. It was becoming a problem. The Cadillac's windshield was going opaque. He fumbled around and found the wiper stalk and flicked the blades right, left, right, left, and cleared it. Which made the rear screen all the worse in comparison. It was completely dewed over. Even a car with its headlights on would be hard to recognize. Its lights would be atomized into a million separate shards, into a single blinding mess. Worse than useless.

Mahmeini's man kept one eye on the road ahead and groped around for the rear defogger button. It was hard to find. With the lights off outside, the dash and all the consoles were unlit inside. And there were a lot of buttons. It was a luxury car, fully equipped. He ducked his head and found a button with zigzag symbols on it. It looked like something to do with heating. And it had a red warning lens laid into it. He pressed it, and waited. Nothing happened to the rear window, but his ass got hot. It was the seat warmer, not the defogger. He turned it off and found another button, one eye on the console, one eye on the road ahead. He pressed the button. The radio came on, very loud. He shut it down in a hurry and tried again, another button close by, a satisfying tactile click under his fingertip.

The trunk lid clunked and popped and raised itself up, slowly and smoothly, damped and hydraulic, all the way open, completely vertical.

Now he had no view at all out the back.

Not good.

And presumably there was a courtesy light in the trunk, in reality quite weak and yellow, but no doubt looking like a million-watt searchlight in the dark of the night.

Not good at all.

He pressed the button again, not really thinking. Afterwards he realized he had half expected the trunk lid to close again, slowly and obediently, like the seat warmer and the radio had gone off again. But of course the trunk lid didn't close again. The release mechanism merely clicked and whirred one more time, and the trunk lid stayed exactly where it was.

Wide open.

Blocking his view.

He was going to have to get out and close it by hand.

FORTY-FIVE

Roberto Cassano and Angelo Mancini had been in the area three whole days, and they figured their one real solid-gold advantage over Mahmeini's crew was their local knowledge. They knew the lie of the land, literally. Most of all, they knew it was flat and empty. Like a gigantic pool table, with brown felt. Big fields, for efficiency's sake, no ditches, no hedges, no other natural obstacles, the ground frozen firm and hard. So even though their car was a regular street sedan, they could drive it cross-country without a major problem, pretty much like sailing a small boat on a calm open sea. And they had seen the Duncan compound up close. They had been in it. They knew it well. They could loop around behind it in the car, slow and quiet, lights off, inky blue and invisible in the dark, and then they could get out and climb the crappy post-and-rail fence, and storm the place from the rear. Surprise was everything. There might be eyeballs to the front, but in back there would be nothing at all except the Duncans and Mahmeini's guys all sitting around in one of the kitchens, probably toasting each other with cheap bourbon and sniggering about their newly streamlined commercial arrangements.

Two handgun rounds would take care of that happy conversation.

Cassano came south on the two-lane and switched off his lights level with the motel. The Ford was still burning in the lot, but only just. The remains of the tyres were still giving off coils of greasy rubber smoke, and small flames were licking out of the gravel all around where oil had spilled. Safir's boys were dark shrunken shapes about half their original size, both fused to the zigzag springs that were all that was left of the seats, their mouths forced open like awful shrieks, their heads burned smooth, their hands up like talons. Mancini smiled and Cassano rolled slowly past them and headed on down the road, cautiously, navigating by the light of the moon.

Four miles south of the motel and one mile north of the Duncan place he slowed some more and turned the wheel and bumped across the shoulder and struck out across the open land. The car lurched and pattered. In a geological sense the ground was dead flat, but down there where the rubber met the dirt it was rutted and lumpy. The springs creaked and bounced and the wheel jumped and chattered in Cassano's hands. But he made steady progress. He kept it to about twenty miles an hour and held a wide curve, aiming to arrive about half a mile behind the compound. Two minutes, he figured. At one point he had to brake hard and steer around a bramble thicket. Just beyond it they saw the burned-out shell of an SUV. It loomed up at them out of the dark, all black and ashen grey. Reacher's work, from earlier in the day. But after that it was easy all the way. They could see a pool of faint yellow light ahead, like a homing beacon. A kitchen window, almost certainly, spilling warmth. The southernmost house, probably. Jacob Duncan's place. The big cheese.

Mahmeini's man climbed out of the Cadillac and stood for a second in the night-time cold. He looked all around, east, west, north, south, and he saw nothing stirring. He closed his door, to kill the interior light. He took a step towards the trunk. He had been right. There was a light in the trunk. It was throwing a pale sphere of yellow glow into the mist. Not serious from the front, but a problem from behind. The human eye was very sensitive.

He took another step, past the rear passenger door, and he raised his left hand, palm flat, somehow already feeling the familiar sensations associated with an action he had performed a thousand times before, his palm on the metal maybe a foot from the edge of the lid, so that the force of his push would act on both hinges equally, so that the panel would not buckle, so that both calibrated springs would stretch together with soft creaks, whereupon the lid would go down smooth and easy until the upmarket mechanism grabbed at it and sucked it all the way shut.

He got as far as putting his palm on the panel.

Subconsciously he leaned into the motion, not really intending to slam the lid, not at all bad-tempered, just seeking a little physical leverage, and his change of position hunched his shoulders a little, which brought his head forward a little, which changed his eye line a little, which meant he had to look somewhere, and given the choice of the lit interior of a previously closed space or a featureless length of dark blacktop, well, any human eye would opt for the former over the latter.

Asghar Arad Sepehr stared back at him.

His sightless eyes were wide open. His olive skin was pale with death and yellow in the light. Forces from braking and accelerating and turning had jammed him awkwardly into the far rear corner of the trunk. His limbs were in disarray. His neck was bent. His look was quizzical.

Mahmeini's man stood absolutely still, his hand on the cold metal, his mouth open, not really breathing, his heart hardly beating. He forced himself to look away. Then he looked back. He wasn't hallucinating. Nothing had changed. He started breathing again. Then he started panting. His heart started thumping. He started to shake and shiver.

Asghar Arad Sepehr stared up at him.

Mahmeini's man took his hand off the trunk lid and shuffled all the way around to the rear of the car. He stood there with the idling exhaust pooling around his knees and with his fingers steepled against his forehead, looking down, not understanding. Asghar was stone dead, but there was no blood. No gunshot wound between the eyes. No blunt-force trauma, no caved-in skull, no signs of strangulation or suffocation, no knife wounds, no defensive injuries. Nothing at all, except his friend, dead in the trunk, all slack and undignified, all thrown about and jumbled up.

Mahmeini's man walked away, ten feet, then twenty, and then he turned back and raised his head and raised his arms and howled silently at the moon, his eyes screwed tight shut, his mouth wide open in a desperate snarl, his feet stamping alternately like he was running in place, all alone in the vast empty darkness.

Then he stopped and swiped his hands over his face, one after the other, and he started thinking. But the subtleties were almost completely beyond him. His friend had been killed sixty miles away, by an unknown person and an unknown method with no visible signs, and then locked in the trunk of a car that could have absolutely nothing at all to do with either Rossi's boys, or Safir's. Then his own rental had been taken away, so that he had been forced to steal the very same car, the only possible choice in an entire town, inevitably and inexorably, like a puppet being manipulated from afar by a grinning intelligence much greater than his own.

It was incomprehensible.

But, facts were facts. He walked back to the trunk and steeled himself to investigate further. He pushed and pulled and hauled Asghar into the centre of the space and began a detailed examination, like a pathologist leaning over a mortuary table. The trunk light burned bright and hot, but it revealed nothing. Asghar had no broken bones, and no bruises. His neck was intact. He had no wounds, no cuts, no scrapes, no scratches, and there was nothing under his fingernails. His gun and his knife and his money were missing, which was interesting. And all around him in the trunk were the usual kinds of things a person might expect to find in a trunk, which was odd. No attempt had been made to clean it up. No incriminating evidence had been removed. There was an empty grocery bag with a week-old register receipt inside, and a month-old local newspaper never read and still neatly folded, and some browned and curled leaves and some crumbs of dirt as if items had been hauled home from a plant nursery. Clearly the car belonged to someone who used it in a fairly normal manner, and who had not prepared it in any special way for its current gruesome task.

So, whose car was it? That was the first question. The licence plates would reveal the answer, of course, assuming they were genuine. But there might be a faster way to find out, given the fact that nothing seemed to have been sanitized. Mahmeini's man stepped away to the front passenger door, and opened it, and leaned in, and opened the glove box. He found a black leather wallet the size of a hardcover book, stamped on the front with the Cadillac shield in gold. Inside it he found two instruction books, one thick, one thin, one for the car and one for the radio, and a salesman's business card clipped into four angled slots, and a registration document, and an insurance document. He pulled out both documents and dropped the wallet in the foot well and held the documents close to the light inside the glove box.

The car was Seth Duncan's.

Which was logical, in a sudden, awful, spectacular way. Because everything had been utterly, utterly miscalculated, right from the start. There was no other possible explanation. There was no giant stranger on the rampage. No one had seen him and no one could describe him, because he didn't exist. He was an invention. He was imaginary. He was bait. He was a ruse. The whole delivery delay was bullshit. It had been staged, from beginning to end. The purpose had been to lure everyone to Nebraska, to be cut out, to be eliminated, to be killed. The Duncans were removing links, severing the chain, intending to remake it with nobody between themselves at the bottom and the Saudis at the top, with a truly massive increase in profit as their prize. Audacious, but obvious, and clearly feasible, clearly within their grasp, because clearly their abilities had been grotesquely underestimated by everyone. They were not the clueless rural hicks everyone thought they were. They were ruthless strategists of stunning and genuine quality, subtle, sophisticated, capable of great insight and penetrating analysis. They had foreseen Mahmeini as their strongest opponent, quite correctly and accurately and realistically, and they had absolutely crippled his response from the get-go by taking Asghar down, somehow, mysteriously, before the bell had even sounded, and then by leaving his untouched body in a car they knew for sure would be found and identified as one of their own.

So, not just a coup, but a message too, brazenly and artfully and subtly delivered. A message that said: *We can do anything we want. We can reach out and touch anyone, anywhere, any time, and you won't even begin to understand how we did it.* And in case subtlety didn't impress, they had reached out and burned Safir's guys to death in the motel lot, in a brutal demonstration of range and power. Rossi's boys hadn't done that. Rossi's boys were probably already dead themselves, some-where else, somehow else, maybe dismembered or bled out or even crucified. Or buried alive. Rossi's spokes-man had used those very words, on the subject of the Duncans' tastes.

Mahmeini's man felt completely alone. He *was* completely alone. He was the last survivor. He had no friends, no allies, no familiarity with the terrain. And no idea what to do next, except to lash out, to fight back, to seek revenge.

No desire to do anything else, either.

He stared through the darkness at the three Duncan houses. He closed the trunk lid on Asghar, reverently, with soft pressure from eight gentle fingertips, like a sad chord on a church organ. Then he walked along the dirt on the shoulder, back to the passenger door, and he leaned in and picked up his Glock from where it lay on the seat. He closed the door, and skirted the hood, and crossed the road, and stepped on to the dirt of some-one's fallow field, and walked a straight line, parallel with the Duncans' fenced driveway, their three houses a hundred yards ahead of him, his gun in his right hand, his knife in his left.

Half a mile behind the Duncan houses, Roberto Cassano slowed and hauled the Chevrolet through a tight turn and let it coast onward towards the compound. A hundred yards out he brought it to a stop with the parking brake. He reached up and switched the dome light so it would stay off when the doors opened. He looked at Angelo Mancini next to him, and they both paused and then nodded and climbed out into the night. They drew their Colts and held them behind their backs, so that the moon glinting off the shiny steel would not be visible from the front. They walked forward together, shoulder to shoulder, a hundred yards to go.

FORTY-SIX

The doctor and his wife and Dorothy Coe were sitting quiet in the dining room, but the football player with the shotgun had moved out of the doorway and gone into the living room, where he was sprawled out full-length on the sofa, watching recorded NFL highlights in high definition on the doctor's big new television set. His partner had moved off the basement door and was leaning comfortably on the hallway wall, watching the screen at an angle, from a distance. They were both absorbed in the programme. The sound was low but distinct, grumbling richly and urgently through the big loudspeakers. The room lights were off, and bright colours from the screen were dancing and bouncing off the walls. Outside the window, the night was dark and still. The phone had rung three times, but no one had answered. Apart from that, all was peaceful. It could have been the day after Christmas, or late on a Thanksgiving afternoon.

Then all the power in the house went out.

The TV picture died abruptly and the sound faded away and the subliminal hum of the heating system disappeared. Silence clamped down, elemental and absolute, and the temperature seemed to drop, and the walls seemed to dissolve, as if there was no longer a difference between inside and out, as if the house's tiny footprint had suddenly blended with the vast emptiness on which it stood.

The football player in the hallway pushed off the wall and stood still in the centre of the space. His partner in the living room swivelled his feet to the floor and sat up straight. He said, 'What happened?'

The other guy said, 'I don't know.'

'Doctor?'

The doctor got up from behind the dining table and fumbled his way to the door. He said, 'The power went out.'

'No shit, Sherlock. Did you pay your bill?'

'It's not that.'

'Then what is it?'

'Could be the whole area.'

The guy in the living room found his way to the window and peered into the blackness outside. He said, 'How the hell would anyone know?'

The guy in the hallway asked, 'Where are the circuit breakers?'

The doctor said, 'In the basement.'

'Terrific. Reacher's awake. And he's playing games.' The guy crept through the dark to the basement door, feeling his way with his fingertips on the hallway wall. He identified the door by touch and pounded on it. He called, 'Turn it back on, asshole.'

No response.

Pitch black throughout the house. Not even a glimmer, anywhere.

'Turn the power back on, Reacher.'

No response.

Cold, and silence.

The guy from the living room found his way out to the hallway. 'Maybe he isn't awake. Maybe it's a real outage.'

His partner asked, 'Got a flashlight, doctor?'

The doctor said, 'In the garage.'

'Go get it.'

'I can't see.'

'Do your best, OK?'

The doctor shuffled down the hallway, hesitantly, fingers brushing the wall, colliding with the first guy, sensing the second guy's hulking presence and avoiding it, making it to the kitchen, stumbling against a chair with a hollow rattle of wood, hitting the edge of the table with his thighs. The world of the blind. Not easy. He trailed his fingers along the countertops, passing the sink, passing the stove, making it to the mud room lobby in back. He turned ninety degrees with his hands out in front of him and found the door to the garage. He groped for the knob and opened the door and stepped down into the chill space beyond. He found the workbench and reached up and traced his fingers over the items clipped neatly above it. A hammer, good for hitting. Screwdrivers, good for stabbing. Wrenches, stone cold to the touch. He found the flashlight's plastic barrel and pulled it out from its clip. He thumbed the switch and a weak yellow beam jumped out. He rapped the head against his palm and the beam sparked a little brighter. He turned and found a football player standing right next to him. The one from the living room.

The football player smiled and took the flashlight out of his hand and held it under his chin and made a face, like a Halloween lantern. He said, 'Good work, doc,' and turned away and used the beam up and down and side to side to paint his way back into the house. The doctor followed, using the same lit memories a second later. The football player said, 'Go back in the dining room now,' and shone the beam ahead, showing the doctor the way. The doctor went back to the table and the football player said, 'All of you stay right where you are, and don't move a muscle,' and then he closed the door on them.

His partner said, 'So what now?'

The guy with the flashlight said, 'We need to know if Reacher is awake or asleep.'

'We hit him pretty hard.'

'Best guess?'

'What's yours?'

The guy with the flashlight didn't answer. He stepped back down the hallway to the basement door. He pounded on it with the flat of his hand. He called, 'Reacher, turn the power back on, or something bad is going to happen up here.'

No response.

Silence.

The guy with the flashlight hit the door again and said, 'I'm not kidding, Reacher. Turn the damn power back on.'

No response.

Silence.

The other guy asked again, 'So what now?'

The guy with the flashlight said, 'Go get the doctor's wife.' He aimed the beam at the dining room door and his partner went in and came back out holding the doctor's wife by the elbow. The guy with the flashlight said, 'Scream.'

She said, 'What?'

'Scream, or I'll make you.'

She paused a beat and blinked in the light of the beam, and then she screamed, long and high and loud. Then she stopped and dead silence came back and the guy with the flashlight hammered on the basement door again and called, 'You hear that, asshole?'

No response.

Silence.

The guy with the flashlight jerked the beam back towards the dining room and his partner led the doctor's wife back down the hallway and pushed her inside and closed the door on her again. He said, 'So?'

The guy with the flashlight said, 'We wait for daylight.'

'That's four hours away.'

'You got a better idea?'

'We could call the mothership.'

'They'll just tell us to handle it.'

'I'm not going down there. Not with him.'

'Me either.'

'So what do we do?'

'We wait him out. He thinks he's smart, but he isn't.

383

We can sit in the dark. Anyone can. It ain't exactly rocket science.'

They followed the dancing beam back to the living room and sat side by side on the sofa with the old Remington propped between them. They clicked off the flashlight, to save the battery, and the room went pitch dark again, and cold, and silent.

Mahmeini's man walked parallel with the driveway for a hundred yards and then came up against a length of fence that ran south directly across his path. It defined the lower left-hand part of the crossbar of the hollow T that was the Duncans' compound. It was made of five-inch rails, all of them a little gnarled and warped, but easy enough to climb. He got over it without any difficulty and paused for a second with the three pick-up trucks and the Mazda parked to his left, and the southernmost house straight in front of him. The centre house was the only one that was dark. The southernmost and the northernmost houses both had light in them, faint and a little secondhand, as if only back rooms were in use and stray illumination was finding its way out to the front windows through internal passageways and open doors. There was the smell of wood smoke in the air. But no sound, not even talking. Mahmeini's man hesitated, choosing, deciding, making up his mind. Left or right?

Cassano and Mancini came on the compound from the rear, out of the dark and dormant field, and they stopped on the far side of the fence opposite the centre house, which was Jonas's, as far as they knew. It was closed up and dark, but both its neighbours had light in their kitchen windows, spilling out in bright bars across the weedy backyard gravel. The gravel was matted down into the dirt, but it was still marginally noisy, Cassano knew. He had walked across it earlier in the day, to find undisturbed locations for his phone conversations with Rossi. Their best play would be to stay on the wrong side of the fence, in the last of the field, and then head directly for their chosen point of entry. That would reduce the sound of their approach to a minimum. But which would be their chosen point of entry? Left or right? Jasper's place, or Jacob's?

All four Duncans were in Jasper's basement, hunting through old cartons for more veterinary anaesthetic. The last of the hog dope had been used on Seth's nose, and his busted hand was going to need something stronger anyway. Two fingers were already swollen so hard the skin was fit to burst. Jasper figured he had something designed for horses, and he planned to find it and flood Seth's wrist joint with it. He was no anatomist, but he figured the affected nerves had to pass through there somewhere. Where else could they go?

Seth was not complaining at the delay. Jasper figured he was taking it very well. He was growing up. He had been petulant after the broken nose, but now he was standing tall. Because he had captured his assailant all by himself, obviously. And because he was planning what to do with the guy next. The glow of achievement and the prospect of revenge were anaesthetics all by themselves.

Jonas asked, 'Is this it?' He was holding up a round pint bottle made of brown glass. Its label was stained and covered in long technical words, some of them Latin. Jasper squinted across the dim space and said, 'Good man. You found it.'

Then they heard footsteps on the floor above their heads.

FORTY-SEVEN

Jacob was first up the cellar stairs. His first thought was that a football player was checking in, but the floors in their houses were typical of old-style construction in rural America, built of boards cut from the hearts of old pines, thick and dense and heavy, capable of transmitting noise but not detail. So it was not possible to say who was in the house by sound alone. He saw no one in the hallway, but when he got to the kitchen he found a man in there, standing still, small and wiry, dark and dead-eyed, rumpled, not very clean, wearing a buttoned shirt without a tie, holding a knife in his left hand and a gun in his right. The knife was held low, but the gun was pointing straight at the centre of Jacob's chest.

Jacob stood still.

The man put his knife on the kitchen table and raised his forefinger to his lips.

Jacob made no sound.

Behind him his son and his brothers crowded into the kitchen, too soon to be stopped. The man moved the muzzle of his gun, left and right, back and forth. The four Duncans lined up, shoulder to shoulder. The man turned his wrist and moved the muzzle down and up, down and up, patting the air with it. No one moved.

The man said, 'Get on your knees.'

Jacob asked, 'Who are you?'

The man said, 'You killed my friend.'

'I didn't.'

'One of you Duncans did.'

'We didn't. We don't even know who you are.'

'Get on your knees.'

'Who are you?'

The little man picked up his knife again and asked, 'Which one of you is Seth?'

Seth Duncan paused a beat and then raised his good hand, like a kid in class.

The little man said, 'You killed my friend and you put his body in the trunk of your Cadillac.'

Jacob said, 'No, Reacher stole that car this afternoon. It was him.'

'Reacher doesn't exist.'

'He does. He broke my son's nose. And his hand.'

The gun didn't move, but the little man turned his head and looked at Seth. The aluminium splint, the swollen fingers. Jacob said, 'We haven't left here all day. But Reacher was at the Marriott. This afternoon, and this evening. We know that. He left the Cadillac there.'

'Where is he now?'

'We're not sure. Close by, we think.'

'How did he get back?'

'Perhaps he took your rental car. Did your friend have the key?'

The little man didn't answer.

Jacob asked, 'Who are you?'

'I represent Mahmeini.'

'We don't know who that is.'

'He buys your merchandise from Safir.'

'We don't know anyone of that name either. We sell to an Italian gentleman in Las Vegas, name of Mr Rossi, and after that we have no further interest.'

'You're trying to cut everyone out.'

'We're not. We're trying to get our shipment home, that's all.'

'Where is it?'

'On its way. But we can't bring it in until Reacher is down.'

'Why not?'

'You know why not. This kind of business can't be done in public. You should be helping us, not pointing guns at us.'

The little man didn't answer.

Jacob said, 'Put the gun away, and let's all sit down and talk. We're all on the same side here.'

The little man kept the gun straight and level and said, 'Safir's men are dead too.'

'Reacher,' Jacob said. 'He's on the loose.'

'What about Rossi's boys?'

'We haven't seen them recently.'

'Really?'

'I swear.'

The little man was quiet for a long moment. Then he said, 'OK. Things change. Life moves on, for all of us. From now on you will sell direct to Mahmeini.'

Jacob Duncan said, 'Our arrangement is with Mr Rossi.'

The little man said, 'Not any more.'

Jacob Duncan didn't answer.

Cassano and Mancini opted to try Jacob Duncan's place first. A logical choice, given that Jacob was clearly the head of the family. They backed off the fence a couple of paces and walked parallel with it to a spot opposite Jacob's kitchen window. The bar of yellow light coming out of it laid a bright rectangle on the gravel, but it fell six feet short of the base of the fence. They climbed the fence and skirted the rectangle, quietly across the gravel, Cassano to the right, Mancini to the left, and then they flattened themselves against the back wall of the house and peered in.

No one there.

Mancini eased open the door and Cassano went in ahead of him. The house was silent. No sound at all. No one awake, no one asleep. Cassano and Mancini had searched plenty of places, plenty of times, and they knew what to listen for.

They slipped back out to the yard and retraced their steps. They climbed back into the field and walked north in the dark and lined up again opposite Jasper's window. They climbed the fence and skirted the light. They flattened themselves against the wall and peered inside.

Not what they expected.

Not even close.

There was only one Iranian, not two. There was no

happy conversation. No smiles. No bourbon toasts. Instead, Mahmeini's man was standing there with a gun in one hand and a knife in the other, and all four Duncans were cowering away from him. The glass in the window was wavy and thin in places, and Jacob Duncan's urgent voice was faintly audible.

Jacob Duncan was saying, 'We have been in business a long time, sir, based on trust and loyalty, and we can't change things now. Our arrangement is with Mr Rossi, and Mr Rossi alone. Perhaps he can sell direct to you, in the future, now that Mr Safir seems to be out of the picture. Perhaps that might be of advantage. But that's all we can offer, not that such a thing is even ours to offer.'

The little man said, 'Mahmeini won't take half a pie when the whole thing is on the table.'

'But it isn't on the table. I repeat, we deal with Mr Rossi only.'

'Do you really?' the little man asked. He changed his position and stood sideways, and raised his arm level with his shoulder, and closed one eye, and tracked the gun slowly and mechanically back and forth, left and right along the line of men, like a great battleship turret traversing, pausing first on Seth, then on Jasper, then on Jonas, then on Jacob, and then back again, to Jonas, to Jasper, to Seth, and then back again once more. Finally the gun came to rest aimed square at Jonas. Right between his eyes. The little man's finger whitened on the trigger.

Then simultaneously the window and the little man's

head exploded, and the crowded room filled with powdered glass and smoke and the massive barking roar of a .45 gunshot, and blood and bone and brain slapped and spattered against the far wall, and the little man fell to the floor, and first Mancini and then Cassano stepped in from the yard.

After less than an hour the two football players were thoroughly bored with sitting in the dark. And not just bored, either, but unsettled and a little anxious, too, and irritated, and exasperated, and humiliated, because they were very aware that they were being beaten on a minute-to-minute basis, and being beaten on any basis did not come easy to them. They were not submissive people. They never came second. They were the big dogs, and being denied heat and light and NFL highlights was both insulting and totally inappropriate.

One said, 'We have a shotgun, damn it.'

The other said, 'It's a big basement. He could be any-where.'

'We have a flashlight.'

'Pretty weak.'

'Maybe he's still unconscious. It could be an actual fault, and we're sitting here like idiots.'

'He has to be awake by now.'

'So what if he is? He's one guy, and we have a shotgun and a flashlight.'

'He was a soldier.'

'That doesn't give him magic powers.'

'How would we do it?'

'We could tape the flashlight to the shotgun barrel.

Go down, single file, like they do in the movies. We'd see him before he sees us.'

'We're not supposed to kill him. Seth wants to do that himself, later.'

'We could aim low. Wound him in the legs.'

'Or make him surrender. That would be better. And he'd have to, wouldn't he? With the shotgun and all? We could tape him up, with the tape we use for the flashlight. Then he couldn't mess with the power again. We should have done that in the first place.'

'We don't have any tape, for either thing.'

'Let's look in the garage. If we find some tape, we'll think about doing it.'

They found some tape. They followed the flashlight beam through the hallway, through the kitchen, through the mud room, all the way to the garage, and right there on the workbench was a fat new roll of silver duct tape, still wrapped up, fresh from the store. They carried it back with them, not really sure if they were pleased or not. But they had promised themselves in a way, so they pulled off the plastic wrap and picked at the end of the tape and unwound a short length. They tried the flashlight against the shotgun barrel, working in the dim light of reflections off the walls. The flashlight fit pretty well, ahead of the forestock, and underslung because of the front sight above the muzzle, and jutting out a little because of its length. The plastic lens was about an inch in front of the gun. Satisfactory. But to get it secure they were going to have to wrap tape right over the thumb switch, which was a point of no return, of sorts. If they were going to do that, then they were going to have to act. No point in leaving the light burning and running the battery down all for nothing.

One asked, 'Well?'

Three hours before daylight. Boredom, irritation, exasperation, humiliation.

The other said, 'Let's do it.'

He propped the gun across his knees and held the flashlight in place. The first guy juggled the roll of tape, making sticky tearing noises, winding it around and around, like he was binding broken ribs with a bandage, until the whole assembly was fat and mummified. He ducked his head and bit off a nine-inch tail and pressed it down securely, and then he squeezed everything hard between his palms, and smoothed the edges of the tape with his fingers. The other guy lifted the gun off his knees and swung it left and right and up and down. The flashlight stayed solidly in place, its beam moving faithfully with the muzzle.

'OK,' he said. 'Cool. We're good to go. The light is like a laser sight. Can't miss.'

The first guy said, 'Remember, aim low. If you see him, jerk the barrel down and fire at his feet.'

'If he doesn't surrender first.'

'Exactly. First choice is to immobilize him. But if he moves, shoot him.'

'Where will he be?'

'Could be anywhere. Probably out of sight at the bottom of the stairs. Or hiding behind the water heater. It's big enough.'

They followed the light out to the hallway and stopped near the basement door. The guy with the gun said, 'You open it and step back and then get behind me. I'll go down slowly and I'll move the light around as much as I can. Tell me if you see him. We need to talk each other through this.'

'OK,' the first guy said. He put his hand on the knob. 'We sure about this?'

'I'm ready.'

'OK, on three. Your count.'

The guy with the gun said, 'One.'

Then, 'Two.'

The first guy said, 'Wait. He could be right behind the door.'

'At the top of the stairs?'

'Just waiting to jump out at us before we're ready.'

'You think? That would mean he's been waiting there a whole hour.'

'Sometimes they wait all day.'

'Snipers do. This guy wasn't a sniper.'

'But it's possible.'

'He's probably behind the water heater.'

'But he might not be.'

'I could fire through the door.'

'If he isn't there, that would alert him.'

'He'll be alerted anyway, as soon as he sees the flashlight beam coming down.'

'The door has a steel core. You heard what Seth said.'

The guy with the gun asked, 'So what do we do?'

The first guy said, 'We could wait for daylight.'

Boredom, irritation, exasperation, humiliation.

The guy with the gun said, 'No.'

'OK, so I'll open up real fast, and you fire one round immediately, right where his feet are. Or where they would be. Just in case. Don't wait and see. Just pull the trigger, whatever, right away.'

'OK. But then we'll have to go down real fast.'

'We will. He'll be in shock. I bet that gun is pretty loud. Ready?'

'I'm ready.' The guy with the gun estimated the arc of the swinging door and shuffled a foot closer and braced himself, the stock to his shoulder, one eye closed, his finger tight on the trigger.

The first guy said, 'Aim low.'

The oval of light settled on the bottom quarter of the door.

'On three. Your count.'

'One.'

'Two.'

'Three.'

The first guy turned the knob and flung the door wide open and the second guy fired instantly, with a long tongue of flame and a huge roaring twelve-gauge boom.

FORTY-EIGHT

Reacher had studied the electrical panel and had decided to cut all the circuits at once, because of human nature. He was pretty sure that the football players would turn out to be less than perfect sentries. Practically all sentries were less than perfect. It was any army's most persistent problem. Boredom set in, and attention wandered, and discipline eroded. Military history was littered with catastrophes caused by poor sentry performance. And football players weren't even military. Reacher figured the two in the house above him would stay on the ball for about ten or fifteen minutes, and then they would get lazy. Maybe they would make coffee or turn on the television, and relax, and get comfortable. So he gave them half an hour to settle in, and then he cut all the power at once, to be sure of killing whatever form of entertainment they had chosen.

Whereupon human nature would take over once again. The two in the house above him were used to dominance, used to getting their own way, used to having what they wanted, and accustomed to winning. Being denied television or warmth or coffee wasn't a major defeat or the end of the world, but for guys like that it was a proxy version of a poke in the chest on a sidewalk outside a bar. It was a provocation. It would eat away at them, and it would not be ignored for ever. Ultimately they would respond, because of ego. The response would start with anger, and then threats, and then intervention, which would be inexpert and badly thought out.

Human nature.

Reacher hit the circuit breakers and found the stairs in the dark and crept up to the top step and listened. The door was thick and tight in its frame, so he didn't hear much, except the bouts of hammering an inch from his ear, and then the scream from the doctor's wife, which he discounted immediately, because it was clearly staged. He had heard people scream before, and he knew the difference between real and fake.

Then he waited in the dark. All went quiet for the best part of an hour, which was longer than he expected. All bullies are cowards, but these two had a little more pussy in them than he had guessed. They had a shotgun, for God's sake, and he assumed they had found a flashlight. What the hell were they waiting for? Permission? Their mommies?

He waited.

Then eventually he sensed movement and deliberation on the other side of the door. He imagined that one guy would be holding the shotgun, and the other would be holding the flashlight. He guessed they would plan to shuffle down slowly behind the gun, like they had seen in the movies. He figured their primary intention would be to capture him and restrain him, not to kill him, partly because there was a large conceptual gap between sacking a quarterback and murdering a fellow human being, and partly because Seth Duncan would want him alive for later entertainment. So if they were going to shoot, they were going to aim low. And if they were smart, they were going to shoot immediately, because sooner or later they would have to realize that his own best move would be to be waiting right there at the top of the stairs, for the sake of surprise.

He felt the doorknob move, and then there was a pause. He put his back flat on the wall, on the hinge side of the door, and he put one foot on the opposite wall, at waist height, and he straightened his leg a little, and he clamped himself tight, and then he lifted his other foot into place, and he walked himself upward, palms and soles, until his head was bent against the stairwell ceiling and his butt was jammed four feet off the ground.

He waited.

Then the door flung open away from him and he got a split-second glimpse of a flashlight taped to a shotgun barrel, and then the shotgun fired instantly, at point-blank range and a downward angle, right under his bent knees, and the stairwell was instantly full of deafening noise and flame and smoke and dust and wood splinters from the stairs and shards of plastic from where the muzzle blast blew the protruding flashlight apart. Then the muzzle flash died and the house went pitch dark again and Reacher vaulted out of his clamped position, his right foot landing on the top stair, his left foot on the second, balanced, ready, using the bright fragment of visual memory his eyes had retained, leaning down to where he knew the shotgun must be, grabbing it two-handed, tearing it away from the guy holding it, backhanding it hard into where he knew the guy's face must be, achieving two results in one, making the guy disappear backward and recycling the shotgun's pump action both at once, loudly, *CRUNCH-crunch*, and then shouldering the swinging door away and feeling it crash against the second guy, and bursting out of the stairwell and firing into the floor, not really seeking to hit anyone but needing the brief light from the muzzle flash, seeing one guy down on his left and the other still up on his right, launching himself at that new target, clubbing the gun at the guy, cycling the action again against his face, *CRUNCH-crunch*, bringing him down, kicking hard against his fallen form, head, ribs, arms, legs, whatever he could find, then dancing back and kicking and stamping on the first guy in the dark, head, stomach, hands, then back to the second guy, then the first again, all unaimed and wild, overwhelming force indiscriminately applied, not giving up on it until well after he was sure no more was required.

Then he finally stopped and stepped back and stood still and listened. Most of what he heard was panicked breathing from the room on his left. The dining room. He called, 'Doctor? This is Reacher. I'm OK. No one got shot. Everything is under control now. But I need the power back on.'

No response.

Pitch dark.

'Doctor? The sooner the better, OK?'

He heard movement in the dining room. A chair scraping back, a hand touching a wall, a stray foot kicking a table leg. Then the door opened and the doctor came out, more sensed than seen, a presence in the dark. Reacher asked him, 'Do you have another flashlight?'

The doctor said, 'No.'

'OK, go switch on the circuit breakers for me. Take care on the stairs. They might be a little busted up.'

The doctor said, 'Now?'

'In a minute,' Reacher said. Then he called out, 'You two on the floor? Can you hear me? You listening?'

No response. Pitch dark. Reacher moved forward, carefully, sliding his feet flat on the floor, feeling his way with the toes of his boots. He came up against the first guy's head, and worked out where his gut must be, and jammed the shotgun muzzle down into it, hard. Then he pivoted onward, like pole vaulting, and found the second guy a yard away. They were on their backs, roughly in a straight line, lying symmetrically, feet to feet. Reacher stood between them and kicked the side of his left boot against one guy's sole and his right boot against the other's. He got set and aimed the shotgun at the floor in front of him and rehearsed a short arc, left and then right and back again, like a batter in the box loosening up his swing ahead of a pitch. He said, 'If you guys move at all, I'm going to shoot you both in the nuts, one after the other.'

No response.

Nothing at all.

Reacher said, 'OK, doctor, go ahead. Take care now.' He heard the doctor feel his way along the wall, heard his feet on the stairs, slow cautious steps, fingertips trailing, the creak and crack of splintered boards underfoot, and then the confident click of a heel on the solid concrete below.

Ten seconds later the lights came back on, and the television picture jumped back to life, and the excited announcers started up again, and the heating system clicked and caught and hummed and whirred. Reacher screwed his eyes shut against the sudden dazzle and then forced them open to narrow slits and looked down. The two guys on the floor were battered and bleeding. One was out cold, and the other was dazed. Reacher fixed that with another kick to the head, and then he looked around and saw the roll of duct tape on the sofa. Five minutes later both guys were trussed up like chickens and bound together back to back by their necks and their waists and their ankles. Together they were far too heavy to move, so Reacher left them right where they were, on the hallway floor, hiding the ruined patch of parquet where he had fired into the ground.

Job done, he thought.

Job done, Jacob Duncan thought. Seth's Cadillac had been retrieved from the road, and both dead Iranians had been stripped to the skin and their clothes had been dumped in the kitchen woodstove. Their bodies had been hauled to the door and left in the yard for later disposal. Then the kitchen wall and the floor had been wiped clean, and the broken glass had been swept up, and the busted window had been patched with tape and wax paper, and Seth's hand had been taken care of, and then Jasper had dragged extra chairs in from another room, and now all six men were sitting close together around the table, the four Duncans plus Cassano and Mancini, all of them tight and collegial and elbow to elbow. The Knob Creek had been brought out, and toasts had been drunk, to each other, and to success, and to future partnership.

Jacob Duncan had leaned back and drunk with considerable private satisfaction and personal triumph, because he felt fully vindicated. He had glimpsed Cassano at the window, had seen the aimed .45, and had talked a little longer and louder than was strictly necessary, proclaiming his undying loyalty to Rossi, cementing the relationship beyond a reasonable doubt, all the while keeping his nerve and waiting for Cassano to shoot, which he had eventually. Quick thinking, courage under pressure, and a perfect result. Doubled profits stretched ahead in perpetuity. Reacher was locked safely underground, with two good men on guard. And the shipment was on its way, which was the most wonderful thing of all, because as always a small portion of it would be retained for the family's personal use. A kind of benign shrinkage. It made the whole crazy operation worthwhile.

Jacob raised his glass and said, 'Here's to us,' because life was good.

Reacher found a paring knife in a kitchen drawer and cut the decapitated remains of the flashlight off the shotgun barrel. Laymen misunderstood gunpowder. A charge powerful enough to propel a heavy projectile through the air at hundreds of miles an hour did so by creating a shaped bubble of exploding gas energetic enough to destroy anything it met on its way out of the barrel. Which was why military flashlights were made of mctal and mounted with the lens behind the muzzle, not in front of it. He tossed the shattered plastic in the trash, and then he looked around the kitchen and asked, 'Where's my coat?'

The doctor's wife said, 'In the closet. When we came back in I took all the coats and hung them up. I kind of scooped yours up along the way. I thought I should hide it. I thought you might have useful stuff in it.'

Reacher glanced into the hallway. 'Those guys didn't search my pockets?'

'No.'

'I should kick them in the head again. It might raise their IQ.'

The doctor's wife told him to sit down in a chair. He did, and she examined him carefully, and said, 'Your nose looks really terrible.'

'I know,' Reacher said. He could see it between his eyes, purple and swollen, out of focus, an unexpected presence. He had never seen his own nose before, except in a mirror.

'My husband should take a look at it.'

'Nothing he can do.'

'It needs to be set.'

'I already did that.'

'No, seriously.'

'Believe me, it's as set as it's ever going to get. But you

404

could clean the cuts, if you like. With that stuff you used before.'

Dorothy Coe helped her. They started with warm water, to sponge the crusted blood off his face. Then they got to work with the cotton balls and the thin astringent liquid. The skin had split in big U-shaped gashes. The open edges stung like crazy. The doctor's wife was thorough. It was not a fun five minutes. But finally the job was done, and Dorothy Coe rinsed his face with more water, and then patted it dry with a paper towel.

The doctor's wife asked, 'Do you have a headache?'

'A little bit,' Reacher said.

'Do you know what day it is?'

'Yes.'

'Who's the president?'

'Of what?'

'The Nebraska Corn Growers.'

'I have no idea.'

'I should bandage your face.'

'No need,' Reacher said. 'Just lend me a pair of scissors.'

'What for?'

'You'll see.'

She found scissors and he found the roll of duct tape. He cut a neat eight-inch length and laid it glue-side up on the table. Then he cut a two-inch length and trimmed it to the shape of a triangle. He stuck the triangle glue-side to glue-side in the centre of the eight-inch length, and then he picked the whole thing up and smoothed it into place across his face, hard and tight, a broad silver slash that ran from one cheekbone to the other, right under his eyes. He said, 'This is the finest field dressing in the world. The Marines once flew me from the Lebanon to Germany with nothing but duct tape keeping my lower intestine in.'

'It's not sterile.'

'It's close enough.'

'It can't be very comfortable.'

'But I can see past it. That's the main thing.'

Dorothy Coe said, 'It looks like war paint.'

'That's another point in its favour.'

The doctor came in and stared for a second. But he didn't comment. Instead he asked, 'What happens next?'

FORTY-NINE

They went back to the dining room and sat in the dark, so they could watch the road. There were three more Cornhuskers out there somewhere, and it was possible they would come in and out on rotation, swapping duties, spelling each other. Like shift work. Reacher hoped they all showed up sooner or later. He kept the duct tape and the Remington close by.

The doctor said, 'We haven't heard any news.'

Reacher nodded. 'Because you weren't allowed to use the phone. But it rang, and so you think something new has happened.'

'We think three new things have happened. Because it rang three times.'

'Best guess?'

'The gang war. Three men left, three phone calls. Maybe they're all dead now.'

'They can't all be dead. The winner must still be alive, at least. Murder-suicide isn't normally a feature of gang fights.'

'OK, then maybe it's two dead. Maybe the man in the Cadillac got the Italians.'

Reacher shook his head. 'More likely the other way around. The man in the Cadillac will get picked off very easily. Because he's alone, and because he's new up here. This terrain is very weird. It takes some getting used to. The Italians have been here longer than him. In fact they've been here longer than me, and I feel like I've been here for ever.'

The doctor's wife said, 'I don't see how this is a gang war at all. Why would a criminal in Las Vegas or wherever just step aside because two of his men got hurt in Nebraska?'

Reacher said, 'The two at the motel got more than hurt.'

'You know what I mean.'

'Think about it,' Reacher said. 'Suppose the big guy is at home in Vegas, taking it easy by the pool, smoking a cigar, and his supplier calls him up and says he's cutting him out of the chain. What does the big guy do? He sends his boys over, that's what. But his boys just got beat. So he's bankrupt now. He's fresh out of threats. He's powerless. It's over for him.'

'He must have more boys.'

'They all have more boys. They can choose to fight two on two, or ten on ten, or twenty on twenty, and there's always a winner and there's always a loser. They accept the referee's decision and they move on. They're like rutting stags. It's in their DNA.'

'So what kind of gangs are they?'

'The usual kind. The kind that makes big money out of something illegal.'

'What kind of something?'

408

'I don't know. But it's not gambling debts. It's not something theoretical on paper. It's something real. Something physical. With weight, and dimensions. It has to be. That's what the Duncans do. They run a transportation company. So they're trucking something in, and it's getting passed along from A to B to C to D.'

'Drugs?'

'I don't think so. You don't need to truck drugs south to Vegas. You can get them direct from Mexico or South America. Or California.'

'Drug money, then. To be laundered in the casinos. From the big cities in the East, maybe coming through Chicago.'

'Possible,' Reacher said. 'Certainly it's something very valuable, which is why they're all in such an uproar. It has to be the kind of thing where you smile and rub your hands when you see it rolling in through the gate. And it's late now, possibly, which is why there are so many boots on the ground up here. They're all anxious. They all want to see it arrive, because it's physical, and valuable. They all want to put their hands on it and babysit their share. But first of all, they want to help bust up the logjam.'

'Which is what?'

'Me, I think. Either the Duncans are late for some other reason and they're using me as an excuse, or this is something a stranger absolutely can't be allowed to see. Maybe the area has to be sanitized before it can come in. Have you ever been told to stay away from anywhere for periods of time?'

'Not really.'

'Have you ever seen any weird stuff arrive? Any big unexplained vehicles?'

'We see Duncan trucks all the time. Not so much in the winter.'

'I heard the harvest trucks are all in Ohio.'

'They are. Nothing more than vans here now.'

Reacher nodded. 'One of which was missing from the depot. Three spaces, two vans. So what kind of a thing is valuable and fits in a van?'

Jacob Duncan saw that Roberto Cassano's mind had been changed once and for all by the dead man in the Cadillac's trunk. Mancini's, too. Now they both accepted that Reacher was a genuine threat. How else could they react? The dead man had no marks on him. None at all. So what had Reacher done to him? Frightened him to death? Jacob could see both Cassano and Mancini thinking about it. So he waited patiently and eventually Cassano looked across the table at him and said, 'I apologize, most sincerely.'

Jacob looked back and said, 'For what, sir?'

'For before. For not taking you seriously about Reacher.'

'Your apology is accepted.'

'Thank you.'

'But the situation remains the same,' Jacob said. 'Reacher is still a problem. He's still on the loose. And nothing can happen until he's accounted for. We have three men looking for him. They'll work all night and all day if necessary. Just as long as it takes. Because we don't want Mr Rossi to feel we're in any way the junior partner in this new relationship. That's very important to us.'

Cassano said, 'We should go out too.'

'All of us?'

'I meant me and Mancini.'

'Indeed,' Jacob Duncan said. 'Perhaps you should. Perhaps we should turn the whole thing into a competition. Perhaps the prize should be to speak first when we sit down to renegotiate the profit share.'

'There are more of you than us.'

'But you are professionals.'

'You know the neighbourhood.'

'You want a fairer fight? Very well. We'll send our three boys home to bed, and I'll send my son out in their place. Alone. That's one against two. As long as it takes. May the best man win. To the victor, the spoils, and so on, and so forth. Shall I do that?'

'I don't care,' Cassano said. 'Do whatever you want. We'll beat all of you, however many you put out there.' He drained his glass and set it back on the table and stood up with Mancini. They walked out together, through the back door, to their car, which was still parked in the field, on the other side of the fence. Jacob Duncan watched them go, and then he sat back in his chair and relaxed. They would waste some long and fruitless hours, and then all in good time Reacher would be revealed, and Rossi would take the small subliminal hit, and the playing field would tilt, just a little, but enough. Jacob smiled. Success, triumph, and vindication. Subtlety, and finesse.

*   *   *

The road outside the dining room window stayed dark. Nothing moved on it. The two Cornhusker vehicles were still parked on the shoulder beyond the fence. One was an SUV and one was a pick-up truck. Both looked cold and inert. Overhead the moon came and went, first shining faintly through thin cloud, and then disappearing completely behind thicker layers.

The doctor said, 'I don't like just sitting here.'

'So don't,' Reacher said. 'Go to bed. Take a nap.'

'What are you going to do?'

'Nothing. I'm waiting for daylight.'

'Why?'

'Because you don't have street lights here.'

'You're going out?'

'Eventually.'

'Why?'

'Places to go, things to see.'

'One of us should stay awake. To keep an eye on things.'

'I'll do that,' Reacher said.

'You must be tired.'

'I'll be OK. You guys go get some rest.'

'Are you sure?'

'Positive.'

They didn't need much more persuading. The doctor looked at his wife and they headed off together, and then Dorothy Coe followed them, presumably to a spare room somewhere. Doors opened and closed and water ran and toilets flushed, and then the house went quiet. The heating system whirred and the taped-up football players muttered and grunted and snored on the hallway floor, but apart from that Reacher heard nothing at all. He sat upright on the hard chair and kept his eyes open and stared out into the dark. The duct tape bandage itched his face. He did OK for ten or twenty minutes, and then he slipped a little, like he knew he would, like he often had before, into a kind of trance, like suspended animation, half awake and half asleep, half effective and half useless. He was a less than perfect sentry, and he knew it. But then, practically all sentries were less than perfect. It was any army's most persistent problem.

Half awake and half asleep. Half effective and half useless. He heard the car and he saw its lights, but it was a whole stubborn second before he understood he wasn't dreaming.

FIFTY

The car came in from the right, from the east, preceded by headlight beams and road noise. It slowed to a walk and passed behind the parked Cornhusker pick-up, and then it rolled on and passed behind the parked SUV. Then it turned and nosed into the driveway, with a crunch and a squelch from its wheels on the gravel, and then it stopped.

And then Reacher saw it.

There was enough light scatter and enough reflection to identify it. It was the dark blue Chevrolet. The Italians. Reacher picked up the Remington. The car stayed where it was. No one got out. It was sixty yards away, half in and half out of the driveway mouth. Just sitting there, lights on, idling. A tactical problem. Reacher had three innocent non-combatants in a wood-frame house. There were two parked cars on the driveway and two on the road, for cover. There were two opponents and the house had windows and a door both front and back.

Not ideal conditions for a gun battle.

Best hope would be for the Italians to approach the front door on foot. Game over, right there. Reacher could swing the door open and fire point blank. But the Italians weren't approaching on foot. They were just sitting in the car. Doing nothing. Talking, maybe. And scouting around. Reacher could see dim flashes of white as necks craned and heads turned. They were discussing something.

Angelo Mancini was saying, 'This is a waste of time. He ain't in there. He can't be. Not unless he's hanging out with three of their football players.'

Roberto Cassano nodded. He glanced over his shoulder at the pick-up truck and the SUV on the shoulder, and then he glanced ahead at the gold GMC Yukon on the driveway. It was parked in front of an older truck. He said, 'That's the old woman's ride, from the farm.'

Mancini said, 'Sleepover time.'

'I guess Mahmeini's boy was right about something. They know the doctor is the weak link. They've got him staked out.'

'Not much of a trap, all things considered. Not with their cars parked out front. No one is going to walk into that.'

'Which is good for us, in a way. They're wasting their resources. Which gives us a better chance somewhere else.'

'Do you want to check here? Just in case?'

'What's the point? If he's in there, he's already their prisoner.'

'That's what I was thinking. But then I thought, not necessarily. They could be his prisoner.'

415

'One against three?'

'You saw what he did to the guy in the Cadillac's trunk.'

'I don't know. I kind of want to check, I guess. And maybe we should. But you heard the man. This is a competition now. We can't waste time.'

'Wouldn't take much time.'

'I know. But we'll look like idiots if he's not in there. The football players will be straight on the phone to the Duncans, all yukking it up about how we came looking in a place he couldn't possibly be.'

'No one said there are style points involved.'

'But there are. There are always style points involved. This is a long game. There's a lot of money involved. If we lose face we'll never get it back.'

'So where?'

Cassano looked again at the old woman's truck. 'If she's here, then her house is empty tonight. And people looking for places to hide love empty houses.'

Reacher saw them back out and drive away again. At first he didn't understand why. Then he concluded they were looking for Seth Duncan. They had pulled up, they had eyeballed the parked cars, they had seen that the Mazda wasn't among them, and they had gone away again. Logical. He put the Remington back on the floor, and planted his feet, and straightened his back, and stared out into the darkness.

Nothing else happened for ninety long minutes. No one came, no one stirred. Then pale streaks of dawn started showing in the sky to Reacher's right. They came in low and silver and purple, and the land slowly lightened from black to grey, and the world once again took solid shape, all the way to the far horizon. Rags of tattered cloud lit up bright overhead, and a knee-high mist rose up off the dirt. A new day. But not a good one, Reacher thought. It was going to be a day full of pain, both for those who deserved it, and for those who didn't.

He waited.

He couldn't get his Yukon out, because he had no key for Dorothy Coe's pick-up truck. It was possibly in her coat, but he wasn't inclined to go look for it. He was in no hurry. It was wintertime. Full daylight was still an hour away.

Five hundred miles due north, up in Canada, just above the 49th Parallel, because of the latitude, dawn came a little later. The first of the morning light filtered down through the needles of the towering pine and touched the white van in its summer picnic spot at the end of the rough grassy track. The driver woke in his seat, and blinked, and stretched. He had heard nothing all night long. He had seen nothing. No bears, no coyotes, no red foxes, no moose, no elk, no wolves. No people. He had been warm, because he had a sleeping bag filled with down, but he had been very uncomfortable, because panel vans had small cabs, and he had spent the night folded into a seat that didn't recline very far. It was always on his mind that the cargo in the back was treated better than he was. It rode more comfortably. But then, it was expensive and hard to get, and he wasn't. He was a realistic man. He knew how things worked.

He climbed out and took a leak against the pine's ancient trunk. Then he ate and drank from his meagre supplies, and he pushed his palms against his aching back, and he stretched again to work out the kinks. The sky was brightening. It was his favourite time for a run to the border. Light enough to see, too early for company. Ideal. He had just twenty miles to go, most of them on an unmapped forest track, to a point a little less than four thousand yards north of the line. The transfer zone, he called it. The end of the road for him, but not for his cargo.

He climbed back in the cab and started the engine. He let it warm and settle for a minute while he checked the dials and the gauges. Then he selected first gear, and released the parking brake, and turned the wheel, and moved away slowly, at walking speed, lurching and bouncing down the rough grassy track.

Reacher heard sounds at the end of the hallway. A toilet flushing, a faucet running, a door opening, a door closing. Then the doctor came limping past the dining room, stiff with sleep, mute with morning. He nodded as he passed, and he skirted the football players, and he headed for the kitchen. A minute later Reacher heard the gulp and hiss of the coffee machine. The sun was up enough to show a reflection in the window of the SUV parked beyond the fence. Webs of frost were glinting and glittering in the fields.

The doctor came in with two mugs of coffee. He

was dressed in a sweater over pyjamas. His hair was uncombed. The damage on his face was lost in general redness. He put one mug in front of Reacher and threaded his way around and sat in a chair on the opposite side of the table.

He said, 'Good morning.'

Reacher said nothing.

The doctor asked, 'How's your nose?'

Reacher said, 'Terrific.'

The doctor said, 'There's something you never told me.'

Reacher said, 'There are many things I never told you.'

'You said twenty-five years ago the detective neglected to search somewhere. You said because of ignorance or confusion.'

Reacher nodded, and took a sip of his coffee.

The doctor asked, 'Is that where you're going this morning?'

'Yes, it is.'

'Will you find anything there after twenty-five years?'

'Probably not.'

'Then why are you going?'

'Because I don't believe in ghosts.'

'I don't follow.'

'I hope you never have to. I hope I'm wrong.'

'Where is this place we're talking about?'

'Mrs Coe told me that fifty years ago two farms were sold for a development that never happened. The out-buildings from one of them are still there. Way out in a field. A barn, and a smaller shed.'

The doctor nodded. 'I know where they are.'

'People plough right up to them.'

'I know,' the doctor said. 'I guess they shouldn't, but why let good land go to waste? The subdivisions were never built, and they're never going to be. So it's something for nothing, and God knows these people need it. It's yield that doesn't show up on their mortgages.'

'So when Detective Carson came up here twenty-five years ago, what did he see? In the early summer? He saw about a million acres of waist-high corn, and he saw some houses dotted around here and there, and he saw some outbuildings dotted around here and there. He stopped in at every house, and every occupant said they'd searched their outbuildings. So Carson went away again, and that old barn and that old shed fell right between the cracks. Because Carson's question was, did you search *your* outbuildings? Everyone said yes, probably quite truthfully. And Carson saw the old barn and the old shed and quite naturally assumed they must belong to someone, and that therefore they had indeed been looked at, as promised. But they didn't belong to anyone, and they hadn't been looked at.'

'You think that was the scene of the crime?'

'I think Carson should have asked that question twenty-five years ago.'

'There won't be anything there. There can't be. Those buildings are ruins now, and they must have been ruins then. They've been sitting there empty for fifty years, in the middle of nowhere, just mouldering away.'

'Have they?'

'Of course. You said it yourself, they don't belong to anyone.'

'Then why have they got wheel ruts all the way to the door?'

'Have they?'

Reacher nodded. 'I hid a truck in the smaller shed my first night. No problem getting there. I've seen worse roads in New York City.'

'Old ruts? Or new ruts?'

'Hard to tell. Both, probably. Many years' worth, I would say. Quite deep, quite well established. No weeds. Not much traffic, probably, but some. Some kind of regularity. Enough to keep the ruts in shape, anyway.'

'I don't understand. Who would use those places now? And for what?'

Reacher said nothing. He was looking out the window. The light was getting stronger. The fields were turning from grey to brown. The parked pick-up beyond the fence was all lit up by a low ray.

The doctor asked, 'So you think someone scooped the kid up and drove her to that barn?'

'I'm not sure any more,' Reacher said. 'They were harvesting alfalfa at the time, and there will have been plenty of trucks on the road. And I'm guessing this whole place felt a bit happier back then. More energetic. People doing this and that, going here and there. The roads were probably a little busier than they are now. Probably a lot busier. Maybe even too busy to risk scooping a kid up against her will in broad daylight.'

'So what do you think happened to her?'

Reacher didn't answer. He was still looking out the

window. He could see the knots in the fence timbers. He could see clumps of frozen weeds at the base of the posts. The front lawn was dry and brittle with cold.

Reacher said, 'You're not much of a gardener.'

'No talent,' the doctor said. 'No time.'

'Does anyone garden?'

'Not really. People are too tired. And working farmers hardly ever garden. They grow stuff to sell, not to look at.'

'OK.'

'Why do you want to know?'

'I'm asking myself, if I was a little girl with a bicycle, and I loved flowers, where would I go to see some? No point coming to a house like this, for instance. Or any house, probably. Or anywhere at all, really, because every last inch of ground is ploughed for cash crops. I can think of just three possibilities. I saw two big rocks in the fields, with brambles around them. Nice wild flowers in the early summer, probably. There may be more just like them, but it doesn't matter anyway, because in the early summer they would be completely inaccessible, because you'd have to wade a mile through growing corn just to get to them. But there was one other place I saw the same kind of brambles.'

'Where was that?'

'Around the base of that old barn. Windblown seeds, I guess. People plough close, but they leave some space.'

'You think she rode there on her own?'

'I think it's possible. Maybe she knew the one place she was sure to see flowers. And maybe someone knew she knew.'

422

FIFTY-ONE

The Duncans had moved on to Jonas's kitchen, because the taped window in Jasper's was leaking cold air, and the burning fabric in the stove was making smoke and smells. They had stopped drinking bourbon and had started drinking coffee. The sun was up and the day was already forty minutes old. Jacob Duncan checked the clock on the wall and said, 'The sun is up in Canada too. Dawn was about ten minutes ago. I bet the shipment is already rolling. I know that boy. He likes an early start. He's a good man. He doesn't waste time. The transfer will be happening soon.'

The road that led south from Medicine Hat petered out after Pakowki Lake. The blacktop surface finished with a ragged edge, and then there was a quarter-mile of exposed roadbed, just crushed stone bound with tar, and then that finished too, in a forest clearing with no apparent exit. But the white van lined up between two pines and drove over stunted underbrush and found itself on a rutted track, once wide, now neglected, a firebreak running due south, designed with flames and westerly winds in mind. The van rolled slowly, tipping left and right, its wheels moving up and down independently, like walking. Ahead of it was nothing but trees, and then the Montana town of Hogg Parish. But the van would stop halfway there, a little more than two miles short of the border, at the northern limit of the safe zone, exactly symmetrical with its opposite number in America, which was no doubt already in place and waiting, all fresh and energetic and ready for the last leg of the journey.

The doctor went back to the kitchen and returned with more coffee. He said, 'It could have been an accident. Maybe she went inside the barn.'

Reacher said, 'With her bicycle?'

'It's possible. We don't know enough about her. Some kids would dump a bike on the track, and others would wheel it inside. It's a matter of personality. Then she might have injured herself on something in there. Or gotten stuck. The door is jammed now. Maybe it was baulky then. She could have gotten trapped. No one would have heard her shouting.'

'And then what?'

'An eight-year-old without food or water, she wouldn't have lasted long.'

'Not a pleasant thought,' Reacher said.

'But preferable to some of the alternatives.'

'Maybe.'

'Or she might have gotten hit by a truck. Or a car. On the way over there. You said it yourself, the roads could have been busy. Maybe the driver panicked and hid the body. And the bike with it.'

'Where?'

'Anywhere. In that barn, or miles away. In another county. Another state, even. Maybe that's why nothing was ever found.'

'Maybe,' Reacher said again.

The doctor went quiet.

Reacher said, 'Now there's something you're not telling me.'

'There's time.'

'How much?'

'Probably half an hour.'

'Before what?'

'The other three Cornhuskers will come here for breakfast. Their buddies are here, so this is their temporary base. They'll make my wife cook for them. They enjoy feudal stuff like that.'

'I figured,' Reacher said. 'I'll be ready.'

'One of them is the guy who broke your nose.'

'I know.'

The doctor said nothing.

Reacher said, 'Can I ask you a question?'

'What?'

'Is your garage like your garden or like your television set?'

'More like my television set.'

'That's good. So turn around and watch the road. I'll be back in ten.' Reacher picked up the Remington and found his way through the kitchen to the mud room lobby. He found the door that led to the garage. It was a big space, empty because the Subaru was still at the motel, and neat and clean, with a swept floor and no visible chaos. There were shelving racks all along one wall, loaded with the stuff that hadn't been in the basement. There was a workbench along a second wall, well organized, again neat and clean, with a vice, and a full-width pegboard above, loaded with tools logically arrayed.

Reacher unloaded the Remington, five remaining shells from the magazine and one from the breech. He turned the gun upside down and clamped it in the vice. He found an electric jigsaw and fitted a woodcutting blade. He plugged it in and fired it up and put the dancing blade on the walnut and sawed off the shoulder stock, first with a straight cut across the narrowest point, and then again along a curving line that mirrored the front contour of the pistol grip. Two more passes put a rough chamfer on each raw edge, and then he found a rasp and cleaned the whole thing up, with twists of walnut falling away like grated chocolate, and then he finished the job with a foam pad covered with coarse abrasive. He blew off the dust and rubbed his palm along the result, and he figured it was satisfactory.

He swapped the jigsaw blade for a metal cutter, a fine blued thing with tiny teeth, and he laid it against the barrel an inch in front of the forestock. The saw screeched and screamed and howled and the last foot of the barrel fell off and rang like a bell against the floor. He found a metal file and cleaned the burrs of steel off the new muzzle, inside and out. He released the vice and lifted the gun out and pumped it twice, *crunch-crunch*, *crunch-crunch*, and then he reloaded it, five in the magazine and one in the breech. A sawn-off with a pistol grip, not much longer than his forearm.

He found the coat closet on his way back through the house and retrieved his winter parka. The Glock and the switchblade were still in the pockets, along with the two screwdrivers and the wrench. He used the switchblade to slit the lining inside the left-hand pocket, so the sawn-off would go all the way in. He put the coat on. Then he unlocked the front door, and went back to the dining room to wait.

The Cornhuskers came in separately, one by one, the first of them right on time, exactly thirty minutes after the doctor had spoken, in a black pick-up truck he left on the road. He jogged up the driveway and pushed in through the door like he owned the place, and Reacher laid him out with a vicious blow to the back of the head, from behind, with the wrench. The guy dropped to his knees and toppled forward on his face. Reacher invested a little time and effort in dragging him onward across the shiny wood, and then he taped him up, quick and dirty, not a permanent job, but enough for the moment. The crunch of the wrench and the thump of the guy falling and Reacher's grunting and groaning woke the doctor's wife and Dorothy Coe. They came out of their rooms wearing bathrobes. The doctor's wife looked at the new guy on the floor and said, 'I guess they're coming in for breakfast.'

Reacher said, 'But today they're not getting any.'

Dorothy Coe asked, 'What about tomorrow?'

'Tomorrow is a new day. How well do you know Eleanor Duncan?'

'She's not to blame for anything.'

'She'll be hauling your harvest this year. She's going to be in charge.'

Dorothy Coe said nothing.

The doctor's wife said, 'You want us to stay out of the way?'

'Might be safer,' Reacher said. 'You don't want one of these guys falling on you.'

'Another one coming,' the doctor called from the dining room, soft and urgent.

The second guy went down exactly the same as the first, and in the same place. There was no room left to drag him forward. Reacher folded his legs at the knees so the door would close, and then he taped him up right there.

The last to arrive was the guy who had broken Reacher's nose.

And he didn't come alone.

FIFTY-TWO

Awhite SUV parked on the road beyond the fence, and the guy who had broken Reacher's nose climbed out of the driver's seat. Then the passenger door opened and the kid called John got out. The kid Reacher had left at the depot. *Go to bed*, Reacher had said. But the kid hadn't gone to bed. He had hung out until he heard that things were safe, and then he had come out to claim his share of the fun.

Dumb, dumb, dumb.

The hallway was almost too crowded to move. It was full of football players, four of them lying around like carcasses, like beached whales, limbs tapcd, heads flopping. Reacher picked his way around them and watched out a window. The two late arrivals were making their way past Dorothy Coe's pick-up, past John's own Yukon, hustling through the damp and the cold, heading for the door, full of high spirits.

Reacher opened the door and stepped out to meet them head on. He drew his sawn-off across his body, a long high exaggerated movement like a pirate drawing an ancient flintlock pistol, and he held it right-handed, elbow bent and comfortable, and he aimed it at the guy who had hit him. But he looked at John.

'You let me down,' he said.

Both guys came to a dead stop and stared at him a little more urgently than he thought was warranted, until he remembered the duct tape on his face. Like war paint. He smiled and felt it pucker. He looked back at the guy who had hit him and said, 'It was nothing that couldn't be fixed. But I'm not certain you'll be able to say the same.'

Neither guy spoke. Reacher kept his eyes on the guy who had hit him and said, 'Take out your car keys and toss them to me.'

The guy said, 'What?'

'I'm bored with John's Yukon. I'm going to use your truck the rest of the day.'

'You think?'

'I'm pretty sure.'

No response.

Reacher said, 'It's make-your-mind-up time, boys. Either do what I tell you, or get shot.'

The guy dipped into his pocket and came out with a bunch of keys. He held them up briefly, to prove what they were, and then he tossed them underhand to Reacher, who made no attempt to catch them. They bounced off his coat and landed on the gravel. Reacher wanted his left hand free and his attention all in one place. He looked at the guy again and asked, 'So how does your nose feel right now?'

The guy said, 'It feels OK.'

'It looks like it has been busted before.'

The guy said, 'Two times.'

Reacher said, 'Well, they say three is a lucky number. They say the third time's the charm.'

Nobody spoke.

Reacher said, 'John, lie face down on the ground.'

John didn't move.

Reacher fired into the ground at John's feet. The gun boomed and kicked and the sound rolled away across the land, loud and dull, like a quarry explosion. John howled and danced. Not hit, but stung in the shins by fragments of gravel kicked up by the blast. Reacher waited for quiet and pumped the gun, a solid *crunch-crunch*, probably the most intimidating sound in the world. The husk of the spent cartridge ejected and flew through the air and landed near the car keys and skittered away.

John got down on the ground. First he got on his knees, awkwardly, like he was in church, and then he spread his hands and lowered himself face down, reluctantly, like a bad-tempered coach had demanded a hundred push-ups. Reacher called over his shoulder, 'Doctor? Bring me the duct tape, would you?'

No response from inside the house.

Reacher called, 'Don't worry, doctor. There won't be any comebacks. Never again. This is the last day. Tomorrow you'll be living like normal people. These guys will be unemployed, heading back where they came from, looking for new jobs.'

There was a long, tense pause. Then a minute later the doctor came out with the tape. He didn't look at the two guys. He kept his face averted and his eyes down.

431

Old habits. He gave the roll to Reacher and ducked back inside. Reacher tossed the tape to the guy who had hit him and said, 'Make it so your buddy can't move his arms or legs. Or I will, by some other method, probably including spinal injury.'

The guy caught the roll of tape and got to work. He wrapped John's wrists with a tight three-layer figure of eight, and then he wrapped the waist of the eight in the other direction, around and around. Plastic handcuffs. Reacher had no idea of the tensile strength of duct tape in terms of engineering numbers, but he knew no human could pull it apart lengthways. The guy did the same to John's ankles, and Reacher said, 'Now hog-tie him. Join it all up.'

The guy folded John's feet up towards his butt and wrapped tape between the wrist restraints and the ankle restraints, four turns, each about a foot long. He squeezed it all tight and stood back. Reacher took out his wrench and held it up. There was a little blood and hair on it, from the previous two guys. He dropped it on the ground behind him. He took out his switchblade. He dropped it on the ground behind him. He took out his Glock pistol. He dropped it on the ground behind him. Then he turned and laid the sawn-off next to it. He shrugged out of his coat and let it fall. It covered all four weapons. He looked at the guy who had hit him and said, 'Fair fight. You against me. Second-string Nebraska football against the U.S. Army. Bare knuckles. No rules. If you can get past me, you're welcome to use anything you can find under my coat.'

The guy looked blank for a second, and then he smiled

a little, as if the sun had come out, as if an unbelievable circumstance had unveiled itself right in front of him, as if a hole had opened up in a tight defence, as if suddenly he had a straight shot to the end zone. He came up on his toes, and angled his body, and bunched his right fist up under his chin, and got ready to lead with his left.

Reacher smiled too, just a little. The guy was dancing around like the Marquess of Queensberry. He had no idea. No idea at all. Maybe the last fight he had seen was in a Rocky movie. He was six-seven and three hundred pounds, but he was nothing more than a prize ox, big and dumb and shiny, going up against a gutter rat.

A 250-pound gutter rat.

The guy stepped in and bobbed and weaved for a minute, up on his toes, jiggling around, ducking and diving, wasting time and energy. Reacher stood perfectly still and gazed at him, wide-eyed with peripheral vision, focusing nowhere and everywhere at once, hyper-alert, watching the guy's eyes and his hands and his feet. And soon enough the left jab came in. The obvious first move, for a right-handed man who thought he was in a boxing ring. Any guy's left jab followed the same basic trajectory as his straight left, but much less forcefully, because it was powered by the arm only, snapping out from the elbow, with no real contribution from the legs or the upper body or the shoulders. No real power. Reacher watched the big pink knuckles getting closer, and then he moved his own left hand, fast, a blur, whipping it in and up and out like a man flailing backhanded at a wasp, and he slapped at the inside of the guy's wrist, hard enough to alter the line of the incoming jab, hard enough to deflect

433

it away from his face and send it buzzing harmlessly over his moving shoulder.

His shoulder was moving because he was already driving hard off his back foot, jerking forward, twisting at the waist, building torque, hurling his right elbow into the gap created by turning the guy counterclockwise an inch, aiming to hit him with the elbow right on the outer edge of his left eye socket, hoping to crack his skull along the line of his temple. *No rules.* The blow landed with all 250 pounds of moving mass behind it, a solid, jarring impact Reacher felt all the way down to his toes. The guy staggered back. He stayed on his feet. Evidently his skull hadn't cracked, but he was feeling it. He was feeling it bad, and his mouth was opening ready to howl, so Reacher shut it again for him with a vicious uppercut under the chin, convulsive, far from elegant, but effective. The guy's head snapped back in a mist of blood and bounced forward again off his massive deltoids and Reacher tried for his other eye socket with his left elbow, a ferocious in-and-out snap from the waist, and then he put a forearm smash from the right into the guy's throat, a real home run swing, and then he kneed him in the groin, and danced behind him and kicked him hard in the back of the knees, a sweeping, scything action, so that the guy's legs folded up under him and he went down heavily on his back on the path.

Six blows, three seconds.

No rules.

Second-string Nebraska football against the U.S. Army.

But the guy was tough. Or afraid. Or both. Either way, he didn't quit. He started scrabbling around on his back, like a turtle, trying to get up again, making botched snow angels in the gravel, his head snapping left and right. Maybe the decent thing would have been to let him take an eight-count, but having your opponent on the floor is gutter rat heaven, the absolute object of the exercise, a precious gift never to be spurned, so Reacher stilled him by kicking him hard in the ear, and then he stamped down hard with his heel in the guy's face, like an appalled homeowner stomping a cockroach, and the crunch of the guy's shattering nose was clearly audible over all the generalized panting and grunting and groaning and moaning.

Game over. Eight blows in six seconds, which was grievously slow and laborious by Reacher's standards, but then, the guy was huge, and he had an athlete's tone and stamina, and he was accustomed to a certain amount of physical punishment. He had been competitive, just barely. In the ballpark, almost. Not the worst Reacher had ever seen. Four years of college ball was probably equivalent to four days of Ranger training, and plenty of people Reacher had known hadn't even made day three.

He taped the guy up where he lay, with plastic handcuffs linked to four turns around the guy's own neck and ankle restraints linked to four turns around John's neck. Then he stepped back into the hallway and did a better job on the two who had come in first. He slid them around on the shiny parquet and taped them together, back to back, like the two from the middle of the night. He stood up and caught his breath.

Then a phone rang, muted and distant.

The phone turned out to be Dorothy Coe's cell. Its ring was muted and distant because it was with her, behind a closed door, in her room. She came out with it in her hand, and looked between it and the four taped guys on the hallway floor, and then she smiled, as if at a hidden irony, as if normality was intruding on a thoroughly abnormal day. She said, 'That was Mr Vincent at the motel. He wants me to work this morning. He has guests.'

Reacher asked, 'Who are they?'

'He didn't say.'

Reacher thought for a moment, and said, 'OK.' He told the doctor to keep a medical eye on all six of the captured football players, and then he went back out to the gravel path and put his coat back on. He reloaded the pockets with his improvised arsenal, and he found the car keys where they lay on the stones, and then he headed down the driveway to the white SUV parked beyond the fence.

Eldridge Tyler moved, just a little, but enough to keep himself comfortable. He was into his second hour of daylight. He was a patient man. His eye was still on the scope. The scope was still trained on the barn door, six inches left of the judas hole, six inches down. The rifle's forestock was still bedded securely on the bags of rice. The air was wet and thick, but the sun was bright and the view was good.

But the big man in the brown coat hadn't come.

Not yet.

And perhaps he never would, if the Duncans had been successful during the night. But Tyler was still fully on the ball, because he was cautious by nature, and he always took his tasks seriously, and maybe the Duncans hadn't been successful during the night. In which case the big man would show up very soon. Why would he wait? Daylight was all he needed.

Tyler took his finger off the trigger, and he flexed his hand, once, twice, and then he put his finger back.

FIFTY-THREE

The white SUV turned out to be a Chevy Tahoe, which seemed to Reacher's untutored eye the exact same thing as a GMC Yukon. The cabin was the same. All the controls were the same. All the dials were the same. It drove just the same, big and sloppy and inexact, all the way back to the two-lane, where Reacher turned right and headed south. There was mist, but the sun was well up in the east. The day was close to two hours old.

He slowed and coasted and then parked on the shoulder, two hundred yards short of the motel. From the north he could see nothing of it except the rocket sign and the big round lounge. He got out of the truck and walked on the blacktop, slow and quiet. His angle changed with every step. First he saw the burned-out Ford. It was in the main lot, down on its rims, black and skeletal, with two shapes behind the glassless windows, both of them burned as smooth and small as seals. Then he saw the doctor's Subaru, outside room six, jagged and damaged, but still a living thing in comparison to the Ford.

Then he saw the dark blue Chevrolet.

It was parked beyond the Subaru, outside room seven, or eight, or both, at a careless angle, at the end of four short gouges in the gravel. Frustrated men, tired and angry, jamming to a stop, ready for rest.

Reacher came in off the road and walked to the lounge door, as quietly as he could on the loose stones, past the Ford. It was still warm. The heat of the fire had scorched fantastic whorls into the metal. The lounge door was unlocked. Reacher stepped inside and saw Vincent behind the reception desk. He was in the act of hanging up the telephone. He stopped and stared at Reacher's duct-tape bandage. He asked, 'What the hell happened to you?'

'Just a scratch,' Reacher said. 'Who was on the phone?'

'It was the morning call. The same as always. Like clockwork.'

'The phone tree?' Reacher asked.

Vincent nodded.

'And?'

'Nothing to report. Three Cornhusker vehicles were tooling around all night, kind of aimlessly. Now they've gone somewhere else. All four Duncans are in Jacob's house.'

'You have guests here,' Reacher said.

'The Italians,' Vincent said. 'I put them in seven and eight.'

'Did they ask about me?'

Vincent nodded. 'They asked if you were here. They asked if I had seen you. They're definitely looking for you.'

'When did they get here?'

'About five this morning.'

Reacher nodded in turn. A wild goose chase all night long, no success, eventual fatigue, no desire to drive an hour south to the Marriott and an hour back again, hence the local option. They had probably planned to nap for a couple of hours, and then saddle up once more, but they were oversleeping. Human nature.

'They woke me up,' Vincent said. 'They were very bad-tempered. I don't think I'm going to get paid.'

'Which one of them shot the guys in the Ford?'

'I can't tell them apart. One did the shooting, and the other one set fire to the car.'

'And you saw that with your own eyes?'

'Yes.'

'Would you go to court and say so?'

'No, because the Duncans are involved.'

'Would you if the Duncans weren't involved?'

'I don't have that much imagination.'

'You told me.'

'Privately.'

'Tell me again.'

'One of them shot the guys and the other one burned their car.'

'OK,' Reacher said. 'That's good enough.'

'For what?'

'Call them,' Reacher said. 'One minute from now. In their rooms. Talk in a whisper. Tell them I'm in your lot, right outside your window, looking at the wreck.'

'I can't be involved in this.'

'This is the last day,' Reacher said. 'Tomorrow will be different.'

'Forgive me if I prefer to wait and see.'

'Tomorrow there are going to be three kinds of people here,' Reacher said. 'Some dead, some sheepish, and some with a little self-respect. You need to get yourself in that third group.'

Vincent said nothing.

'You know Eleanor Duncan?' Reacher asked.

'She's OK,' Vincent said. 'She was never part of this.'

'She'll be taking over. She'll be hauling your stuff tomorrow.'

Vincent said nothing.

'Call the Italians one minute from now,' Reacher said. He stepped back out to the lot and walked on the silver baulks of timber, past room one, past room two, past three and four and five and six, and then he looped around behind room seven and room eight, and came out again near room nine. He stood in a narrow gap shaped like an hourglass, the circular bulk of room eight right there in front of him, close enough to touch, room seven one building along, the Chevy and the Subaru and the burned-out Ford trailing away from him, south to north, in a line. He took out the dead Iranian's Glock and checked the chamber.

All set.

He waited.

He heard the room phones ring, first one, then the other, both of them faint behind walls and closed doors. He pictured men rolling over on beds, struggling awake, sitting up, blinking, checking the time, looking around the unfamiliar spaces, finding the phones on the night-stands, answering them, listening to Vincent's urgent whispered messages.

He waited.

He knew what was going to happen. Whoever opened up first would wait in the doorway, half in and half out, gun drawn, leaning, craning his neck, watching for his partner to emerge. Then there would be gestures, sign language, and a cautious joint approach.

He waited.

Room eight opened up first. Reacher saw a hand on the jamb, then a pistol pointing almost vertical, then a forearm, then an elbow, then the back of a head. The pistol was a Colt Double Eagle. The forearm and the elbow were covered with a wrinkled shirtsleeve. The head was covered in uncombed black hair.

Reacher backed off a step and waited. He heard room seven's door open. He sensed more than heard the rustle of starched cotton, the silent debate, the pointing and the tapped chests assigning roles, the raised arms indicating directions, the spread fingers indicating timings. The obvious move would be for the guy from room eight to leapfrog ahead and then duck around behind room six and circle the lounge on the blind side and hit the lot from the north, while the guy from room seven waited a beat and then crept up directly from the south. A no-brainer.

They went for it. Reacher heard the farther guy step out and wait, and the nearer guy step out and walk. Eight paces, Reacher thought, before the latter passed the former. He counted in his head, and on six he stepped out, and on seven he raised the Glock, and on eight he screamed FREEZE FREEZE FREEZE and both men froze, already surrendering, guns held low near their thighs, tired, just woken up, confused and disoriented. Reacher stayed with the full-on experience and screamed DROP YOUR WEAPONS PUT YOUR WEAPONS ON THE GROUND and both men complied instantly, the heavy stainless pieces hitting the gravel in unison. Reacher screamed STEP AWAY STEP AWAY STEP AWAY and both men stepped away, out into the lot, isolated, far from their rooms, far from their car.

Reacher breathed in and looked at them from behind. They were both in pants and shirts and shoes. No jackets, no coats. Reacher said, 'Turn around.'

They turned around.

The one on the left said, 'You.'

Reacher said, 'Finally we meet. How's your day going so far?'

No answer.

Reacher said, 'Now turn out your pants pockets. All the way. Pull the linings right out.'

They obeyed. Quarters and dimes and bright new pennies rained down, and tissues fluttered, and cell phones hit the gravel. Plus a car key, with a bulbous black head and a plastic fob shaped liked a big number one. Reacher said, 'Now back away. Keep going until I tell you to stop.'

They walked backward, and Reacher walked forward with them, keeping pace, eight steps, ten, and then Reacher arrived at where their Colts had fallen and said, 'OK, stop.' He ducked down and picked up one of the guns. He ejected the magazine and it fell to the ground and he saw it was full. He picked up the other gun. Its magazine was one short.

'Who?' he asked.

The guy on the left said, 'The other one.'

'The other what?'

'The Iranians. You got one, we got the other. We're on the same side here.'

'I don't think so,' Reacher said. He moved on towards the small pile of pocket junk and picked up the car key. He pressed the button set in the head and he heard the Chevy's doors unlock. He said, 'Get in the back seat.'

The guy on the left asked, 'Do you know who we are?'

'Yes,' Reacher said. 'You're two jerks who just got beat.'

'We work for a guy named Rossi, in Las Vegas. He's connected. He's the kind of guy you can't mess with.'

'Forgive me if I don't immediately faint with terror.'

'He's got money, too. Lots of money. Maybe we could work something out.'

'Like what?'

'There's a deal going down here. We could cut you in. Make you rich.'

'I'm already rich.'

'You don't look it. I'm serious. Lots of money.'

'I've got everything I need. That's the definition of affluence.'

The guy paused a beat, and then he started up again, like a salesman. He said, 'Tell me what I can do to make this right for you.'

'You can get in the back seat of your car.'

'Why?'

'Because my arms are sore and I don't want to drag you.'

'No, why do you want us in the car?'

'Because we're going for a drive.'

'Where?'

'I'll tell you after you get in.'

The two men glanced at a spot in the air halfway between them, not daring to let their eyes meet, not daring to believe their luck. An opportunity. Them in the back, a solo driver in the front. Reacher tracked them with the Glock, all the way to the car. One got in on the near side, and the other looped around the trunk. Reacher saw him glance onward, at the road, at the open fields beyond, and then Reacher saw him give up on the impulse to run. Flat land. Nowhere to hide. A modern nine-millimetre sidearm, accurate out to fifty feet or more. The guy opened his door and ducked his head and folded himself inside. The Impala was not a small car, but it was no limousine in the rear. Both guys had their feet trapped under the front seats, and even though they were neither large nor tall, they were both cramped and close together.

Reacher opened the driver's door. He put his knee on the seat and leaned inside. The guy who had spoken before asked, 'So where are we going?'

'Not far,' Reacher said.

'Can't you tell us?'

'I'm going to park next to the Ford you burned.'

'What, just up there?'

'I said not far.'

'And then what?'

'Then I'm going to set this car on fire.'

The two men glanced at each other, not understanding. The one who had spoken before said, 'You're going to drive with us in the back? Like, loose?'

'You can put your seat belts on if you like. But it's hardly worth it. It's not very far. And I'm a careful driver. I won't have an accident.'

The guy said, 'But,' and then nothing more.

'I know,' Reacher said. 'I'll have my back turned. You could jump me.'

'Well, yes.'

'But you won't.'

'Why not?'

'You just won't. I know it.'

'Why wouldn't we?'

'Because you'll be dead,' Reacher said, and he shot the first guy in the forehead, and then the second, a brisk double tap, no pause, *bang bang*, no separation at all. The rear window shattered and blood and bone and brain hit the remains of the glass, delayed, slower than the bullets, and the two guys settled peacefully, slower still, like afterthoughts, like old people falling asleep, but with open eyes and fat beads of purple welling out of the neat holes in their brows, welling and lengthening and becoming slow lazy trickles that ran down to the bridges of their noses.

Reacher backed out of the car and straightened up and looked north. Nine-millimetre Parabellums. Fine ammunition. The two slugs were probably hitting the ground right about then, a mile farther on, burning their way into the frigid dirt.

Reacher checked room seven and found a wallet in a coat. There was a Nevada driver's licence in it, made out in the name of Roberto Cassano, at a local Las Vegas address. There were four credit cards and a little more than ninety dollars in cash. Reacher took sixty and got in the Impala and drove forty yards and parked tight up against the shell of the Ford. He gave the sixty bucks to Vincent in the lounge, two rooms, one night, and then he borrowed rags and matches, and as soon as the fuse was set in the Chevy's filler neck he hustled back to the Tahoe he had left on the shoulder. The first major flames were showing as he drove by, and he saw the fuel tank go up in his mirror, about four hundred yards later. The angle he was at and the way the fireball rose and then smoked and died made the motel sign look real, like it was a genuine working rocket, like it was blasting off for the infinite emptiness of space.

Eldridge Tyler heard the gunshots. Two faint pops, rapid, a double tap, very distant, really nothing more than vague percussive holes in the winter air. Not a rifle. Not a shotgun. Tyler knew firearms, and he knew the way their sounds travelled across the land. A handgun, he thought, three or four miles away. Maybe the hunt was over. Maybe the big man was down. He moved again, easing one leg, easing the other, stretching one arm, stretching the other, rolling his shoulders, rotating his neck. He dug into his canvas tote bag and came out with a bottle of water and a brown-bread sandwich. He put both items within easy reach. Then he peered out through the space left by the missing louvre, and took a careful look around. Because maybe the big man wasn't down. Tyler took nothing for granted. He was a cautious man. His job was to watch and wait, and watch and wait he would, until he was told different.

He leaned up on his hands and craned around and looked behind him. The sun had moved a little south of east and low slanting light was falling on the shelter's entrance. The tripwire's plastic insulation had dewed over with dawn mist and was glistening faintly. Ten minutes, Tyler thought, before it dried and went invisible again.

He turned back and lay flat and snuggled behind the scope again, and he put his finger on the trigger.

FIFTY-FOUR

Dorothy Coe used the guest bathroom and showered fast, ready for work at the motel. She stopped in the kitchen to drink coffee and eat toast with the doctor and his wife, and then she changed her mind about her destination. She asked, 'Where did Reacher go?'

The doctor said, 'I'm not sure.'

'He must have told you.'

'He's working on a theory.'

'He knows something now. I can feel it.'

The doctor said nothing.

Dorothy Coe asked, 'Where did he go?'

The doctor said, 'The old barn.'

Dorothy Coe said, 'Then that's where I'm going too.'

The doctor said, 'Don't.'

Reacher drove south on the two-lane road and coasted to a stop a thousand yards beyond the barn. It stood on the dirt a mile away to the west, close to its smaller companion, crisp in the light, canted down at one corner like it was kneeling. Reacher got out and grasped the roof bar and stood on the seat and hauled himself up

449

and stood straight, like he had before on the doctor's Subaru, but higher this time, because the Tahoe was taller. He turned a slow circle, the sun in his eyes one way, his shadow immense the other. He saw the motel in the distance to the north, and the three Duncan houses in the distance to the south. Nothing else. No people, no vehicles. Nothing was stirring.

He stepped down on the hood and jumped down to the ground. He ignored the tractor ruts and walked straight across the dirt, a direct line, homing in, aiming for the gap between the barn and the smaller shelter.

Eldridge Tyler heard the truck. Just the whisper of faraway tyres on coarse blacktop, the hiss of exhaust through a catalytic converter, the muted thrash of turning components, all barely audible in the absolute rural silence. He heard it stop. He heard it stay where it was. It was a mile away, he thought. It was not one of the Duncans with a message. They would come all the way, or call on the phone. It was not the shipment, either. Not yet. The shipment was still hours away.

He rolled on his side and looked back at the tripwire. He rehearsed the necessary moves in his head, should someone come: snatch back the rifle, roll on his hip, sit up, swivel around, and fire point blank. No problem.

He faced front again and put his eye on the scope and his finger on the trigger.

Ten minutes later Reacher was halfway to the barn, assessing, evaluating, counting in his head. He was alone. He was the last man standing. All ten football players were down, the Italians were down, the Arabs in the Ford were down, the remaining Iranian was accounted for, and all four Duncans were holed up in one of their houses. Reacher felt he could trust that last piece of information. The local phone tree seemed to be an impeccable source of human intelligence. Humint, the army called it, and the army Reacher had known would have been crazy with jealousy at such vigilance.

He walked on, bending his line a little to centre himself in the gap between the buildings. The barn was on his right, and the smaller shelter was on his left. The brambles at their bases looked like hasty freehand shading on a pencil drawing. Dry sticks in the winter, possibly a riot of colour and petals in the summer. Possibly an attraction. Kids' bikes could handle the tractor ruts. Balloon tyres, sturdy frames.

He walked on.

Eldridge Tyler stilled his breathing and concentrated hard and strained to hear whatever sounds there were to be heard. He knew the land. The earth was always moving, heating, cooling, vibrating, suffering tiny tremors and microscopic upheavals, forcing small stones upward through its many layers to the broken surfaces above, where they lay in the ruts and the furrows, waiting to be stepped on, to be kicked, to be crunched together, to be sent clicking one against the other. It was not possible to walk silently across open land. Tyler knew that. He kept his eye to the scope, his finger on the trigger, and his ears wide open.

*   *   *

Reacher stopped fifty yards out and stood absolutely still, looking at the buildings in front of him and juggling circular thoughts in his head. His theory was either all the way right or all the way wrong. The eight-year-old Margaret Coe had come for the flowers, but she hadn't gotten trapped by accident. The bike proved the proposition. A child impulsive enough to drop a bike on a path might have dashed inside a derelict structure and injured herself badly. But a child earnest and serious enough to wheel her bike in with her would have taken care and not gotten hurt at all. Human nature. Logic. If there had been an accident, the bike would have been found outside. The bike had not been found outside, therefore there had been no accident.

And: she had gone to the barn voluntarily, but she had not gone inside the barn voluntarily. Why would a child looking for flowers have gone inside a barn? Barns held no secrets for farm children. No mysteries. A kid interested in colours and nature and freshness would have felt no attraction for a dark and gloomy space full of decaying smells. Had the slider even worked twenty-five years ago? Could a kid have moved it? The building was a century old, and it had been rotting since the day it was finished. The slider was jammed now, and it might have been jammed then, and in any case it was heavy. Alternatively, could an eight-year-old kid have lifted a bike through the judas hole? A bike with big tyres and a sturdy frame and awkward pedals and handlebars?

No, someone had done it for her.

A fifth man.

Because the theory didn't work without the existence

of a fifth man. The barn was irrelevant without a fifth man. The flowers were meaningless without a fifth man. The Duncans were alibied, but Margaret Coe had disappeared even so. Therefore someone else had been there, either by chance or on purpose.

Or not.

Circular logic.

All the way right, or all the way wrong.

To be all the way wrong would be frustrating, but no big deal. To be all the way right meant the fifth man existed, and had to be considered. He would be bound to the Duncans, by a common purpose, by a terrible shared secret, always and for ever. His cooperation could be assumed. His loyalty and service were guaranteed, either by mutual interest or by coercion. In an emergency, he would help out.

Reacher looked at the barn, and the smaller shelter.

If the theory was right, the fifth man would be there.

If the fifth man was there, the theory was right.

Circular logic.

Reacher had seen the buildings twice before, once by night, and once by day. He was an observant man. He had made his living by noticing details. He was *living* because he noticed details. But there was nothing much to be seen from fifty yards. Just a side view of two old structures. Best move would be for the guy to be inside the barn, off centre, maybe six feet from the door, sitting easy in a lawn chair with a shotgun across his knees, just waiting for his target to step through in a bar of bright light. Second-best move would put the guy in the smaller shelter a hundred and twenty yards away, prone with a rifle on the mezzanine half-loft, his eye to a scope, watching through the ventilation louvres Reacher had noticed on both his previous visits. A harder shot, but maybe the guy thought of himself more as a rifleman than a close-quarters brawler. And maybe the inside of the barn was sacrosanct, never to be seen by an outsider, even one about to die. But in either case, the smaller shelter would have to be checked first, as a matter of simple logic.

Reacher headed left, straight for the long east wall of the smaller shelter, not fast, not slow, using an easy cadence halfway between a march and a stroll, which overall was quieter than either rushing or creeping. He stopped six feet out, where the dry brambles started, and thought about percentages. Chances were good the fifth man had served, or at least had been exposed to military culture through friends and relatives. A heartland state, big families, brothers and cousins. Probably not a specialist sniper, maybe not even an infantryman, but he might know the basics, foremost among which was that when a guy lay down and aimed forward, he got increasingly paranoid about what was happening behind him. Human nature. Irresistible. Which was why snipers operated in two-man teams, with spotters. Spotters were supposed to acquire targets and calculate range and windage, but their real value was as a second pair of eyes, and as a security blanket. All things being equal, a sniper's performance depended on his breathing and his heart rate, and anything that helped quiet either one was invaluable.

So would the fifth man have brought a spotter of

his own? A sixth man? Probably not, because there was already a sixth man away driving the grey van, so a spotter would be a seventh man, and seven was a large and unwieldy number for a local conspiracy. So the fifth man was most likely on his own, and therefore at the minimum he would have set up a physical early-warning system, either fresh gravel or broken glass scattered along the approaches, or possibly a tripwire at the shelter's entrance, something noisy, something definitive, something to help him relax.

Reacher stepped back from the brambles and walked towards the entrance. He stopped a foot short of level, and listened hard, but he heard nothing at all. He breathed the air, hoping to detect the kind of faint chemical tang that would betray the presence of a parked vehicle, benzenes and cold hydrocarbons riding the earthier organic odours of dirt and old wood, but his broken nose was blocked with clots of blood and he had no sense of smell. None at all. So he just drew the sawn-off with his right hand and the Glock with his left and inched forward and peered right.

And saw a tripwire.

It was a length of thin electrical cable, low voltage, like something a hobbyist would buy at Radio Shack, insulated with black plastic, tied tight and shin-high across the open end of the structure. It was filmy with the part-dried remains of the morning dew, which meant it had been in place for at least two hours, since before dawn, which in turn meant the fifth man was a serious, cautious person, and patient, and committed, and fully invested. And it meant he had been contacted the day before, by the Duncans, maybe in the late afternoon, as a belt-and-suspenders back-up plan, which confirmed, finally, that the barn was indeed important.

Reacher smiled.

All the way right.

He stayed clear of the tangled vine and walked a silent exaggerated curve. He worked on the assumption that most people were right-handed, so he wanted to be on the guy's left before he announced himself, because that would give the guy's rifle a longer and more awkward traverse before it came to bear on target. He watched the ground and saw nothing noisy there. He saw a truck deep inside the shelter, parked halfway under the mezzanine floor. Its tailgate was open, the dirty white paint on its edge pale in the gloom. He approached within six inches of the wire and stood absolutely still, letting his eyes adjust. The inside of the shelter was dark, except for thin random bars of sunlight coming through gaps between warped boards. The truck was still and inert. It was a Chevy Silverado. Above it, a long step up from its crew-cab roof, was the loft, and there was a humped shape up there, butt and legs and back and elbows, all preceded by the soles of a pair of boots, all brightly backlit by daylight coming in through the ventilation louvres. The fifth man, prone with a rifle.

Reacher stepped over the tripwire, left foot, then right, high and careful, and eased into the shadows. He inched along the left-hand tyre track, where the earth was beaten smooth, like walking a tightrope, slow and cautious, holding his breath. He made it to the back of the truck. From there he could see the fifth man's feet, but nothing more. He needed a better angle. He needed to be up in the truck's load bed, which meant that a silent approach was no longer an option. The sheet metal would clang and the suspension would creak and from that point onward the morning would get very noisy very fast.

He took a deep breath, through his mouth, in and out.

FIFTY-FIVE

Eldridge Tyler heard nothing at all until a sudden shattering cacophony erupted ten feet behind him and eight feet below. There was some kind of heavy metal implement beating on the side of his truck and then footsteps were thumping into the load bed and a loud nasal voice was screaming STAY STILL STAY STILL and then a shotgun fired into the roof above his back with a pulverizing blast in the closed space and the voice yelled STAY STILL STAY STILL again and the shotgun *crunch-crunched* ready for the next round and hot spent buckshot pattered down on him and wormy sawdust drifted off the damaged boards above him and settled all around him like fine khaki snow.

Then the shelter went quiet again.

The voice said, 'Take your hands off your gun, or I'll shoot you in the ass.'

Tyler took his right forefinger off the trigger and eased his left hand out from under the barrel. The voice was behind him, to the left. He jacked up on his palms and turned a little, arching his back, craning his neck. He saw a big guy, six-five at least, probably two-fifty, wearing a big brown parka and a wool cap. He was holding himself awkwardly, like he was stiff. Like he was hurting, exactly as advertised, except for a length of duct tape stuck to his face. Nobody had mentioned that. He was holding a sawn-off shotgun and a big metal wrench. He was right-handed. His shoulders were broad. The centre of his skull was about seventy-three inches off the floor of the Silverado's load bed. Exactly as calculated.

Tyler closed his eyes.

Reacher saw a man somewhere between sixty and seventy years old, broad and not tall, with thin grey hair and a seamed, weather-beaten face. He was dressed in multiple layers topped by an old flannel shirt and wool pants. Beyond him and beneath him was the gleam of fine walnut and smooth gunmetal. An expensive hunting rifle, resting on what looked like stacked bags of rice. There was a bottle of water next to the rice, and what looked like a sandwich.

Reacher said, 'Your tripwire worked real well, didn't it?'

The guy didn't answer.

Reacher asked, 'What's your name?'

The guy didn't answer.

Reacher said, 'Come down from there. Leave your rifle where it is.'

The guy didn't move. His eyes were closed. He was thinking. Reacher saw him running through the same basic calculation any busted man makes: *How much do they know?*

Reacher told him, 'I know most of it. I just need the last few details.'

The guy said nothing.

Reacher said, 'Twenty-five years ago a little girl came here to see flowers. Probably she came every Sunday. One particular Sunday you were here too. I want to know if you were here by chance or on purpose.'

The guy opened his eyes. Said nothing.

Reacher said, 'I'm going to assume you were here on purpose.'

The guy didn't answer.

Reacher said, 'It was early summer. I don't know much about flowers. Maybe they hadn't been open long. I want to know how fast the Duncans picked up on the pattern. Three weeks? Two?'

The guy moved a little. His head stayed where it was, but his hands crept back towards the gun. Reacher said, 'Fair warning. I'll shoot you if that muzzle starts turning towards me.'

The guy stopped moving, but he didn't bring his hands back.

Reacher said, 'I'm going to assume two weeks. They noticed her the first Sunday, they watched for her the second Sunday, they had you in place for the third go-round.'

No response.

Reacher said, 'I want you to confirm it for me. I want to know when the Duncans called you. I want to know when they called those boys to build the fence. I want to hear about the plan.'

No response.

Reacher said, 'You want to tell me you don't know what I'm talking about?'

No reply.

'OK,' Reacher said. 'I'm going to assume you do know what I'm talking about.'

No comment.

Reacher said, 'I want to know how you knew the Duncans in the first place. Was it a matter of shared enthusiasms? Were you all members of the same disgusting little club?'

The guy didn't answer.

Reacher asked, 'Had you done it before somewhere?'

No reply.

Reacher asked, 'Or was it your first time?'

No reply.

Reacher said, 'You need to talk to me. It's your only way of staying alive.'

The guy said nothing. He closed his eyes again, and his hands started creeping back under his body again, blindly, all twisted and awkward. He was up on one hip and one elbow, curled around, the bottom of his ribcage facing Reacher like the open mouth of a bucket. The muzzle of the rifle jerked left a little. The guy had his hand on the forestock. He didn't want to stay alive. He was going to commit suicide. Not with the rifle, but by moving the rifle. Reacher knew the signs. Suicide by cop, it was called. Not uncommon, after arrests for certain kinds of crimes.

Reacher said, 'It had to come to an end sometime, right?'

461

The guy nodded. Just a tiny movement of his head, almost not there at all. The rifle kept on moving, sudden inch after sudden inch, pulling and snagging, trapped between the wooden boards and the guy's awkward clothing.

Reacher said, 'Open your eyes. I want you to see it coming.'

The guy opened his eyes. Reacher let him fumble the rifle through ninety degrees, and then he shot him with the sawn-off, in the gut, another tremendous twelve-gauge blast in the stillness, at an angle that drove the small steel buckshot balls upward through the guy's stomach and deep into his chest cavity. He died more or less instantly, which was a privilege Reacher figured had not been offered to young Margaret Coe.

Reacher waited a long moment and then he stepped up on the roof of the Silverado's cab and climbed on to the half-loft shelf and squatted next to the dead man. He rolled him off the rifle and climbed down with it. It was a fancy toy, custom built around a standard Winchester bolt action. Very expensive, probably, but as good a way of wasting money as any other. There was a .338 Magnum in the breech and five more in the magazine. Reacher thought the .338 was overkill at a hundred and twenty yards against a human target, but he figured the firepower was about to be useful.

He carried the rifle to the mouth of the shelter and stepped over the tripwire again and stood with the cold sun on his face. Then he looped around and headed for the barn.

The judas hole was hinged to open outward and was secured with the kind of lock normally seen on a suburban front door. There was a corroded brass keyhole plate the diameter of an espresso cup, and there would be a steel tongue behind it, which would be snicked into a pressed steel receptacle, which would be rabbeted into the jamb and held by two screws. The jamb was the main slider itself, which was a sturdy item. Reacher aimed the fancy rifle from a foot away and fired twice, at where he thought the screws might be, and then twice more, at a different angle. The Magnums did a pretty good job. The door sagged open half an inch before catching on splinters. Reacher jammed his fingertips in the crack and pulled hard. A jagged piece of wood the length of his arm split off and fell to the floor and the door came free. Reacher folded the door all the way back, and then he stood in the sun for a second, and then he stepped inside the barn.

FIFTY-SIX

Reacher stepped out of the barn again eleven minutes later, and saw Dorothy Coe's truck driving up the track towards him. There were three people in the cab. Dorothy herself was at the wheel, and the doctor was in the passenger seat, and the doctor's wife was jammed in the space between them. Reacher stood absolutely still, completely numb, blinking in the sun, the captured rifle in one hand, the other hand hanging free. Dorothy Coe slowed and stopped and waited thirty feet away, a cautious distance, as if she already knew.

A long minute later the truck doors opened and the doctor climbed out. His wife slid across the vinyl and joined him. Then Dorothy Coe got out on her side. She stood still, shielded by the open door, one hand on its frame. Reacher blinked one last time and ran his free hand over his taped face and walked down to meet her. She was quiet for a moment, and then she started the same question twice, and stopped twice, before getting it all the way out on the third attempt.

She asked, 'Is she in there?'

Reacher said, 'Yes.'

'Are you sure?'

'Her bike is in there.'

'Still? After all these years? Are you sure it's hers?'

'It's as described in the police report.'

'It must be all rusted.'

'A little. It's dry in there.'

Dorothy Coe went quiet. She was staring at the western horizon, a degree or two south of the barn, as if she couldn't look directly at it. She was completely still, but her hand was clenched hard on the truck's door frame. Her knuckles were white.

She asked, 'Can you tell what happened to her?'

Reacher said, 'No,' which was technically true. He was no pathologist. But he had been a cop for a long time, and he knew a thing or two, and he could guess.

She said, 'I should go look.'

He said, 'Don't.'

'I have to.'

'Not really.'

'I want to.'

'Better if you don't.'

'You can't stop me.'

'I know.'

'You have no right to stop me.'

'I'm asking you, that's all. Please don't look.'

'I have to.'

'Better not.'

'I don't have to listen to you.'

'Then listen to her instead. Listen to Margaret. Pretend she grew up. Imagine what she would have become. She wouldn't have been a lawyer or a scientist. She loved

465

flowers. She loved colours and forms. She would have been a painter or a poet. An artist. A smart, creative person. In love with life, and full of common sense, and full of concern for you, and full of wisdom. She'd look at you and she'd shake her head and smile and she'd say, come on, mom, do what the man says.'

'You think?'

'She'd say, mom, trust me on this.'

'But I have to see. After all these years of not knowing.'

'Better if you don't.'

'It's just her bones.'

'It's not just her bones.'

'What else can be left?'

'No,' Reacher said. 'I mean, it's not just *her* bones.'

Up on the 49th Parallel, the transfer was going exactly to plan. The white van had driven slowly south, through the last of Canada, and it had parked for the final time in a rough forest clearing a little more than two miles north of the border. The driver had gotten out and stretched and then taken a long coil of rope from the passenger foot well and walked around to the rear doors. He had opened them up and gestured urgently and the women and the girls had come on out immediately, with no reluctance, with no hesitation at all, because passage to America was what they wanted, what they had dreamed about, and what they had paid for.

There were sixteen of them, all from rural Thailand, six women and ten female children, average weight close to eighty pounds each, for a total payload of 1,260 pounds. The women were slim and attractive, and the girls were all eight years old or younger. They all stood and blinked in the morning light and looked up and around at the tall trees, and shuffled their feet a little, stiff and weary but excited and full of wonderment.

The driver herded them into a rough semicircle. He couldn't speak Thai and they couldn't understand English, so he started the same dumb show he had performed many times before. It was probably faster than talking anyway. First he patted the air to calm them down and get their attention. Then he raised a finger to his lips and twisted left, twisted right, tracking the whole length of the semicircle, a big exaggerated pantomime, so that they all saw, so that they all understood they had to be silent. He pointed at a spot on the ground and then cupped a hand behind his ear. *There are sensors. The earth listens.* The women nodded, deferential, keen to let him know they understood. He pointed to himself, and then to all of them, and then pointed south, and wiggled his fingers. *Now we all have to walk.* The women nodded again. They knew. They had been told at the outset. He used both hands, one and then the other, palms down, stepping on the air gently and delicately. He kept the gesture going and looked along the semicircle, making eye contact with each of his charges. *We have to walk softly and keep very quiet.* The women nodded eagerly, and the girls looked back at him shyly from behind their hair.

The driver uncoiled his rope and measured off six feet from the end and wrapped that point around the first woman's hand. He measured another six feet and wrapped the rope around the first girl's hand, and then the next, and then the second woman, and so on, until he had all sixteen joined together safely. The rope was a guide, that was all, not a restraint. Like a mobile handrail. It kept them all moving at the same pace in the same direction and it prevented any of them from wandering off and getting lost. The forest transfer was dangerous enough without having to double back and crash around, hunting for stragglers.

The driver picked up the free end of the rope and wrapped it around his own hand. Then he led them off, like a train, snaking south between bushes and trees. He walked slowly and softly and listened out for commotion behind him. There was none, as usual. Asian people knew how to keep quiet, especially illegals, especially women and girls.

But as quiet as they were, twenty minutes later they were clearly heard, in two separate locations, both more than six hundred miles away, first in Fargo, North Dakota, and then in Winnipeg, Manitoba. Or more accurately they were seen in both places, in that remote seismograph needles flickered a little as they passed over a buried sensor. But the deflection was minor, barely above the level of background noise. In Fargo, an employee of the U.S. Department of Homeland Security checked back on his graph and thought: *Deer. Maybe whitetails. Maybe a whole family.* His counterpart in Canada checked his own graph and thought: *A breeze, bringing clumps of snow down off the trees.*

*   *   *

They walked on, slowly and carefully, treading lightly, patiently enduring the third of the four parts of their adventure. First had come the shipping container, and then had come the white van. Now came the hike, and then there would be another van. Everything had been explained beforehand, in great detail, in a small shipping office above a store in a town near their home. There were many such offices, and many such operations, but the one they had used was widely considered the best. The price was high, but the facilities were excellent. Their contact had assured them his only concern was that they arrive in America in the best of condition, as fresh as daisies. To that end, the shipping container, which would be their home for the longest of the four phases, was equipped with everything necessary. There were lamps inside with bulbs that simulated daylight, wired to automobile batteries. There were mattresses and blankets. There was plenty of food and water and there were chemical toilets. There was medicine. There were ventilation slots disguised as rust holes, and in case they weren't enough there was a fan that ran off the same batteries as the lights, and there were oxygen cylinders that could be bled slowly if the air got stuffy. There was an exercise machine, so they could keep in shape for the four-mile hike across the border itself. There were washing facilities, and lotions and moisturizers for their skin. They were told that the vans were equipped with the same kind of stuff, but less of it, because the road trips would be shorter than the sea voyage.

An excellent organization, that thought of everything.

And the best thing was that there was no bias shown against families with girl children. Some organizations would smuggle adults only, because adults could work immediately, and some allowed children, but older boys only, because they could work too, but this organization welcomed girls, and wasn't even upset if they were young, which was considered a very humane attitude. The only downside was that the sexes always had to travel separately, for the sake of decorum, so fathers were separated from mothers, and brothers from sisters, and then on this particular occasion they were told at the very last minute that the ship the men and the boys were due to sail on was delayed for some reason, so the women and the girls had been obliged to go on ahead. Which would be OK, they were told, because they would be well looked after at their destination, for as long as it took for the second ship to arrive.

They had been warned that the four-mile hike would be the hardest part of the whole trip, but it wasn't, really. It felt good to be out in the air, moving around. It was cold, but they were used to cold, because winter in Thailand was cold, and they had warm clothes to wear. The best part was when their guide stopped and raised his finger to his lips again and then traced an imaginary sideways line on the ground. He pointed beyond it and mouthed, 'America.' They walked on and passed the line one after the other and smiled happily and picked their way onward, across American soil at last, slowly and delicately, like ballet dancers.

*   *   *

470

The Duncan driver in the grey van on the Montana side of the border saw them coming about a hundred yards away. As always his Canadian counterpart was leading the procession, setting the pace, holding the rope. Behind him the shipment floated along, seemingly weightless, curving and snaking through the gaps between the trees. The Duncan driver opened his rear doors and stood ready to receive them. The Canadian handed over the free end of the rope, like he always did, like the baton in a relay race, and then he turned about and walked back into the forest and was lost to sight. The Duncan driver gestured into the truck, but before each of his passengers climbed aboard he looked at their faces and smiled and shook their hands, in a way his passengers took to be a formal welcome to their new country. In fact the Duncan driver was a gambling man, and he was trying to guess ahead of time which kid the Duncans would choose to keep. The women would go straight to the Vegas escort agencies, and nine of the girls would end up somewhere farther on down the line, but one of them would stay in the county, at least for a spell, or actually for ever, technically. Buy ten and sell nine, was the Duncan way, and the driver liked to look over the candidates and make a guess about which one was the lucky one. He saw four real possibilities, and then felt a little jolt of excitement about a fifth, not that she would be remotely recognizable by the time she was passed on to him.

Dorothy Coe stood behind her truck's open door for ten whole minutes. Reacher stood in front of her, watching her, hoping he was blocking her view of the barn, happy to keep on standing there as long as it took, ten hours or ten days or ten years, or for ever, anything to stop her going inside. Her gaze was a thousand miles away, and her lips were moving a little, as if she was rehearsing arguments with someone, look or don't look, know or don't know.

Eventually she asked, 'How many are in there?'

Reacher said, 'About sixty.'

'Oh my God.'

'Two or three a year, probably,' Reacher said. 'They got a taste for it. An addiction. There are no ghosts. Ghosts don't exist. What the stoner kid heard from time to time was real.'

'Who were they all?'

'Asian girls, I think.'

'You can tell that from their bones?'

'The last one isn't bones yet.'

'Where were they all from?'

'From immigrant families, probably. Illegals, almost certainly, smuggled in, for the sex trade. That's what the Duncans were doing. That's how they were making their money.'

'Were they all young?'

'About eight years old.'

'Are they buried?'

Reacher said, 'No.'

'They're just dumped in there?'

'Not dumped,' Reacher said. 'They're displayed. It's like a shrine.'

There was a long, long pause.

Dorothy Coe said, 'I should look.'

'Don't.'

'Why not?'

'There are photographs. Like a record. Like mementos. In silver frames.'

'I should look.'

'You'll regret it. All your life. You'll wish you hadn't.'

'You looked.'

'And I regret it. I wish I hadn't.'

Dorothy Coe went quiet again. She breathed in, and breathed out, and watched the horizon. Then she asked, 'What should we do now?'

Reacher said, 'I'm going to head over to the Duncan houses. They're all in there, sitting around, thinking everything is going just fine. It's time they found out it isn't.'

Dorothy Coe said, 'I want to come with you.'

Reacher said, 'Not a good idea.'

'I need to.'

'Could be dangerous.'

'I hope it is. Some things are worth dying for.'

The doctor's wife said, 'We're coming too. Both of us. Let's go, right now.'

FIFTY-SEVEN

Dorothy Coe got behind the wheel of her truck again and the doctor and his wife slid in beside her. Reacher rode in the load bed, with the captured rifle, holding tight over the tractor ruts, a long slow mile, back to where he had left the white Tahoe he had taken from the football player who had broken his nose. It was still there, parked and untouched. Reacher got in and drove it and the other three followed behind. They went south on the two-lane and then coasted and stopped half a mile shy of the Duncan compound. The view from there was good. Reacher unscrewed the Leica scope from the rifle and used it like a miniature telescope. All three houses were clearly visible. There were five parked vehicles. Three old pick-up trucks, plus Seth Duncan's black Cadillac, and Eleanor Duncan's red Mazda. All of them were standing in a neat line on the dirt to the left of the southernmost house, which was Jacob's. All of them were cold and inert and dewed over, like they had been parked for a long time, which meant the Duncans were holed up and isolated, which was pretty much the way Reacher wanted it.

He climbed out of the Tahoe and walked back to meet the others. He took the sawn-off from his pocket and handed it to Dorothy Coe. He said, 'You all head back and get car keys from the football players. Then bring me two more vehicles. Choose the ones with the most gas in the tank. Get back here as fast as you can.'

Dorothy Coe backed up a yard and turned across the width of the road and took off north. Reacher got back in the Tahoe and waited.

Three isolated houses. Wintertime. Flat land all around. Nowhere to hide. A classic tactical problem. Standard infantry doctrine would be to sit back and call in an artillery strike, or a bombing run. The guerilla approach would be to split up and attack with rocket-propelled grenades from four sides simultaneously, with the main assault from the north, where there were fewest facing windows. But Reacher had no forces to divide, and no grenades or artillery or air support. He was on his own, with a middle-aged alcoholic man and two middle-aged women, one of whom was in shock. Together they were equipped with a bolt-action rifle with two rounds in it, and a Glock nine-millimetre pistol with sixteen rounds, and a sawn-off twelve-gauge shotgun with three rounds, and a switchblade, and an adjustable wrench, and two screwdrivers, and a book of matches. Not exactly overwhelming force.

But time was on their side. They had all day. And the terrain was on their side. They had forty thousand un-obstructed acres. And the Duncans' fence was on their side. The fence, built a quarter of a century before, as an alibi, still strong and sturdy. The law of unintended consequences. The fence was about to come right back and bite the Duncans in the ass.

Reacher put the Leica to his eye again. Nothing was happening in the compound. It was still and quiet. Nothing was moving, except smoke coming from the chimneys on the first house and the last. The smoke was curling south. A breeze, not a wind, but the air was definitely in motion.

Reacher waited.

Fifteen minutes later Reacher checked the Tahoe's mirror and saw a little convoy heading straight for him. First in line was Dorothy Coe's truck, and then came the gold Yukon Reacher had taken from the kid called John. It had the doctor at the wheel. Last in line was the doctor's wife, driving the black pick-up the first Cornhusker of the morning had arrived in. They all slowed and parked nose to tail behind the Tahoe. They all looked left, away from the Duncan compound, studiously averting their eyes. Old habits.

Reacher climbed out of the Tahoe and the other three gathered around and he told them what they had to do. He told Dorothy Coe to keep the sawn-off, and he gave the Leica scope to the doctor's wife, and he took her scarf and her cell phone in exchange. As soon as they understood their roles, he waved them away. They climbed into Dorothy Coe's truck and headed south. Reacher was left alone on the shoulder of the two-lane, with the white Tahoe, and the gold Yukon, and the black pick-up, with the keys for all of them in his pocket. He counted to ten, and then he got to work.

The black pick-up truck was the longest of the three vehicles, by about a foot, so Reacher decided to use it second. The white Tahoe had the most gas in it, so Reacher decided to use it first. Which left John's gold Yukon to use third, which Reacher was happy about, because he knew it drove OK.

He walked back and forth along the line and started all three vehicles and left them running. Then he started leapfrogging them forward, moving them closer to the mouth of the Duncan driveway, a hundred yards at a time, getting them in the right order, hoping to delay detection for as long as possible. Without the scope, his view of the compound was much less detailed, but it still looked quiet. He got the black pick-up within fifty yards, and he left the gold Yukon waiting right behind it, and then he jogged back and got in the white Tahoe and drove it all the way forward. He turned it into the mouth of the driveway and lined it up straight and eased it to a stop.

He slid out of the seat and crouched down and clamped the jaws of his adjustable wrench across the width of the gas pedal. He corrected the angle so that the stem of the wrench stuck up above the horizontal, and then he turned the knurled knob tight. He ducked back and hustled around the tailgate and opened the fuel filler door and took off the gas cap. He poked the end of the borrowed scarf down the filler neck with the longer screwdriver, and then he lit the free end of the scarf with his matches. Then he hustled back to the driver's door and leaned in and put the truck in gear. The engine's idle speed rolled it forward. He kept pace and put his finger on the button and powered the driver's seat forward. The cushion moved, slowly, an inch at a time, through its whole range, past the point where a person of average height would want it, on towards where a short person would want it, and then the front of the cushion touched the end of the wrench, and the engine note changed and the truck sped up a little. Reacher kept pace and kept his finger where it was and the seat kept on moving, and the truck kept on accelerating, and Reacher started running alongside, and then the seat arrived at the limit of its travel and Reacher stepped away and let the truck go on without him. It was rolling at maybe ten miles an hour, maybe less, not very fast at all, but enough to overcome the wash of gravel under its tyres. The ruts in the driveway were holding it reasonably straight. The scarf in the filler neck was burning pretty well.

Reacher turned and jogged back to the road, to the black pick-up, and he got in and drove it forward beyond the mouth of the driveway, and then he backed it up and in and parallel-parked it across the width of the space, between the fences, sawing it back and forth until he had it at a perfect ninety degrees, with just a couple of feet of open space at either end. The white Tahoe was rolling steadily, already halfway to its target, tramlining left and right in the ruts, trailing a bright plume of flame. Reacher pulled the black pick-up's keys and jogged back to the road. He leaned on the blind side of the gold Yukon's hood and watched.

The white Tahoe was well ablaze. It rolled on through

its final twenty yards, dumbly, unflinchingly, and it hit the front of the centre house and stopped dead. Two tons, some momentum, but no kind of a major crash. The wood on the house split and splintered, and the front wall bowed inward a little, and glass fell out of a ground floor window, and that was all.

But that was enough.

The flames at the rear of the truck swayed forward and came back and settled in to burn. They roiled the air around them and licked out horizontally under the sills and climbed up the doors. They spilled out of the rear wheel wells and fat coils of black smoke came off the tyres. The smoke boiled upward and caught the breeze and drifted away south and west.

Reacher leaned into the Yukon and took the rifle off the seat.

The flames crept onward towards the front of the Tahoe, slow but urgent, busy, seeking release, curling out and up. The rear tyres started to burn and the front tyres started to smoke. Then the fuel line must have ruptured because suddenly there was a wide fan of flame, a new colour, a fierce lateral spray that beat against the front of the house and rose up all around the Tahoe's hood, surging left and right, licking the house, lighting it, bubbling the paint in a fast black semicircle. Then finally flames started chasing the bubbling paint, small at first, then larger, like a map of an army swarming through broken defences, fanning out, seeking new ground. Air sucked in and out of the broken window and the flames started licking at its frame.

Reacher dialled his borrowed cell.

He said, 'The centre house is alight.'

Dorothy Coe answered, from her position half a mile west, out in the fields.

She said, 'That's Jonas's house. We can see the smoke.'

'Anyone moving?'

'Not yet.' Then she said, 'Wait. Jonas is coming out his back door. Turning left. He's going to head around to the front.'

'Positive ID?'

'A hundred per cent. We're using the telescope.'

'OK,' Reacher said. 'Stay on the line.'

He laid the open cell phone on the Yukon's hood and picked up the rifle. It had a rear iron sight just ahead of the scope mount, and a front iron sight at the muzzle. Reacher raised it to his eye and leaned forward and rested his elbows on the sheet metal and aimed at the gap between the centre house and the southernmost house. Distance, maybe a hundred and forty yards.

He waited.

He saw a stocky figure enter the gap from the rear. A man, short and wide, maybe sixty years old or more. Round red face, thinning grey hair. Reacher's first live sighting of a Duncan elder. The guy hustled stiffly between the blank ends of the two homes and came out in the light and stopped dead. He stared at the burning Tahoe and started towards it and stopped again and then turned and faced front and stared at the pick-up truck parked across the far end of the driveway.

Reacher laid the front sight on the guy's centre mass and pulled the trigger.

FIFTY-EIGHT

The .338 hit high, a foot above Jonas Duncan's centre mass, halfway between his lower lip and the point of his chin. The bullet drove through the roots of his front incisors, through the soft tissue of his mouth and his throat, through his third vertebra, through his spinal cord, through the fat on the back of his neck, and onward into the corner of Jacob Duncan's house. Jonas went down vertically, claimed by gravity, his stiff fireplug body suddenly loose and malleable, and he ended up sprawled in a grotesque tangle of limbs, face up, eyes open, the last of his brain's oxygenated blood leaking from his wound, and then he died.

Reacher shot the rifle's bolt and the spent shell case clanged against the Yukon's hood and rolled down its contour and fell to the ground. Reacher picked up the cell phone and said, 'Jonas is down.'

Dorothy Coe said, 'We heard the shot.'

'Any activity?'

'Not yet.'

Reacher kept the phone against his ear. Jonas's house

was burning nicely. The whole front wall was on fire, and there were flames inside, throwing orange light and shadows all around, curling flat and angry against the ceilings, gleaming wetly behind intact panes of glass, spilling out through the broken windows and leaping up and merging into the general conflagration. Smoke was still blowing south, and heat too, towards the southernmost building.

Dorothy Coe's voice came back: 'Jasper is out. He has a weapon. A long gun. He sees us. He's looking right at us.'

Reacher asked, 'How far back are you?'

'About six hundred yards.'

'Stand your ground. If he fires, he'll miss.'

'We think it's a shotgun.'

'Even better. The round won't even reach you.'

'He's running. He's past Jonas's house. He's heading for Jacob's.'

Reacher saw him, flitting right to left across the narrow gap between Jonas's house and Jacob's, a short wide man very similar to his brother. On the phone Dorothy Coe said, 'He's gone inside. We see him in Jacob's kitchen. Through the window. Jacob and Seth are in there too.'

Reacher waited. The fire in Jonas's house was burning out of control. In front of it the white Tahoe was a blackened wreck inside a ball of flame. Glass was punching out of the house's windows ahead of flames that followed horizontally like arms and fists before boiling upward. The roof was alight. Then there was a loud sound and the air inside the house seemed to shudder and cough and a hot blue shimmer gasped out through the ground floor, like an expelled breath, clearly visible, like a force, and it rose slowly upward, one second, two, three, and then the flames came back even stronger behind it.

Dorothy Coe said, 'Something just blew up in Jonas's kitchen. The propane tank, maybe. The back wall is burning hard.'

Reacher waited.

Then the ground floor itself burned through and there was another cough and shudder as the flaming timbers tumbled through to the basement. The left-hand gable tilted inward and the right-hand gable fell outward, across the gap to Jasper's house. Sparks showered all around and thermals caught them and sent them shooting a hundred feet in the air. Jonas's right-hand wall collapsed into the gap and piled high against Jasper's left-hand wall, and gales of new air hit fresh unburned surfaces and vivid new flames leapt up.

Reacher said, 'This is going very well.'

Then Jonas's second floor fell in with an explosion of sparks and his left-hand wall came unmoored and folded slowly and neatly in half, the top part falling inward into the fire and the bottom part angling outward and propping itself against Jacob's house. Burning timbers and bright red embers spilled and settled and sucked oxygen towards them and huge new flames started licking upward and outward and sideways. Even the weeds in the gravel were on fire.

Reacher said, 'I think we're three for three. I think we got them all.'

Dorothy Coe said, 'Jasper is out again. He's heading for his truck.'

Reacher watched over the front sight of his rifle. He saw Jasper run for the line of cars. Saw him slide into a white pick-up. Saw him start it up and back it out. It stopped and turned and aimed straight for the driveway. It blew through a shower of sparks, right past Jonas's body, and headed straight towards the two-lane. Straight towards Reacher. Straight towards the parked black truck. It braked hard and stopped short just behind it, and Jasper scrambled out. He opened the black truck's passenger door and ducked inside.

Then a second later he ducked out again.

No key.

The key was in Reacher's pocket.

Reacher put the phone on the Yukon's hood.

Jasper Duncan stood still, momentarily unsure. Distance, maybe forty yards. Which was really no distance at all.

Reacher shot him through the head and he went straight down the same way his brother had before him, leaving a small pink cloud in the air above him, made of pulverized blood and bone, which drifted an inch and then disappeared in the breeze.

Reacher picked up the phone and said, 'Jasper is down.'

Then he dropped the empty gun on the road behind him and climbed inside the Yukon. Lack of replacement ammunition meant that phase one was over, and that phase two was about to begin.

FIFTY-NINE

Reacher drove the Yukon a hundred yards beyond the mouth of the driveway, and then he turned right, on to the open dirt. Lumps and stones squirmed and pattered under his tyres. He drove a wide circle until he was level with the compound itself and then he stopped, facing the houses, the engine idling, his foot on the brake. From his new angle he saw that Jacob's south wall was so far untouched by the fire, but judging by the backdrop of smoke and flame the north end of the house was burning. Ahead and far to the left he could see Dorothy Coe's truck, waiting six hundred yards west in the fields, similarly nose-in and pent-up and expectant, like a gundog panting and crouching.

He raised the phone to his ear and said, 'I'm end-on now. What do you see?'

Dorothy Coe said, 'Jonas's house is about gone. All that's left is the chimney, really. The bricks are glowing red. And Jasper's house is on its way. His propane just blew up.'

'How about Jacob's?'

485

'It's burning north to south. Pretty fierce. Has to be getting hot in there.'

'Stand by, then. It won't be long now.'

It was less than a minute. Dorothy Coe said, 'They're out,' and a second later Reacher saw Jacob and Seth Duncan spill around the back corner of the house. They ran ducked down and bent over, zigzagging, afraid of the rifle they thought was still out there. They made it to one of the remaining pick-up trucks and Reacher saw them open the doors from a crouch and then climb in and hunker down low. Behind them the north end of Jacob's house swelled and bellied and came down, quite slowly and gracefully, with sparks shooting up and out like fireworks, with burning timbers tumbling and spreading like lava from a volcano, reaching almost to the boundary fence, a vertical mass made horizontal, and then the south end of the house fell slowly backward and collapsed into the fire, leaving only the chimney upright.

Reacher asked, 'How does it look?'

Dorothy Coe answered, 'Just like you said it would.'

Reacher saw Jacob Duncan at the wheel of the pick-up, shorter and broader than Seth in the passenger seat. Seth still had his splint taped to his face. The truck backed up ten yards, almost into the fire behind it, and then it drove forward and hit the fence, butting against it, trying to break through. The pick-up's front bumper bent out of shape and the hood crumpled a little, and the fence shuddered and rattled, but it held. Deep holes for the posts, sturdy timbers, strong rails. A big production. The law of unintended consequences.

Jacob Duncan tried again. He backed up, much less than ten yards this time because the fire was spreading behind him, and then he shot forward once more. The truck hit the fence and he and Seth bounced around in the cab like rag dolls, but the fence held. Reacher saw Jacob glance backward again. There was no space for a longer run-up. The fire and the mean allocation of land did not permit it.

Jacob changed his tactics. He manoeuvred until the nose of the truck was exactly halfway between two posts, and then he came in slow, in a low gear, pushing the grille into the rails, firming up the contact, then easing down on the gas, pushing harder and harder, hoping that sustained pressure would achieve what a sharp blow had not.

It didn't. The rails bent, and they bowed, and they trembled, but they held. Then the pick-up's rear tyres lost traction and spun and howled in the dirt and the fence pushed back and the truck eased off six inches.

The doors opened up again and Jacob and Seth spilled out and hustled over and tried the Cadillac instead. A heavier car, better torque, better power. But worse tyres, built for quiet and comfort out on the open road, not for traction over loose surfaces. Seth drove, hardly backing up at all for fear of putting his gas tank right in the flames behind him. Then he rolled four feet forward and the chrome grille hit the rails and the tyres spun almost immediately.

Game over.

'Here they come,' Reacher said.

Behind them the last vestigial support under the blazing structure gave way and the burning pile settled slowly and gently into a lower and wider shape, blowing gales of sparks and gases outward. Big curled flames danced free, burning the air itself, twisting and splitting and then vanishing. Heat distorted the air and gouts of fire hurled themselves a hundred feet up. Jacob and Seth shrank back and shielded their faces with their arms and ducked away.

They climbed the fence.

They dropped into the field.

They ran.

SIXTY

Jacob and Seth Duncan ran thirty yards, a straight line away from the fire, pure animal instinct, and then they stopped and glanced back and spun in place, alone and insignificant in the empty acres. They saw the parked Yukon as if for the first time, and they stared at it in confusion, because it was one of theirs, driven by one of their own damn boys, and the guy wasn't coming to help them. Then they saw Dorothy Coe's truck far off in another direction and they glanced back at the Yukon and they understood. They looked at each other one last time, and they ran again, in different directions, Jacob one way, and Seth another.

Reacher raised his phone.

He said, 'If I'm nine o'clock on a dial and you're twelve, then Jacob is heading for ten and Seth is heading for seven. Seth is mine. Jacob is yours.'

Dorothy Coe said, 'Understood.'

Reacher took his foot off the brake and steered one-handed, following a lazy clockwise curve, heading first north and then east, bumping across the washboard surface, feeling the heat of the fires on the glass next to his face. Ahead of him Seth was stumbling through the dirt, heading for the road, still seventy yards short of getting there. Reacher saw something in his right hand, and then he heard Dorothy Coe's voice on the phone: 'Jacob has a gun.'

Reacher asked, 'What kind?'

'A handgun. A revolver, I think. We can't see. We're bouncing around too much.'

'Slow down and take a good look.'

Ten long seconds later: 'We think it's a regular six-shooter.'

'Has he fired it yet?'

'No.'

'OK, back off, but keep him in sight. He's got nowhere to go. Let him get tired.'

'Understood.'

Reacher laid the phone on the seat next to him and followed Seth south, staying thirty yards back. The guy was really hustling. His arms were pumping. Reacher had no scope, but he was prepared to bet the thing in Seth's right hand was a revolver too, probably half of a matched pair his father had shared.

Reacher steered and accelerated and pushed on to within twenty yards. Seth was racing hard, knees pumping, arms pumping, his head thrown back. The thing in his hand was definitely a gun. The barrel was short, no longer than a finger. The two-lane road was forty yards away. Reacher had no idea why Seth wanted to get there. No point in it. The road was just a blacktop ribbon with no traffic on it and nothing but more dirt beyond. Maybe it was a generational thing. Maybe the youngest Duncan thought municipal infrastructure was going to save him. Or maybe he was heading home. Maybe he had more weapons in the house. He was going in roughly the right direction. In which case he was either terminally desperate or the world's biggest optimist. He had more than two miles to go, and he was being chased by a motor vehicle.

Reacher stayed twenty yards back and watched. Way behind his left shoulder a last propane tank cooked off with a dull thump. The Yukon's mirror filled with sparks. Up ahead, Seth kept on running.

Then he stopped running and whirled around and planted his feet and aimed his revolver two-handed, eye-high, with his aluminium mask right behind it. His chest was heaving and all four of his limbs were trembling and despite the two-handed grip the muzzle was jerking through a circle roughly the size of a basketball. Reacher slowed and changed gear and backed up and stood thirty yards off. He felt safe enough. He had a big V-8 engine block between himself and the gun, and anyway the chances of a panting untrained man even hitting the truck itself with a short-barrelled handgun at ninety feet were slight. The chances of a successful head shot through a windshield were less than zero. The chances of putting the round in the right zip code were debatable.

Seth fired, three times, well spaced, with a jerky trigger action and plenty of muzzle climb and no lateral control at all. Reacher didn't even blink. He just watched the three muzzle flashes with professional interest and tried to identify the gun, but he couldn't at thirty yards.

Too far away. He knew there were seven- and eight-shot revolvers in the world, but they weren't common, so he assumed it was a six-shooter and that therefore there were now three rounds left in it. Beside him the phone squawked with concern and he picked it up and Dorothy Coe asked, 'Are you OK? We heard shots fired.'

'I'm good,' Reacher said. 'Are you OK? He's as likely to hit you as me. Wherever you are.'

'We're good.'

'Where's Jacob?'

'Still heading south and west. He's slowing down.'

'Stay on him,' Reacher said. He put the phone back on the seat. He kept his Glock in his pocket. The problem with being a right-handed man in a left-hand-drive truck was that he would have to bust out the windshield to fire, which used to be easy enough back in the days of pebbly safety glass, but modern automotive windshields were tough, because they were laminated with strong plastic layers, and anyway his heavy wrench was in the burned-out Tahoe, probably all melted back to ore.

Seth rested, bending forward from the waist, his head coming down almost to his shins, and he forced air into his lungs, and he panted once, then twice, and he straightened up and held his breath and aimed the gun again, this time with much more concentration and much better control. Now the muzzle was moving through a circle the size of a baseball. Reacher turned the wheel and stamped on the gas and took off to his right, in a fast tight circle, and then he feinted to come back on his original line but wrenched the wheel the other way and rocked the truck through a figure eight. Seth fired once into empty space and then aimed again and fired again. A round smacked into the top of the Yukon's windshield surround, on the passenger side, six feet from Reacher's head.

One round left, Reacher thought.

But there were no rounds left. Reacher saw Seth thrashing at the trigger and he saw the gun's wheel turning and turning to no effect at all. Either the gun was a six-shooter that hadn't been fully loaded, or it was a five-shooter. Maybe a Smith 60, Reacher thought. Eventually Seth gave up on it and looked around desperately and then just hurled the empty gun at the Yukon. Finally, a decent aim. The guy would have been better off throwing rocks. The gun hit the windshield dead in front of Reacher's face. Reacher flinched and ducked involuntarily. The gun bounced off the glass and fell away. Then Seth turned and ran again, and the rest of it was easy.

Reacher stamped on the gas and accelerated and lined up carefully and hit Seth from behind doing close to forty miles an hour. A car might have scooped him up and tossed him in the air and sent him cartwheeling backward over the hood and the roof, but the Yukon wasn't a car. It was a big truck with a high blunt nose. It was about as subtle as a sledgehammer. It caught Seth flat on his back, everywhere from his knees to his shoulders, like a two-ton bludgeon, and Reacher felt the impact and Seth's head whipped away out of view, instantaneously, like it had been sucked down by amazing gravity, and the truck bucked once, like there was something passing under the rear left wheel, and then the going got as smooth as the dirt would let it.

Reacher slowed and steered a wide circle and came back to check if any further attention was required. But it wasn't. No question about it. Reacher had seen plenty of dead people, and Seth Duncan was more dead than most of them.

Reacher took the phone off the passenger seat and said, 'Seth is down,' and then he lined up again and drove away fast, south and west across the field.

SIXTY-ONE

Jacob Duncan had gotten about two hundred yards from his house. That was all. Reacher saw him up ahead, all alone in the vastness, with nothing but open space all around. He saw Dorothy Coe's truck a hundred yards farther on, well beyond the running man to the north and the west. It was holding a wide slow curve, like a vigilant sheepdog, like a destroyer guaranteeing a shipping lane.

On the phone Dorothy said, 'I'm worried about the gun.'

Reacher said, 'Seth was a lousy shot.'

'Doesn't mean Jacob is.'

'OK,' Reacher said. 'Pull over and wait for me. We'll do this together.'

He clicked off the call and changed course and crossed Jacob's path a hundred yards back and headed straight for Dorothy Coe. When he arrived she got out of her truck and headed for his passenger door. He dropped the window with the switch on his side and said, 'No, you drive. I'll ride shotgun.'

He got out and stepped around and they met where

the front of the Yukon's hood was dented. No words were exchanged. Dorothy's face was set with determination. She was halfway between calm and nervous. She got in the driver's seat and motored it forward and checked the mirror, like it was a normal morning and she was heading out to the store for milk. Reacher climbed in beside her and freed the Glock from his pocket.

She said, 'Tell me about the photographs. In their silver frames.'

'I don't want to,' Reacher said.

'No, I mean, I need to know there's no doubt they implicate the Duncans. Jacob in particular. Like evidence. I need you to tell me. Before we do this.'

'There's no doubt,' Reacher said. 'No doubt at all.'

Dorothy Coe nodded and said nothing. She fiddled the selector into gear and the truck took off, rolling slow, jiggling and pattering across the ground. She said, 'We were talking about what comes next.'

Reacher said, 'Call a trucker from the next county. Or do business with Eleanor.'

'No, about the barn. The doctor thinks we should burn it down. But I'm not sure I want to do that.'

'Your call, I think.'

'What would you do?'

'Not my decision.'

'Tell me.'

Reacher said, 'I would nail the judas hole shut, and I would leave it alone and never go there again. I would let the flowers grow right over it.'

*   *   *

There was no more conversation. They got within fifty yards of Jacob Duncan and switched to operational shorthand. Jacob was still running, but not fast. He was just about spent. He was stumbling and staggering, a short wide man limited by bad lungs and stiff legs and the aches and pains that come with age. He had a revolver in his hand, the same dull stainless and the same stubby barrel as Seth's. Probably another Smith 60, and likely to be just as ineffective if used by a weak man all wheezing and gasping and trembling from exertion.

Dorothy Coe asked, 'How do I do this?'

Reacher said, 'Pass him on the left. Let's see if he stands and fights.'

He didn't. Reacher buzzed his window down and hung the Glock out in the breeze and Dorothy swooped fast and close to Jacob's left and he didn't turn and fire. He just flinched away and stumbled onward, a degree or two right of where he had been heading before.

Reacher said, 'Now come around in a big wide circle and aim right for him from behind.'

'OK,' Dorothy said. 'For Margaret.'

She continued the long leftward curve, winding it tighter and tighter until she came back to her original line. She coasted for a second and straightened up and then she hit the gas and the truck leapt forward, ten yards, twenty, thirty, and Jacob Duncan glanced back in horror and darted left, and Dorothy Coe flinched right, involuntarily, a civilian with forty years of safe driving behind her, and she hit Jacob a heavy glancing blow with the left headlight, hard in his back and his right shoulder, sending the gun flying, sending him tumbling, spinning him around, hurling him to the ground.

'Get back quick,' Reacher said.

But Jacob Duncan wasn't getting up. He was on his back, one leg pounding away like a dog dreaming, one arm scrabbling uselessly in the dirt, his head jerking, his eyes open and staring, up and down, left and right. His gun was ten feet away.

Dorothy Coe drove back and stopped and stood off ten yards away. She asked, 'What now?'

Reacher said, 'I would leave him there. I think you broke his back. He'll die slowly.'

'How long?'

'An hour, maybe two.'

'I don't know.'

Reacher gave her the Glock. 'Or go shoot him in the head. It would be a mercy, not that he deserves it.'

'Will you do it?'

'Gladly. But you should. You've wanted to for twenty-five years.'

She nodded slowly. She stared down at the Glock, laid flat like an open book on both her hands, like she had never seen such a thing before. She asked, 'Is there a safety catch?'

Reacher shook his head.

'No safety on a Glock,' he said.

She opened the door. She climbed down, to the sill step, to the ground. She looked back at Reacher.

'For Margaret,' she said again.

'And the others,' Reacher said.

'And for Artie,' she said. 'My husband.'

She stepped sideways around her open door, touching it with one hand as she went, slowly, with reluctance, and then she crossed the open ground, small neat strides on the dirt, ten of them, twelve, turning a short distance into a long journey. Jacob Duncan went still and watched her approach. She stepped up close and pointed the gun straight down and to one side, holding it a little away from herself, making it not part of herself, separating herself from it, and then she said some words Reacher didn't hear, and then she pulled the trigger, once, twice, three four five six times, and then she stepped away.

SIXTY-TWO

The doctor and his wife were waiting in Dorothy Coe's truck, back on the two-lane road. Reacher and Dorothy parked ahead of them and they all got out and stood together. The Duncan compound was reduced to three vertical chimneys and a wide horizontal spread of ashy grey timbers that were still burning steadily, but no longer fiercely. Smoke was coming up and gathering into a wide column that seemed to rise for ever. It was the only thing moving. The sun was as high as it was going to get, and the rest of the sky was blue.

Reacher said, 'You've got a lot of work to do. Get everyone on it. Get backhoes and bucket loaders and dig some big holes. Really big holes. Then gather the trash and bury it deep. But save some space for later. Their van will arrive at some point, and the driver is just as guilty as the rest of them.'

The doctor said, 'We have to kill him?'

'You can bury him alive, for all I care.'

'You're leaving now?'

Reacher nodded.

'I'm going to Virginia,' he said.

'Can't you stay a day or two?'

'You all are in charge now, not me.'

'What about the football players at my house?'

'Turn them loose and tell them to get out of town. They'll be happy to. There's nothing left for them here.'

The doctor said, 'But they might tell someone. Or someone might have seen the smoke. From far away. The cops might come.'

Reacher said, 'If they do, blame everything on me. Give them my name. By the time they figure out where I am, I'll be somewhere else.'

Dorothy Coe drove Reacher the first part of the way. They climbed back in the Yukon together and checked the gas gauge. There was enough for maybe sixty miles. They agreed she would take him thirty miles south, and then she would drive the same thirty miles back, and then after that filling the tank would be John's own problem.

They drove the first ten miles in silence. Then they passed the abandoned roadhouse and the two-lane speared onward and empty ahead of them and Dorothy asked, 'What's in Virginia?'

'A woman,' Reacher said.

'Your girlfriend?'

'Someone I talked to on the phone, that's all. I wanted to meet her in person. Although now I'm not so sure. Not yet, anyway. Not looking like this.'

'What's the matter with the way you look?'

'My nose,' Reacher said. He touched the tape, and

smoothed it down, two-handed. He said, 'It's going to be a couple of weeks before it's presentable.'

'What's her name, this woman in Virginia?'

'Susan.'

'Well, I think you should go. I think if Susan objects to the way you look, then she isn't worth meeting.'

They stopped at a featureless point on the road that had to be almost exactly halfway between the Apollo Inn and the Cell Block bar. Reacher opened his door and Dorothy Coe asked him, 'Will you be OK here?'

He nodded.

He said, 'I'll be OK wherever I am. Will you be OK back there?'

'No,' she said. 'But I'll be better than I was.'

She sat there behind the wheel, a solid, capable woman, about sixty years old, blunt and square, worn down by work, worn down by hardship, fading slowly to grey, but better than she had been before. Reacher said nothing, and climbed out to the shoulder, and closed his door. She looked at him once, through the window, and then she looked away and turned across the width of the road and drove back north. Reacher pulled his hat down over his ears and jammed his hands in his pockets against the cold, and got set to wait for a ride.

He waited a long, long time. For the first hour nothing came by at all. Then a vehicle appeared on the horizon, and a whole minute later it was close enough to make out some detail. It was a small import, probably Japanese, a Honda or a Toyota, old, with blue paint faded by

502

the weather. A sixth-hand purchase. Reacher stood up and stuck out his thumb. The car slowed, which didn't necessarily mean much. Pure reflex. A driver's eyes swivel right, and his foot lifts off the gas, automatically. In this case the driver was a woman, young, probably a college student. She had long fair hair. Her car was piled high inside with all kinds of stuff.

She looked for less than a second and then accelerated and drove by at sixty, trailing cold air and whirling grit and tyre whine. Reacher watched her go. A good decision, probably. Lone women shouldn't stop in the middle of nowhere for giant unkempt strangers with duct tape on their faces.

He sat down again on the shoulder. He was tired. He had woken up in Vincent's motel room early the previous morning, when Dorothy Coe came in to service it, and he hadn't slept since. He pulled his hood up over his hat and lay down on the dirt. He crossed his ankles and crossed his arms over his chest and went to sleep.

It was going dark when he woke. The sun was gone in the west and the pale remains of a winter sunset were all that was lighting the sky. He sat up, and then he stood. No traffic. But he was a patient man. He was good at waiting.

He waited ten more minutes, and saw another vehicle on the horizon. It had its lights on against the gloaming. He flipped his hood down to reduce his apparent bulk and stood easy, one foot on the dirt, one on the blacktop, and he stuck his thumb out. The approaching vehicle was bigger than a car. He could tell by the way the headlights were spaced. It was tall and relatively narrow. It had a big windshield. It was a panel van.

It was a grey panel van.

It was the same kind of grey panel van as the two grey panel vans he had seen at the Duncan depot.

It slowed a hundred yards away, the automatic reflex, but then it kept on slowing, and it came to a stop right next to him. The driver leaned way over and opened the passenger door and a light came on inside.

The driver was Eleanor Duncan.

She was wearing black jeans and an insulated parka. The parka was covered in zips and pockets and it gleamed and glittered in the light. Its threads had been nowhere near any living thing, either plant or animal.

She said, 'Hello.'

Reacher didn't answer. He was looking at the truck, inside and out. It was travel-stained. It had salt and dirt on it, all streaked and dried and dusty. It had been on a long journey.

He said, 'This was the shipment, right? This is the truck they used.'

Eleanor Duncan nodded.

He asked, 'Who was in it?'

Eleanor Duncan said, 'Six young women and ten young girls. From Thailand.'

'Were they OK?'

'They were fine. Not surprisingly. It seems that a lot of trouble had been taken to make sure they arrived in marketable condition.'

'What did you do with them?'

'Nothing.'

'Then where are they?'

'They're still in the back of this truck.'

'What?'

'We didn't know what to do. They were lured here under false pretences, obviously. They were separated from their families. We decided we have to get them home again.'

'How are you going to do that?'

'I'm driving them to Denver.'

'What's in Denver?'

'There are Thai restaurants.'

'That's your solution? Thai restaurants?'

'It isn't nearly as dumb as it sounds. Think about it, Reacher. We can't go to the police. These women are illegal. They'll be detained for months, in a government jail. That would be awful for them. We thought at least they should be with people who speak their own language. Like a supportive community. And restaurant workers are connected, aren't they? Some of them were smuggled in themselves. We thought perhaps they could use the same organizations, but in reverse, to get out again.'

'Whose idea was this?'

'Everybody's. We discussed it all day, and then we voted.'

'Terrific.'

'You got a better idea?'

Reacher said nothing. He just looked at the blank grey side of the van, and its salt stains, all dried in long feathered aerodynamic patterns. He put his palm on the cold metal.

Eleanor Duncan asked, 'You want to meet them?'

Reacher said, 'No.'

'You saved them.'

Reacher said, 'Luck and happenstance saved them. Therefore I don't want to meet them. I don't want to see their faces, because then I'll get to thinking about what would have happened to them if luck and happenstance hadn't come along.'

There was a long pause. The van idled, the breeze blew, the sky darkened, the air grew colder.

Then Eleanor Duncan said, 'You want a ride to the highway at least?'

Reacher nodded and climbed in.

They didn't talk for twenty miles. Then they rumbled past the Cell Block bar and Reacher said, 'You knew, didn't you?'

Eleanor Duncan said, 'No.' Then she said, 'Yes.' Then she said, 'I thought I knew the exact opposite. I really did. I thought I knew it for absolute sure. I knew it so intensely that eventually I realized I was just trying to convince myself.'

'You knew where Seth came from.'

'I told you I didn't. Just before you stole his car.'

'And I didn't believe you. Up to that point you had answered fourteen consecutive questions with no hesitation at all. Then I asked you about Seth, and you stalled. You offered us a drink. You were evasive. You were buying time to think.'

'Do you know where Seth came from?'

'I figured it out eventually.'

She said, 'So tell me your version.'

Reacher said, 'The Duncans liked little girls. They always had. It was their lifelong hobby. People like that form communities. Back in the days before the internet they did it by mail and clandestine face to face meetings. Photo swaps, and things like that. Maybe conventions. Maybe guest participation. There were alliances between interest groups. My guess is a group that liked little boys was feeling some heat. They went to ground. They fostered the evidence with their pals. It was supposed to be temporary, until the heat went away, but no one came back for Seth. The guy was probably beaten to death in jail. Or by the cops, in a back room. So the Duncans were stuck. But they were OK with it. Maybe they thought it was kind of cute, to get a son without the involvement of a real grown woman. So they kept him. Jacob adopted him.'

Eleanor Duncan nodded. 'Seth told me he had been rescued. Back when we still talked. He said Jacob had rescued him out of an abusive situation. Like an act of altruism and charity. And principle. I believed him. Then over the years I sensed the Duncans were doing something bad, but what turned out to be the truth was always the last thing on my mental list. Always, I promise you. Because I felt they were so opposed to that kind of thing. I felt that rescuing Seth had proved it. I was blind for a long time. I thought they were shipping something else, like drugs or guns, or bombs, even.'

'What changed?'

'Things I heard. Just snippets. It became clear to me they were shipping people. Even then I thought it was just regular illegals. Like restaurant workers and so on.'

'Until?'

'Until nothing. I never knew for sure, until today. I promise you that. But I was getting more and more suspicious. There was too much money. And too much excitement. They were practically drooling. Even then I didn't believe it. Especially with Seth. I thought he would find that kind of thing totally repulsive, because he had suffered it himself. I didn't want to think it could cut the other way. But I guess it did. I suppose ultimately it was all he knew. And all he ever enjoyed.'

Reacher said, 'I'm no psychologist either.'

'I'm so ashamed,' Eleanor said. 'I'm not going back. They think I am, but I'm not. I can't face them. I can't be there ever again.'

'So what are you going to do?'

'I'm going to give this truck to whoever helps the people in it. Like a donation. Like a bribe. Then I'm going somewhere else. California, maybe.'

'How?'

'I'm going to hitchhike, like you. Then I'm going to start over.'

'Take care on the road. It can be dangerous.'

'I know. But I don't care. I feel like I deserve whatever I get.'

'Don't be too hard on yourself. At least you called the cops.'

She said, 'But they never came.'

Reacher didn't answer.

She said, 'How do you know I called the cops?'

'Because they came,' Reacher said. 'In a manner of speaking. That's the one thing no one ever asked me. No one put two and two together. Everyone knew I was hitchhiking, but no one ever wondered why I had been let out at a crossroads that didn't lead anywhere. Why would a driver stop there? Either he wouldn't have gotten there at all, or he would have carried on south for another sixty miles at least.'

'So who was he?'

'He was a cop,' Reacher said. 'State Police, in an unmarked car. He didn't say so, but it was pretty obvious. Nice enough guy. He picked me up way to the north. Almost in South Dakota. He told me he would have to drop me off in the middle of nowhere, because all he was doing was heading down and back. We didn't talk about reasons, and I didn't know he meant he was going back immediately. But that's what he did. He pulled over, he let me out, and then two seconds later he turned around and took off again, right back the way we had come.'

'Why would he?'

'GPS and politics,' Reacher said. 'That was my first guess. A big state like Nebraska, I figured there could be bitching and moaning about which parts get attention, and which don't. So I thought maybe they were defending themselves in advance. They could come out with still frames from their GPS systems to show they've been everywhere in the state at one time or another. Cop cars all have trackers now, and all that kind of stuff can be subpoenaed if they get called in front of a committee. Then a little later on I changed my mind. I wondered if they'd had a bullshit call from someone, and they knew they weren't going to do anything about it, but they still needed to cover their asses by being able to prove they had showed up, at least. Then later still I wondered if it hadn't been such a bullshit call after all, and whether it was you who had made it.'

'It was me. Four days ago. And it wasn't a bullshit call. I told them everything I was thinking. Why didn't the guy even get out of his car?'

'Prejudice and local knowledge,' Reacher said. 'I bet you mentioned Seth beat you.'

'Well, yes, I did. Because he did.'

'Therefore they ignored everything else you said. They put it down to a wronged wife making stuff up to get her husband in trouble. Cops can be like that sometimes. It ain't right, but that's how it is. And they certainly weren't going to tackle the domestic issue itself. Not against the Duncans. Because of local knowledge. Dorothy Coe told me some neighbourhood kids join the State Police. So either they were asked, or else the story had already gotten around some other way, but in either case the message was the same, which was, in that corner of that county, you can't mess with the Duncans.'

'I don't believe it.'

'You tried,' Reacher said. 'Along with everything else, you have to remember that. You tried to do the right thing.'

They drove on and blew through what counted as the downtown area, past the Chamber of Commerce billboard, past the aluminium coach diner, past the gas station with its Texaco sign and its three service bays, past the hardware store, and the liquor store, and the bank, and the tyre shop and the John Deere dealership and the grocery and the pharmacy, past the water tower, past McNally Street, past the signpost to the hospital, and onward into territory Reacher hadn't seen before. The van's engine muttered low, and the tyres hummed, and from time to time Reacher thought he heard sounds from the load space behind him, people moving around, talking occasionally, even laughing. Beside him Eleanor Duncan concentrated on the dark road ahead, and he watched her in the corner of his eye.

Then an hour and sixty miles later they saw bright vapour lights at the highway cloverleaf, and big green signs pointing west and east. Eleanor slowed and stopped and Reacher got out and waved her away. She used the first ramp, west towards Denver and Salt Lake City, and he walked under the bridge and set up on the eastbound ramp, one foot on the shoulder and one in the traffic lane, and he stuck out his thumb and smiled and tried to look friendly.

Exclusive extract

from the new
Jack Reacher thriller

THE AFFAIR

Published 29 September 2011
in hardcover

Six months before the events in *Killing
Floor*, Major Jack Reacher of the US
Military Police goes undercover in
Mississippi, to investigate a murder…

ONE

The Pentagon is the world's largest office building, six and a half million square feet, thirty thousand people, more than seventeen miles of corridors, but it was built with just three street doors, each one of them opening into a guarded pedestrian lobby. I chose the southeast option, the main concourse entrance, the one nearest the Metro and the bus station, because it was the busiest and the most popular with civilian workers, and I wanted plenty of civilian workers around, preferably a whole long unending stream of them, for insurance purposes, mostly against getting shot on sight. Arrests go bad all the time, sometimes accidentally, sometimes on purpose, so I wanted witnesses. I wanted independent eyeballs on me, at least at the beginning. I remember the date, of course. It was Tuesday, the eleventh of March, 1997, and it was the last day I walked into that place as a legal employee of the people who built it.

A long time ago.

The eleventh of March 1997 was also by chance exactly four and a half years before the world changed, on that other future Tuesday, and so like a lot of things in the old days the security at the main concourse entrance was serious without being hysterical. Not that I invited hysteria. Not from a distance. I was wearing my Class A uniform, all of it clean, pressed, polished and spit-shined, all of it covered with thirteen years' worth of medal ribbons, badges, insignia and citations. I was thirty-six years old, standing tall and walking ramrod straight, a totally squared away U.S. Army Military Police major in every respect, except that my hair was too long and I hadn't shaved for five days.

Back then Pentagon security was run by the Defense Protective Service, and from forty yards I saw ten of their guys in the lobby, which I thought was far too many, which made me wonder whether they were all theirs or whether some of them were actually ours, working undercover, waiting for me. Most of our skilled work is done by Warrant Officers, and they do a lot of it by pretending to be someone else. They impersonate colonels and generals and enlisted men, and anyone else they need to, and they're good at it. All in a day's work for them to throw on DPS uniforms and wait for their target. From thirty yards I didn't recognize any of them, but then, the army is a very big institution, and they would have chosen men I had never met before.

I walked on, part of a broad wash of people heading across the concourse to the doors, some men and women in uniform, either Class As like my own or the old woodland-pattern BDUs we had back then, and some men and women obviously military but out of uniform, in suits or work clothes, and some obvious civilians, some of each category carrying bags or briefcases or packages, all of each category slowing and sidestepping and shuffling as the broad wash of people narrowed to a tight arrowhead and then narrowed further still to lonely single file or collegial two-by-two, as folks got ready to stream inside. I lined up with them, on my own, single file, behind a woman with pale unworn hands and ahead of a guy in a suit that had gone shiny at the elbows. Civilians, both of them, desk workers, probably analysts of some kind, which was exactly what I wanted. Independent eyeballs. It was close to noon. There was sun in the sky and the March air had a little warmth in it. Spring, in Virginia. Across the river the cherry trees were about to wake up. The famous blossom was about to break out. All over the innocent nation airline tickets and SLR cameras lay on hall tables, ready for sightseeing trips to the capital.

I waited in line. Way ahead of me the DPS guys were doing what security guys do. Four of them were occupied with specific tasks, two manning an inquiry counter and two checking official badge holders and then waving them through an open turnstile. Two were standing directly behind the glass inside the doors, looking out, heads high, eyes front, scanning the approaching crowd. Four were hanging back in the shadows behind the turnstiles, just clumped together, shooting the shit. All ten were armed.

It was the four behind the turnstiles that worried me. No question that back in 1997 the Department of Defense was seriously puffed up and overmanned in relation to the threats we faced then, but even so it was unusual to see four on-duty guys with absolutely nothing to do. Most commands at least made their surplus personnel look busy. But these four had no obvious role. I stretched up tall and peered ahead and tried to get a look at their shoes. You can learn a lot from shoes. Undercover disguises often don't get that far, especially in a uniformed environment. The DPS was basically a beat cop role, so to the extent that a choice was available, DPS guys would go for cop shoes, big comfortable things appropriate for walking and standing all day. Undercover MP Warrant Officers might use their own shoes, which would be subtly different.

But I couldn't see their shoes. It was too dark inside, and too far away.

The line shuffled along, at a decent pre-9/11 clip. No sullen impatience, no frustration, no fear. Just old-style routine. The woman in front of me was wearing perfume. I could smell it coming off the nape of her neck. I liked it. The two guys behind the glass noticed me about ten yards out. Their gaze moved off the woman and on to me. It rested on me a beat longer than it needed to, and then it moved on to the guy behind.

Then it came back. Both men looked me over quite openly, up and down, side to side, four or five seconds, and then I shuffled forward and their attention moved behind me again. They didn't say anything to each other. Didn't say anything to anyone else, either. No warnings, no alerts. Two possible interpretations. One, best case, I was just a guy they hadn't seen before. Or maybe I stood out because I was bigger and taller than anyone within a hundred yards. Or because I was wearing a major's gold oak leaves and ribbons for some heavy-duty medals including a Silver Star, like a real poster boy, but because of the hair and the beard I also looked like a real caveman, which visual dissonance might have been enough reason for the long second glance, just purely out of interest. Sentry duty can be boring, and unusual sights are always welcome.

Or two, worst case, they were merely confirming to themselves that some expected event had indeed happened, and that all was going according to plan. Like they had prepared and studied photographs and were saying to themselves: *OK, he's here, right on time, so now we just wait two more minutes until he steps inside, and then we take him down.*

Because I was expected, and I was right on time. I had a twelve o'clock appointment and matters to discuss with a particular colonel in a third-floor office in the C ring, and I was certain I would never get there. To walk head-on into a hard arrest was a pretty blunt tactic, but sometimes if you want to know for sure whether the stove is hot, the only way to find out is to touch it.

The guy ahead of the woman ahead of me stepped inside the doors and held up a badge that was attached to his neck by a lanyard. He was waved onward. The woman in front of me moved and then stopped short, because right at that moment the two DPS watchers chose to come out from behind the glass. The woman paused in place and let them squeeze out in front of her, against the pressing flow. Then she resumed her progress and stepped inside, and the two guys stopped and stood exactly where she had been, three feet in front of me, but facing in the opposite direction, towards me, not away from me.

They were blocking the door. They were looking right at me. I was pretty sure they were genuine DPS personnel. They were wearing cop shoes, and their uniforms had eased and stretched and moulded themselves to their individual physiques over a long period of time. These were not disguises, snatched from a locker and put on for the first time that morning. I looked beyond the two guys, inside, at their four partners who were doing nothing, and I tried to judge the fit of their clothes, by way of comparison. It was hard to tell.

In front of me the guy on my right said, 'Sir, may we help you?'

I asked, 'With what?'

'Where are you headed today?'

'Do I need to tell you that?'

'No sir, absolutely not,' the guy said. 'But we could speed you along a little, if you like.'

Probably via an inconspicuous door into a small locked room, I thought. I figured they had civilian witnesses on their mind too, the same way I did. I said, 'I'm happy to wait my turn. I'm almost there, anyway.'

The two guys said nothing in reply to that. Stalemate. Amateur hour. To try to start the arrest outside was dumb. I could push and shove and turn and run and be lost in the crowd in the blink of an eye. And they wouldn't shoot. Not outside. There were too many people on the concourse. Too much collateral damage. This was 1997, remember. March eleventh. Four and a half years before the new rules. Much better to wait until I was inside the lobby. The two stooges could close the doors behind me and form up shoulder to shoulder in front of them while I was getting the bad news at the desk. At that point theoretically I could turn back and fight my way past them again, but it would take me a second or two, and in that second or two the four guys with nothing to do could shoot me in the back about a thousand times.

And if I charged forward they could shoot me in the front. And where would I go anyway? To escape *into* the Pentagon was no kind of a good idea. The world's largest office building. Thirty thousand people. Five floors. Two basements. Seventeen miles of corridors. There are ten radial hallways between the rings, and they say a person can make it between any two random points inside a maximum seven minutes, which was presumably calculated with reference to the army's official quick-march pace of four miles an hour, which meant if I was running hard I could be anywhere within about three minutes. But where? I could find a broom closet and steal bag lunches and hold out a day or two, but that would be all. Or I could take hostages and try to argue my case, but I had never seen that kind of thing succeed.

So I waited.

The DPS guy in front of me on my right said, 'Sir, you be sure and have a nice day now,' and then he moved past me, and his partner moved past me on my other side, both of them just strolling slow, two guys happy to be out in the air, patrolling, varying their viewpoint.

Maybe not so dumb after all. They were doing their jobs and following their plan. They had tried to decoy me into a small locked room, but they had failed, no harm, no foul, so now they were turning the page straight to plan B. They would wait until I was inside and the doors were closed, and then they would jump into crowd control mode, dispersing the incoming people, keeping them safe in case shots had to be fired inside. I assumed the lobby glass was supposed to be bulletproof, but the smart money never bets on the DoD having gotten exactly what it paid for.

The door was right in front of me. It was open. I took a breath and stepped into the lobby. *Sometimes if you want to know for sure whether the stove is hot, the only way to find out is to touch it.*

TWO

The woman with the perfume and the pale hands was already deep into the corridor beyond the open turnstile. She had been waved through. Straight ahead of me was the two-man inquiry desk. To my left were the two guys checking badges. The open turnstile was between their hips. The four spare guys were still doing nothing beyond it. They were still clustered together, quiet and watchful, like an independent team. I still couldn't see their shoes.

I took another breath and stepped up to the counter.

Like a lamb to the slaughter.

The desk guy on the left looked at me and said, 'Yes, sir.' Fatigue and resignation in his voice. A response, not a question, as if I had already spoken. He looked young and reasonably smart. Genuine DPS, presumably. MP Warrant Officers are quick studies, but they wouldn't be running a Pentagon inquiry desk, however deeply under they were supposed to be.

The desk guy looked at me again, expectantly, and I said, 'I have a twelve o'clock appointment.'

'Who with?'

'Colonel Frazer,' I said.

The guy made out like he didn't recognize the name. The world's largest office building. Thirty thousand people. He leafed through a book the size of a telephone directory and asked, 'Would that be Colonel John James Frazer? Senate Liaison?'

I said, 'Yes.'

Or: *Guilty as charged.*

Way to my left the four spare guys were watching me. But not moving. Yet.

The guy at the desk didn't ask my name. Partly because he had been briefed, presumably, and shown photographs, and partly because my Class A uniform included my name on a nameplate, worn as per regulations on my right breast pocket flap, exactly centred, its upper edge exactly a quarter of an inch below the top seam.

Seven letters: *REACHER.*

Or, eleven letters: *Arrest me now.*

The guy at the inquiry desk said, 'Colonel John James Frazer is in 3C315. You know how to get there?'

I said, 'Yes.' Third floor, C ring, nearest to radial corridor number three, bay number fifteen. The Pentagon's version of map coordinates, which it needed, given that it covered twenty-nine whole acres of floor space.

The guy said, 'Sir, you have a great day,' and his guileless gaze moved past my shoulder to the next in line. I stood still for a moment. They were tying it up with a bow. They were making it perfect. The general common law test for criminal culpability is expressed by the Latin *actus non facit reum nisi mens sit rea*, which means, roughly, doing things won't necessarily get you in trouble unless you actually mean to do them. Action plus intention is the standard. They were waiting for me to prove my intention. They were waiting for me to step through the turnstile and into the labyrinth. Which explained why the four spare guys were on their side of the gate, not mine. Crossing the line would make it real. Maybe there were jurisdiction issues. Maybe lawyers had been consulted. Frazer wanted my ass gone for sure, but he wanted his own ass covered just as much.

I took another breath and crossed the line and made it real. I walked between the two badge checkers and squeezed between the cold alloy flanks of the turnstile. The bar was retracted. There was nothing to hit with my thighs. I stepped out on the far side and paused. The four spare guys were on my right. I looked at their shoes. Army regulations are surprisingly vague about shoes. Plain black lace-up Oxfords or close equivalents, conservative, no designs on them, minimum of three pairs of eyelets, closed toe, maximum two-inch heel. That's all the fine print says. The four guys on my right were all in compliance, but they weren't wearing cop shoes. Not like the two guys outside. They were sporting four variations on the same classic theme. High shines, tight laces, a little creasing and wear here and there. Maybe they were genuine DPS. Maybe they weren't. No way of telling. Not right then.

I was looking at them, and they were looking at me, but no one spoke. I looped around them and headed deeper into the building. I used the E ring counter-clockwise and turned left at the first radial hallway.

The four guys followed.

They stayed about sixty feet behind me, close enough to keep me in sight, far enough back not to crowd me. A maximum seven minutes between any two points. I was the meat in a sandwich. I figured there would be another crew waiting outside 3C315, or as close to it as they decided to let me get. I was heading straight for them. Nowhere to run, nowhere to hide.

I used some stairs on the D ring and went up two flights to the third floor. I changed to a clockwise direction, just for the fun of it, and passed radial corridor number five, and then four. The D ring was busy. People were bustling from place to place with armfuls of khaki files. Blank-eyed men and women in uniform were stepping smartly. The place was congested. I dodged and sidestepped and kept on going. People looked at me every step of the way. The hair, and the beard. I stopped at a water fountain and bent down and took a drink. People passed me by. Sixty feet behind me the four spare DPS guys were nowhere to be seen. But then, they didn't really need to tail me. They knew where I was going, and they knew what time I was supposed to get there.

I straightened up and got going again and turned right into radial number three. I made it to the C ring. The air smelled of uniform wool and linoleum polish and very faintly of cigars. The paint on the walls was thick and institutional. I looked left and right. There were people in the corridor, but no big cluster outside bay fifteen.

Maybe they were waiting for me inside. I was already five minutes late.

I didn't turn. I stuck with radial three and walked all the way across the B ring to the A ring. The heart of the building, where the radial corridors finish. Or start, depending on your rank and perspective. Beyond the A ring is nothing but a five-acre pentagonal open courtyard, like the hole in an angular doughnut. Back in the day people called it Ground Zero, because they figured the Soviets had their biggest and best missile permanently targeted on it, like a big fat bull's-eye. I think they were wrong. I think the Soviets had their five biggest and best missiles targeted on it, just in case strikes one through four didn't work. The smart money says the Soviets didn't always get what they paid for, either.

I waited in the A ring until I was ten minutes late. Better to keep them guessing. Maybe they were already searching. Maybe the four spare guys were already getting their butts kicked for losing me. I took another big breath and pushed off a wall and tracked back along radial three, across the B ring, to the C. I turned without breaking stride and headed for bay fifteen.

THREE

There was no one waiting outside bay fifteen. No special crew. No one at all. The corridor was entirely empty, too, both ways, as far as the eye could see. And quiet. I guessed everyone else was already where they wanted to be. Twelve o'clock meetings were in full swing.

Bay fifteen's door was open. I knocked on it once, as a courtesy, as an announcement, as a warning, and then I stepped inside. Originally most of the Pentagon's office space was open plan, boxed off by file cabinets and furniture into bays, hence the name, but over the years walls had gone up and private spaces had been created. Frazer's billet in 3C315 was pretty typical. It was a small square space with a window without a view, and a rug on the floor, and photographs on the walls, and a metal DoD desk, and a chair with arms and two without, and a credenza and a double-wide storage unit.

And it was a small square space entirely empty of people, apart from Frazer himself in the chair behind the desk. He looked up at me and smiled.

He said, 'Hello, Reacher.'

I looked left and right. No one there. No one at all.

There was no private bathroom. No large closet. No other door of any kind. The corridor behind me was empty. The giant building was quiet.

Frazer said, 'Close the door.'

I closed the door.

Frazer said, 'Sit down, if you like.'

I sat down.

Frazer said, 'You're late.'

'I apologize,' I said. 'I got hung up.'

Frazer nodded. 'This place is a nightmare at twelve o'clock. Lunch breaks, shift changes, you name it. It's a zoo. I never plan to go anywhere at twelve o'clock. I just hunker down in here.' He was about five-ten, maybe two hundred pounds, wide in the shoulders, solid through the chest, red-faced, black-haired, in his middle forties. Plenty of old Scottish blood in his veins, filtered through the rich earth of Tennessee, which was where he was from. He had been in Vietnam as a teenager and the Gulf as an older man. He had combat pips all over him like a rash. He was an old-fashioned warrior, but unfortunately for him he could talk and smile as well as he could fight, so he had been posted to Senate Liaison, because the guys with the purse strings were now the real enemy.

He said, 'So what have you got for me?'

I said nothing. I had nothing to say. I hadn't expected to get that far.

He said, 'Good news, I hope.'

'No news,' I said.

'Nothing?'

I nodded. 'Nothing.'

'You told me you had the name. That's what your message said.'

'I don't have the name.'

'Then why say so? Why ask to see me?'

I paused a beat.

'It was a shortcut,' I said.

'In what way?'

'I put it around that I had the name. I wondered who might crawl out from under a rock, to shut me up.'

'And no one has?'

'Not so far. But ten minutes ago I thought it was a different story. There were four spare men in the lobby. In DPS uniforms. They followed me. I thought they were an arrest team.'

'Followed you where?'

'Around the E ring to the D. Then I lost them on the stairs.'

Frazer smiled again.

'You're paranoid,' he said. 'You didn't lose them. I told you, there are shift changes at twelve o'clock. They come in on the Metro like everyone else, they shoot the shit for a minute or two, and then they head for their squad room. It's on the B ring. They weren't following you.'

I said nothing.

He said, 'There are always groups of them hanging around. There are always groups of everyone hanging around. We're seriously overmanned. Something is going to have to be done. It's inevitable. That's all I hear about on the Hill, all day, every day. There's nothing we can do to stop it. We should all bear that in mind. People like you, especially.'

'Like me?' I said.

'There are lots of majors in this man's army. Too many, probably.'

'Lots of colonels too,' I said.

'Fewer colonels than majors.'

I said nothing.

He asked, 'Was I on your list of things that might crawl out from under a rock?'

You were the list, I thought.

He said, 'Was I?'

'No,' I lied.

He smiled again. 'Good answer. If I had a beef with you, I'd have you killed down there in Mississippi. Maybe I'd come on down and take care of it myself.'

I said nothing. He looked at me for a moment, and then a smile started on his face, and the smile turned into a laugh, which he tried very hard to suppress, but he couldn't. It came out like a bark, like a sneeze, and he had to lean back and look up at the ceiling.

I said, 'What?'

His gaze came back level. He was still smiling. He said, 'I'm sorry. I was thinking about that phrase people use. You know, they say, that guy? He couldn't even get arrested.'

I said nothing.

He said, 'You look terrible. There are barbershops here, you know. You should go use one.'

'I can't,' I said. 'I'm supposed to look like this.'

Five days earlier my hair had been five days shorter, but apparently still long enough to attract attention.

531

Leon Garber, who at that point was once again my commanding officer, summoned me to his office, and because his message read in part *without repeat without attending to any matters of personal grooming* I figured he wanted to strike while the iron was hot and dress me down right then, while the evidence was still in existence, right there on my head. And that was exactly how the meeting started out. He asked me, 'Which army regulation covers a soldier's personal appearance?'

Which I thought was a pretty rich question, coming from him. Garber was without a doubt the scruffiest officer I had ever seen. He could take a brand new Class A coat from the quartermaster's stores and an hour later it would look like he had fought two wars in it, then slept in it, then survived three bar fights in it.

I said, 'I can't remember which regulation covers a soldier's personal appearance.'

He said, 'Neither can I. But I seem to recall that whichever, the hair and the fingernail standards and the grooming policies are in chapter one, section eight. I can picture it all quite clearly, right there on the page. Can you remember what it says?'

I said, 'No.'

'It tells us that hair grooming standards are necessary to maintain uniformity within a military population.'

'Understood.'

'It mandates those standards. Do you know what they are?'

'I've been very busy,' I said. 'I just got back from Korea.'

'I heard Japan.'

'That was a stopover on the way.'

'How long?'

'Twelve hours.'

'Do they have barbers in Japan?'

'I'm sure they do.'

'Do Japanese barbers take more than twelve hours to cut a man's hair?'

'I'm sure they don't.'

'Chapter one, section eight, paragraph two, says the hair on the top of the head must be neatly groomed, and that the length and the bulk of the hair may not be excessive or present a ragged, unkempt, or extreme appearance. It says that instead, the hair must present a tapered appearance.'

I said, 'I'm not sure what that means.'

'It says a tapered appearance is one where the outline of the soldier's hair conforms to the shape of his head, curving inward to a natural termination point at the base of his neck.'

I said, 'I'll get it taken care of.'

'These are mandates, you understand. Not suggestions.'

'OK,' I said.

'Paragraph two says that when the hair is combed, it *will not* fall over the ears or the eyebrows, and it *will not* touch the collar.'

'OK,' I said again.

'Would you not describe your current hairstyle as ragged, unkempt, or extreme?'

'Compared to what?'

'And how are you doing in relation to the thing

with the comb and the ears and the eyebrows and the collar?'

'I'll get it taken care of,' I said again.

Then Garber smiled, and the tone of the meeting changed completely.

He asked, 'How fast does your hair grow, anyway?'

'I don't know,' I said. 'A normal kind of speed, I suppose. Same as anyone else, probably. Why?'

'We have a problem,' he said. 'Down in Mississippi.'

WANT TO READ ON?

The Affair, the brand new Jack Reacher thriller, is out in hardback on 29th September 2011.

KILLING FLOOR

By Lee Child

Introducing Jack Reacher

Killing Floor is the first book in the internationally popular Jack Reacher series. It presents Reacher for the first time, as the tough ex-military cop of no fixed abode: a righter of wrongs, the perfect action hero.

Jack Reacher jumps off a bus and walks fourteen miles down a country road into Margrave, Georgia. An arbitrary decision he's about to regret.

Reacher is the only stranger in town on the day they have had their first homicide in thirty years. The cops arrest Reacher and the police chief turns eyewitness to place him at the scene. As nasty secrets leak out, and the body count mounts, one thing is for sure.

They picked the wrong guy to take the fall.

'All [Reacher thrillers] are ripping yarns, but since this is the first, it seems the logical place to start'
Stephen King

'One of the genre's finest practitioners'
Independent

DIE TRYING

By Lee Child

A Jack Reacher thriller

'Not content with writing a rip-roaring thriller,
Child also gives us one of the truly memorable
tough-guy heroes in recent fiction'
Jeffery Deaver

Jack Reacher, alone, strolling nowhere.

A Chicago street in bright sunshine.
A young woman, struggling on crutches.
He offers her a steadying arm.

And turns to see a handgun aimed at his stomach.

Chained in a dark van racing across America, Reacher doesn't
know why they've been kidnapped. The woman claims to be
FBI. She's certainly tough enough. But at their
remote destination, will raw courage be enough
to overcome the hopeless odds?

'Jack Reacher is a wonderfully epic hero: tough,
taciturn, yet vulnerable . . . irresistible'
People

TRIPWIRE

By Lee Child

A Jack Reacher thriller

**'A slickly effective thriller which confirms Child's ability
to keep the reader guessing – and sweating'**
The Times

For Jack Reacher being invisible has become a habit.

He spends his days digging swimming pools by hand and his
nights as the bouncer in the local strip club in the Florida Keys.

He doesn't want to be found.

But someone has sent a private detective to seek him out.
Then Reacher finds the guy beaten to death with his fingertips
sliced off. It's time to head north and work out who
is trying to find him and why.

'Gives new meaning to what a page-turner should be'
Michael Connelly

'Bang-on suspense'
Houston Chronicle

THE VISITOR

By Lee Child

A Jack Reacher thriller

'Lee Child writes edgy American thrillers to rival the likes of Thomas Harris and John Grisham. You'll bomb through it and enjoy every second'
Mirror

Sergeant Amy Callan and Lieutenant Caroline Cooke
have a lot in common.

Both were army high-flyers.
Both were acquainted with Jack Reacher.
Both were forced to resign from the service.

Now they're both dead.

Found in their own homes, naked, in a bath full of paint.
Apparent victims of an army man. A loner, a smart guy
with a score to settle, a ruthless vigilante.

A man just like Jack Reacher.

'Reacher is the sort of hero no woman could help falling for . . . Relentlessly fast-paced'
Daily Mail

ECHO BURNING

By Lee Child

A Jack Reacher thriller

**Jack Reacher, adrift in the hellish
heat of a Texas summer.**

Looking for a lift through the vast empty landscape.
A woman stops, and offers a ride.
She is young, rich and beautiful.

**But her husband's in jail.
When he comes out, he's going to kill her.**

Her family's hostile, she can't trust the cops, and the lawyers
won't help. She is entangled in a web of lies and
prejudice, hatred and murder.

Jack Reacher never could resist a lady in distress.

'To die for'
Mirror

**'The best mystery I have read this year: best written,
best plotted, best just about every way. Compelling'**
Boston Globe

WITHOUT FAIL

By Lee Child

A Jack Reacher thriller

**'Jack Reacher is a most magnetic creation,
tough, cool and ultimately moral'**
Irish Independent

Jack Reacher walks alone.

No job, no ID, no last known address. But he never turns down
a plea for help. Now a woman tracks him down. A woman
serving at the very heart of US power. A woman who needs
Reacher's assistance in her new job.

Her job?

Protecting the Vice-President of the United States.

Her problem?

Someone wants the VP dead.

**'Jack Reacher is a hero in the Dirty Harry style, a
man who lives by his own principles . . . Produces a
surprising twist when it's least expected'**
Sunday Telegraph

PERSUADER

By Lee Child

A Jack Reacher thriller

'Reacher on top form'
Sunday Telegraph

Never forgive, never forget.

Jack Reacher lives for the moment. Without a home.
Without commitment. But he has a burning desire to right
wrongs – and rewrite his own agonizing past.

Never apologize. Never explain.

When Reacher witnesses a brutal kidnap attempt, he takes
the law into his own hands. But a cop dies. Has
Reacher lost his sense of right and wrong?

'May be the best thriller writer in the business'
Boston Globe

**'Reacher is a seriously tough but unbending
moral loner . . . violent and exciting'**
Irish Independent

THE ENEMY

By Lee Child

A Jack Reacher thriller

'Jack Reacher is utterly irresistible'
Observer

New Year's Day, 1990.

A soldier is found dead in a sleazy motel bed. Jack Reacher is the officer on duty. The soldier turns out to be a two-star general. The situation is bad enough, then Reacher finds the general's wife.

This stomach-churning thriller turns back the clock to a younger Reacher, in dogtags. A Reacher who still believes in the service. A Reacher who imposes army discipline. Even if only in his own pragmatic way . . .

'The thing about Lee Child's books is that you can't put the damn things down . . . there's something about his writing that's addictive. *The Enemy* is no exception . . . superb'
Independent on Sunday

ONE SHOT

By Lee Child

A Jack Reacher thriller

'One of the best in the genre . . . nobody does it better'
Sunday Telegraph

Six shots. Five dead.

A heartland city thrown into terror. But within hours the cops
have it solved. A slam-dunk case. Apart from one thing. The
accused gunman refuses to talk except for a single phrase:

Get Jack Reacher for me.

Reacher lives off the grid. He's not looking for trouble.
But sometimes trouble looks for him. What could connect
the ex-military cop to this psychopathic killer?

**'The thing about Lee Child's books is that
you can't put the damn things down'**
Independent on Sunday